ONE

JEWEL E. ANN

This book is a work of fiction. Any resemblances to actual persons, living or dead, events, or locales are purely coincidental.

ISBN 978-1-7359982-3-7

Second Print Edition

Cover Designer: Jennifer Beach

DEDICATION

For true lovers of life.

AUTHOR'S NOTE

One is a spinoff of the Jack & Jill Series—*End of Day, Middle of Knight, Dawn of Forever*. It can be read as a standalone, however, there are many spoilers to the Jack & Jill Series.

CHAPTER ONE

10,000 LAKES AND ONE MYTHICAL GOD

THREE MONTHS after landing in Minneapolis, a Greek god moved into the apartment across from mine. Okay, maybe not an actual god, but close. The view from my peephole might not have been entirely accurate. Nevertheless, my eyeball remained glued to it with no signs of blinking; I had a peephole addiction—along with Netflix, marshmallows, and cinnamon.

"It's not gonna fit," I narrated the situation to myself.

Two scrawny, pale-skinned boys danced with an oversized, black leather chair, working to maneuver it through the doorway. Apollo stood just opposite my door with his tree-trunk arms crossed over his chest. The guy could carry the chair on his pinky finger with Beavis and Butt-Head sitting atop, yet he gave them nothing more than a slight head shake.

My mumblings continued. "Turn it the other way."

"Don't scratch the legs," he said, eliciting a whole new round of sweat from the movers.

Left. Right. Up. Down.

"Gah!" Enough was enough. I threw open my door. "Flip it the other way. That's the only way it will fit."

After a few seconds of frozen silence and three who-the-hell-are-you looks, the moving guys angled it back out, flipped it, and had it inside the apartment in less than ten seconds.

I turned. He wasn't a god.

Stupid peephole.

He was a mountain of muscles wrapped in dark skin perfection.

"Men are supposed to have better spatial abilities than women, but I have yet to witness it firsthand." I shrugged and smiled.

His eyes shifted down to mine, arms still crossed over the continent of his chest. He quirked an eyebrow.

"*I'm* a man."

No words had ever been truer. The *man* before me stood close to 6'5" and maybe 275 pounds, with calves the circumference of my waist. A solid rock with a few scattered tattoos on biceps partially covered by his gray T-shirt. And that voice ... it vibrated my body in all the places that weren't already awakened by the slight scent of spice, which had to be something lingering on his skin. Whatever it was, my nose approved.

"That was my first guess." My tight-lipped smile accompanied a resolute nod.

His eyes shifted to my chest.

Please don't squint.

With a subtle arch of my back, I attempted to look confident, because nothing said confidence like a good push-up bra. My boobs weren't the ripest mangoes on the tree, but they were a step above fleshy acorns. It seemed unlikely that Apollo was the kind of guy to be impressed by barely average-sized ta-tas, but a girl could hope.

A subtle smirk pulled at his lips. I knew they hid a beautiful set of white teeth ... I just knew. However, he didn't indulge me with as much as a glimpse. Too bad.

His gaze moved to my legs—my real one and my prosthetic one on full display beneath my green running shorts.

"You lost your leg."

"Genius. You're two for two today." I winked.

He stared and stared, cocking his head from one side to the other like it was a puzzle to solve. I wasn't a puzzle, just a below-the-knee amputee with a kick-ass robotic leg.

"Hmm ..." He pushed a quick breath out of his nose while shaking his head. "Bummer."

I narrowed my eyes, tracking his path past me to his door as the two moving guys squeezed by him. "Bummer?"

"Yup." He turned, taking in my leg once more. "Never seen any leg quite like that."

"It's a prototype. By the way, I'm Lake Jones."

"Okay," he called, his back already to me. Two seconds later his door shut.

Biting my lips together, I tapped them with my finger then huffed out a laugh. "That went well."

After returning to the sanctity of my apartment, nestled in a quaint neighborhood just outside of downtown Minneapolis, I typed out a message to my BFF, Lindsay.

Lake: *Hot guy alert.*

I pitched my phone on my alabaster and Spanish yellow striped ottoman and walked to the window. Opening my peacock blue curtains—because it was the best shade of blue ever—I frowned at the dismal clouds shadowing the city, confirming the April afternoon rain shower prediction. My phone chimed. I smiled while retrieving it. There was a lot to be said for independence, spreading one's wings, and moving to a new place with no family and friends.

Words like daring, adventurous, and driven described my frame of mind when I decided to leave behind everything that was familiar. Two months later ... bored out of my fucking mind was the accurate description of how my newfound freedom felt.

What person, with an ounce of sanity, moves to Minnesota in the middle of February? Stubborn twenty-four-year-old girls who want to exert their independence at the worst possible time, that's who. I shrugged off all offers to help me move. The need to overcompensate in everything was a tragic side effect of living with a disability. People without disabilities would accept help; it was the normal thing to do. Me? Not so much.

My brother, psychiatrist extraordinaire, called me contumacious—stubbornly disobedient. Whatever. I made it with the help of a moving company, who arrived three days late. That minor detail was omitted when I told my parents the move went off without a hitch.

Lindsay: *Sex?*

Lake: *No. I think there are security cameras in the hall. But I love that you believe after a year of not having sex that I'd jump my new neighbor in the hall upon our first meeting.*

Lindsay: *That's exactly why. You have to be so desperate.*

Lake: *Thx for keeping it real.*

Lindsay: *Always. I need details!*

Lake: *I've given up on my vibrator. It makes me feel like a complete loser. I still question the existence of God. If he exists, then that means there is a Heaven and Ben is there, watching me*

shove vibrating plastic into myself with one hand while I stimulate my nipples with the other. I know he's thinking "WTF" but it means something more spiritual like "Why This, Father?"
Lindsay: *LMAO – I meant details about the hot guy, but thx for the visual.*
Lake: *Awkward*
Lindsay: *A bit. The guy. Tell me about the guy!*

"The guy." I wished there were a guy. All-encompassing statements like "the worst" were reserved for drama queens. I didn't use them much, but when it came to guys, I reserved the right to say, "I have the worst luck with men." It was safe to say I'd never find "the one," because I'd met two "the ones," which went against all mathematical laws of nature. Two perfect guys and I lost them both.

Ben ...

This was what I learned from him. Life was a peculiar journey—a marathon for some, a sprint for others. One day I woke up and discovered the shitty part was nobody knew which one. A marathon required a different frame of mind than a sprint.

Live for the moment. What did that mean? Which one? How many? With whom?

Ben died and I lived.

Three months later I awoke from a coma, with an infinity of blank space below my left knee. The shitty part? The pinky toe on my right foot suffered two different breaks years earlier, and it was painful to wear pretty, yet completely impractical, shoes because it never healed properly. But no ... I had to lose the foot with the good pinky toe. It was an embarrassing yet completely human thought that went through my head, because the thought that wanted to take up residency in my brain was just too unbearable: Ben died and I lived.

A second chance at life deserved a profound purpose, a commitment to changing the world. Don't waste a single minute. Don't take anything for granted. Don't ever forget ...

Ben died and I lived.

The problem: I wasn't living. I wasn't sleeping. I wasn't changing the world.

Over four years later, everything around me remained black and white with the occasional splash of color that quickly faded. I'm not sure if it was grief or guilt, but everything around me, everything I held dear—family, friends, my favorite city by the bay—became suffocating.

So I left.

Lake: *Nothing to tell. He's 2.5 x my size. Looked at my boobs and my leg then said, "Bummer."*

Lindsay: *To your boobs or your leg?*

Lake: *Lol, my leg. I hope.*

Lindsay: *A guy that size could break you. I don't think a relationship would work if he could never give you more than just the tip.*

Lake: *Thx for going there.*

Lindsay: *Anytime. ;) Gotta run, babe. Keep me apprised and don't think about God or Ben in Heaven when you're getting yourself off. Too weird.*

SOUNDPROOF WALLS MY ASS!

Apollo liked his music deafeningly loud, with an extra side of bass, and he liked it during the hours of my best sleep.

bang bang bang

ONE

I rapped my fist against his door until my knuckles protested such aggression.

The door eased open. His manly pheromones, cologne, or over-all sex appeal wafted in my direction. I breathed out of my mouth to keep my brain from liquefying. He brought a tall glass of something that looked like blood to his lips and took a slow sip before licking them.

"Sup?"

"*Sup*?" I planted my fists on my hips. "What's up is I'm trying to sleep and it sounds like you're running a nightclub in here! Am I seriously the first person who has complained?"

He held up his glass, uncurling his index finger from it, and then he turned, disappearing around the corner. I took a step inside, straining my neck to see where he went.

Stark white walls. He needed a decorator. Then again, the walls probably had ten coats of stain-blocking primer on them to cover up the blood. Rumor was the previous tenant shot his wife in the head, then himself. I figured that's why the place sat vacant for so long. Who wants to live in an apartment where a murder/suicide took place? Talk about bad chi.

I made a mental note to offer my services. Peacock blue. He needed the window wall painted peacock blue with pewter blinds. The music cut off, and I shuffled back into the hallway.

"Sorry, what were you saying?"

My eyes narrowed. "The music. It's too loud. You're waking up the whole damn neighborhood."

There it was—and no less brilliant than I thought it would be—a smile. Large, perfectly-aligned pearly whites. I sort of had a thing for smiles.

"Listen, Stick ... it's eleven-thirty in the morning. I

reckon you're the only one in the neighborhood still sleeping." He took another sip of blood.

If he knew what had happened in that apartment, he would not have chosen beet juice, or tomato juice, or whatever the hell he had in that glass.

My nose wrinkled at the glass then my eyes shifted to his. "Did you just call me *stick*?"

He nodded once, his gaze making another assessment of my whole body. "Angry Bird, huh?" He shrugged. "Fitting, I suppose. But that shirt is the worst fucking thing I've ever seen."

Yes, I wore Angry Bird women's boxer shorts and a 49ers T-shirt.

"What's wrong with the 49ers?"

"You're in Minnesota Kings country. That's what's wrong with them."

I shook my head. "It's a nightshirt. And who cares? It was a gift. I don't follow football."

"Are we done, Stick?"

"Why are you calling me stick?"

"Why ya sleepin' at 11:30 a.m.?"

"I work nights." That was a stretch of the truth.

He grinned, an enticing one that made the rest of my body wake up, even if my eyes still needed the sleep rubbed out of them. I wanted to climb him like a tree and—

"Doing what?"

"What?" I shook my head. I was halfway up the tree. "Oh ... video chatting."

"Porn?"

"None of your business." I huffed. No. No was the answer. Why didn't I just say no? Did I want him to think I liked porn?

Resting his shoulder against the door frame, he sipped his drink again, then smirked. "Now I'm curious."

My chin jutted forward as I narrowed my eyes. "Are ya, Apollo? Are ya really curious?"

"Apollo?" A boisterous laugh rumbled from his chest. "As in Creed?"

"What?" My eyes narrowed. "Creed what?"

"Apollo Creed. Rocky?"

"Rocky?" My head tilted to the side, eyes still narrowed.

"For fuck's sake, Stick. Please don't tell me you've never watched Rocky."

"Boxing movie? No. I have not."

"Then why the hell are you calling me Apollo?"

"Well, you have not told me your name. And you're well ... um ... fit of sorts. Strong looking. Not exactly ugly. So Apollo came to mind. You know ... mythical god, son of Zeus?"

He fisted his free hand at his mouth.

"You're laughing at me?"

He shook his head, but his massive fist still wasn't big enough to hide his grin. "See the color of my skin? Do I look Greek to you? If you must call me Apollo, let's go with Creed, even though I'm not a boxer either." He chuckled a little more.

"That's it!" I pointed a stiff finger at him. "I'm not going to stand here and take this." My stubborn personality grasped for a phantom shred of dignity. Pivoting, I returned to my apartment with as much confidence as an amputee wearing Angry Bird boxers could have.

"Hope this isn't your way of playing hard to get, Stick. It's not happening between us. You're not my type."

The nerve of him ...

"I'm not playing hard to get, and I never implied I

wanted anything to happen." I may have thought about his tip, but nothing beyond that. "It's very arrogant of you to assume I thought something was going to happen between us. AND I don't have a *stick* up my ass!"

I slammed my door and opened it again two seconds later. "And just to be clear ... why exactly am I not your type?"

He finished the last of the blood drink and wiped his mouth with the back of his hand. " 'Cause you're a skinny-as-a-*stick* white girl without a damn thing to hold on to."

I slammed the door again.

I LANDED a dream job two years ago—a dream job because when I had two complete legs I never would have *dreamed* of being a "subject" or "tester" of prosthetic legs. However, using the label "prosthetic leg" around my boss was off limits.

A designer in England made me several pretty legs with painted nails. They looked freakishly real. My boss hated them. He said they were as 'fucking impractical as a pair of high-heeled shoes.' Those legs were 'prosthetics,' and wearing them only revealed my vanity. He designed robotic legs, and comparing them to the average prosthesis was the ultimate insult.

"Hey love, tell me about my baby." Thaddeus "Thad" Westbrook wasn't British, but he always called me love. Why? No idea. I was not his baby, but I think his baby ranked higher than his love. The "smart limb" aka my bionic leg was his baby. I had a lot of his babies, yet we'd never had sex.

Thad was my first date from a matchmaking site. And

for the record, he was not one of the "ones." We should have had sex. He took me to the brink of an orgasm, yet he had no clue what he did to me. I was open about my disability on the dating site, he was not. Thad lost one hand and two fingers from his other hand in a farm equipment accident when he was twelve.

He invited himself into my apartment after dinner, and then he removed my leg. It wasn't exactly a first-base move, but as his hands skimmed over my flesh, inspecting my residual limb. I shivered, heart racing. At first it tickled my knee, but then it shot tingling goose bumps up along my skin while the much neglected area between my thighs screamed, *YES!* But, no—we never happened.

I put him on speaker phone and combed through my wet hair after a long run and a shower. "I like her ... a lot. In fact, I think I'm keeping her. She's not sexy, but she's smooth. No limp, not even when taking the stairs. I got caught in the rain the other day and worried about the sensory electrode shorting out, but—"

"She's waterproof, love."

"Yeah, where have I heard that before? Oh that's right, with your last baby that shorted out and nearly set my pants on fire. That shit would never happen with a *prosthetic* leg."

"My smart limbs are made to mimic a human's movement in every way, only better. But much like the human body, sometimes there can be a few glitches. That's why I have you."

"The guinea—"

"My test subject, not guinea pig, love."

"Whatever, so why'd you call?"

My memories of Thad were surreal. People just didn't meet like that. I had an official paying job by the end of our first and only date. I also fingered myself into a sweaty mess that night in bed, but it was a small sacrifice. Thad admitted he was looking for a "subject" to join his geek team experts in prosthetics, robotics, machine learning, and biomechanics —geek being my word not his—to "test the future of robotics that would make physical disabilities obsolete." He also confessed that his attraction to me was unplanned and not going to work out if I took the job. Thad was a stickler on not mixing business and pleasure.

Job versus male-induced orgasm—I mean boyfriend. It was a toughie, but in the end, I made the right decision. Thanks to Thad and his ingenious team of geeks, I felt like a superhero, not a young woman with a disability. Thanks to Thad, my disability was non-existent.

"I already booked your flight and hotel," he said with his usual passive voice. Always multi-tasking. The guy could do brain surgery while practicing his golf swing and reciting Pi to infinity.

"For?" I stopped mid-comb and stared at my phone.

"Beijing. Next Wednesday. You'll be there about a week or so."

I rolled my eyes. "Jerry Chu. I was up half the night video chatting with him. I showed him our latest baby, and he needs to tweak his before I give it a go."

"Yes, love, I know. I just got off the phone with him, and he needs you there for the tweaking. It's supposed to be the best one yet for rock climbing. Besides, half the parts of *my* baby that you have were designed by Jerry."

"I hate flying to China."

"You told me you love Beijing."

"I do. I hate getting there. Fourteen hours on a plane. I get restless."

"Take a friend."

"I don't have that many friends here yet."

"Take a sedative."

"I don't like how they make me feel."

"You're being difficult, love."

"Strong. I'm being strong-willed. That's why you hired me."

"I hired you because you're active yet submissive."

"Pardon me?"

"Don't act offended. Who lets a guy get away with, 'I want to take your leg off,' on the first date—before so much as a kiss?"

"You were handsome."

"Were?"

"Yes. Now you're just bossy, and that's not very attractive on you."

"Next Wednesday. Ass on the plane, love."

"Bossy cow." I sighed, plugging in the dryer.

"Mmm hmm." He disconnected our call.

I aimed the hairdryer at my phone and blasted it on high with an evil glare.

CHAPTER TWO

UNFORGETTABLE

APOLLO BECAME MY NEW OBSESSION. I needed to get out, find a date, and make friends, but I couldn't leave my apartment during peak watch-hours, which happened to be from seven to eleven at night. That's when my neighbor was home with visitors coming and going.

The peephole wasn't going to watch itself.

With stubborn reluctance, I met a guy on a dating site. Tucker Bailey was a twenty-eight-year-old chiropractor from St. Paul who enjoyed swimming, biking, and traveling.

Check.

Check.

Check.

We were a near-perfect match according to the dating website. However, it was his profile picture that sold me: lean, fit guy wearing a huge smile while crossing the finish line of a marathon ... pushing a young man in a wheelchair.

A guy that wouldn't act all weird about my superhero leg was hard to come by. Committing to my look for the evening was difficult too.

Ponytail.

No ponytail.

Bangs braided and pinned back.

Bangs tucked behind my ear.

I should have taken a night off 'Apollo watch' to get a haircut. The downside to my long, stick-straight, black hair, that rejected all efforts by a curling iron, was the split ends that stood out.

The strong magnetic force of the peephole sucked my eye right to it. "Whatcha doing, Apollo? Big party tonight?" I murmured to myself.

Mr. You're Not My Type had an unusual amount of traffic around his place. Did he know I had a date and wouldn't be able to spy ... I mean, man my neighborhood-watch post?

All normal pre-date jitters, including a last-minute outfit change and a check of my teeth, were forgotten. Tucker would have to accept my first choice of black jeans and a white V-neck, button-down blouse with my favorite leather ankle boots. Thad's robotic leg was benched for the night so I could feel more like a lady and less like a hybrid human.

Meow

"Trzy, I'll feed you when I get home. We both know it will be before ten."

She purred, slamming her body against my leg and prancing around it like a seductive pole dancer. I had to give her credit, for the world's ugliest cat, she dripped with confidence.

"Be good." I blew her a kiss, grabbed my phone, and opened the door. "Purse ... might need my purse." I rolled my eyes at my forgetfulness as I stepped back inside to grab it.

"AHH!"

"EEK!"

"OH MY GOD!"

I whipped around as the shrill cries from across the hall were heard by half the city.

"WHAT IS THAT?"

"SHIT!"

"MOTHERFUCKER GET IT OUT OF HERE!"

After a quick scan of the room, I grimaced. "Trzy," I said through gritted teeth.

Two women in short dresses and high heels shuffled like ducks running from hunting dogs out of Apollo's apartment while the cries for help continued. I jockeyed my way through the crowd of large bodies. There must have been a minimum weight limit to be invited to his place. It was like a bouncer convention, except for the few remaining women that I didn't notice right away because they were all perched on the counters and the back of the sofa with terror etched into their makeup-caked faces.

"Excuse me. Pardon me. Excuse me." I spotted my little feline slut hunched back ready to jump on the couch and give the two cornered damsels in distress strokes or heart attacks.

"Come on, Trzy." I scooped her up. "You weren't invited to the party. Neither was I," I mumbled.

"Stick, what in God's name is that?"

I hugged her closer to me, looking up at Apollo blocking the exit. "Stupid question, Apollo. Clearly, Trzy is a cat."

"She has no hair."

"She's hypoallergenic."

"You're allergic to cats?"

"I'm not."

"She has three legs."

I shrugged. "Hence the name Trzy, and it's two more than I have."

He narrowed his eyes. "Part of her ear is missing."

"She was in an accident. Apparently she got tangled up in a group of bikers. I think that's why she won't go biking with me."

"You bike?"

"I do."

"With a cat?"

"Gah! No, Apollo! I just said she won't go with me."

"Apollo? Like Creed?" a guy behind me said with a chuckle.

I glanced over my shoulder. The Hulk hid his smirk behind his arm, masking his laugh as a cough. The testosterone in the room dissolved my panties. Hulk's blond man bun held my gaze a few extra seconds, and he smelled like sex felt. I didn't even know what that meant, but it crossed my mind as I took a second whiff. Visiting a gynecologist was on my to-do list. There was a ninety-percent chance that I was in heat.

"Trzy means three?" the Hulk asked with a smirk.

"Yes. That's what the card said when she was delivered to me. It's the Polish word for three.

Hulk shook his head. "I don't even want to know what kind of person gives you that..." he nodded to Trzy "...as a gift. But I can tell you the number three in Polish is pronounced 'shi' not "tr-zy"

I squinted one eye. "The note said T-r-z-y. Tr-zy."

Hulk shook his head. "It's 'shi'"

"'Shi? Like shit without the *T*?"

"No. Like shit with the T at the beginning. Shi."

I couldn't hear him pronounce the T and, in general, it

sounded like the noise Trzy made when she was hacking up a fur ball.

I shook my head. "Doesn't matter. She responds to tr-zy."

Hulk smiled. "It was a nice one too."

Wetting my lips, I returned my attention to Apollo. Cocking my head a bit, a grin claimed the corners of my mouth. "He won't tell me his name. So I'm stroking his ego with the name of a mythical god. I figure it's the only thing he gets stroked."

My comment was met with laughter from everyone but the large, tatted black man blocking my escape.

"Don't take it personal, Stick. I won't let you stroke other parts of me because you're still not my type." He stepped aside.

I glared at his arrogant smirk while I brushed past him.

"Oh sweet Jesus! What the—" A woman gasped.

"What's with you people, Trzy's just a—"

While the blonde with a wrinkle of disgust on her face was a sight to behold, she vanished the second I saw the man behind her.

"You," I whispered.

He—my other "one"—stared at me for a long moment. The star of all my dreams for the past three years stood before me, and I couldn't see an ounce of recognition in his eyes. Was I really that forgettable?

"Banks, do you know her?" The blonde continued to grimace at Trzy.

"Stick lives across the hall," *Banks* answered.

I whipped my head around, giving him the stink eye. "Banks Apollo or Apollo Banks?"

He grinned, holding his lips in a tight seal.

"Everson Banks. Seriously, you don't know your neighbor? How can you live next to a sports star and not know it?" The blonde sucked in a breath and turned sideways to squeeze past me and Trzy without touching us. "Cage, you coming?"

"In a minute," Cage answered.

"Monaghan, you know Stick?" Everson asked.

Cage smiled. I died a little because really ... I could barely breathe. Maybe I wasn't so forgettable.

"Yes, I know Lake."

He remembered my name. He remembered my name! HE REMEMBERED MY NAME!

I bit my tongue so those words didn't actually vomit from my mouth. The tall, hunky blond with dimples remembered my name. That meant he had to remember the kiss.

His eyes shifted to my lips as I rubbed them together. Yeah, he remembered the kiss.

We both grinned.

"Ya know, you're not allowed to have pets in these apartments, Stick."

"Bite me, *Everson*." I couldn't tear my eyes away from Cage, nor could I wipe the ridiculous smile from my face. My cheeks hurt, but I kept smiling.

The door shut, leaving just us two grinning fools in the hallway.

Three years earlier I met Cage Monaghan, college star quarterback for Nebraska, under the worst circumstances. My brother's fiancée, Jessica, disappeared and our search for her took us to Omaha, where she had been living under the name Jillian Knight and in a relationship with Cage's father. Our lives were at risk because there were some dangerous people who didn't want her to be found.

It was one day.

We met.

There was a connection.

We didn't find Jessica that day. Instead, we found the man of my dreams, and he'd just lost his father to cancer. I'd lost both Ben and my leg a year earlier. I was a hot mess, literally and figuratively stumbling my way through life. My need to state the obvious "I have a prosthetic leg" was cringe-worthy. Cage was Cool Joe. To protect lives, I couldn't tell him that I lived in San Francisco, so he believed I lived in New York.

We talked much ado about nothing, ate pizza, drank beer, and then I had to leave for New York, which was actually San Francisco. He asked for my number, but I couldn't give it to him. I wanted to—really, really, really bad. But ... lives at risk and all that jazz.

"Give me your phone number," he called as I walked to the car.

I stopped and closed my eyes for a moment, wanting to just savor the feeling. Then I turned. "I can't"

Cage deflated. "You can't or you won't?"

"Both. No, really just ... I can't"

"So you're just going to leave me with nothing?"

My mind screamed "screw it." I walked back and grabbed his face with both of my gloved hands, pulling his cheek toward my lips. At the last second he turned and his lips pressed to mine. I wasn't going to kiss him on the lips. He did it. He turned into my kiss. Neither of us moved. It wasn't a passionate, open-mouthed kiss, but it wasn't a peck either. Our lips simply locked, idle like a statue, neither one wanting to end the feeling because it was The. Best. Feeling.

I knew him for a few hours.

One day.

One kiss.

One moment.

One unforgettable memory.

"How..." Cage shook his head "...how long have you lived here?"

"Few months."

"What brings you to Minnesota from New York?"

"Oh, well ..." Just then it occurred to me he didn't know the whole truth. He didn't know Jillian Knight became Jessica Jones. He didn't know New York was a lie. His dad died, Jillian left, and Cage moved on with his life.

Lives were no longer at risk, but the story behind it was too long to explain with an antsy Trzy in my arms and my date waiting for me at the restaurant.

"There's more to my New York story, but I'm here looking for a change—freedom of sorts. My family wasn't too thrilled, but ..." I shrugged. "So ... are you still playing football?" I really didn't know. After our one day, I stalked him and his college football career online for a solid year before I decided two things: he was a fantasy—a reason to avoid reality—and I hated football.

Cage chuckled, shoving his hands into the back pockets of his jeans. "Uh ... yeah." His brow furrowed. "I take it you don't follow football."

My nose wrinkled. "Not so much." Not at all. Worst game ever.

He nodded. "I'm the Minnesota Kings' quarterback. Banks is a defensive end."

Not surprising, but awkward, so very awkward. It was an enormous physical feat to not grimace.

"Oh ... wow." I laughed. "You must think I'm—"

"It's fine."

"No, I mean ... you're a sports star. I should, I don't

know—ask for your autograph or something. Maybe we should get a selfie together."

A brilliant idea. Face-palm. What was wrong with me?

"Wait right here."

"Lake—"

I hurried into my apartment, depositing Trzy on the sofa before grabbing a marker from my kitchen drawer.

"What to sign, what to sign, what to sign?" I whispered to myself, in frantic search for something to sign.

"Lake?"

"One second!" I grabbed the first thing I spotted on the counter. "Here." Stepping back into the hallway I handed him the marker.

"Crispy Rice?" He stared at the box of generic cereal I handed him with the marker. "You want me to sign a box of cereal?"

No. I didn't. But there was no turning back so I owned my moment of insanity.

"Yes. I mean, you're not on the box yet, but maybe someday." Because all NFL quarterbacks dreamed of having their picture on the front of a generic brand of crispy rice cereal.

I was stubborn to the point of my own demise. Had I grabbed a tampon box, I would have held my chin up and insisted he sign it.

Cage shook his head, but he signed it.

I held up my camera. "Selfie?"

He bit back his smirk and handed me the cereal and marker then took my camera. I jumped when he snaked his left arm around me.

"You okay?"

I nodded with a gulp.

"Crispy rice on three." He held up my camera with his right hand.

I gave my best I'm-a-cheeseball smile while holding up the box of cereal.

Dork. Such a dork.

"Thanks." I slipped the phone into my back pocket then hugged the crispy rice box to my chest. "I'd love to stay and chat or completely embarrass myself some more, but I'm late for a date."

Cage jabbed his thumb toward Everson's door. "Yeah, they're probably wondering what's taking me so long."

I nodded.

"It was good to see you again." He smiled and it was genuine, not the broad-is-bat-shit-crazy smirk he had earlier.

"You too. Maybe I'll see ya around sometime. Everson and I are pretty close."

He squinted. "Really?"

"Oh yeah. I think he has a crush on me. It's sweet."

I loved the look of humor mixed with confusion on Cage's face, especially since it brought out his dimples.

"Anyway ... I'm off. Wish me luck." I headed to the elevator.

"You're taking the cereal on your date?"

I stepped into the elevator and turned back to him. "Hell yes. The quarterback for Minnesota just signed my box of crispy rice. I'm showing everyone I see tonight." The elevator doors began to close. "And the selfie too!" It meant absolutely nothing to me to have an NFL quarterback's signature, but since it was Cage Monaghan's, there was a good chance of me humping the box later that night.

CHAPTER THREE

TOOTH FAIRIES AND DOLLS

MY DATE SUCKED. Yeah, Tucker pushed his buddy's wheelchair in a marathon, but he also had an actual fetish with missing limbs, or more accurately ... the prosthetic itself. Before dessert was served, he asked how many prosthetics I owned and if I had any old ones that he could have because he just sort of "liked" them.

I considered offering to shove the one I had on up his ass, but a creepy little voice in my head warned me that he'd probably like it.

Skipped dessert.

Faked a migraine.

Paid my half of the bill because there was no way Twisted Tucker would think I owed him anything.

Drove home in a crazy zigzagging, backtracking pattern to make sure Freak Fetish wasn't following me.

"Stiiiick ..." Everson slurred from his doorway as I stuck my key in the lock.

I grinned, keeping my back to him. "You're drunk."

"A bit. It's my birthday."

"Happy birthday. How was your party?" I turned.

He tipped back an amber bottle of beer then rubbed his lips together. "It was good after your rat left."

"Trzy is a cat. I told you that. Everyone gone?"

He nodded. Drunk Everson didn't look at me like I wasn't his type.

"I had a crappy date. You should invite me over for a beer."

"Let me guess ... the prick was scared of your leg."

I liked drunk Everson's take on things. Sober Everson needed to take a few pointers from him.

"Aw ... you do like me." Stepping in front of him, I peered up at his glassy eyes.

He shook his head. "Never said that."

"You really did. If being scared of my leg makes my date a *prick*, then ... you like me."

He smirked, retreating a few steps to allow me into his apartment.

Plastic red cups, paper plates, and empty alcohol bottles dotted the premises.

Everson snagged a beer from his refrigerator. "You're still not my type, even drunk." He popped the top and handed me the cold bottle.

"Cool your balls, hot stuff. I'm not going to jump ya." I took a long pull of my beer. "Tell me about your quarterback?"

Everson quirked a brow. "You tell me. You seemed to know him earlier."

I shrugged. "We met. I wasn't available at the time." I was ... I was available like a sofa at the end of a driveway. But ... lives at risk.

"Ain't that a bummer. He's not available now."

His response led to me chugging the rest of my beer. After catching my breath and suppressing an unladylike burp, I smiled to hide my disappointment. Seeing the man of my dreams for the first time in three years while holding Trzy was not the best time to size up my competition. She insulted my cat and my lack of knowing who my neighbor was, but I couldn't focus on her because ... Man. Of. My. Dreams.

"Married?"

"Nah, girlfriend."

I nodded. "Serious?"

He chuckled while collecting some of the trash on the counter. "Listen, Stick, we're not going to braid each other's hair and talk about this shit."

I snatched one of the empty trash bags he set out and went to work on the living room.

"What about you?" We weren't done talking about Cage. I just needed to work it from a different angle.

"What about me?"

"You have a girlfriend—a non-white, non-skinny one with things to grab or hold on to?"

Everson erupted into a belly laugh. "Don't you worry about me. I get mine."

I nodded. "Yeah ... well, I get mine too." I didn't. Or maybe I did; I wasn't one hundred percent sure what he meant by that. Dates? Sex? Both? "You could use some color in here. White walls. Black furniture. Are you color blind?"

"I'm not here enough to need color, and when I am here, my ass is planted on that sofa, eyes glued to the television. Why? You some type of decorator or something?"

"No. But your home is your sanctuary so—"

"The stadium is my sanctuary. This is where I sleep and fuck."

I mouthed, "OK ... Wow."

"Tell me, Stick, how you afford to live in this place and drive the wheels you do?"

"Wheels? You've been spying on me?"

"I notice things, that's all."

"I run an amputee porn site."

Everson stilled, looking over his shoulder, trash bag dangling from his huge hand. "You're a freak. I knew you were a freak." Turning back to his task, he shook his head and chuckled like he had the whole world figured out.

There was definitely a freak in the monochrome room, but it wasn't me. Just as I opened my mouth to confess my dry humor that he seemed to miss, there was a knock at his door.

"Who's that?"

I shrugged. "Sorry, my super powers don't extend past my bionic leg."

He sighed like it was somehow my fault that my road to recovery didn't include x-ray vision.

"I think you have the wrong apartment," Everson said to the person at his door.

I continued to clean up the mess.

"Do you speak? Is someone here with you? What's this?"

"Please take care of her!" a woman's voice sounded in the distance.

"Wait! What the hell? Where are you going?" Everson yelled into the hall, then he banged his fist against the door frame.

The suspense was too much to take. I peeked around his massive body. "Hi." I smiled at the little girl.

Her brown eyes held my gaze for a moment before she tucked her chin and stared at her feet. Tight, dark curls curtained her face. Stains soiled her yellow T-shirt with a glitter rainbow, and her jeans were about two sizes too big, hanging from her tiny waist. She looked about six or seven.

Everson shook his head slowly while reading the wrinkled piece of paper in his hand. She had to be his daughter. I had my speech all planned out.

One night.

One sperm.

One forgotten condom.

One huge responsibility for the rest of his life.

I would give him the gentle version of the lecture since his glazed-over expression conveyed complete shock. He would not escape without any lecture. Men could impregnate the whole world without a damn clue. They should at very least have their dicks shrink a quarter inch for every egg fertilized.

"Well, we'll talk tomorrow, Everson, after you get her settled in."

The girl looked at me with big hazelnut eyes, and so did Everson. Did I say something shocking? I'd never seen a black man look so white.

"Nice to meet you. I'm Lake, by the way." I offered my hand to the girl. She hiked her over-stuffed, red backpack onto her narrow shoulders and rested her small hand in mine.

"Shayna," she whispered.

"Shayna." I smiled. "That's a beautiful name."

She smiled back. It was faint, but I saw it.

"Good night, Miss Shayna. Maybe I'll see you around."

Tipping her chin down, she nodded.

"Night, Everson. Happy birthday and thanks for the beer."

His tongue seemed to be paralyzed, jaw stuck open.

After locking my door, I tossed my purse on the counter

and realized I forgot my signed crispy rice box in my car and had nothing to hump.

"Gah! You scared me!" I jumped, opening my door to Everson towering over me.

"Where you going?"

"To my car," I answered with my hand still plastered over my heart.

"I need a favor."

I squinted. "A favor?"

"Can you watch her in the morning while I get all this figured out?"

"You're going to just leave her with a stranger?"

"You're my neighbor."

"I could be a serial killer."

"Are you?"

"If I were, I certainly wouldn't tell you, would I?"

Everson sighed as if my legitimate argument somehow irritated him. "I'll take my chances. So you'll do it?"

"Fine! But after you get back tomorrow we are having a serious conversation about condoms."

Everson's head jerked back, then he turned, looking at Shayna standing just inside his doorway. "She's not ..." He brought his attention back to me and lowered his voice. "She's not my daughter. She's my sister."

I had no response. Didn't see that coming.

"If you're trying to do the math in your head, let me help you out. My mom was fourteen when she had me. I'm twenty-five. She was thirty-eight when she died last year." His voice broke at the end. Then he cleared his throat and glanced up at the ceiling. "Just do me this favor, *please*."

When he looked at me, I nodded. Still, no words came. My heart held them captive.

"Eight too early?"

I shook my head. It was way too early, but telling him that required speech, so eight it was.

THE KNOCK at my door startled me from my naked quarterback dream. I thought I set my alarm. Apparently not.

"Just a minute!" I yelled. "Give a girl a minute to put her leg on, antsy pants," I mumbled.

"You forgot." Everson inspected my shorts and shirt: plaid Hello Kitty.

"Yes, in less than seven hours I forgot." I narrowed my eyes. *Really?* "I didn't forget, I just didn't get up. Good morning, Shayna." I smiled. "Come in."

Her eyes remained fixed to my leg, which wasn't obvious last night under my pants.

"It does cool tricks. I'll show you later."

Darting her gaze to mine, she sucked in a breath like I'd caught her doing something wrong.

"I'm serious. I get paid to play with robotic legs." I winked at her, and she smiled on a sigh.

"And not in a kinky way?" Everson quirked a brow.

I laughed. "No. Not in a kinky way. Clearly you didn't catch my humor."

He nodded, maybe a bit relieved, maybe disappointed. Everson Banks was a hard man to read. "So, uh ... I appreciate this. I guess I owe you."

"Yup." I popped my lips. "You owe me a hair-braiding session while I talk about boys I like."

He shook his head. "Still won't make him available."

"But he's not married. Is he engaged?"

"No time for this, Stick." Everson turned and headed toward the elevator.

The guy was a beast. A sexy, I'm-not-interested-in-the-girl-next-door beast, but still ... a beast.

"Just answer me! Is he engaged or living with her?"

Stepping into the elevator, he turned and gave me a smirk. It was a "no" smirk. I just knew it. The man of my dreams was not officially off the market yet. I would not pursue him or try and steal him from the cat-hater. That wasn't classy, and everyone who knew me would attest to my classiness.

OK, no one would call me classy. Who was I kidding?

My plan: just be the girl he turned his head for three years earlier, the girl whose lips he wanted to kiss. It was a brilliant plan except for the he's-an-impossibly-inaccessible-super-star part. Even the best plans had a few bumps to smooth out.

"Hungry?" I motioned for Shayna to come inside.

She nodded, taking slow steps like ice cracking beneath her.

"Trzy!" I grimaced as my slut cat pounced in Shayna's direction. The harrowing scream I anticipated never came.

"Pretty kitty." Shayna dropped her backpack at her feet and bent down, picking up Trzy.

Pretty kitty? Maybe Shayna needed glasses. I almost passed out when she brushed her lips over Trzy's hairless, wrinkly skin, stopping to kiss her partial ear. Trzy purred like someone starting a lawnmower.

"You like kitties?"

Shayna peeked up at me, hugging Trzy to her chest. "I do like kitties."

"Me too." I pointed to my Hello Kitty jammies and smiled. "Toast? Eggs? Cereal? What do you want to eat?"

"Toast."

"Toast it is. I love toast ... and waffles with chocolate hazelnut butter."

Shayna's eyes grew when I said chocolate.

"We'll save waffles for another day."

She nodded with a huge grin.

We enjoyed butter, cinnamon, and sugar toast while lounging on the sofa; Trzy sprawled out between us.

"Yellow pillows." She bounced a little against the decor pillow. "I like yellow. I like red too."

The kid had excellent taste.

"How old are you?"

"Six."

I nodded. If she would have been seven, I might have explained the many shades of yellow, including my Spanish yellow pillow, a bit brighter than saffron which my mother loved. Maybe once she felt more settled, we'd discuss color swatches. One thing was for certain: Shayna was the resplendent kaleidoscope Everson needed in his life.

"Who brought you to Everson's last night?" It wasn't any of my business, but my favorite pastime was peepholing, so of course I had to ask her.

"Judy." She licked sugar from her finger.

"Did you live with Judy?"

Shayna nodded.

"Is Judy your family?"

She nodded. "Ne-ma's sissy."

"Where is your Ne-ma?"

"With Jesus." Shayna didn't hesitate. She said it like her Ne-ma ran to the grocery store.

I, however, fought back tears while the lump in my throat began to swell.

"Evson's gonna take care of me. Judy says he buy me dolls."

The only thing uglier than the hairless feline between us was the cry I fought back.

"Evson's my family now. He gonna love me."

I blinked and swatted away my tears before she saw them. For someone so little, she could pack a hard punch to the feels. I could barely breathe.

"So did you sleep well last night?" I cleared my throat and wiped the remaining moisture from my eyes.

"I got scared on the couch, so I sneak-ed into Evson's bed." Her eyes grew big with excitement. "It's the biggest bed I ever seen!"

I laughed. "Did he wake up?"

She shook her head. "No. I just hugged his arm until mama visit me. She only come if I sleepin'... in my dreams. She's always in my dreams."

Aaannd ... more tears! I jumped up and took our plates to the kitchen, grabbing a wad of paper towels to deal with my out-of-control emotions.

Shayna slid off the sofa, lugging Trzy with her. My diva cat proved to be quite submissive. I never would have guessed. They plopped on the floor by Shayna's backpack.

"What happened to your leg?" she asked, keeping her focus on the contents of the bag she dumped onto my floor.

I put our plates in the dishwasher. "I had something bad happen to it and I lost part of it. Now I have this cool new leg, and I have others in my closet. I'll show you sometime."

"I lost two teef."

"Did the tooth fairy come?"

"What's a toof fairy?"

Everson needed to get his shit done before his little sister completely wrecked me.

"If you put your tooth under your pillow at night, then the tooth fairy takes it when you're asleep and leaves money for you. I'm sure the next time you lose a tooth the tooth fairy will come."

The kid had me promising things I couldn't guarantee, but I just couldn't stop myself. Major diarrhea mouth. I wanted to see her smile, that and I didn't want to cry anymore. Despite the missing leg and boyfriend-died part of my life, I had it good.

The best parents ever!

Four siblings.

A gaggle of nieces and nephews.

Friends.

A job.

Money.

Independence.

The man of my dreams in. The. Same. City!

Among Shayna's few clothes, a toothbrush with gnarled bristles, several broken crayons, and a Matchbox car that looked like it had been run over by an actual car, there was a photo of a woman kissing a younger Shayna on the cheek. I picked up the photo.

"Mama and Shay."

"This is your mama?" I narrowed my eyes, looking at Shayna and then back at the photo.

She nodded.

"Your mama was beautiful."

And *white*.

And *skinny* ... with nothing to hold on to.

"Mama love Shay."

I smiled, handing the picture to her. "Yes, I'm sure your mama loved you very much."

Shayna would be a heartbreaker, with her perfect, light mocha skin, and long curls that bounced with every move she made. But those eyes ... they held a lifetime, and they made me want to give her back every ounce of innocence I could give. Tooth fairies. Santa Claus. The Easter Bunny.

We played with Trzy, giggling at the never-ending fun she had with a laser pointer for almost an hour before there was a knock at the door.

"Oh!" I looked at Shayna with wide eyes. "I bet that's Everson."

She grinned and I knew everything would be OK for her.

"Hey!" I greeted Everson.

"Yeah, hey, how's it going?"

"Good." I narrowed my eyes a bit.

The man I'd come to recognize as nothing but muscle and confidence looked different. Weak? Shy? He wouldn't hold eye contact with me. Instead, he shifted his weight from one foot to the other, looking only at them.

"Listen this is kind of a big team event day starting with a charity golf outing, so would you mind waiting with her in my apartment until they come to get her?"

"They?"

"My attorney is handling it. Someone with CPS will be here within the hour to get her."

I turned to check on Shayna. She smiled then kissed Trzy on the head. "I'll just be in the hall for a second, okay, sweetie?"

She smiled and nodded.

Closing the door behind me, I glared up at Everson. "Child Protective Services?"

"Yeah."

"And why are they coming to get her?"

"Because her grandmother died the other day and she's an orphan."

"She's your sister, not an orphan." I gritted my teeth.

"I met her last night. I'm not in any position to raise a child."

"You probably make more money in a week than most people make in a year. I think you're in a pretty damn good position to take care of her."

He shook his head. "I didn't say take care of her. I'll make sure she's taken care of. I can't *raise* her. I'm never here. She deserves a family, a yard with a swing set ... I'll make sure she gets that. It just won't be with me."

Fuck you, tears! Keep it together!

I swallowed past my anger and raw emotion. "You are her only family. She needs you."

"She doesn't even know me and in a week she won't remember me. Here..." he reached into his pocket and pulled out a wad of cash and held it out to me "...for your trouble today and here's a key to my place. Make sure she grabs her hairbrush by the bathroom sink."

Stunned.

I was speechless, and heartbroken, and angry, and just ... *stunned.* He grabbed my hand and shoved the money and key into it.

"We'll have that chick-talk about Monaghan later." He turned and left.

A war of emotions throbbed in my head. Even after the elevator doors closed, I just stood there waiting for one emotion to emerge as the dominate one, the one that would guide my next move.

Livid. That's the one that broke from the pack as the leader.

CHAPTER FOUR

JAILBIRD

I DROVE to Target like a granny. Since Ben died and I lived, Sunday drives and joyrides vanished from my life. It was all about getting from point A to point B without dying. My red Acura SUV rated high in all safety tests, but I didn't have a booster seat. Shayna said she didn't need one. I disagreed.

After finding the best booster seat with the minimal time I had to do any sort of research on the safest brand, I Googled and hash-tagged the hell out of every possible connection to Minnesota and golf charity events, found the location, drove there, and parked ... *then* it occurred to me I may have kidnapped a child. At least, CPS and the police would think I did.

knock knock knock

I opened my door, forcing the police officer to step back.

"Miss, you can't park here."

"Well the parking lot is gated off. Where am I supposed to park?"

He stared at my leg.

I sighed. Normally my patience level was much higher,

as well as my respect for men in uniform. "Yes. I have a bionic leg, and I could literally crush your junk beyond recognition if I kicked you between the legs—"

"Miss, are you threatening a police officer?"

"Not at all. I'm simply stating a fact. This leg is designed and has a pending patent by Thaddeus Westbrook, and *he* told me it could literally crush a man's junk beyond recognition. I'm no more threatening you than a car salesman telling you a certain model gets eighteen miles to the gallon and goes zero to sixty in under three seconds. I'm stating a fact."

I opened the back door and unfastened Shayna, hoping he wouldn't slap handcuffs on me. My brain was not working properly. Adrenaline fed everything I did.

"Miss, I told you this is a no-parking zone, and the club is closed today for a private event."

"Listen..." I pulled Shayna in front of me and covered her ears with my hands then lowered my voice to a whisper "...see this little girl? Her grandmother just died and her only living relative is playing golf here today, but he's not answering his phone." Because, of course, I didn't have his number. "So this is sort of an emergency situation."

His gaze flitted between me and Shayna. Conflict etched his face. "I ticket you in thirty minutes. I have your vehicle towed in an hour."

I smiled. "Thank you kindly for your condolences." I didn't care about the ticket, so we had an hour. Having my vehicle towed was on my list of things to avoid. Landing in jail for child abduction was on that list too.

"Let's go, sweetie."

"Where's Evson?"

I led her through the barriers and parking lot filled with luxury vehicles, but the security guard at the entrance looked a little smarter and meaner than Mr. I Wear a Uniform and Give Out Parking Tickets.

"Everson's here. We're going to see him soon." Another promise I couldn't guarantee. How did my morning turn into a segue to Hell?

Lies. Lies. Lies. Just the day before, I would have called myself a pretty honest person.

"Do you have a press pass or invitation?" the security guard asked.

No. I had a kidnapped child.

"My name is Lake Jones, Everson Banks's nanny, and this is his..." I covered Shayna's ears again because there had to be brownie points with God for not letting a young child hear my lies "...daughter." Sister seemed too unbelievable. "There has been a family emergency and Everson is not answering his phone. Could you contact him for me?"

"Miss, this is a televised event. I'll need to know what kind of emergency you have."

"Death in the family." I uncovered her ears once the lies were over.

He narrowed his eyes at me then looked at Shayna.

Don't you dare ... you unemotional bastard!

"Hey, darling ... did someone die?" He leaned down a few inches from her face.

Who the hell asks a child that? I wanted to scream!

Shayna nodded. "Mama and Ne-ma went to see Jesus."

He grimaced, standing back to his full height. "I'm very sorry for your loss. I'll have someone track Mr. Banks right away."

"Thank you." I gave him my best grievance-laden smile as the top of my knee twitched, like the doctor tapping to check my reflex only more intense—much more intense. My bionic leg jerked forward landing squarely into his shin.

"Ah!" he cried, bending down to grab his leg.

"Oh my gosh! I'm so sorry." Before I could make sense of why I kicked him—because I didn't try to kick him—a police officer had me in handcuffs.

We were escorted inside the building while they found Everson. I sat handcuffed to a chair in the manager's office with my chin down, whispering, "*shh*, everything's going to be okay" to a teary-eyed Shayna sitting next to me. The injured guard was hauled off for medical attention while the disapproving police officer watched over me.

I had a feeling my next seat would be the back of a police cruiser. So much for avoiding my car being towed. What were the chances of Thaddeus flying to Minneapolis to bail me out of jail and testify before a judge that kicking the guard was not my fault but rather a malfunction of his invention?

"Lake? Want to tell me what the hell is going on?" Everson called me Lake. I imagined it sounding sexier. I also imagined not being in handcuffs. Scratch that ... there were handcuffs, but I was handcuffed to a bed, not a chair in the manager's office at a golf course.

"Mr. Banks, your nanny assaulted one of the security guards."

"Run that by me again? Who did what?"

"Miss Jones demanded we find you to notify you of a family emergency, then she struck a guard with her ..."

I looked up at the officer with his mouth hanging open as if the politically-correct word for my prosthetic leg, which didn't look like a prosthetic leg, would magically fall from his lips.

"Leg? Is that the word you're looking for? Real leg. Fake leg. Prosthetic leg. Bionic leg. Any way you look at it ... the word is leg, because it replaces the part of my body that's missing. Does anyone know what part of my body is missing?"

tick tick tick

The wall clock was the only sound in the room.

"Leg ... Lake's leg is fun." The child in the room was the only one not afraid to call it like she saw it.

"Could I please speak with *Miss Jones* alone about the family emergency?" Everson eyed the officer. "Maybe you could get this little girl a snack or something?"

The officer stood his ground, jaw set, eyes narrowed.

"Ten minutes?" Everson asked.

"Five." The officer grunted.

Everson motioned for Shayna to go with the police officer. "He's going to get you a snack."

"Everson—"

"Shut it, Lake."

I glared at him as Shayna followed the officer out of the office.

It didn't matter that my Apollo was dressed in blindingly bright plaid shorts and a white collared short-sleeved shirt. I wouldn't let his looks distract me from my anger.

"He could be molesting her as we speak. You don't send your child off with a stranger, even if they're wearing a badge."

"That's just it!" he roared, bending at the waist so his face was level and a few inches from mine. "She's not my kid. She shouldn't be here. You shouldn't be here. I paid you to stay with her until CPS arrived and you couldn't fucking follow my simple instructions! What is your problem?"

My teeth hurt from grinding them so hard. My pulse raced. My skin burned.

"You're her family." I had a million answers, but that was the only one that mattered.

"We share a few genes. She doesn't think of me as her family—"

"She does."

He stood straight, planted his hands on his hips, and paced the small room.

"She does. She knows you're her family, and she thinks you're going to take care of her. That little girl has lost the two most important people in her life. She's lost two teeth and doesn't know who the tooth fairy is ... and dolls ... she doesn't have any dolls."

"This is none of your business." He continued to pace.

I stared at my lap. "I know," I whispered.

Guilt. I felt guilt. Regret? None. I couldn't picture Shayna or hear her little voice in my head and regret one thing I did that morning. Okay, maybe assaulting the guard, but that really wasn't my fault.

"There's a slew of press out there waiting to find out why I'm not teeing it up on the third hole."

"I know."

"My PR people are on their way, and they're going to want to know what the deal is with you and that girl."

"Shayna."

"What?" He stopped in front of me again.

"Shayna. Her name is Shayna, not 'that girl.'"

"I know her fucking name!"

I flinched.

He blew out a big breath. "What was your point of coming here? What is this family emergency?"

Those were really good questions. An hour earlier, while running on pure adrenaline from my livid emotions, I had a whole spiel in my head. It sounded good at the time, the kind of good that would make Everson rethink his rash decision to give away his sister.

Under the intensity of his gaze and the heat radiating from the nearness of his body, my entire case for doing what I did just sort of ... crumbled. I would say the words because just like the box of crispy rice cereal, I owned my craziness at all cost.

"Shayna's Ne-ma ... your Ne-ma, died a few days ago. Your mother died two years ago. You have friends, a team, a family of sorts, and money. Shayna has nothing but a promise from Judy that you are going to love her, take care of her, and buy her dolls. If you take that away, she'll have nothing. And I worry that no matter how wonderful the family that might adopt her will be, she will never recover from the abandonment she will surely feel when you, too, disappear from her life."

Yes, it sounded better in my head. Coming from my mouth it sounded childish. Everson had a job that required his undivided attention. He wouldn't have much time to spend with her. She would be raised by a nanny and how would that be better than a loving family with a big yard, other kids to play with, and maybe a big, fluffy dog who chased rabbits?

The officer opened the door to the office. Shayna sat beside me, holding a soft pretzel with salt.

"We're taking Miss Jones to the station now."

Shayna looked up at me with pleading eyes, the kind that asked a million heartbreaking questions without a single word. I don't think she knew what exactly was about to happen, but she sensed something. I felt her fear as much as I saw it in those eyes.

I leaned forward, my handcuffed wrists drawing my shoulders back. Then I kissed her on the forehead. "Shayna," I whispered. "Repeat after me. 'I'm beautiful.'"

She blinked several times but never stopped looking into my eyes.

"I'm bootiful."

I smiled, nodding. "Say, 'I'm loved.'"

"I'm loved."

Another nod. "Say, 'I'll be happy.'"

Her eyes shifted to Everson for a brief moment then back to me. "I'll be happy."

After depositing one last kiss on her head, I stood.

I nodded to the officer.

"I'll get you bailed ..." Everson started.

"Don't worry about it." I didn't look back as the officer led me out of the room.

A MOB of press waited by the entrance. Only a few snapped photos of me. After all, who was I? I should have been humiliated, but no one knew me.

"Lake?"

I looked over my shoulder as the officer escorted me to the police cruiser.

"No." I grimaced and whipped my head forward, chin down so my hair covered my face.

Eighteen holes spread out over many acres. How did I manage to make my criminal exit while Cage Monaghan strolled up to the tee just over the fence to my right?

He drew near. I knew it from the photographers scrambling for their cameras and vying for the best position to get photos of *us*! Just like that I went from no one to the handcuffed amputee attracting the attention of a famous quarterback. This was *not* how I wanted to capture his attention.

"Lake? Officer, can you hold up a minute?"

I closed my eyes, took a deep breath, then looked up with my absolute best smile ever. "Cage! Hey, how's it going? Ya having a good golf game today? The weather couldn't be better for this time of year in Minnesota."

He narrowed his eyes, like not a single word I just spoke was in English. "Are you being arrested?"

I tugged against the handcuffs. "Oh, this?" I sucked air in through my bared-teeth smile. "Yeeaah, there was a glitch of sorts with my leg." Camera flashes closed in on us as the officer opened the door to the back of the police car. "You should go. I'm not good publicity today."

I took one last look at the man of my dreams in his royal blue polo shirt that brought out the heavens in his eyes and accented the bronzy tones of his blond hair. The grimace on his face hid his dimples; that was unfortunate. The door closed and the car pulled away from the curb.

"Nothing embarrassing about that," I mumbled to myself. I couldn't say for sure, but I think the bald man in uniform behind the steering wheel smirked. Yeah, I was always good for a laugh.

"You've been sprung, Jones."

That was quick. I didn't even get my phone call.

The officer opened the holding cell.

"By whom? I didn't call anyone."

"Beats me. I just do as I'm told." I followed the stocky, gray-haired officer. He returned my purse and its contents to me in a bag then nodded to the entrance. "That guy."

I squinted. "I don't know him."

"You're out. Who cares? The guy got the charges dropped before they were officially filed. You don't have to go with him, but I'd say at least a thank-you is in order."

My hero with perfectly-parted black hair and a suit that fit too well to not be tailored leaned against the wall next to the door, one ankle crossed over the other as he swiped his finger along the screen of his phone. The gold watch, the confident way he held his shoulders back, and the blinding shine to his flawlessly polished shoes spelled money and power.

As I approached, he kept his head down. I expected nothing less of a man who exuded such confidence. The world waited for him.

"I'm not posing naked for you, so if you have some weird amputee fetish then you've sprung the wrong girl."

A smirk pulled at his lips, but I still hadn't earned his eye contact. "How'd you lose your leg?"

"Car accident."

"How'd you land in jail?" He clicked off his phone and slipped it into the inside pocket of his jacket. Golden brown eyes met mine.

"A brilliant engineer had a glitch with his latest invention. Who are you?"

He stared at me for a few seconds like the answer was on its way but hadn't arrived yet. "I'm Flint. My boy asked me to clear up this confusion and escort you home."

"Everson sent you?" I adjusted my purse strap on my shoulder then crossed my arms over my chest.

"Are you ready?"

"What makes you think I need a ride? I have a car, you know."

He mirrored my stance and it looked better on him. A sexy guy named Flint wanted to take me home. Best offer

I'd had in weeks. Unfortunately, I still abided by the Stranger Danger rule.

"Yes, I know, and it was towed over an hour ago, but I'm working on that too. It will be returned to you by the end of the day if you give me the key."

"Really? You think I'm just going to hand over my key so you can steal my car?"

He cocked his head to the side. "Yes. I made this whole arrested-for-assaulting-a-security-guard thing disappear just so I could steal your car."

I shook my head but dug my fob out of my purse anyway.

"Great." He took it from me. "I'll drive you home now."

Presumptuous. However, I did admire his take-charge personality.

"You're quite handsome." I twisted my lips, waiting for his response. Even the tough ones responded to compliments.

His smirk grew until his pearly whites peeked through his parted lips, brows raised a fraction.

Predictable. I winked at him. "But I can't go with you. Thank you and thank Everson if you see him before I do, but I'll catch a cab. What do I owe you?"

"Owe me?" He chuckled, shaking his head. "You don't owe me anything. Just doing my job, keeping my boy's reputation squeaky clean."

I nodded. "You do his dirty work?"

He shrugged. "Something like that."

"What about Shayna?"

Intense eyes stayed glued to mine. He had a killer poker face. I didn't expect anything less from a sharp-suited guy named Flint. My eyes? They begged him to tell me that Everson changed his mind about giving up Shayna.

"So no ride?"

"He let her go, didn't he?" My heart sank. It already knew the answer.

"Have a nice day, Miss Jones." He slid on his sunglasses and pushed the front door open.

I called a cab.

CHAPTER FIVE

POWERFUL THOUGHTS

AS PROMISED, my car was returned to me. Flint wasn't the delivery man, it was a younger guy who couldn't answer a single question I asked him—not one single question out of the dozen I asked. He gave me my key fob and a note card then walked away.

CHAPTER ONE

Chapter one? I was used to weird. I was raised on weird. The note took a step past weird. I slapped it on the refrigerator and stabbed it with a magnet then went for a jog to clear my head. Shayna's commanding eyes and innocent smile haunted me with every step. I couldn't save the world—every child, every stray animal—but that reality didn't make it any less heartbreaking.

After my shower, Thad called me while I melted marshmallows and butter in the microwave.

"I quit."

"Now, love, don't be so rash. I gathered from the ten

messages you left me earlier that we have a monumental breakthrough on our hands."

I laughed. "A monumental breakthrough? It's possible a security guard will be in a cast for the next few months because of your monumental *mistake*. Oh, and you did catch the part about me going to jail, right?"

"Yeah, yeah, yeah, let's get to the good part. You said you didn't mean to kick him, that you felt a muscle twitch and then it just happened, but you *thought* about kicking him. Correct?"

"Yes, but—"

"Fuck Einstein, love. Do you get how incredible that is? Your thoughts alone made it happen. That sensory chip detected the twitch and bang! Just like that, my baby went into action."

"Stop calling a part of me your baby. It's creepy. And stop celebrating what is a serious and dangerous defect. Do you get what this really means? I have to control my thoughts! People can't control their thoughts, only their actions, but I can't do either. What if every time you saw an attractive woman and you imagined having sex with her, you couldn't control your body and the next thing you know you have her pinned to the wall with your dick in her. You'd be in prison for rape. That's not a breakthrough, that's a felony!"

I took my bowl from the microwave and stirred the melted marshmallows and butter.

"I never said it's perfect. It needs some tweaking, but this is big, very big. I'm booking a flight for myself to Beijing too. I'll meet you there next week. Jerry's testicles are going to explode when he finds out."

A trip to China to watch a man's balls explode, what more could I have asked for?

"I'm not wearing it until I'm there." I poured crispy rice cereal into my gooey concoction—microwaved rice crispy treats, my weakness and obsession.

"You have to wear it through security. If you pack it, some luggage troll with a TSA badge will steal it and have it on eBay by sunset."

"I could bring down the plane with my robotic kung-fu leg."

Thad chuckled. "Only if you're thinking about it."

"Well, since we're having this conversation, it's all I'll think about because that's how the mind works. Don't think about food. Yep, that's all I'll think about. Snakes? Spiders? Sex? My mind is going to go there on its own, especially if it knows it's not supposed to!" I shoved a spoonful into my mouth.

"Sex, huh?"

"Shut up," I mumbled over my crunching.

"Just focus on happy, kind, nonviolent things. I don't think you can bring down a plane with one leg if your other three limbs know better. But if you choose to use your 'glitch' to get some nookie on the plane, that's your prerogative. I'll text you your hotel information in a few days. Gotta run, love."

"Thad—"

Aannd that was that.

I stared at the celebrity signature on my cereal box. How far back did this morning's events set my plan to make the man of my dreams fall in love with me? It was hard to say. I collapsed on the sofa, set my bowl beside me, and grabbed my laptop.

"Back away, Trzy." I gave her the stink eye when she poked her nose near my marshmallow treat.

A quick internet search for Cage Monaghan brought up picture after picture of *me*.

Minnesota's Quarterback Shows Concern for Disabled Woman Arrested at Charity Golf Tournament

Unidentified Woman Threatens Security at Charity Golf Tournament – Monaghan Helps Police Catch Her.

Yeah, sure, that really happened. After more of the same and photos to accompany every headline, I shut my laptop and fed my face while watching *Sons of Anarchy* on Netflix. Some days reality sucked. Netflix was the perfect drug and my addiction to binge-watching series on it was borderline committable.

I missed my friend Lindsay, but I didn't miss being her roommate. There were those in life who were destined to live productive lives, real "Be the Change" people, then there were those who subscribed to Netflix like a religion. Lindsay was a nurse who traveled with Doctors without Boarders. I streamed shows on Netflix. To each their own.

Just as the show hit a good part and my purring cat was draped over my lap, there was a knock at my door. I paused my show. "Jax, Jax, Jax, I love that ass of yours." I winked at the screen which was paused on Charlie Hunnam's naked backside.

Everson was on the opposite side of my peephole. "Be nice, Lake. He did get you bailed out," I mumbled to myself.

I opened the door, forcing a smile. "Yes?"

His gaze moved along my face without looking at my eyes, then down my neck and to my chest as his head inched forward a bit, eyes slightly squinted.

"Dandruff?"

"What?" I looked down at my chest. "Oh, no it's ..." I brushed the crumbs away then wiped my mouth and cheeks with the back of my hand because I was just. That. Sexy. "They're crispy treat crumbs."

Everson always looked at me the same way, the way I imagined he'd look at a train wreck.

"About this morning—"

"Don't." I shook my head and held up my hand. "I got too emotionally invested in a situation that wasn't any of my business and I apologize. I have a terrible habit of lighting a match before looking to see if anything around me is flammable. I just ... react on impulse. I appreciate you sending Flint to get me out of jail and dealing with my impounded vehicle. Honestly, I didn't know what I was going to do. I don't have any family here and I haven't really made friends yet."

Another downside to being a Netflix addict.

"Flint?"

"Yes."

Everson shook his head. "Flint said I sent him?"

"Yes ... well, come to think of it, he never said your name, just that he was protecting his boy, which wasn't that hard to figure out, it had to be you. I assume he's PR? Agent? Personal Assistant?"

"Yeah, Flint takes care of his boy, that's for sure."

"Lucky you."

"Not exactly, but it doesn't matter. You a Twins fan?" He held up a ticket. "Suite behind home plate. Game starts in an hour. I'd suggest you cover the leg, pull your hair up, and buy a hat to wear as soon as you get there."

"What are you talking about?"

"Minnesota Twins. It's baseball."

"I know who the Twins are, I'm talking about the rest.

Why are you offering me a ticket and telling me to cover my leg and—"

"I can't go. Thought I'd offer it to you for helping Shay, but after the media frenzy I think it's best for you to not draw any more attention to yourself today."

"It's one ticket."

He chuckled. "Best seat in the house and you're getting greedy on me?"

"I won't know anyone."

"You will."

"I wi—Cage? He's going? Are you serious?"

"Take it." He grinned, handing me the ticket. "Go brush yourself off and get out of here."

I snatched the ticket. "His girlfriend? Will she be there?"

He walked toward his door and shrugged. "There will be a lot of women there. It's an opportunity, Stick. The rest is on you."

"Everson?'

He turned before closing his door.

"Thank you."

He nodded. "For the record, I'd planned on coming to get you myself, but something came up."

I smiled and shut the door.

"EEEEK!" Everson heard me, hell, the whole neighborhood probably heard me, but I didn't care. In an hour I would see Cage again. "An hour. Shit! I've got to get ready."

CHAPTER SIX

CHEATER BOYFRIEND

FROM THE SLAMMER to a suite behind home plate at a Twin's game. Not bad. Thaddeus's robotic leg got benched for the night. I dug out one of my pretty prosthetic legs that fit under my jeans and tall boots. Comfort wise it was like downgrading from a Cadillac to a Ford Escort, but Everson was right; I couldn't show up with my superhero leg that stood out in any crowd, not after it had been plastered all over the internet earlier that morning.

I pulled my hair back in a ponytail and bought a Twins hat before making my way to the suite. My nerves stripped my confidence. I might as well have been naked. The fluttering in the pit of my stomach brought about a slight sensation of nausea. I tried to wet my lips, but my mouth was too dry. As the guard let me into the suite, I nearly fainted from shortness of breath and heart palpitations. Had they asked me to sing the National Anthem before the game, I wouldn't have been as nervous as I was when I saw *him*.

Cage's back was to me as he stood by the large windows overlooking the private balcony seating and a spectacular view of the field. His black, long-sleeved T-shirt hugged him the way I wanted to hug him; the jealousy I felt for his hands that were shoved into the back pockets of his dark jeans was a little unhealthy. The chestnut-haired guy standing next to him looked back at me first. Then Cage glanced over his shoulder as if to see what had caught his friend's attention.

I gave a small wave like a beauty queen, then dropped my hand and balled it into a fist to fight off the shakes. He made his way back to me, twisting the cap back onto his water bottle.

"Jailbird."

I laughed.

He smiled so big my heart exploded. I loved the way his dark bronzy hair fell across his forehead, like yesterday it was too short and tomorrow it would be too long, but today it was perfect. I loved his blue eyes that reflected mine. More than anything, I loved how with one look he stilled my jitters.

"I think to earn the official title of jailbird I have to be a repeat offender. This morning was my first arrest."

He nodded, grazing his teeth along his lower lip. "Well the night is still young." He tugged on the bill of my hat.

I felt it in between my legs. The guy made me wet just by touching my baseball cap. In reality, he made me wet by just existing.

"Funny." I rolled my eyes.

"I take it Everson gave you his ticket?"

I held up the stub. "Yep."

"So do you follow baseball more than football?"

I cocked my head to one side and then the other while pursing my lips. "I'd say about the same."

He laughed. Yeah, I loved that too.

"What are you drinking tonight?"

I shrugged. "Probably just water since I'm driving."

"Water it is." He stepped over to the bar area to get me a water.

"Thanks." I twisted off the top and took a small swig.

"So do you know anyone else here?"

Nothing quite like being put on the spot. However, "Nope, I just came here to make you love me," didn't seem like an appropriate answer.

"Um ... I recognize a few people from Everson's birthday party."

"Yeah? Who did you to talk to there?"

"Oh, well ..." Heat crawled up my neck until I could feel it stinging my cheeks.

The crowd erupted into cheers. We both looked out the windows.

"You want to sit outside?" Cage asked.

"Sure." Anything. I wanted to do literally anything but discuss who I did or didn't meet at a party I wasn't invited to, yet ended up there because my scary cat crashed it.

We sat down and Cage introduced me to a few of his teammates and their spouses, ones I of course didn't get around to meeting at Everson's party.

"So how did you two meet?" Brea, one of the wives, asked me as Cage and her husband chatted. She must have thought we were there together. The way she stared at me with her bottom lip protruding out in a you-poor-thing expression told me she also thought I looked less than presentable compared to all the other women there. With my hair back and hat pulled down low on my head to shadow my face, I did look like my next stop might be robbing a convenience store.

"It's a long and really weird story, but it happened by

chance several years ago and we hadn't seen each other since, until we ran into each other at Everson's birthday party."

She leaned in close to me, looking past the shadows of my hat. "Oh my God, you're that cat lady!"

There it was, that label that would stick forever.

"You had that cat that looked like ... like ... uh ..."

I let her fumble her words. If she thought I would jump in and admit to being the cat lady, she was so very wrong.

Every nerve along my skin shot up goose bumps as Cage's hot breath bathed my ear. "Brea and her husband, Michael, role play during sex. She wears her hair in a beehive and he sucks a pacifier and calls her mommy," he whispered.

I giggled. Brea gave us both a curious look. Then I giggled some more, and I just couldn't stop. She shook her head and turned her attention back to the game. I covered my mouth with my hand, but the laughter continued. Cage put his arm around my shoulders and pulled me into his chest to help hide my laughing fit.

"I was just kidding." He chuckled.

"What?" I jerked up.

"Shh ..." He grinned, tapping the side of his finger over his lips.

At the same time, our smiles faded. I don't know what it was for him. I imagined thoughts of his girlfriend came to mind. For me, it was my body fully registering his arm around my shoulders, my hands fisting his shirt, and our faces just inches apart. The bill of my hat grazed his forehead. It wasn't a good idea to stare at his lips, but I couldn't help it because he stared at mine. I pulled back an inch and watched his Adam's apple bob as he took a deep swallow.

Why did I feel so comfortable with him touching me and me touching him? We'd had brief interactions on three different occasions over the course of more than three years, yet I kissed him the first time, took a goofy fan-girlish selfie the second time, and lingered too close to his lips the third time. The problem was that it didn't feel too close.

I released his shirt and sat up straight. He removed his arm from me. We sat silent for a few minutes, staring at the field. I jumped when his shoulder bumped mine as he leaned in closer.

"Brea was being a bitch by calling you the cat lady. I just wanted to see you smile again so I made that shit up," he whispered.

Keeping my eyes focused on the second player in a row to strike out, I nodded. "It was funny shit. Well done, you." I smirked and through the corner of my eye, I could see him smiling too.

It took everything I had to keep from asking about his girlfriend. I didn't want to bring it to his attention that I even realized he had a girlfriend. After all, he didn't introduce me to her the night of Everson's party.

"So ... I never lived in New York."

"What?"

My eyes remained focused on the game. "In Omaha, I told you I was from New York. My brother Luke and I were looking for 'Jillian,' and she was in danger ... we were kind of in danger too. I'm from Tahoe and moved here from San Francisco—"

"She called me. Jillian ... she called me." Cage's jagged-edge voice sliced through my train of thought.

I didn't know that. Our family rarely discussed Jessica/Jillian's time in Omaha. She faked her death and fell in love with another man. Both she and Luke spent many months in counseling to piece back together their relationship after everything was over. As much as I wanted to ask her about Cage, I never did. I loved her and Luke too much to mention anything related to that time in our lives.

"So she told you everything?"

"She told me virtually nothing. She offered, but I didn't want to know about her new life. I know that sounds bad, but I just couldn't deal with it—any of it."

"She's my sister-in-law now."

"Don't ..."

I looked over at him.

He forced an apologetic smile. "I'm sorry. I don't want to know. Not yet, just ... not yet."

I nodded. "I understand." It was the truth, but it still made me sad. It had been three years, but his wounds weren't healed. It's like he just buried them without any sort of closure, and they'd forever feel raw as long as he ignored them. In my own way, I really did understand. After all, I still couldn't go a day without thinking: Ben died and I lived.

We didn't talk much the rest of the game. One minute I felt the events of our pasts like a wedge between us, and the next minute I felt some pull—a sexual tension. To be honest, it might have just been me. Going a really long time without sex, having Everson as a neighbor, and watching naked Charlie Hunnam didn't help my situation.

The Twins were killing it, so the crowd started to thin out before the end. I thought it would be best for me to slip out, as well. Cage had gone back inside. As I made my way to him, several guys gave me an easy nod and said, "Hi." I stopped behind Cage, feeling like a fool because I wanted to say goodbye, but I didn't want to interrupt his conversation.

Finally one of the guys in their little circle nodded toward me, and Cage turned around.

"Sorry, I'm not trying to interrupt. I'm leaving and I just wanted to say goodbye."

"Oh, the game's not over. You have a hot date or something?" Cage wiggled his brows.

Yes, naked Charlie, but after the close encounter with the man of my dreams, I would be watching Charlie but thinking of Cage while I touched myself. In that moment I prayed he couldn't read my filthy mind.

"More like a Netflix addiction." I shrugged. "That's what us cat ladies do."

After observing me for a few moments, maybe to see if I was just kidding—sadly I wasn't—he turned back to his buddies. "I'm heading out. I'll catch up with you guys next week."

There were some fist bumps and a few "laters."

"You ready?"

"Ready?"

"To go?"

I shook my head. "You don't have to leave too. I can find my way out just fine."

"You sure? 'Cause the last time I saw you exiting a building you were in handcuffs."

"Such a funny guy." I grinned.

"Such a beautiful smile."

That's *not* what I expected him to say. His face didn't hold one bit of regret. How could he say that to me without thinking of *her*? I wanted his attention, but with him standing in front of me, giving it so freely, I felt nothing but guilt. It wasn't a kiss or anything physical, it was a compliment, but that compliment in that moment felt as intimate as his lips on mine or his hand grazing my breast. Not that I thought about his hand on my breast ... Who was I kidding? Of course I thought about his hand on my breast.

I need to do the right thing.

"Okay, I'll let you escort me from the building." That wasn't the right thing.

Cage chuckled. "Sounds so formal, but all right, let's go." He nodded toward the door.

It was formal. It had to be formal.

No touching.

No flirting.

No kissing.

No grazing my breasts.

He pressed his hand to the small of my back, and just like that, he broke rule number one. We made it to the lower level before anyone stopped him for an autograph and picture. I kept walking like we weren't together.

He tugged at my ponytail as I exited the building. "You didn't have to run off on me."

I shrugged. "I didn't. This isn't my running leg, it's my sexy leg. I mean—"

"Your sexy leg, huh?"

"No. I didn't mean it that way, like I think I'm sexy. It's just the one that looks more like an actual leg, not that you can tell with my jeans and boots covering it. It's the leg that makes me feel sexy. Gah!" I shook my head and tried to keep a few steps ahead of him so he wouldn't see my flushed face.

"That sounds bad too. The leg doesn't actually do anything to make me feel sexy, like vibrate or something weird like that. Not that I'm suggesting vibrating things make me feel good."

"They don't?" He chuckled.

I unlocked my door and turned before getting inside.

"I'm so embarrassed." Slapping my hands over my face, I tipped my chin down.

"I think you're refreshing."

A few creepers began to inch their way closer to my vehicle, pens and camera phones in hand. I tugged down on the bill of my hat. Cage opened my door and I climbed in the driver's seat. He blocked their view of me with his large frame then ducked his head inside.

"Give me your number, Lake."

Why did he have to destroy the perfect image I had of him? The man of my dreams was not a cheater.

"I can't."

"Again?" He laughed, shaking his head.

Years ago when he asked for my number I said the same thing but for different reasons—lives at risk and all that jazz.

I sighed. "I like you. I've liked you for longer than is probably healthy, given the minimal amount of time we've spent together, but I like to win the guy fair and square. I don't want to be the dirty little secret. And if you're willing to cheat on one girl, then you're willing to cheat on any girl, and that just makes me sad because I've had you on this huge pedestal since we first met. Now that you've asked me for my number, you've just been knocked down quite a few notches, and while you're still incredibly sexy —excessively so really—I think what you're trying to do here is just ugly."

"Cage, can we get your autograph?" one of the groupies asked, standing directly behind him.

He turned, not looking the least bit upset about their intrusion, and autographed a purse, a hat, and a shirt, although not on the bust where the skank requested he sign it. After a few quick pictures, they took off in a fit of squeals and giggles.

"So..." he turned back to me "...you won't give me your phone number this time because of my 'girlfriend?'"

I nodded. "Don't get me wrong. I don't even like her. The night of Everson's party she acted like Trzy was the plague and anyone who doesn't like Trzy will most likely not like me, so she can choke to death on her uppityness for all I care, but that still doesn't mean I want to take her cheater boyfriend."

Cage narrowed his eyes a little. Why did he have to smell as good as he looked? It was like sitting at the dinner table staring at my favorite dessert and listing all the reasons I should not eat it. I wanted to eat him. Yes, that's what I thought. I. Wanted. To. Eat. Him.

"Trzy is your cat?"

"Uh huh."

"And I'm the cheater boyfriend?"

I shrugged, giving him the if-the-shoe-fits grimace.

He nodded slowly, eyes pinning me with a world of thought behind them. "Well, here's the thing: I don't have a girlfriend, so either you're going to give me your number or you're going to kiss me again. What's it going to be?"

Poof. There went my panties.

Two big gulps later ... "She wasn't your girlfriend?"

"She was."

"But she's not now?"

"She's not."

"Why?"

The one! He was available. It was too much to take. Inside I died a little. There was a ninety-nine percent chance of me blowing my second chance at one of my *two* ones, which was a mathematical phenomenon.

He smirked. "You're nosy."

"I am." I bit my lips together.

"We weren't that serious, and I wanted to ask for Lake Jones's number without being a cheater boyfriend."

I continued to bite back my smile along with my need to run, jump, and scream. On the outside I remained Iceland. Okay, maybe not Iceland because there were cooler places than Iceland.

Antarctica. I was just that cool.

"Choose."

"You choose." My grin broke free before I could catch it.

Cage inched his head toward mine. The kiss, he wanted the kiss. All the air got sucked out of the car. My lungs called 9-1-1 while the gallop of my heart made it impossible to hear anything but my own pulse. I closed my eyes.

"I want your number," he whispered over my lips without touching them.

What a sadist. My libido self-combusted. I would need a 5-in-1 to scrape it off my leather seat later.

My eyes popped open. His danced with amusement.

"My number?"

He nodded, not moving an inch from my face like he dared me to kiss him.

"I'm not going to kiss you," I whispered. Shoving him into the back seat and having sex with him was another thing, but I could do that without kissing him.

"No?"

"No."

He moved back and my lungs screamed *YES!* as they drew in a breath. Cage retrieved his phone from his pocket, unlocked it, and handed it to me.

"I'm leaving for Beijing in a few days." I typed my name and number into his contacts.

"Really? What for?"

I handed his phone back to him. "My job. In layman's

terms, I test robotic legs. The company has engineers all around the world who make prototypes for amputees. Jerry Chu, twenty-eight and just barely over five foot with an affinity for answering all questions with 'excellent' or 'you'll see,' has two new prototypes to fit me—one for swimming and one for rock climbing. So basically I'm going to China to swim and climb."

"You rock climb?"

"I do a little bit of everything. That's why my boss, Thaddeus Westbrook, hired me. Different limbs for different activities which is nothing new, but his are unique. They 'sense' or respond to my muscle reflexes. You could call them smart limbs, of sorts. Although, the one I had on this morning was too smart for its own good when it landed on the security guard's shin."

"Jailbird." He grinned, looking at my mouth.

"Shut up." My eyes shifted to his lips, begging him to just kiss me.

"Is your sexy prosthetic also smart?"

I laughed while rubbing my hand down over it. "No, she's clueless. My smart ones are not sexy. Thaddeus says function before fashion. He hopes to someday make physical disabilities obsolete."

"Big dreams."

"Yes, but he's wicked smart, so I don't doubt him."

Cage shoved his phone in his pocket. "Well, safe travels."

I smiled. "Thanks."

I waited for him to shut my door, but he just stared at me. No one looked at me like Cage Monaghan. I thought it the first time we laid eyes on each other, and years later it still felt the same. He looked at me like people looked at puppies, cooing babies, ocean-view sunsets, and ... miracles.

Not one ounce of pity.

Not one reservation.

Not one hint of anything but total admiration.

"I'll call you."

"Pfft." I rolled my eyes. "You won't remember me in the morning."

"I won't forget you when I'm dead." He shut the door.

CHAPTER SEVEN

RUB A DUB DUB

Several days later a familiar *bang bang bang* brought me out of the best dream, one with a sexy NFL quarterback who may or may not have been wearing any clothes.

"Trzy, get the door. I need to finish my dream."

Meow

"You're really worthless, you know that, right? But I love you anyway."

The banging continued as I made my way to the peephole, but I knew it was Everson. He had the weirdest knock: knock knock (ten seconds later) knock knock knock knock knock. The same pattern continued without variation. The guy knew I had to assemble myself before I could get the door.

"Yes, I'm marrying Cage."

Everson grinned—the full-on smile I loved. It was the best because I knew he didn't really want to admit that he genuinely liked me. Or that he was amused by me—same thing.

"Monaghan is married to the team. He won't be taking a

wife anytime soon if he knows what's best for him. Too distracting."

"Good morning to you, too." I crossed my arms over my chest.

"It's nearly noon, Stick."

"I had a late night."

He held his hand up. "I don't need to hear about you getting your freak on."

"*Sons of Anarchy* until 2:00 a.m. is hardly getting my freak on. What do you want?"

"Conditioner."

My gaze shifted to his short, buzzed hair. He rolled his eyes.

"Ooohhh ..." I nodded. "You had a lady friend stay over last night."

"A lady friend? Really, Stick? No one says that. And no, that's not it."

"First of all, I just said it, so you can't say 'no one' says it. I'm someone, you know? And as for your *stick* ... I saw a picture of Shayna's mom—*your* mom."

His brow peaked.

I narrowed my eyes, but he shook off my comment.

After a few seconds of silence that he refused to fill with elaborating on his mom, I sighed. "If the conditioner is not for hair, then I have a good idea what you're going to do with it and I'll give you some lotion instead. I splurge on good conditioner. I'm sure some sort of cooking oil would work just as good. Ya ever thought about trying that?"

Everson shook his head. "Porn site or not, you're a freak, woman, that's all there is to it."

"Evson?"

The door to his apartment cracked open.

I came so close to bursting into tears. I couldn't even speak past the lump in my throat.

"I'm not sure what the rules are on helping her bathe. I'm a guy, her brother, not her dad, and—"

I shook my head until he stopped talking, then I nodded. "I've got her," I choked out, blinking back my tears.

"Get your clothes," he told her then turned to me when she went back inside his apartment. "Don't give me that look. I'm not making any promises. One day at a time. That's all I've got to give. Don't get too attached to her, Stick. Got it?"

I nodded, completely lying. Shayna already had me with her very first smile.

As Shayna played in the bathtub, I sat on the vanity and scrolled through my emails looking for my flight confirmation. My phone vibrated and a text popped up at the top of my screen.

This is me wanting to call you, but I'm not alone. Hi.

I wasted no time typing my future husband's name into my contacts with the text number.

Lake: *Hi. It's rude to text me with someone else in your bed.*
Cage: *It's afternoon. Who's still in bed?*
Lake: *Never mind.*
Cage: *What are you doing?*
Lake: *Giving the cutest little girl a bath.*
Cage: *You have a child?*
Lake: *No. She's Everson's.*

Cage: *Banks has a daughter?*

Lake: *No. It's his sister. Long story and you didn't hear it from me.*

Cage: *Clearly, since you didn't actually tell me the story.*

Lake: *What are you doing?*

Cage: *Getting a massage.*

Lake: *Rough life.*

Cage: *Not like a spa massage. Sports therapy.*

Lake: *Isn't it off season?*

Cage: *I still train in the off season.*

Lake: *Coach's pet.*

Cage: *So I've heard.*

I laughed. Shayna looked up from her soapy abyss and grinned.

"You ready to get rinsed off and get out?"

She shook her head.

I shrugged. "Okay, but the water won't stay warm forever."

She grabbed one of the plastic cups I gave her and dumped water through my kitchen strainer.

Cage: *When do you leave for China?*

Lake: *EARLY tomorrow morning.*

Cage: *Need a ride to the airport?*

Lake: *No. My boss pays for parking.*

Cage: *::clearing my throat:: Do you WANT me to take you to the airport?*

"I love him," I whispered to myself as my heart fluttered in my chest to the same rhythm as the butterflies in my stomach.

Lake: *You'd have to get up too early.*

Cage: *You still haven't answered my question.*

Lake: *The sun won't be up.*

Cage: *And???*

I trapped my lips between my teeth and took a deep breath.

Lake: *I'd love for you to take me to the airport.*

Cage: *Time?*

Lake: *My flight leaves at 10:05 so you'll need to be here by 7:30.*

CHAPTER EIGHT

THE KISS

CAGE

I COULDN'T CONTAIN my laughter. She thought 7:30 a.m. was early.

"Something funny?" Kevin, my massage therapist, asked as he kneaded the hell out of my calves.

"Yeah. I'm taking a friend to the airport in the morning, and she thinks it's still dark out at 7:30. I wonder what time she normally wakes up."

"Friend? A she?"

"Officially, yes. *She* is a friend."

"Unofficially?"

I stared at my phone screen. "Unofficially, I can't stop thinking about her. I met her right after my dad died. It was just one day, but she made one hell of an impression on me. I saw her at Banks's birthday party. She lives in the apartment across from his and ... I don't know." I shook my head.

Cage: *How do you like your coffee?*

Lake: *I like it as tea, honey – no milk.*

Cage: *See you in the morning. I might even bring the sun with me.*

Lake: *I fear you're making fun of me.*

Cage: *Never.*

"What about Kelsey?"

"I broke up with her the night of the party. We weren't that serious, so there wasn't any drama or shit like that. But it was impulsive and I'm not impulsive. I saw this girl holding quite possibly the ugliest cat in the world, and she was all-over-the-place crazy, yet I found it so damn sexy." I laughed just thinking about it. "She doesn't follow football so she had no idea what I do."

For some reason I liked that she didn't follow football.

"She ran into her apartment and grabbed a permanent marker and a box of generic cereal then asked me to sign the box."

Kevin laughed. "That had to be a blow to your ego, like she was trying to acknowledge your fame to not offend you."

"Actually, it had the opposite effect on me. She doesn't seem like the type who tries to impress anyone, yet she's one of the most impressive people I've ever met. Crazy, but impressive. Anyway, she was leaving to go on a date and it messed with my head. I tried to enjoy the party, took Kelsey home, and ended it."

"Girls messing with your head two months before training camp probably isn't the best thing for someone in your shoes."

Tossing my phone on my bag, I rested my head on the table and closed my eyes. "You're probably right."

ONE

LAKE

MORE *BANG BANG BANG,* but a different rhythm. Not Everson. Why can't a girl get some decent sleep?

Meow

"Meow yourself. Get the door. Impress me. I don't let *my* disability hold me back." I rolled toward my clock. Mornings were not my thing. My brain refused to work properly until noon.

"Shit!" The half-packed suitcase on the floor gave my memory a quick jolt. "Shit, shit, shit ... I'm so late. Why didn't my alarm go off? Why didn't you wake me, Trzy?"

I scrambled to the door.

Eye.

Peephole.

Shit shit shit!

I threw open the door. There wasn't one single second to spare to look at the man of my dreams standing before me in a pair of dark blue jeans and a blue shirt that matched his eyes, but I took the second anyway.

"You did tell me 7:30, right?"

I jumped out of my daze. "Yes, ugh ... I overslept. Come in." I hurried back to my bedroom. No time for a shower.

"Anything I can do?" Cage called.

"Feed Trzy. Bowl is on the floor, food's in the cabinet by the fridge. And if you wouldn't mind sifting the shit out of her litter box, it's in the laundry room. Trash bag is under the sink."

When I decided to impress a guy, I went all out.

The worst day ever to oversleep? The day I flew to China and NFL hottie offered me a ride. I threw myself together and it wasn't pretty. Then I threw the rest of my stuff in my suitcases. By the time I made it to the kitchen, Trzy had her nose buried in her food dish and Cage waited by the door with a spark of amusement lighting up his face.

I gave him a weak, very apologetic smile. "I'm aware that I just crossed a line by asking you to scoop cat poop for me, but Mrs. Leonard in 2A just had back surgery; she'll feed Trzy for me, but I didn't want her to have to scoop poop, so I thought it best to leave with it clean this morning."

"It's fine."

Double checking for my passport in my purse, I shook my head. "It's not fine. I don't know how I manage to oversleep all the time, and you got up extra early to do this for me this morning—"

"I'm up before six every morning. I got in a run, showered, and ate breakfast already."

I looked up, slinging my purse over my shoulder. "Wow, you must go to bed really early."

Cage shrugged. "Eleven most nights."

"Early." I wheeled my two suitcases to the door.

"Eleven is early?"

"A bit, but what do I know? Ready?"

He took my bags while I said goodbye to Trzy and locked the door.

"Your place—the decorating is really cool. Did you hire someone?"

"Nope." I beamed as the elevator descended. "I used to love fashion, decorating, designing ... all that artsy stuff. That's what I started studying in college before the accident." I laughed. "Shoes. I *loved* shoes—sexy, beautiful, ankle-breaking, toe-mangling shoes. I spent every paycheck on shoes. Stupid."

I shook my head. "It's crazy how life puts things into

perspective. My mom hauled off all my fancy shoes after the accident. I couldn't even look at them. Then one day..." I gave him a shy glance as we stepped off the elevator "...I met this guy. It was just one day, but he changed my whole world. He was the guy girls would sell their souls to be with, and he flirted with me and then he kissed me. And even though I feared I would never see him again, I walked away with this crazy confidence that I'd totally lost the day of the accident. I wanted a new leg, one that I could use with high heels and that I could paint the toenails. And shoes ... I wanted sexy shoes again."

Cage opened the door to the front of the building. "Me? That was me?"

I nodded with an enormous grin. "Yep."

He shook his head with a smile that rivaled mine. "That's just ... so crazy."

Parked in front of the building was the same truck he had in Omaha.

"Wow. You still have this truck? No ridiculously expensive sports car for Mr. NFL?"

Cage loaded my bags in back. "Not yet."

He shot me a frown when I didn't wait for him to open my door. I shrugged with a grin. As he climbed in, I fastened my seatbelt, adjusted the strap, and tugged it several times. Then, I reached over and gave his seatbelt a firm tug. It was instinct. He looked at me with narrowed eyes for a moment. I looked straight ahead.

"Here." He pulled a cup from the holder between us. "Tea with honey, no milk."

My mouth said *thank you*, but my heart said *I love you*. My brain was removed from the equation.

"Anyway..." he continued, pulling away from the curb "...I can't trade my truck in until I can no longer imagine my father's disapproving face. He was the epitome of practical. I already know I'll be grounded in the afterlife for the house I purchased, and compared to other players' homes, it's quite conservative."

"As conservative as Everson's?"

He chuckled. "You both live in luxury apartments, emphasis on luxury. All I can say is testing prosthetics must pay quite well." He gave me a quick sideways glance.

I smirked.

"Everson has one more year before he becomes a free agent. I have no doubt we'll keep him, but he had an offer on his mansion—and it was a mansion—so he sold it and leased the apartment until he knows for sure where he'll be in another year."

"It must be hard to put down roots as a professional athlete."

"Depends. Some players stay with the same team for their entire career."

"Is that what you hope to do?"

"Sure. If I'm on a good team and getting to play, that's the dream."

I nodded. After a few minutes, I reached for the radio. "No docking station for your phone in here. You're so old-school in this truck. Time to get personal. What's programmed into your radio?" Flashing him a devilish grin I turned on the radio. "Country?" I grimaced.

He shrugged, keeping his eyes on the road, a small grin teasing his lips.

I pressed the next preset button. "Country." I shook my head and pushed the next button.

"Country."

Next button.

"Country."

Next button. "Oh thank God. Pop-rock."

"I ran out of country stations in this area."

I chuckled. "Wow ... so you're a country boy."

Cage smiled. "Not in the cowboy sense, but yes, I like country music. I take it you don't?"

"I like some of the crossover artists, but most of it is too twangy for me and some of the lyrics are just too sad—my girl left me, my guy cheated on me, my truck has big tires, and my dog died."

He coughed a laugh. "Because cock-rock is so much better. Let's see ... I'm pretty sure most of those songs are about sex, drugs, prostitution, and rich people buying shit."

The tea in my mouth tried to come out of my nose as laughter filled my chest. "*Cock-rock*? Like ... getting your cock rocked?"

"So you've heard the term?"

"No." I giggled some more. "That's not a real term." Tapping my finger on the console between us, I shrugged. "But at least the voices are sexy, not twangy."

"So it's not what someone says, it's how they say it?"

"Exactly." My head bobbed in an exaggerated nod.

"So I could call you a whore, and tell you to bend over while I snort a line off your sweet ass with a hundred dollar bill before I fuck you, and if I said it in the right voice it would sound sexy to you?"

"Pfft ... no." I rolled my eyes. Then, of course, I wondered if the "sweet ass" comment was literal or just a lyrical example.

Okay, it might have sounded sexy to me. I wasn't going to ask him to actually say that in his sexiest voice, but it sure left me thinking about the songs I liked. Then I focused on the actual lyrics ... yeah, he could have said that to me and made me want to let him do it. The religious sector was right: music was corrupting young minds, and I was one of them. A unique and catchy beat could make people dance and celebrate some really terrible shit. Not. Good.

"So …" I found a quick change of subject that made me feel less like a tramp. "Thaddeus is quite wealthy. He has tons of patents on things beyond robotic technology. He pays me well, but I received a hefty settlement from my accident, too. I've also been photographed for various fitness and technology magazines. Thad lines all that stuff up for me. It's good publicity for him as well, and the money that comes from the photo releases is pretty good."

"Sounds like you've got everything going for you."

Not everything.

He pulled into my airline's terminal drop-off and got my luggage out of the back.

"So how long will you be in Beijing?"

"A week to ten days. It depends on how much tweaking they do." I shrugged. "So if you find yourself in the Beijing area give me a call. We can grab dinner or something."

Cage grinned. "Sure, I'll check my schedule. Somehow I think my six-day-a-week workouts, pre-season training, and fishing will prevent me from being in your neighborhood."

"Fishing? You fish?"

"Ten thousand lakes, of course I fish."

I nodded, imagining Cage on a fishing boat, listening to country music. It surprised me how much I liked that visual. "I'd better go. Who knows how long it will take me to get through security with my metal parts. Thank you for the ride."

"My pleasure." He didn't move.

I didn't move.

What were we waiting for? A kiss? I hoped so. He

stepped closer to me. I held my breath. The ground shook. The clouds parted. Angels played their trumpets. Okay, that may have been a slight exaggeration, but inside that's how I felt until the world's biggest dickhead honked his horn at us.

"This isn't a parking lane," he yelled out his window.

Cage stepped back.

No, don't step back!

"We'll text."

I smiled, but it felt more like a grimace. "Bye." Turning, I made sure to give dickhead an evil glare before making my way to the entrance.

First-class. Thaddeus took care of me, but even with some extra room and extra attention, the flight would be brutal. No one sat next to me on the flight to Seattle; I could only hope to have as much luck on the plane from Seattle to Beijing.

With my two-hour layover in Seattle, I grabbed a sandwich, SmartWater, and a bag of BBQ potato chips, then claimed my seat by the gate, propping my legs up on my carry-on suitcase. After licking off the BBQ flavoring, I took my phone off airplane mode and a text dinged right away.

Cage: *I should have just kissed you. Stupid me.*

"Why, why, why!" I closed my eyes as my chin dipped to my chest.

When I opened them, several people around me gave me that are-you-okay-or-just-crazy look.

"Sorry," I whispered then shoved my sandwich into my mouth, ripping off a very unladylike-sized bite.

Lake: *I haven't left the states. How soon can you get to Seattle?*

Lake: *Do you remember our first kiss?*

Lake: *You turned your head. I wasn't going to kiss you on the lips.*

Lake: *Thank you for turning your head. Best. Kiss. Ever.*

Lake: *Are you still there?*

Cage: *Just being polite and listening to you.*

Lake: *Sorry. I talk a lot.*

Cage: *I noticed, especially to yourself.*

Lake: *I don't talk to myself.*

Cage: *You do. The day we met? You used the bathroom at my dad's house, and I heard you talking to yourself.*

He heard me. I couldn't believe he heard me. So. Embarrassing.

After shutting the bathroom door, I rested my hands on the edge of the sink, looking in the mirror at the flushed face of a girl who hadn't given a second glance to a guy since her accident. "He's gorgeous, Lake. Stop thinking stupid shit about a gorgeous guy that lives a million miles away, and oh yeah ... he's naturally going to be attracted to gorgeous women with all their limbs intact."

I may have had some self-esteem issues right after my accident.

Lake: *I don't talk to myself. Sometimes I just think out loud. Why were you eavesdropping on my thoughts?*

Cage: *Lol, because you think so loud.*

Lake: *I'm ashamed.*

Cage: *Why?*

Lake: *Because you were grieving your dad that day. I ached for you, but it didn't stop me from pining for you too. I was lonely and insecure.*

Cage: *And now?*

He asked some really good questions. I took a few minutes to enjoy the rest of my lunch while I thought about it. Cage didn't text me again. He waited for me. I loved his patience.

Lake: *Now I'm alone, but I'm no longer lonely—Netflix, Trzy, etc., and I'm not insecure about my body.*

Half-truths. A cat and Netflix were a stretch for defining companionship. It had been so long since I'd been intimate with anyone, that I couldn't honestly say how insecure I would feel lying on a bed naked in front of a sexy man like Cage. Clearly, my thoughts were jumping ahead to ... maybe never.

Cage: *When did you get Trzy? She's quite the cat.*

I grinned.

Lake: *She was a gift.*

Cage: *Was she in one piece when you got her?*

Lake: *Lol! No. They say the truth is more unbelievable than fiction, well, here it is ... she was a gift from a date I met on an online dating website. I knew right away my leg made him nervous and there wouldn't be a second date, but I think he mistook my kindness for attraction. The next day he had a friend* *of his deliver me a package with a note that said, "Sorry we didn't work out, hope she keeps you company until you find the right guy. Her name is Trzy, which means three in Polish. I'm half-Polish and you are missing a leg so I thought it was a fitting reminder of our date. The rescue shelter said she lost her leg and part of her ear when she got tangled up in a group of bikers. I hope you two bond and you think of me often."*

Cage: *LMFAO. You have to be joking.*

Lake: *Sadly ... no. I've had her in the car and halfway to the shelter to return her, at least a dozen times. But I can't do it. It pisses me off that she's so attached to me.*

Cage: *Are you sure it's not that you're so attached to her?*

I shook my head.

Lake: *I can board my plane. TTYL.*

Cage: *Safe travels. And, Lake ... I remember the kiss. I remember it well.*

I floated onto the plane. My head was huge and way up in the clouds. It was a miracle that I even fit onto the aircraft. After tossing my purse onto my seat, I unzipped the front pocket of my carry-on to get my headphones. As I pulled them out, something fell to the ground. An older gentleman, waiting for me to move out of the aisle, bent down and picked it up.

"You dropped this."

"Thank you." I looked at it without recognition and stepped back out of his way. It was a blank white notecard, then I flipped it over.

CHAPTER TWO

I shook my head. Flint? Everson? It didn't make sense. Cage was the only one near my carry-on, but he didn't have anything to do with the first notecard. It had to be him, yet it couldn't be him. It was very weird and mysterious. I settled into my seat and for the next twelve hours, and I thought non-stop about the notecards and the missed kiss while listening to some country music I had downloaded at the airport.

CHAPTER NINE

JET LAG

THE TYPICAL STRANGER holding a sign with my name on it at the Beijing airport didn't exist. Instead, I was greeted with the cocky grin I knew too well. His lower teeth were a bit crowded like he didn't wear his retainer long enough as a boy, but the dirty-blond version of Einstein's hair and hazel-green eyes made up for that minor imperfection. At nearly six-foot-six, it was impossible to miss Thaddeus Westbrook waiting on the other side of security, grinning like a complete goofball.

"Love!"

I rolled my tired eyes. Early afternoon Beijing time was early morning, aka my bedtime in the States.

"Thrilled to see you didn't take down the plane with my baby."

"Shut up." I released my carry-on and collapsed into his arms. "I'm tired. Hotel. Now."

"Sorry, love. Jerry awaits. Come, we'll stop for coffee on the way."

"I don't drink coffee."

"Yes, yes ... tea. Well, you're in the right place for that."

"What the hell is with your hand?"

He held his new invention out in front of him as we made our way to baggage claim. "You like?"

"It has eight fingers."

"Indeed it does. Technology isn't limited to biological standards. Have you ever heard someone say they needed another hand?"

"They're fingers, Thad."

"It's just an example. Trust me. The ladies love it."

"You're a pervert."

"I'm a gentleman and you know it."

"It's not fair. I think women look at amputee men differently than men look at amputee women."

"We're visual creatures, love. Don't worry, you'll find your man ... he may only have five fingers to give you, but if he's good with them—"

"Enough, jeez." My mind latched onto Thad's stupid comment and all my thoughts jumped to Cage and five of his fingers.

The driver took us straight to Jerry's lab, in spite of my protesting and desperate pleas for sleep. We didn't stop for tea, but Jerry had a cast-iron pot of Oolong and three small cups waiting for us when we arrived.

"Excellent! You made it!" Little Jerry bowed as we removed our shoes at the door.

"I'm a zombie, Jerry. Can we do this in say ... six to eight hours?" I tossed my purse on the wood floor.

"No, no ... I'll be asleep."

"This time change kills me every time I visit." I glared at Thad as he wiggled his eight metal fingers at Jerry. "From now on you need to give me twenty-four hours to acclimate before we do any work."

They both ignored me, their enamored gazes fixed only to the crazy hand.

"Stop whining, love. You're much too beautiful to walk around with your lip sticking out."

I sighed. "Whatever. Let's blow up Jerry's balls so we can get back to the hotel."

Jerry stopped messing with Mr. Eight Fingers and tipped his chin down, rolling his eyes up to give us both a disapproving look. "I'm not gay. So if that's some American expression for implying that I'm gay, then—"

"It's not." Thad shook his head.

"Because I'm not."

My grin, although buried under my deep need for sleep, managed to make a brief appearance. "Oh, I'm sure you get yours, Jerry."

Nothing ruined a good line quite like two intellectual over-achievers giving the dopey girl in the room a WTF look.

"Is that street talk, love?"

No. It was Everson talk, but apparently I failed to deliver it accurately or in the right context.

"You two would never survive in the wild. You know that, right?" It was a weak recovery, but sleep deprivation left my brain functioning at less than twenty percent.

"Our dear Lake has been in Minnesota too long." Thad drew out the "O" like sooo-da. "I fear she's morphed into a throwback from the nineties. Lake, my love, do the women there still wear scrunchies in their hair?"

"Really, Thad? You grew up in Kansas."

Thad whipped his head around to Jerry.

"Kansas?" Jerry asked. "You said you grew up in Boston and went to MIT."

Thad shrugged, staring at his prosthetic hand like a

woman contemplating her need for a manicure. "True and true."

"Explain." Jerry crossed his arms over his chest.

I tried to stifle a laugh. It was quite the sight, seeing a guy who was tall enough to play center in the NBA looking proverbially much smaller than the Asian man who was not tall enough to ride most rollercoasters at Six Flags.

"I did go to MIT and technically I didn't 'grow up' until my last year in college, which happened to be in Boston. But if we're being technical..." Thad gave me a quick glance with the stink eye "...then one could say I was born and spent my childhood in Kansas."

I snorted. "Duh, Jerry. How many farming accidents do you suppose happen around Boston?"

"You said you lost your hand and fingers from frostbite while climbing Everest."

"It was cold that year at harvest time and the machine that nearly took my life was big ... and tall, much like Everest."

Jerry deflated like he'd just discovered his idol was a fraud.

"In all fairness to Thaddeus, he did summit Everest, but that was after the accident." I nodded big, attempting to rally Thad's number one fan.

Jerry looked to Thad for confirmation, a sliver of hope that Thaddeus the Great was not a complete sham.

"It's true."

"So why did you lie?"

Thad sighed. "I don't know. It sounded better on my resumé."

"*You* hired *me*."

"True, but I wanted you to take the job. I needed you, and I thought I needed to look impressive because I knew for a fact that at least ten other companies were trying to recruit you."

Jerry smiled, his face flushing a bit as he fluttered his eyelashes. "I'm touched."

Thad shook his head. "Great. Fabulous. Wonderful. Now can we get to work? I have to tell you about Lake's reason for landing in jail. *That's* what will make your testicles explode. It's the biggest breakthrough I've ever had and it's going to change the future."

By the time the two geeks finished feeling me up—fitting me for Jerry's climbing robotic leg—and testing the thought-to-action of Thad's rebel baby, my battery was dead. I'm not sure how we got to the hotel, but I think Thad may have tossed me over his shoulder, palming my ass with all eight fingers. One minute I was swaying by Jerry's door waiting for them to stop their endless ramblings and the next I was waking up in a big bed. The red numbers on the digital clock read: 11:30.

I sat up wearing nothing but my bra and panties.

"Pervert," I mumbled.

The dimly lit street lights below cast a hazy glow along the edge of the curtains where they didn't meet the wall. I hopped over to the desk to grab my phone then hopped back in bed.

Five hours of sleep gave me enough brain function to want to call a certain dimpled boy in Minnesota.

"Having trouble adjusting to the time change?" he answered on the second ring.

"I'm so screwed. I don't know which end is up. I just

woke up, but the rest of Beijing is turning out their lights for the night."

"How was your flight?"

It sucked, but the voice on the other end of the line erased all that.

"Long and strange."

"Strange?"

"Yeah. The day I got arrested and Everson's guy bailed me out then returned my car? Well, the kid who brought the car back handed me this notecard that read: CHAPTER ONE. Then on the plane I found another notecard in my carry-on that read: CHAPTER TWO. I think I'm being stalked by a writer. Is that crazy?"

"Undoubtedly."

I grinned, running my fingers through my tangled hair. Cage's voice had true personality. If words could smile, then his did.

"Enough about me and my literary stalker. Tell me what you've been doing."

"Let's see ... I exercised this morning, helped out at youth camp, and then I spent an hour on the phone with my mom. My sisters have a birthday coming up, and she wants me to fly home for it, but my schedule is crazy and taking a shit is frowned upon at this point. Leaving town? It wouldn't be good."

"Omaha?"

"No. They live in Portland."

"Hmm, I didn't know you had sisters."

"Half-sisters, twins. My mom remarried after she and my dad divorced."

"How old are your sisters?"

"They're turning eight."

"Well that sounds like fun. You should go."

"I should, huh? You did hear me say it's not a great time to leave town, right?"

"Family is not a career. It's why you have a career. If you can't be there for the big moments, then why are you doing it? Besides, I have no doubt that your sisters look up to you, Mr. NFL Sensation."

"How do you know I'm a sensation? You don't follow football."

"Google told me."

"Google?"

"Yes." I flipped onto my stomach, propped up my elbows. "Google told me Cage Monaghan won the Heisman Trophy *and* went number one in the draft. I also know your jersey number is one, which is cool because one is the best number."

His chuckle tickled my skin. Yes, I could *feel* him laugh and the way it made me feel was indescribable, truly like nothing I had ever felt before.

"Tell me why one is the best."

"One is enough. It's unique. It's a chance, an opportunity, an experience. One is never greedy. One is independent. One can change everything."

"One is the best."

I trapped my lower lip between my teeth and nodded. "Yes. It is."

"So I'm going to win the Super Bowl this season?"

"*One* day I believe you will."

"What if I want to win it more than once?"

"Then you're just being greedy."

"Are you ever greedy?"

"Undoubtedly."

"When?"

"I don't know, lots of times. I'm human. We're greedy.

I'm not sure if it's nature or nurture, but everyone has their greedy moments."

"Like when?"

"Stop." I laughed.

"Just *one*. Give me one of your greedy instances."

"Why?"

"Because I want to know your weakness."

"So if I say it's chocolate, are you going to send me a huge box of truffles?"

"Yes."

I giggled. "You're terrible."

"I'm waiting."

"Netflix."

"Doesn't count. Give me something more tangible."

I squeezed my eyes shut and jumped off the bridge. "Your kiss."

The line went silent, even my heart stopped for a few seconds—waiting.

"My kiss?"

We weren't on the same continent. How could I be so embarrassed? My hand covered my face. Why? Because that was my level of complete craziness.

"Well ... sort of ... yeah."

"Hmm, I really like—"

"Monaghan, let's go!" a man's voice echoed.

"Yeah, yeah, give me thirty seconds."

"Twenty," the man replied.

The interruption left me panting, on the verge of an all-out drool. He really liked what? The kiss? Me? Pizza? Dogs? Three-legged cats?

"I've gotta run. I have an interview."

"No." I shook my head. I needed to practice not

sounding so desperate. "I mean, okay. I'll be here, maybe indefinitely since I said what I did."

"Oh, Lake ..." He chuckled. "I'll call you later."

"Bye." I pressed *End* and hammered my head into the pillow. "You're not this girl, Lake. Stop being so gaga stupid like a fifteen-year-old at a Justin Bieber concert."

CHAPTER TEN

IMPULSIVITY

THE BLUE DEPTHS of the Olympic pool haunted me, along with the bystanders snapping photos of the girl with a fin leg swimming laps. I had to remind myself that the near drowning incident the previous year, when Thad saved me, was a weak moment. I wasn't that girl anymore.

In the afternoon we were at the climbing facility.

Fit the leg.

Climb the wall.

Make adjustments.

Climb the wall again.

Repeat. Repeat. Repeat.

Three days passed with no word, no "later" call from Cage. I said too much. My mouth and brain functioned independently. Jerry and Thad tap danced on my last nerve. They bickered like a married couple after fifty years of marriage.

"We're going to dinner, love. You coming?" Thad asked, like he and Jerry hadn't just been on the verge of killing each other over a sensory setting on the new leg.

"I think I need a break from..." I smiled "...people."

"You mean us." Jerry didn't have to look up from his computer. The guy was perceptive. Heterosexual and perceptive.

Thad narrowed his eyes in a say-it-ain't-so way.

"You both are just really ..."

"Really?" Thad prodded.

"Draining." Jerry deadpanned, eyes still focused on his screen. "We suck the life out of everything and everyone around us, Thaddeus."

"Is this true, Lake?"

I grimaced, lifting my shoulders. "It's not entirely false."

"Fine." Thad's chin jutted out. "Go. We'll just see you tomorrow. We don't need you cock blocking us tonight anyway."

"For the last time! I'm. Not. Gay!"

I bit back my grin while Thad rolled his eyes. "Not with each other, you idiot! With women at bars or clubs. We don't want to look attached if we want to get laid."

"Oh." Jerry peeked up from his computer. "Sorry."

I had a better chance of spontaneously growing a new leg before Jerry would get laid, but I kept that theory to myself.

I had many theories. They were correct half of the time.

"Well, I hope you and your cocks have a lovely night." I grabbed my purse and slipped on my shoe.

"Funny, love. Only not really. Enjoy your freedom. I'll be knocking on your hotel room door early tomorrow morning. Try to be at least a little coherent when you open the door."

"Sorry, I don't have 'masseuses' coming to my room late at night to read me a bedtime story and release my tension from the day."

"I'll come to your room, Lake."

"I get it, Jerry, you're not gay. Wouldn't care if you were. But stay the hell away from my hotel room."

"Oh, love, the sexual tension between you and Jerry could trigger a major earthquake. For the sake of twenty million people, try to control yourselves."

I needed a raise.

"Go to Capital M, tell them I sent you. They'll seat you right away. The nighttime view of Tiananmen Square is excellent. Do you have a company credit card? Make sure Thaddeus pays," Jerry instructed.

I grinned. "I never travel without it."

Thad shook his head.

JERRY CHU's name didn't mean anything to me when I first met him, but the staff at Capital M treated just the mention of his name like the secret code to a buried treasure. As promised, the nighttime view of Tiananmen Square was most excellent.

My vibrating phone drew my attention away from the view and my table filled with too much food and expensive wine. Thad's credit card, of course.

Cage: *Do you speak Chinese?*

I grinned.

Lake: *Sorry. Who are you again? I vaguely remember some guy with your name.*
Cage: *I've been busy.*
Lake: *Sorry, your royal quarterback-ness.*
Cage: *Are you mad at me?*

Yes. No. A little. Why didn't he call?

Lake: *I'm just tired and stressed from spending so much time with my boss and his runt of a sidekick, and the TV sucks at my hotel. I'm bored.*
Cage: *You should go sightseeing.*
Lake: *Been there. Done that. This isn't my first rodeo in Beijing.*
Cage: *They have the rodeo in China?*
Lake: *har har har*
Cage: *Where are you?*
Lake: *Capital M. Too public for phone sex, so don't even ask.*
There it was, exhibit A of *Lake says the most inappropriate things.*
Cage: *Wow … I uh …*
Lake: *Joking. I have a weird sense of humor. Sorry.*
Cage: *What are you eating?*
Lake: *Nothing, but there's a duck and maybe some sort of dumplings on my plate and a really expensive bottle of wine on the table since my boss pays for my meals. Isn't that terrible? I'm already feeling regretful. The whole starving-people thing weighs heavily on my conscience. I should have just grabbed a bag of pretzels at the hotel and called it a night.*

We continued to text for almost forty-five minutes before I tossed Thad's credit card on the table. Cage felt like somebody I'd known my whole life. The conversation came easily.

Lake: *Catching a cab back to my hotel. I'm tired. Fact: I haven't slept well since my accident. I feel chronically sleep deprived. I don't even call what I do falling asleep. It's really just passing out after hitting a wall. I seem to go from 100 to 0 in a matter of seconds.*

Cage: *That sucks.*

I signed for the bill then made my way to the entrance, dodging people and tables while my head was down staring at my phone.

Lake: *Enough about me. What are you doing?*
Cage: *Just enjoying the evening.*
Lake: *It's not evening there.*

"I know."

I hit that wall. I had to have hit that wall. It was a dream. It had to be a dream. I had to be asleep. The mirage standing next to a taxi by the curb in front of the restaurant was the man of my dreams. He smiled. I remained static with my jaw unhinged. I needed to wake from my dream, but I didn't want to, it was too good.

"Of all the places in the world, you had to come here for work. Do you know how impossibly difficult it is to get here? A passport wasn't good enough. I had to expedite a visa. Security violated me on so many levels I'm certain I'll forever be emotionally scarred, and don't even get me started on the impact this little detour could have on my career."

Blink.

Blink.

Blink.

I needed a better response than a blink. Each time I thought he'd disappear because he wasn't fifteen feet from me. There was just no way it was possible.

"You said if I was in the neighborhood ..."

I nodded slowly. It was progress, another sign of life.

"You, you're ... oh my God. You came to Beijing for me?"

Cage returned a guilty shrug like it was no big deal. I was amazed every time a guy returned my phone call. Flowers sent my heart into arrhythmia. Following me to Beijing? Complete cardiac arrest.

"Here's the thing..." he walked toward me "...I should have just kissed you at the baseball game. And after I scooped Trzy's shit, and again at the airport."

Gulp.

He brushed his thumbs along my cheeks then slid his hands back to cup my head. I had to look like the newest addition to The Blue Man Show. I wasn't breathing. There was no oxygen to be had.

Blink.

Blink.

Blink.

Gulp.

"Hi," he whispered over my lips a split second before he kissed me.

I died. The end. Story over.

I vaguely remembered something about public displays of affection being frowned upon, or illegal, or maybe punishable by death in China. It was worth the consequences.

My heart thundered embarrassingly loud. *That* moment was the one that could have triggered the earthquake. Millions of lives were at risk. Was one kiss worth it?

Yes. Oh. Dear. God. Yes!

I wasn't the world's leading expert on kissing, but I knew what I liked, and so did Cage Monaghan. He took his time feeling my lips with his. It wasn't until he'd felt every inch of them several times over before just the tip of his tongue teased my upper lip. I loved that moment when the feeling turned into tasting. I loved the way his hands fisted my hair, holding all of his tension so his lips could remain slow and patient.

More than anything, I loved that as he deepened the kiss, bringing my body flesh to his, his heart hammered against his chest just like mine.

Eventually the need for air trumped the need to kiss. My lungs were such spoil sports. Cage grinned, rubbing his lips together. I grinned too.

"Hi," I whispered.

"Can I offer you a ride back to your hotel before I head back to the airport?"

My eyes popped right out of their sockets. "What? Airport! You just got here."

Cage gave me the textbook what-is-your-point look.

Squeezing my eyes shut, I rubbed my hands over my face. It had to be a dream or a nightmare. I needed to wake up. But when I removed my hands he was still there.

"You applied for a visa and flew to China just to kiss me?"

He nodded. "Totally worth it. Wouldn't you agree?"

"Well, yes ... no ..." I shook my head. "I don't know. Who does that? Who flies halfway around the world to kiss someone they've seen five times in their entire life?"

"So you're counting?" He smirked.

"No."

Yes. I counted every second we spent together since our very first encounter.

I counted the smiles.

The dimple appearances.

The times his eyes wandered down my body.

The butterflies in my stomach.

Every touch. Every look. Every moment that felt like our connection had existed before we ever met.

Yeah, I counted. Every. Single. One.

"Lake?"

I looked up from my absentminded staring at the ground between us. "What?"

"I'm kidding. I didn't fly here just to kiss you."

I smiled. "That would be crazy."

"Probably." He turned and opened the back door to the cab. "But I would have," he said as I slid in the back seat.

There was only one thing left to do. I clenched my fists at the center of my chest like a super hero ripping off their street clothes, but I ripped open my chest instead and silently said, "Here's my heart, just take it."

"You're awfully quiet for someone who thinks so loud."

I turned toward him as the taxi fought through the evening traffic. "You're here and I'm ... speechless. Are you sure you don't have something else going on? Meetings? Therapy? Training?"

He tipped his head back and closed his eyes, a smile grew along his handsome face. "I think Beijing would be a very odd place to hold meetings, therapy, or any sort of NFL training. Is it so hard to believe that I came here just to see you?" He lifted his head and opened his eyes, pinning me with an intense stare that demanded an answer.

"Well ... yeah, it is. Not that I'm not worthy of being followed halfway around the world." I flashed him a flirty smile. "It's just that this is a grand gesture of epic proportions. Are you that guy? The one who's OTT with everything?"

"OTT?" He narrowed his eyes.

"Over the top."

Cage chuckled and looked out his window. "No. I'm the guy who decided to put my career first the day I was drafted. I'm the guy who basically hands a girl a dating agreement that says it will never be anything more than casual because football comes first. I'm the guy who would rather watch game footage than porn. I'm the guy who is focused one hundred percent of the time."

He looked back at me and time seemed to pause while we just gazed at each other.

"You flew to China to kiss me," I whispered.

Cage nodded, but his playful smile vanished. It was as if the reality of his rash behavior finally caught up to him.

I reached between us and took his hand, giving it a tight squeeze. "I won't tell the 'guy' you were just talking about. This will be our little secret."

He stared at our interlaced fingers. "Thanks. He'd be really pissed at me for being so impulsive."

"He sounds like a real downer."

Cage's smile returned and all was right on our side of the world again. "He's just focused. Other than that, he's a pretty good guy."

"Yeah?"

His eyes met mine. "Yeah."

By the time we arrived at my hotel, Cage seemed to be his jovial self again.

"Did you get a room here? And if so, how did you know I was staying here?"

The cabbie retrieved Cage's suitcase from the trunk.

"I didn't know where you were staying, and I don't have a room anywhere yet. I only made the necessary plans to get here."

We stopped at the front desk, but there were no rooms available, not even for an American celebrity.

"You'll stay with me."

"What? No." Cage shook his head.

The guy flew to China to kiss me, but he was too chivalrous to stay in the same room with me. Man, I loved him before it ever made sense.

"I'll just go to another hotel."

"No way."

He smirked.

My skin heated from his what-are-you-implying look. "I'm just saying, it's silly when I have this suite that my boss is paying for and it's not even that late. We could still do something tonight."

Cage's smirk deepened.

"And by something I'm not implying anything like ..."

"Like?"

I rolled my eyes. "I'm not going to jump you. I don't mean any of it in a sexual way."

Yes, in a strip-me-down-and-bury-your-head-between-my-legs sort of way. That was exactly what I meant because I *needed* sex and I *needed* it with him. Sweat began to bead along my skin.

He quirked a brow. "Jump me?"

"I just mean we can share a room without having sex, if that's what you're worried about."

Cage took a quick scan around the lobby. "You think I'm *worried* about having sex with you?" he said in a hushed voice.

"No, I just don't want you to feel obligated to have sex with me. The kiss was enough."

It wasn't enough. Oh my word, I wanted so much more. What had happened to me? When did I become such a liar?

There must have been something in the Minneapolis water, probably pesticide runoff, and nothing was safe to drink in Beijing, at least that's what Thad told me. First Shayna and then Cage. What was my deal with all the lying?

"This is the craziest conversation I have ever had."

I sighed. "Just come."

His eyes widened.

I shook my head. "Come up to my room, er ... just ..." I'd been transported to junior high again where every word meant something sexual in the eyes of immature, giggly girls. How did I become that girl again at twenty-four?

CHAPTER ELEVEN

THE GIFT

CAGE

FLYING to China on a whim was met with a shit-storm of opposition from the people in my life whom I'd hired to keep me focused and out of trouble. I wasn't the guy prone to trouble, but the day I signed with Minnesota, trouble seemed to chase me, usually in the form of greedy people claiming to have been my best buddy in elementary school or women desperate to crawl into my bed.

Seventy-two hours after threatening to fire the very people I hired to keep me from making rash decisions, I found myself in a suite at a Beijing hotel with a woman who made me question my direction in life. That scared me. She scared me.

"So what do you want to do that doesn't involve sex?" Lake tossed her purse on the black couch by the window overlooking the city.

That's where I would sleep. The king-sized bed in the middle of the room looked inviting after my long trip, but I needed to stay as far away from her bed as possible. My time would be equally divided between the couch and cold showers.

I nodded. "I love that the idea of us having sex has now become a joke of sorts." I set my suitcase on the luggage stand.

Lake lifted her shoulders and grinned. "You're staring."

I blinked several times. "Sorry, just ... taking you in."

"Yeah?" She held her arms out to the side for a moment then let them flop back against her body. "And what do you see?"

I crossed my arms over my chest. "You fishing for compliments, Jones?"

"Jones?" She laughed.

My lips twisted to the side as I narrowed my eyes. She didn't melt under my scrutinizing gaze. Lake had her insecurities, they were like small fleeting moments, flashes here and there, but they never appeared to be about her appearance, her leg, or anything on the outside. I couldn't quite figure it out.

"You fit in here. Big, China doll eyes. Long, straight, black hair. Flawless skin. Tiny nose. Petite frame. The ears though ..."

She grabbed her ears. "What's wrong with my ears?"

I shrugged. "They stick out a bit, but don't worry about it. I'm sure no one notices unless you wear your hair back."

"Dumbo ears? Are you suggesting I have Dumbo ears?" Her voice elevated a few octaves.

Fuck me. Lake Jones was the sexiest woman I had ever met, and I think I knew it the moment I laid eyes on her. The space-age looking prosthetic below her knee? It only made her sexier in my eyes. She held her head high, shoulders back, confident smile. She owned herself completely.

"No. I'm not suggesting you can fly."

She squinted. "That's not what I asked."

I stepped closer to her. She didn't flinch. I needed to stop. We needed to sit on separate ends of the couch and watch something like *Schindler's List.* My dick needed to be removed from the equation, but it was hard—in every sense of the word—because if the events of the previous days were to be stripped down to the bare truth ... I flew halfway around the world just to see if her lips tasted the way I remembered from three years earlier. They did, but even better.

My hands flexed; they itched to touch her. I'd stood in the pocket, waiting for a receiver to open up, patient and calm, as my linemen worked to hold off the guys gunning to plant my ass on the ground. I had control. With Lake I was the child running out into the street after a shiny rainbow beach ball. The woman robbed me of all self-preservation by simply existing in my world.

A knock at the door erased the scowl on her face and saved me from my runaway thoughts.

She pointed a stiff finger at me. "You're not off the hook."

Maybe I wasn't saved from anything.

Lake checked the peephole. "I'm not required to see you until morning," she yelled.

A muffled man's voice answered. "Oh come on, love. I'm just stopping by to say goodnight."

"*Love*" didn't sit well with me, neither did the jealousy it evoked.

Lake opened the door, grumbling something under her breath. "Goodnight, Thad." She started to close the door but his hand stopped it.

I moved closer.

"Do you have company?" He peeked past her to me.

She sighed, moving back as Thad took a step inside the room. He held up his hand, an Iron Man-Doc Ock hybrid. Eight fingers.

"He doesn't look Chinese, love." He eyed me.

"He is. It's just poor lighting." She shoved his chest, but her little body made the impact of a fly. "I'll see you in the morning."

Thad smirked, looking down at Lake. I didn't like the way he looked at her. Maybe it was because he called her "love." Maybe one had nothing to do with the other, or maybe they had everything to do with each other. Didn't matter. It left me on edge.

"Are you paying him?"

I fisted my hands, but Lake's left-field reply sidetracked my anger.

"Yes." She shoved toward the door with her whole body, and he stepped back. "I'm paying him for sex, now go because you're wasting my money."

"So you're trying to tell me that Minnesota's Heisman Trophy-winning quarterback turns tricks in Beijing during the offseason?"

Lake grumbled again, louder, but still indiscernible thoughts. She turned to the side, gesturing for Thad to come inside. "Thaddeus Westbrook, meet Cage Monaghan. Cage, this is Thad, my nosy boss."

"Hi." I smiled, making my best effort to give him the benefit of every doubt I held in my head.

"I'm a huge fan." He smiled, but at the same time I saw the protective look in his eyes—the one only another guy would notice. Thad thought I was infringing on his territory, and Lake was oblivious to it.

"Really?" Lake narrowed her eyes at him.

Thad gave her a quick look before returning his attention to me. "Yes. I actually have several patents on knee braces that will put injured players back on the field in half the time with limited risk of further injury." He shrugged. "I watch a lot of sports. It's research."

"I've been pretty lucky so far, no major injuries."

"It's not if, it's *when*, but I'm sure you know that."

I nodded. Of course I knew that, but I didn't like to dwell on the unknown.

"You coming to watch Lake in action tomorrow? Jerry Chu is fitting her for a kick-ass fin and a climbing limb too. She's a natural at everything she attempts to do. That's one of the reasons I hired her. She's fearless." He rested his hand on her lower back.

I didn't like that either.

"I'd love to, but I don't want to be in the way or be a distraction."

Her eyes shifted to me, but she didn't say anything. One of the things I noticed right away when we first met was how her emotions revealed in her eyes or her smile before she ever said a word. She literally looked honest. However, at that moment she revealed nothing.

"Anything else, Thad?"

His tight-browed expression mirrored my own confusion. After a few moments of unspoken words between them, Thad turned toward the door. "Huge pleasure to have met you, Cage." Thad continued to eye Lake.

"You too."

"Be good." He tapped the tip of one of his robotic fingers on Lake's nose twice before disappearing out the door.

She closed it and rested her back against it.

"Sorry, he's ... *him*."

I shrugged. "He seems fine. You don't like him?"

Her brows rose. "No, of course I like him. I would never work for someone I didn't like. Life's too short for that misery. He's just ..." She grazed her teeth along her bottom lip over and over. It was a new side to her, a truly nervous gesture.

"Tell me."

She looked up and blew out a slow breath that made her hair shift away from her forehead. "Thaddeus has seen a very vulnerable side of me. He's watched me stumble and fall more times than I can count. Last year he saved me from drowning in a pool when a fin-type prosthetic fell off during my first lap. Of course I could swim just fine without it, but it freaked me out in that moment. It was not a 'fearless' moment for me."

"He sings your praises quite well."

She nodded slowly.

"I don't have to go tomorrow. This is your job. We can meet up later when you're done."

"Wanna watch TV?"

I took that as a 'yes, we'll meet up later and stop talking about it now.'

"Sure."

LAKE

My mom gave me six months after the accident to grieve, to regret, to feel sorry for myself. I took every single day. Nothing I did during those six months brought Ben back, or my leg, or the dreams I believed to be the purpose of my life. She could have given me ten years and on the first day of the eleventh year the outcome would have been the same: no Ben, no leg, shattered dreams.

Month seven, day one, I tore off my clothes and stood in front of a full-length mirror on my one leg. I said a final, silent goodbye to Ben, my leg, and the dreams they held. Then I introduced myself to the reflection in the mirror. I blinked and in that moment Lake Jones was whole again.

New girl.

Single girl.

Single girl with new dreams.

Cage Monaghan flew to China to kiss me. If he didn't marry me, it would be very awkward for my future husband or children to hear that my greatest memory was another man flying to China to kiss me.

"You're yawning. You look tired," I said as we chilled on the couch watching the worst TV shows ever.

Cage glanced at the clock. "Well, I haven't slept in almost twenty hours, so yeah, I'm a little tired."

"I'll shut off the TV. You get ready for bed."

He shook his head, bringing his fist to his mouth to hide yet another yawn. "It's fine."

I liked his blond hair a little messy, his white T-shirt a little wrinkled, and his bare feet propped up on the coffee table in front of the couch. So. Very. Sexy.

I scooted to the end. "Here, lie down."

I giggled as he tried to maneuver his large body onto the couch without invading my space.

"Put your head on my lap, silly."

He gave me a questioning look.

"I won't shave off an eyebrow or write dork on your forehead in permanent marker." I patted my lap.

Uncoiling his crumpled-up body another foot, he rested his head on my lap.

"No Packers or Bears shit drawn on my face either."

"Shh ..." I pressed my finger to his lips. "Sleep."

Cage wrapped his hand around my wrist, keeping my finger pressed to his lips as he kissed it. Then he kissed the inside of my wrist before laying my hand over his heart and covering it with his own as he closed his eyes. I had to remind myself to breathe. With my other hand I feathered my fingers over his face in random patterns and softly teased his hair. He hummed or maybe purred like Trzy.

After his whole body visibly relaxed and I was certain that he was asleep, I looked in the direction of God and whispered, "Can I keep him? Pretty please?" I didn't want to play the you-owe-me card with the creator of the world, but ... he owed me.

CHAPTER TWELVE

LITERARY STALKER

FOUR HOURS. I spent four hours watching foreign television just so I could stare at Cage and feel his heart beating against the palm of my hand. Eventually, I had to pee. Stupid bladder. My hunky guy—yes, because I'd already claimed him—was dead to the world as I maneuvered myself out from underneath him. After a trip to the bathroom, I decided it was my time to pass out as well. I'd hit my magical wall and the world went black.

The piercing sound of bending metal jolted me from my sleep, panting and sweating. It was the same nightmare. Same sounds. Same feelings.

"Just a dream," I whispered to myself between labored breaths as I sat up.

A sliver of light escaped the bottom of the bathroom door and the shower was running. Yesterday happened, it wasn't a dream. That thought alone eased the anxiety from my nightmare. I reached for my phone on the nightstand.

"No. Way."

Propped up at the base of the lamp was a notecard.

CHAPTER THREE

It made no sense. What? How? Why? I slipped on my leg and went straight to the bathroom, barging in without warning.

"Chapter Three?"

"Fuck! Lake!" In the shower, Cage turned his back toward me.

The condensation-covered glass doors obscured my view of his naked backside, but only a little. My brain made a mental note, as brains do best, to freak-out in the form of a very private happy dance over seeing his *amazing* body. However, my mouth had its own agenda that seemed to be a few steps ahead of actual brain-powered thoughts.

"You're responsible for these notes? The one in my carry-on and the one ... oh my gosh, *you* hired Flint to get me out of jail? You sent that kid to return my car? And you gave me that note?"

Cage cleared his throat. His hands were pressed to the shower wall, head bowed. "I'm in the shower. By any chance is this something we can discuss in maybe five minutes and not in the bathroom with me naked?"

Then it happened. My brain caught up with my impulsiveness. Damn! NFL man of my dreams was so hot. I had to just take a moment and stare. There was physically no other choice. Ass muscles, glutes ... Whatever. I loved a man with defined ass muscles, and his legs, back, and shoulders ... magnificent.

"Lake Jones, are you getting in the shower with me?"

I wiped my brow. Man, it was hot in there. "Wh-what? Um ... no."

"Then get out."

"Oh ... OK."

I left. As soon as I plopped onto the bed, I screamed into the pillow, my body jerked in every direction. It was too much for a girl to take, so I grabbed my phone and texted Lindsay.

Lake: *I'm in Beijing with the man of my dreams and he's in the shower. I saw him naked and we haven't had sex. I'm dying. What do I do?*

I tapped the screen of my phone like my impatience would expedite her response.

Lindsay: *Please tell me it's not that Jerry guy.*
Lake: *No. Football guy from Omaha.*

Sadly, that was Cage's code name between me and Lindsay. She knew the whole "one day, one everything" experience I had three years earlier. However, she didn't know anything about our chance encounter in Minneapolis.

Lindsay: *THE football guy? NFW!!!!*
Lake: *Gotta go. The shower just shut off.*
Lindsay: *Hurry, ride him before he gets dressed. Just do it, babe!*
Lake: *I'll see what I can do.*

Yeah ... no, that wasn't happening. Words were my thing. I pretty much talked nonstop, but "Before you slip on your clothes could you let me ride your cock?" was not in my wheelhouse of phrases I felt confident saying to a guy.

The door opened. The sexiest man alive stepped around the corner in jeans and a faded green T-shirt, hair still dripping.

"Were you serious about me getting in the shower with

you?" Another classic example of my mouth going rogue. That was not on the teleprompter. I was supposed to address the notecards.

Cage rubbed the white towel over his head then tossed it on the back of the desk chair. "Typically if a woman comes into the bathroom while I'm in the shower, it means she wants to join me."

I frowned. "Oh. Is it typical for women to walk in on you while you're showering?" Still, I was way off subject, but a more pressing matter took precedence.

He chuckled, shaking his head. "No."

I tried not to act too relieved, but I most certainly was.

"Why the notecards?" I pulled the sheet up over my chest; it hit me I wasn't wearing a bra. Was it fair that I guarded my T-shirt-covered nipples after gawking at him completely naked? Probably not.

"You don't remember?"

I remembered everything, even things I pretended not to remember because I didn't want to look like a loser with no life. Chapter titles and notecards? That, I didn't remember.

I wrinkled my nose. "I don't. Tell me."

"Nope. You'll eventually remember." He laughed a little. "I'm actually glad you don't remember. It will make a bigger impact when you finally do."

"You cannot be serious. You're not going to tell me."

"Nope." He sat on the edge of the bed, bringing his clean, soapy scent with him. I crossed my legs under the sheet, hoping to ease the miserable ache that developed from his close proximity. "Can I see your leg?"

"Um ..." I rubbed my lips together. I didn't see that request coming. "Sure." I flipped the sheet off and uncrossed my legs. I wasn't embarrassed or ashamed. I'd learned very early on to not hide it. That was me, all of me, one hundred percent complete.

"May I?" His hand hovered over the end of my leg.

I nodded.

Cage brushed the pads of his fingers along my leg, making the occasional glance up to my eyes.

"Does it freak you out?"

He smiled and shook his head. "Nothing about you freaks me out ... well, barging in on me in the shower freaked me out a little." His hand moved up my leg.

I tracked its path, part of me begged him to keep moving north and the other one percent thought he should stop. I considered that one percent a glitch that would work its way to the other ninety-nine percent if he just kept going.

"I didn't see anything. It was too steamy."

Lie. Lie. Lie. Why had it become so addictive?

Cage smirked, meeting my eyes. "You saw nothing?"

CAGE

WHAT ARE YOU DOING? I chanted over and over in my head. I lied. She freaked the living hell out of me and it had nothing to do with her leg. It was the feelings—the goddamn girly-type feelings that I had around her. I couldn't control the things I said or the way I felt any more than I could control my growing erection.

Sure, I wanted to touch her leg as a gesture that it didn't bother me, but I really just wanted to touch her. My hand moved up her leg on its own accord. Lake sucked in a quick breath. I paused, but her expressive, blue eyes told me to keep going.

That was my defense. Her eyes said yes. And her nipples? They gave me a standing ovation. My God, could her light blue T-shirt have been any tighter? Any thinner? The shorts though, they were tiny and with her leg bent I could see her white panties, and I swear they looked wet. I was painfully hard. The room felt over one hundred degrees, and every three seconds I had to gulp down copious amounts of saliva because I craved her so fucking bad.

She wet her lips again and again and again. Each time I wanted to lean in and do it for her. I moved my hand up a little more. Lake sucked in another quick breath, but those eyes still pleaded for me to keep going. I wanted, I *needed* to know if her panties were in fact wet, and I needed to know just how wet I made her. I'd gone rogue, leaving my responsibilities behind and likely my starting position as well—all for a girl.

The only sounds in the room were the echoes of the city outside, my constant swallowing, and her puffy breaths that escaped every time her pink tongue darted out to wet those lips I wanted to taste again.

Another inch or two, my hand worked its way up her leg until my thumb rested on her inner thigh a half inch from those white, *wet* panties. She didn't say anything. Why didn't she tell me to stop or grab my hand? Why didn't I stop on my own? I wanted to kiss her, but my desire to watch her react to my touch won.

"Lake, tell me to stop."

She just stared at me, lips parted.

"Lake, tell me this is too fast. Tell me what's going on between us is crazy because ..." My eyes flitted between hers and my hand high on her leg.

"Because..." she whispered "...it feels like we've known

each other forever. Like that *one* day three years ago held the significance of every day before it. Because on the *one* day you needed to feel a connection to life again, I showed up at your door. I was your connection."

She did. She knocked on my door when the pain, anger, and loss were just too much. I was so mad at my dad for leaving me, for giving up, for dying. Nothing in my world made sense until I opened the door that day, then magically, everything made sense.

"Yes," I whispered.

Lake nodded. "I know because you were mine too. You confirmed what I'd been trying to convince myself of for the previous year—not one single yesterday mattered."

LAKE

I WANTED him to touch me, but more than that, I wanted him to know I felt everything he felt the day we met. Those feelings never went away for me; they became the standard to which I compared all other feelings. Sure, I wanted sex—hell, I was desperate for it—but I wanted more than sex with Cage.

I wanted the man.

I wanted him.

I wanted to always remember that all my yesterdays didn't matter.

When he looked at me, when he touched me ... that became my reality, my truth.

"I haven't had sex in a *long* time and even then it was—" I slapped my hand over my mouth.

Cage started to remove his hand from my leg, and I stopped him with my other hand.

"Don't stop," I mumbled then removed my hand from my mouth, biting my lips together, *hard*.

His expression went from confident and sexy to slightly mortified and utterly confused.

"I'm sorry. I just said that so you wouldn't have high expectations. Not that I don't know what I'm doing ... it's just that when or if we do *that*, it's going to progress quickly for me—like a fifteen-year-old boy with a supermodel."

Cage failed to hide his smirk.

"And just to clarify ... you're the supermodel and I'm the fifteen-year-old boy in that scenario."

"I-I don't know what to say." His eyes flitted between mine and my hand holding his to my leg.

Trzy had nothing on me. My slutty touch-me-pet-me-love-me skills surpassed hers. Desperate. I had to look pathetically desperate. Surrendering to the reality that my big mouth robbed my vagina of some much-needed attention, I released his hand and flopped onto my side, covering my head with a pillow.

"I can't think around you. Gah! Someone just shoot me, please."

"Do you want me to leave?"

I shot up. "No!"

Cage untangled my hair plastered to my face. "No?"

"I'd rather be a blubbering idiot with you here than a well-spoken genius with you gone."

"That's sexy." He threaded his hands through my hair, grasping my head as if preparing to take something that was his. Independent woman, I belonged to no man, blah, blah, blah ... I wanted to be his. The desire to find the one guy that made me want to wave my white flag lived in the non-feminist part of my brain. Cage was white-flag worthy.

I grinned. "It's really not, but it's me and I want you to like *me*."

He pulled me a breath away from his lips. "I'm here, Lake. I think we're good in the 'liking' you department." Then he kissed me.

"My teeth," I mumbled against his lips. "I ... need ... brush ... them ..."

"Shut up," he mumbled back.

Without breaking our kiss, I braced my hands on his biceps while he held my head. Shifting to my knees, my hands slid down and gathered fistfuls of his shirt, tugging it up his torso. I would not speak again. Life was meant to be lived. Ben died, but I lived ... I *lived*.

Cage broke our kiss and smiled so big my heart nearly exploded into a red sea of sparkling glitter. He reached back and grabbed his shirt, removing it in one swift motion. I had to remind myself to breathe. Mr. NFL-followed-me-to-China guy had a ridiculously fit body.

He must have noticed my slack jaw and chest teetering on the edge of hyperventilating. "We don't have to do this."

My eyes flicked to his. "Shut up." I grinned and lunged at him. He fell back onto the bed with me on top of him.

"Oof ..." His mock pain didn't faze me as I kissed his chest and up his neck. Best breakfast ever.

"Please, please, please, tell me you have a condom," I murmured over his jaw, working my way to his lips as he grabbed the back of my legs to straddle me over his cock.

"If I say yes, will it mean I'm too presumptuous?"

I stopped, hovering over his face, our noses nearly touching, my hair falling around us like a curtain. "No. I think if you say yes, then it means you're going to score this morning, Monaghan."

His gaze washed over my face. If only I could have read his expression, but I couldn't. I just knew how it made me feel—somewhere between tipsy and complete nostalgia.

On a sudden jerk, he sat up with me straddling his lap, his hands cupping my waist. "I need you to hear this." A wrinkle of concern lined his forehead.

"O ... K ..." My eyes narrowed a bit.

"I can't define this—us—but you need to know that this means something. Okay?"

I nodded slowly, keeping my gaze locked to his as I raised my arms above my head. He took forever to remove my shirt, inching it up my body so slowly I thought I might orgasm from how damn sexy he made something as simple as taking off my shirt feel. His confidence was rivaled only by his sexiness.

As my shirt fell to the floor and my hair cascaded down my back and chest, I sucked in a shaky breath. Cage didn't move, except for his eyes. They swallowed up every inch of my naked skin.

"Focus, Monaghan ... don't fumble."

The heat in his eyes seared mine, but he still gave up a cocky smile that I'd never seen before. Damn, I was more than ready to eat him alive. Abstinence had made me *very* hungry.

"I've got this."

Aaaannd he claimed my orgasm. Three simple words, said with complete confidence, soaked my panties.

His eyes returned to my bared breasts, no touching, no licking, just ... staring. Complete torture. I squirmed a bit on his lap. The grip he had on my hips tightened. Apparently rubbing myself against his cock wasn't allowed. Just … staring.

Gah! Killing me!

Cage wet his lips. "Tell me, Lake … what part of *my* body should give *you* your first orgasm this morning?"

Gulp.

How embarrassing was it that he was well on his way to giving me one with nothing more than his words? Very. That's how embarrassing it was.

He waited.

Oh God … he really expected me to answer that question.

Just as I opened my mouth to declare my request, a loud rap at the door shattered our moment like a sledge hammer.

"Worst. Timing. Ever!" I yelled loud enough for Thaddeus and the rest of the fifteenth floor to hear.

Hopping off Cage's lap, I retrieved my shirt, slipped it over my head, and threw on my leg before stomping to the door like an errant child being sent to their room.

"Good morning to you too, love." Thad grabbed a white cup with a black lid from a beverage tray. "Tea. Now you have to forgive me for whatever I've done, which of course I have no idea what that is." He stepped inside. "There's our sports star." He held up another cup. "Please tell me you're a coffee man."

I turned and to my disappointment Cage had his shirt back on.

"Yes. Thank you." He took the cup from Thad.

"Why are you not ready to go, love?"

Because I was just about ready to have some really overdue sex with the man of my dreams.

"Twenty minutes. I'll meet you in the lobby."

"And your friend? Is he joining us today?"

It was a reasonable question given my unreasonable reaction to Thad making the offer to Cage the previous night. Some days my job infused me with confidence, some days I freaked out in the pool. It was impossible to predict which Lake Cage would witness that day. The night before I didn't know how I felt about Cage seeing me stumble. However, that morning ...? I just wanted him to see me. Both men looked at me, but I only looked at Cage.

"Yes. I'd love for him to join us today."

We shared knowing smiles.

"Great then ... I'll meet you two downstairs in twenty."

"Thanks again for the coffee," Cage called as Thad walked out.

Thad held up a hand. "Don't mention it."

Cage sipped his coffee, his other hand casually shoved into his jeans pocket as if we hadn't been half naked five minutes earlier.

For a lack of the right words to say, I sighed. Cage grinned. I eased the lid off my tea that was too hot to drink and set it down on the nightstand.

"I need to shower."

He nodded.

"Sorry about Thad's timing."

Cage shrugged, taking another sip of his coffee. "You're here for your job."

"I should quit."

He smirked. "You really should."

CHAPTER THIRTEEN

SLOW TORTURE

CAGE

BEIJING WAS another world away in every sense. It was still technically my off season, not an accurate portrayal of my life. Well, it was my life. I always had an off season, it just wasn't my average day every day. Following a girl to China also wasn't part of my average day or any day for that matter. Was I crazy? Probably.

Flint blew up my phone with texts that I chose to ignore.

Flint: *2 days. I told you 2 days was all you'd have. Obligations …*
Flint: *Every day you're not training, some other quarterback is working to be better than you.*
Flint: *I hope she's worth it.*
Flint: *I hope you get her out of your system before the season starts.*
Flint: *It's driving me fucking mad that you're not responding!*

The hardest part of the day was not envisioning Lake's

breasts because I'd seen them and I couldn't un-see them, not that I wanted to, but it did things to certain parts of my body that made the day less than comfortable. When we arrived at the sports facility with extremely tall climbing walls, Thad said a "team" would be there to evaluate Lake's climbing in the new prototype leg. I didn't expect a large, roped-off area just for her with twenty other people taking photos, video, typing notes on their iPads, and shooting an insane amount of questions at her as she climbed the wall like a monkey.

After several hours of climbing, they whisked her off to the pool, leaving a trail of people with cameras scurrying to catch up to her. Lake emerged from the locker room, and I broke out into a sweat. Dear God ... she fucking owned that swimsuit. I couldn't stop staring at her tits—breasts. Who was I kidding? It was my dick talking, and they were tits.

Everything she did left me without a single coherent thought or articulate word to say. The woman was good—really good. An athlete that showed no disability. She drew a crowd. I hadn't expected that. She laughed, answered all questions, and exchanged playful banter with Thad and Jerry. Lake engaged with everyone around her, and they loved her. I grinned like an idiot, wearing my baseball cap low to ward off recognition, but I was nothing more than the tall guy standing in the way of getting a good picture of Lake Jones.

However, plenty of people still took my picture. Jerry told me it was because I was white and very tall, not that they necessarily recognized me. Apparently, Thad was photographed a lot too. Jerry said most people assumed he was probably an NBA player.

After another two hours with four different versions of the prototype, Thad and Jerry gave Lake the rest of the day off. I thought we should go back to her hotel room because that's what any normal guy would think after focusing on her body all day.

"I'm starving. Lunch?" Lake asked as she came out of the locker room in a pair of jeans, black Nikes, and a tight, white long-sleeved shirt. She'd released her damp hair from its ponytail.

"You're quite the celebrity here."

She rolled her eyes. "It's just because they tape off the area. People are drawn to what they believe is off limits. A dead person in the street with a chalk outline draws a crowd too. Doesn't mean they're a celebrity."

"I know what I saw, and they like watching you, and they love how you interact with them."

We walked to the exit. "I think four of them spoke English. I smile. That's how I interact with them."

"They ate it up."

"Okay, Mr. Actual Celebrity. I noticed you kept your hat down and chin even lower. Are you a big deal over here?"

A driver opened the door to a black, compact SUV. Thad hired a driver for Lake and her "guest" for the rest of the day—anywhere we wanted to go. Lake climbed in and I followed her.

"No. I don't think I'm a big deal here, but to be honest, I didn't think I'd be a big deal the first time I went grocery shopping after I moved to Minneapolis. By the time I autographed my way to my truck and drove home, my perishable items had in fact perished."

"Where to?" the driver asked, in *English*. Well done, Thad.

"Food. I need food, and I'm not picky. Some place nice

but casual, and preferably where there are no American football fans," Lake requested then winked at me.

I shook my head, but I still had to grin as the driver returned an odd look in the rearview mirror then nodded before pulling out of the parking lot.

"Thank you." Lake grabbed my hand.

"For?"

"For being here. For spending hour after boring hour watching me work. The bastard geeks didn't even pull a chair up for you. Sorry."

I kissed the inside of her wrist. "I loved every minute. When you said you were climbing with a prototype leg, I imagined a small bouldering wall with a few crash pads. I didn't anticipate you lead climbing a fifty-foot wall like a kick-ass competitor. You're good. Really good. And the pool ... I was impressed. And for the record, I'm not easily impressed."

My compliment was met with an intense stare and a few moments of silence. The "are you being serious" flashed in neon on her beautiful face. Her hand shook in mine. I squeezed it and she smiled like she believed me. I didn't want her to argue. I didn't want her to question my sincerity. I didn't want her to ever see her reflection as less than amazing.

"Thank you," she whispered.

LAKE

We spent a perfect afternoon sightseeing around Beijing with our personal driver, topping it off with a candlelit dinner and wine. Cage didn't drink. I did, probably too much, but I needed something to numb my nerves that he fed all afternoon with his words, his dimples, and the stolen kisses he took every chance he got.

"Wanna come up to my room for a bit?" I asked when the driver pulled up in front of the hotel.

Cage looked at his non-existent watch on his wrist. "Hmm ... maybe just for a little while. My visa expires in twenty-eight days."

Dimples.

I was such a goner.

In the elevator I shot a text off to Thad.

Lake: *I'll see you tomorrow. If you knock on my hotel room door 2nite you will leave this country in need of prosthetic man parts.*
Thad: *Don't let your sports star impregnate you. The extra weight would require new legs. Basically ... don't have sex. Night, love.*

Thad's text gave me a moment of pause. Don't have sex? Was he being funny or possessive? I knew the idea was ridiculous so I shook it off.

"Texting your Beijing boyfriend to wait a bit before tucking you in bed?"

I giggled, thanks to the extra glass of wine, while looking at my phone screen. "Are you jealous? Pleeease be jealous. I'm not usually into that behavior, but you're different. If I honestly thought you could be jealous, I swear we wouldn't even make it back to the hotel room before ..." I shook my head.

The elevator doors opened. I slipped my phone in my purse and headed toward the room.

"Before what, Lake?" he called behind me.

The bass in my chest kept beat for the song that played

in my body. It was that song that held all of my emotions. It was the song that gave me the courage to turn around.

Thump thump thump ...

It wouldn't be a lie if I said I jumped him in the hallway. That's exactly what I did. I turned and took two steps before demonstrating my high jump abilities. Lucky for me, he caught me. I wrapped my arms and legs around him and kissed him in a way that said, "NOW. RIGHT NOW!"

He grabbed my legs, holding me to him as he shoved my back against the wall. I tore his hat off and fisted my hands in his hair as my tongue invaded his mouth. Trzy would have been proud of me.

His hands moved up my sides and over my breasts. My back arched, breaking our kiss. I couldn't breathe. Desperation was a greedy little oxygen hog. Cage took advantage of my exposed neck when my head thudded against the wall.

"Don't stop ... I want this ... so ... very ... bad ..."

His response was a deep moan that shot straight to my eager kitty.

"Room key," he mumbled over my skin.

"Ph-phone ... purse ..." I said through my heavy panting.

Hormones were little cocktails that trumped the effects of alcohol, public decency, and all reason in general. Cage lowered me to my feet. I retrieved my phone from my purse. The key to my room was on my phone.

I tried it.

It didn't work.

I tried it again and again.

It didn't work.

"Lake ..." Cage pressed himself to my back and splayed his hand over my stomach, the tips of his fingers breaching the waistband of my jeans. "You're killing me."

My forehead fell against the door and I closed my eyes. "It doesn't work."

"Lake ..." Not even the desperation in his voice or the inching of his hand down the front of my pants would magically open the door.

I tried one last time as his middle finger reached the top of my panties. "Work, dammit!" That did it. I just needed to be firm with it.

As soon as the door opened, his lips were back on mine, my feet off the ground, and two seconds later we landed on the bed with his body pressing mine to the mattress.

"We can slow down," Cage whispered in my ear before his tongue flicked my earlobe.

Maybe we could have, but my brain couldn't make sense of that idea or much of anything.

"Fingers, tongue, cock," I whispered with my eyes rolled back in my head as I writhed beneath him, vying for every bit of friction I could get against my most sensitive parts. Simply put, I was grinding my body against his because my need for sex hit the level of shamelessly-desperate.

My eyes opened when I felt his breath over my face.

"What did you just say?"

"It was the answer to your question this morning."

What part of my body do you want me to use to give you your first orgasm?

Thank God, recognition lit up his face. I really didn't want to say it aloud.

"Fingers? Tongue? Cock?"

I nodded. If he'd said it one more time in that same I'm-sexy-and-I-damn-well-know-it voice, then he wouldn't have had to actually *do* anything.

Yeah, I was that aroused—painfully aroused.

My phone rang. God hated me. There really was

no other explanation. He knew I was getting ready to sin. I shook my head when Cage gave me a questioning look.

"Ignore it."

"Are you sure?"

I nodded and grabbed his head bringing him down to my lips. It stopped ringing. I apologized to God and thanked him at the same time. My phone rang again. OK, clearly God was persistent.

"Just get it." Cage rolled off me.

I sat up. "I'll make it quick." I pushed down my shirt that he'd worked halfway up my torso, then grabbed my phone next to my purse on the floor.

"Mom, hi."

"Hey, baby. Thought I'd call you before you went to bed. I have a little time before I need to start making breakfast for our guests."

My parents owned a bed and breakfast in Tahoe, and my mom was always up before dawn.

"Thanks, yeah I'm about ready to go to bed."

Cage laced his fingers behind his head and grinned.

"How's your trip? Do you like the prototypes Jerry made you?"

"Yeah, they're great. I'll have to call you when I get home and tell you all about them."

"Have you talked to your brother or Jessica yet?"

"About?"

"Jessica's pregnant."

"What?" I squealed.

Cage rolled his head to the side, wide eyes looking at me. My smile overtook my face.

"She's due October tenth."

"That's awesome. Grant needs a sister."

"You have to let them tell you and act surprised when they do. Okay?"

I rolled my eyes. "Yeah, yeah."

"Oh, did I tell you about your dad's new project?"

"I don't think so."

My dad's new-project story segued into full updates on all my siblings. My mom was truly my best friend so I didn't have the heart to cut her off. I knew how much she worried about me, and I also knew how much talking to me on the phone helped her feel closer to me, easing her anxiety.

Thirty minutes after I answered my phone, she was still going. In spite of my apologetic looks, Cage disappeared into the bathroom and returned a few minutes later. He gave me a polite smile. Mine still said, "I'm so very sorry."

He mouthed, "it's fine," and stripped down to his black boxer briefs. I heard absolutely nothing my mom said after that point. He grabbed a pillow from the bed and the extra blanket at the end, and then started to make his bed on the couch. When he glanced my way, I shook my head and pointed to the spot in the king-sized bed beside me. We should have been having sex at that very moment; he'd seen my breasts that morning. There was no way I'd let him sleep on the couch.

Cage had the nerve to look conflicted.

I gave him the "really" look, stabbing my finger next to me and mouthing, "bed." He conceded with a small nod.

"Sweetie, are you still there?"

"Uh, yeah, Mom."

She continued. I watched a tall, muscle-bound guy with biceps bigger than my legs get into bed beside me. He turned his back toward me. I wanted to believe it was to give me a sense of privacy that I didn't really need and not that he was upset with me for our second botched attempt at having sex.

My mom droned on for another half hour. Maybe I should have just told her I had someone with me, but that would have only made the conversation longer.

"Well, I'd better get started on breakfast. I love you, Lake. Please be safe. You know I hate you traveling by yourself."

"I'm fine, Mom. I love you too."

I set my phone down and let my eyes wander over Cage's back. The sheet rested low on his hip. He'd fallen asleep, and I couldn't blame him. I eased out of bed and took a much-needed shower, brushed my teeth, then sat on the edge of the bed to rub lotion over my legs and arms.

After shutting off the light, I tried to go to sleep, but I couldn't. It wasn't a big surprise. My body didn't run on the same schedule as normal humans. So many things changed after my accident.

Man of my dreams was next to me in bed. What was I thinking? I shimmied out of my shorts and panties and shrugged off my T-shirt, tossing it to the end of the bed. Easing myself closer to Cage, I rested my head on the edge of his pillow. I brought my hand close to his back, almost touching him, and then I pulled it back. Like the chicken I was, I did the same thing several more times before I worked up the courage to touch him, but it wasn't with my hand. I pressed my lips between his shoulder blades.

He stirred. I pulled away and held my breath as he turned toward me. Stripping was a bad idea; at least that's what my evil friend, Insecurity, said to me. The curtains, that didn't get completely shut, let through enough light that I could see his face, his tired eyes, and the way he blinked them as if to check his vision, because surely the woman beside him wouldn't be naked.

"Hey," he whispered.

I smiled.

My arms were tucked against my breasts. He slowly moved my top arm to my side and then my bottom arm. There was no way to hide the rapid rise and fall of my chest or the unfolding of goose bumps along my skin. It was just meant for him to know exactly what he did to me.

Cage feathered his fingers over my neck then worked his way down to my chest, cupping one breast in his hand as his thumb circled over my nipple. A slow, heavy throb settled between my legs. As if he sensed it too, his fingers brushed down my stomach, stopping an inch above the spot that begged for his touch.

He leaned his head toward me, laying an agonizingly slow kiss on my lips. "Spread your legs," he whispered over my lips.

Oh my hell. How did he make that sound so dirty yet so damn sexy?

I gave him an inch, maybe a half.

His tongue teased my lips as his hand slid further south. "Wider."

Gulp!

I gave him another inch.

He smiled against my lips. "More." He diverted his hand to my inner thigh and opened my legs wider.

My hips jerked off the bed when his fingertip brushed my clit.

"Do you want this?"

I nodded, barely, but it was a nod. His touch paralyzed my whole body.

"Say it."

I swallowed hard again. "I want this."

His mouth covered mine at the same time two of his fingers slid into me. He absorbed my moans as his tongue mimicked the motion of his fingers. I came embarrassingly fast. My fault, not his. As he pulled his fingers out of me, he moved his mouth down my neck to my chest. I rolled onto my back.

"Cage ..." I moaned as his mouth made love to my breasts.

I threaded my fingers into his hair while he positioned his body between my legs. His tongue dipped into my belly button as he shimmied his body toward the end of the bed.

"No." I squirmed beneath him, tightening my grip on his hair.

"You said fingers..." kiss to my abdomen "...tongue..." he licked a path lower "...and cock."

I gave one last unforgiving tug to his hair. He chuckled, but stopped his descent. "No tongue?"

Maybe it was going so long without being with a man. Maybe it was the slow build up and the "almosts" that day. Maybe it was the lingering effects of the first orgasm. Whatever it was, my kitty could not handle his mouth there. I was *so* hypersensitive.

"This is embarrassing," I said in a breathy voice.

Cage crawled up my body. Instant relief washed over me until he settled between my legs. His erection beneath his boxer briefs pressed right *there*.

I gasped.

He dropped soft kisses along my jaw to my ear. "Don't ever be embarrassed with me. We can stop."

It was a terrible idea. Sure, I was a hot mess, but we didn't have to stop. I teased my hands down his back then slipped them into his briefs.

"Jesus ... Lake ..." He moaned as I curled my fingers into his hard glutes.

His pelvis rocked into mine, my breath hitched again. I needed another glass of wine. My mom wrecked my frame of mind and derailed my momentum to just go with it without over thinking.

"I need to know..." he rocked into me again and my fingers curled harder into his flesh "...if I need to get a condom or take a cold shower. I..." he panted into my ear "... I'm OK with whatever you decide." The desperation in his voice betrayed his words.

I smiled. He couldn't see it, but it was huge. That's just what I needed to get out of my head. A small piece of his vulnerability was all it took.

"A cold shower sounds really ... *cold.*"

He laughed a little, pressing his lips to my shoulder. "It really does."

"Maybe ..." I pushed his briefs down just far enough to free his erection.

His breaths at my ear became ragged. "Fuck," he whispered as I wrapped my hand around his cock, warm and hard beneath my fingers.

"Maybe we should work up a sweat before worrying about a shower."

"I love how you think." Our mouths collided and we. Did. Not. Stop.

Sweat. So much sweat.

And his mouth? Once I let go, I begged for it.

Lots of begging.

Muffled screams.

Two condoms later, I passed out in his arms, both of us too exhausted to entertain the shower idea until morning.

CHAPTER FOURTEEN

BOUNCE HOUSES AND BAD TIMING

THREE DAYS IN CHINA. That's how long it took me to officially fall in love with the man of my dreams. Although, by man-of-my-dreams definition, I think I loved him from the first day we met. Love was immune to time. Fuck the naysayers and anti-insta-lovers. They were nothing more than bitter people who had never met their "one."

The morning after we had sex for the first time, I started my period. I blamed Cage at first, claiming he broke my vagina. After he made a sincere offer to take me to the hospital for an X-ray, I conceded the probable explanation was the start of my period. In my dreams—where I controlled the world—men bled out of their penises one week every month. Fair? Yeah, I thought so too.

"My ticket is wrong." I stared at my phone on our way to the airport. "Thad messed up. I need to call him. He has me going to Portland, but that's it. I don't see a ticket to Minneapolis."

"Thad didn't book your flight ... Well, he helped, but I booked our flights."

I glanced over at Cage and his dimply smirk. "Oh?"

"I thought we could stay in Portland for a couple days."

"Oh?" My eyes grew with each "oh."

He rested his hand on my knee, giving it a little squeeze. "Remember I said my sisters have a birthday party they wanted me to attend?"

I nodded.

"It's tomorrow. Perfect timing, right? I may be out of a job but ... *family*." Another squeeze to my knee.

He listened to my family speech. It was so unmanly of him. Guys could hear, but their ability to listen was low. Another theory of mine. "I'm your date to your sisters' birthday party?"

"It's not really a plus-one party, maybe a bounce house, but nothing formal. Are you OK with meeting my family?"

Such a simple question, but the answer was a bit more complicated.

"Are you?"

He laughed. "I'm the reason your ticket ends in Portland. Yes, I think it's fair to say I'm good with introducing you to my family. They'll love you."

Do you love me?

"Then you'll tell them we met like three weeks ago and that you flew to China to kiss me, and they'll think I'm a witch that's cast a spell on you. I do believe you told me you're not impulsive."

"Three *years*. We met three years ago, not three weeks." He winked.

"That's our story? Really?"

"No. The story is in your purse."

I narrowed my eyes. He nodded toward my purse under the seat in front of me. I grabbed it and unzipped the top. A notecard, of course.

CHAPTER FOUR

"Tell me, this is killing me! What does this mean?"

A grin, it's all I got. He seemed quite proud of himself. For what? I had no idea.

"It's official. I'm nervous. This is insane." I squeezed Cage's hand as the cab pulled into his mom's driveway. "You're taking some girl home to meet your family and you've never even mentioned my name."

"You're right. They'll probably make you sleep on the porch with the dogs until they can trust you."

"I'm serious." I glared at him over the roof of the cab as I shut my door.

He paid the cab driver and took our luggage. "So am I. But don't worry about it. The hammock on the porch is ridiculously comfortable and Dora and Diego, the Brittany Spaniels, love the company."

"Dora and Diego?" I followed him to the front door of the two-story brick house. The front porch lights were on as the sun, low in the sky, made its exit.

"My sisters, Hayden and Isa, named them. They were six at the time."

He opened the front door and plopped the luggage inside. "Where's the welcome wagon?" he called.

A stream of high-pitched squeals and barking preceded the tornado of two white and hazelnut-colored dogs jumping on Cage's legs as two girls with long, blond hair practically tackled him to the ground.

"Cage! It's Cage! Mom? It's Cage!" one yelled.

"You came! I can't believe you came! Are you staying

for our birthday party?" the other asked with her arms wrapped around his neck.

"Birthday? What birthday?" he teased.

"It's our birthday tomorrow, silly."

"Oh, well, I think I can stay for a day or two if you're willing to share your cake."

The one attached to him like a monkey, kissed his cheek. "Of course we'll share our cake. Mine is going to be lemon with vanilla frosting, and Isa is having chocolate with cookie frosting."

"There's my favorite boy!" A tall, very thin blonde, clearly their mom, hugged Cage as soon as he set his sister down.

Gorgeous mother.

Beautiful sisters.

And me: scraggly girl hanging out on the porch with hair that looked like it barely survived the long flight and most likely hideous bags sagging under my tired eyes as well.

"Mom, I'd like you to meet Lake Jones." He held out his hand.

I smiled past my overwhelming fear and stepped in the house, accepting his hand.

"Lake, this is my mom, Brooke Hathaway." Cage pulled me into his side.

His mom's eyes moved over our joined bodies and a big smile grew along her face. "Lake, it's a true pleasure to meet you." She held out her hand.

"You too, Mrs. Hathaway." I shook her hand.

"Brooke, only Brooke, dear."

"Brooke." I nodded with a smile.

"This is Hayden and Isa." Brooke rolled her eyes as the girls latched onto Cage again. "Girls, put Dora and Diego on the back porch then go get showered." Brooke motioned us in and shut the door behind me. "They're just a little excited to see you."

Cage grinned. "Well, it worked out perfectly. We're on our way back to Minnesota from Beijing. Lake had a business trip there."

Brooke wrapped her white hoodie jacket around her as if the door being opened had let in too much cool air. "You've been in China?" She gave Cage a wide-eyed look. That confirmed it for me—Cage didn't fly halfway around the world for just any girl.

"Yes." He led me toward the kitchen. "Lake tests robotic legs for this cutting-edge company. She was testing swimming and climbing limbs. She's amazing."

I wanted to crawl under the kitchen table. Amazing was never the word I used to describe myself. Brooke looked at my legs. They were both covered by my jeans and Nikes. I only wore my pretty leg ... well, when I wanted to look and feel pretty which seemed to be quite often since Cage arrived in Beijing.

"Car accident." I pulled up on the left pant leg of my jeans.

Brooke's head jutted forward as her eyes squinted a bit. "Wow, that's a prosthesis?"

"Crazy, right?" Cage grinned. "It has hair-like follicles, veins on the top of the foot; and the heel, and the ball of the foot is slightly pink."

Yes, in those few days, Cage became an expert on my many legs.

"That's incredible."

I shrugged. "It's basically a regular prosthetic leg underneath a cosmetic silicone leg. I call it my pretty leg. I have several to wear with different high heels as well."

"You told me they're your sexy legs."

With my blushing face, I turned to Cage who was biting into an apple, and leaned up against the granite countertop of the kitchen island. "Yes..." I gritted my teeth behind my tight smile "...but since we're talking to your *mom*, I'm using pretty instead of sexy, but thanks for correcting me."

"You're welcome." He winked.

I shook my head while releasing a nervous laugh.

"Cage inherited his father's gift of bluntness." Brooke gave her son a challenging look.

"Mmm, maybe." He didn't appear the least bit bothered by that assessment. "Where's Rob?"

"On call. He had a patient get her tooth knocked out, so he left about an hour ago."

"Dentist," Cage said to me.

I nodded.

"Anyway, he could be a while. I bet you two are exhausted or jet-lagged or something. You'll have to excuse *my* bluntness, but my darling son didn't mention he was bringing a friend, so I'm not sure if I need to get another bed made up or ..."

Nothing awkward about that moment.

"My room is fine, Mom."

I smiled, not sure what or if I needed to add to the uncomfortable conversation. Cage looked completely relaxed as he finished his apple, like discussing sleeping arrangements for his ... *girlfriends?* was a daily occurrence.

"Well, I don't need to tell you to make yourselves at home. I'm going to make sure the girls are getting ready for bed. I'll see you both in the morning."

"Night, Mom."

"Goodnight, Brooke."

She waved while walking toward the stairs.

"You didn't tell her I was coming?"

He shrugged and tossed his core in the trash.

"I like to surprise people."

I tucked my hair behind my ears and nodded. "She looked surprised. Shocked might be the more accurate description."

Grabbing my wrist, he pulled me into his chest then lifted me up on the island, settling his body between my legs. I wrapped my arms around his neck as he nipped teasingly at my lips.

"Tell me you're done with your ..." He kissed along my cheek to my ear, sucking my earlobe into his mouth.

"My?" I laughed. "Period?"

"Mmm hmm. One night with you and then nothing for days. I'm dying a little."

"Would you buy me tampons from the store?"

He pulled back, brows knitted. "Do you need some?"

"Nope. I'm done with my *period.* I just wondered if you were *that* guy."

"That guy?"

"Yes. The guy that buys a woman tampons." I tapped my temple. "In my head, you've always been that guy."

"Pussy-whipped?"

"No." I laughed.

"It's flattering to be in your head, however, I'd rather be naked or part of some fantasy, not shopping for tampons."

"All the best fantasies start off with a guy shopping for tampons."

Cage's eyes grew wide, a smirk teased the corners of his mouth. "Tampons to stop the bleeding after fantasy guy breaks said girl's vagina?"

Biting my top lip, I nodded. "It happens."

"I see. Something tells me that my answer to the tampon question could be a pivotal moment between us."

I shrugged, biting the hell out of my lip to keep from smiling. "A make or break."

"Ouch. We're a little early for ultimatums." He lifted me off the counter. "Come on. My room is downstairs. We have the basement all to ourselves."

I grabbed my carry-on bag, and Cage took our suitcases.

"Wow. Nice basement. Or shrine. It really is more of a shrine."

Cage laughed, taking our luggage into the bedroom.

My eyes remained glued to the wall. "I'm glad you see the humor in it so I won't feel so bad when I say, 'Oh. My. God.' I mean, common sense tells me there has to be a wall behind all these posters and photos, but without that common sense it really does look like the posters and photos *are* the wall." I stepped closer, inspecting the non-existent spacing between the frames.

Cage in high school.

Cage in college.

Cage with Minnesota.

Cage receiving award after award.

Cage.

Cage.

Cage.

"My mom is my number one fan."

"No shit. I'd considered taking on the role myself, but clearly I'm way out of my league."

He swept my hair off to one side and kissed my neck, pressing his body to my back. "Have I told you today how beautiful you are?"

"No. N-not yet." I closed my eyes as his hands slid under my shirt, finding their way to my breasts.

"You are. You're so damn beautiful in every way."

His touch made me crazy. The ending of my cycle made me horny. The combination of both made me not care where we were. I turned in his arms. My grin screamed come hither.

"Couch, Monaghan."

He quirked a brow.

"Don't make me say it again."

He smirked, taking several steps back before flopping onto the enormous brown sectional. I grabbed one of his tennis shoes and pulled it off and then the other. His socks followed suit.

"Can you feel it, Monaghan? You're getting ready to score again. What if your off-season record surpasses your regular-season record?" I shrugged off my shirt.

His gaze dropped to my chest. "I love when you talk my language."

I slipped off my shoe. Each item of clothing got tossed in a different direction for theatrics.

My favorite dimples came out, approving of my strip tease.

"Mind if I lose the leg?" I asked.

He shook his head. There really were no words to describe how his lack of any sort of reaction made me feel.

Not one flinch.

Not one nervous glance at my leg.

Not one second of hesitation.

It was as if I asked whether we could listen to music while having sex. Cage didn't see my disability. He found every version of me sexy. I found my heart hurting from the fear that someday he would look at me and think "Holy, shit! You're missing part of your leg."

With equal flair, I tossed my leg over the back of the

couch and straddled his waist in just my black bra and panties.

"I think we can be honest with each other, Monaghan, so I'm going to let you in on a little female secret."

He tore his eyes from my breasts and met my gaze.

"By the end of a woman's cycle or *period* as you don't like to call it..." he rolled his eyes "...we are horny, as in, there is probably a twenty-four to forty-eight hour gap where you could fuck a woman senseless and she'd still beg for more."

His Adam's apple bobbed, swallowing that little nugget of information. "Shit! I brought you to my mom's house during your fuck-me-senseless time."

I shrugged, reaching behind me and unfastening my bra which got tossed over the couch as well. "Rookie mistake, Monaghan. Now ... the real question is..." I wet my lips while unfastening his jeans "...what part of my body is going to give you your first orgasm tonight?"

"Jesus, Lake ..." His breath caught just as I finished pulling down his zipper.

"AHHHHHHHH!!!!!!"

"AHHHHHHHH!!!!!"

My ears bled from the shrill screams. Trzy was in Minneapolis, so it wasn't her causing the commotion.

"Mom! Dad!" Two little girls' voices screamed in unison.

I dove for the blanket at the other end of the sectional and wrapped it around me. Of course the one blanket available was a cream, loose-knit afghan with quarter-sized holes in the pattern. Cage had his jeans fastened again before two kids and two adults reached the bottom of the stairs.

"It's a leg! It's a leg!" Hayden buried her head in Brooke's shirt while Isa covered her mouth, wide eyes staring at my leg on the floor at the bottom of the stairs. Next. To. My. Bra.

"Sshh ... it's not a real leg. Come on girls." Brooke grimaced at Cage and then at me before ushering the girls back upstairs.

A tall, wiry man with metal-framed glasses and an unfortunate case of male-pattern baldness, assessed the situation with his jaw slack—clearly dumbfounded.

"Rob!" Cage held out his hand.

After a few more awkward seconds, Rob shook Cage's hand. Lovely. The two men greeted each other separated only by my prosthetic limb and black lace bra. I remained balled up in the corner of the couch, wrapped in the most pathetic excuse for a blanket ever.

"Cage, uh ..." Rob gave me a quick glance before focusing his attention back on Cage "...good to see you."

"Rob, this is Lake Jones. Lake, this is my mom's husband, Rob."

"Hi." I wiggled my index finger that poked through one of the large holes. A one-finger wave, beyond embarrassing.

"Nice ... uh ... to meet you."

Biting my lips together, I nodded.

Please let me die.

"I ... just ..." Rob pointed to the bathroom next to Cage's bedroom. "My shaving kit is down here. I'm just going to grab it and we'll chat more in the morning."

"Sure thing." Cage smiled.

Me? Not smiling. Really, I was wondering what Rob had to shave. He was basically bald and I didn't notice any facial hair. Then it hit me—balls. Brooke probably made him manscape. I liked thinking that he needed to get his shaving kit to shave his balls. I liked thinking about anything that made someone else the white elephant in the room. It was a long shot, at best, but I'd take it.

"Got it. Make yourselves at home, er..." Rob made a final glance at my leg and bra "...you know, whatever. Good night." He held up a hand.

I gave a final index-finger wave. It was obvious I'd already made myself right at home. Cage retrieved my leg, bra, and the rest of my clothes then carried them to the bedroom while Rob and his shaving kit escaped up the stairs.

"I'm calling a cab, staying at a hotel, and getting a flight home in the morning. I like you so this really sucks, but we're done because I can never face your family again, and I just don't think you want to waste time on a girl you will never be able to bring home. Thank you for coming to China. Best kiss ever. I wish you luck and happiness in your life. It's been nice knowing ya."

Cage bit back his smirk, making a shitty effort to act serious. "I ... I don't think they even noticed anything out of the ordinary."

"Says the fully-clothed god that everyone in this house pays homage to on these walls. But then there's the naked woman who no one has seen or even heard of before today, just sitting on the couch with like..." I looked down at the blanket "...six measly strands of yarn wrapped around her naked body. Your sisters are going to need therapy. They're going to have nightmares about body parts just ... lying around the house. Your mom has to think I'm a complete slut trying to seduce her son. Probably thinks I'm some disabled gold digger. And don't even get me started on what Rob must be thinking ..."

"Well, let's do this, then." He scooped me up, yarn and all.

"Do what?"

"Fuck you senseless while we wait for your cab."

"Stop mocking me."

Cage deposited me on his bed then shut the door—and locked it. "First, don't ever call yourself disabled. You're the least disabled person I know." He shrugged off his shirt. I didn't object. "Second, in case you missed the Cage Monaghan 'shrine' out there, my mom thinks too highly of me to ever believe I would bring a gold digger home to meet her."

I waited. He didn't say anymore and just stood at the foot of his bed.

"Is there a third?"

He shook his head. "As you were."

My eyes flitted side to side. What was I missing? "As I was what?"

"Before we were interrupted you were unfastening my pants like you had a mission—a plan. Continue on."

My smile faded. I didn't want it to, but feelings were precarious little creatures that swooped in at the worst possible time and insisted on having their way.

"Hey …" Cage sat on the edge of the bed and pulled me and my blankie in for a hug. "What's wrong?"

"Dammit, nothing." I swatted the tears from my cheeks.

"Doesn't look like nothing." He leaned back and tipped my chin up with his finger.

I sniffled and laughed at the stupid timing of it. "Sorry, I can't believe you just offered yourself up to me and I started crying. It's just …" The tip of my tongue rolled along the corner of my mouth as I looked up and blinked away more tears. "I'm not one to work that hard to impress anyone. I had to let that go after my accident. *It* was my biggest disability for a long time, but I want your family to like me because …" I sucked in a shaky breath.

"Because?" he whispered.

My gaze locked to his. "Because I kinda like you—a lot."

The intensity in his eyes broke through all the bullshit, all the self-preservation, and it was him looking at me with my heart, once again, offered up on a silver platter.

After a slow nod for his response to me, he stood and removed the rest of his clothes. I said too much. Stupid blabbering mouth of mine. He wanted sex and I gave him an episode of Oprah. Not cool of me. Not cool at all. In an effort to redeem myself, I tossed the blanket on the floor and offered him my body instead of my heart. He took it again and again, but not once did he say anything to me. Our soft moans were the only sounds that filled the air.

CHAPTER FIFTEEN

SAY IT WITH A TAMPON

***C**RINKLE. Thump. Thump. Crinkle. Thump.*

"Trzy ..." I mumbled. "Not now." I rolled over and that's when the bed didn't feel familiar and my brain jump-started. I peeled open one eye and then the other. "Cage?"

"Good morning. You talk in your sleep." He stood at the end of the bed with his hands shoved into his pockets.

"I don't." I rubbed my eyes.

"You do."

"What is..." I sat up "...all of this?"

Boxes and boxes of tampons covered the foot of the bed.

"I got super, regular, with applicator, without applicator, organic ..."

"Um ... I'm not having my—"

"*Period.* Yes, I know. I witnessed that fact more than once last night." He smirked.

I blushed.

"I want to be the *that* guy."

Tampons. Tampons were my proverbial long-stemmed roses. Tampons took my breath away.

"You bought me tampons," I whispered, still in a daze.

The bed dipped as he sat on the edge. He laced his fingers through my hair and cupped my head as his lips brushed my ear. "I bought you tampons because I kinda like you—a lot."

I loved this man. I loved him so much it brought real pain to my chest.

"Now, since you missed your cab and hotel stay last night, you might as well come up for birthday breakfast."

"Birthday breakfast?"

"Yes." He grabbed the bag and piled the tampons in it. "All food choices belong to Hayden and Isa today, so they agreed on chocolate chip pancakes with bananas and whipped cream for breakfast."

"And my leg?"

He laughed. "No worries. My mom explained it to them last night. Now it's your turn to do what you do best."

"But aren't you about out of condoms and doesn't that seem a little inappropriate for a birthday party?"

"Yes." He adjusted himself. "And so is the hard-on you're giving me by talking about it." He tossed the tampon bag by my suitcase. "I bought condoms too." He winked. "Take your time, pancakes will be waiting, and then you can show my sisters your cool leg. The *other* thing you do best."

COME TO FIND OUT, what I did best was eat chocolate chip pancakes with two eight-year-old girls. Once I showed them my leg and the other two in my suitcase, they wanted to try them on and were bummed that they could not because they had two feet already.

Aww, to be eight again.

"So how did you two meet?" Brooke asked. "Don't take

this the wrong way, but I knew nothing of you until you showed up yesterday."

I dried the dishes from breakfast after she washed them.

"Actually, I met him in Omaha shortly after his father died."

"Oh, really?"

"Yes."

"She's Jillian's sister-in-law," Cage scared me as he snuck up behind me, taking the dry pan from me.

The off-limit topic between us had been breached. I didn't know where to go from there.

The problem was I didn't know Jillian Knight. I knew Jessica Day—Jessica Jones. Of course they were the same person, but lives at risk and all that jazz complicated the situation. My sister-in-law was once involved romantically with Cage's father. It was an extremely weird situation. Cage told me Jessica/Jillian contacted him after his father died. She didn't share much because he didn't want to know, so she offered him her overdue condolences and officially said goodbye.

I assumed he wanted to remember her as Jillian, the woman who in many ways gave his father a life, even if cancer took it in the end. I didn't know what to say. Jessica was my family. Our relationship had nowhere to go if we could never discuss her.

"Jillian got married? That's great." Brooke seemed genuinely happy. "Kids?" She'd already asked more questions than Cage did.

I gave him an uneasy look. He gave me a weak smile, but it felt like an OK to answer his mom. "Yes, a boy. Grant Thomas Orion Jones—GTO Jones. The story is he was conceived in the back of the same vehicle—a red '67 GTO—as my brother, Luke. Grant is 18 months and so stinking cute. He looks just like my brother, but has his mommy's personality—fun." I probably went too far. I didn't even look at Cage. The enthusiasm for my little nephew, and the sister-in-law that I practically worshipped, was too hard to hide.

Cage set the pan down and retrieved his phone from his pocket.

"Banks, what's up?"

I tracked him as he paced the kitchen.

"I am. She is. Hold on." He held out his phone. "Banks. He wants to talk to you."

My eyes narrowed at the phone as I took it. "Everson?"

"It's been more than a week. You said you'd be gone a week. You didn't leave me your cell number."

"I said a week or so. You never asked for my number. What's wrong? Is it Shayna?"

"I've interviewed fifteen different nannies, but I can't decide and that's probably because I don't know what the fuck I'm doing. She hasn't had a bath since you gave her one. That seems bad, right? I can't do this, I can't fucking do this."

"Slow down. It's fine. She's fine. The bath thing is pretty bad, but I'll help you."

"How can you fucking help me when you're not here?"

"Please tell me she's not standing there while you're dropping all these f-bombs."

"She's watching TV in the other room. When are you coming home?"

"Um ... I'm not sure."

"Today. I'll pay for your ticket."

I laughed. "I don't need you to buy me a ticket."

Cage continued drying dishes with Brooke, giving me the occasional narrow-eyed look.

"Not today. I'll get a flight home tomorrow."

"A morning flight."

"An *available* flight. Bye."

I handed Cage his phone.

He pocketed it. "Sooo ... we're flying back tomorrow?"

Brooke pulled the drain on the water and wiped her hands. "I'll give you two some privacy."

"I'm sorry. He's having a rough time with Shayna."

"It's fine."

Were we a couple? Were we having our first fight? It didn't feel like a fight, but his "fine" didn't really sound fine.

"You don't have to leave tomorrow. In fact, you should stay with your family. I'm sure they'd love to spend as much time as possible with you during the offseason."

Cage nodded slowly, more of a processing nod than an approval nod. "That's ... fine." His smile didn't reach his eyes.

I wrapped my arms around his waist. "I'm yours for the day, Monaghan. I do believe you promised me a bounce house and some cake."

He tugged on my ponytail. "Did I mention I kinda like you—a lot?"

I giggled. "You did and you said it with feminine hygiene products. Move over, Prince Charming."

He kissed me, letting his tongue make a leisurely exploration of my mouth. My hands slid down to his ass, giving it a firm squeeze.

He groaned. "Lake ... hands off my ass unless you want me to throw you over my shoulder and haul your sexy ass downstairs."

I kept my hands right where they were.

He chuckled, biting at my lower lip. "I have a love/hate relationship with your stubbornness of calling my bluff."

"You love that I want you to haul my ass downstairs, but you hate that you're not really going to because as we speak there are people gathering out back for kid games."

"Mmm ... later. You've been warned."

It wasn't a warning. It was a promise, one that I intended to ride all night long.

I NEARLY CRIED when Cage drove me to the airport in his mom's car the next morning. For some reason Minneapolis felt like reality, and Beijing and Portland were just a dream —the one that Cage Monaghan starred in as my leading man. Would my carriage turn back into a pumpkin when the plane touched down in Minnesota?

"I'll fly back tomorrow. I'm already on Flint's shit-list for being gone so long ... and probably a few of my coaches' too. Stay out of trouble." He wrapped his arms around me as we stood by the curb.

"And by trouble you mean jail."

"I'll have Flint and Banks keep a close eye on you."

"You ever going to tell me about Flint? Who is he?"

"He was a wide receiver at Nebraska, two years older than me. Called it quits after an ACL injury. Now he's my agent, but the kind that goes above and beyond because we're friends too."

I rubbed my lips together and nodded. He grabbed my ass and squeezed it harder than I'd ever squeezed his. My eyes grew big.

"And should you see Flint before I get home, don't be hitting on him."

My head jerked back.

"And don't give me that look like you don't know what I'm talking about."

"I-I ..."

"He told me the day he bailed you out of jail that you flirted with him." He quirked a brow.

"He's full of himself."

"He said you called him handsome."

I shrugged. "Well he's not *unpleasant* to look at and his name is Flint."

"You like his name?"

"Uh ... yeah." I looked up at him and smirked. "Are you jealous?"

He bit his bottom lip and nodded. "Maybe."

"I like—"

"Don't you dare say you like me jealous. You think that now, but fair warning, guys don't like to be jealous, and I make a living with my hands so busting them against another guy's face is not good."

He was right, but Oh. My. God. That turned me on so much I wanted to shove him into the backseat and have one last good-bye that would most likely have resulted in an arrest.

"Then kiss me like you mean it."

He did. He kissed me like he'd never get to kiss me again.

"Bye," I whispered, completely breathless.

"Bye." He left one last kiss on the tip of my nose before releasing me.

I'm pretty sure I walked like a drunk into the airport.

CHAPTER SIXTEEN

THREE WORDS

CAGE

I WAS DROWNING IN A LAKE. My Lake. Was she mine? God, I wanted her to be. Never in my life had I felt so protective—possessive—of a woman.

"I like Lake, she's real," my mom said then laughed. "Your sisters adore her. I think she sealed the deal when she played in the bounce house more than their friends did. She played all the kids' games, and she braided ribbons into their hair. If you don't keep her, then I'm going to adopt her as their big sister."

We sat in chairs on the front porch watching Hayden and Isa ride their new bikes up and down the long driveway while Rob washed the car.

"I like her too."

She sipped her coffee. "You don't sound too convinced."

"I met her before this life, this ... crazy public life. It's not that she's fragile, she's not. I'm just worried that the publicity, my crazy schedule, and all the crap that comes as a package deal with me could be more than she wants. And honestly, I wouldn't blame her."

"You don't have to get down on one knee, hun. I mean ... I'm going to adopt her, but ..."

I grinned. "Flint thinks I'm insane. I think his words were something like 'worst timing ever.' I told myself I'd give this football career everything, and I'm just getting started, but then ..."

Mom rested her hand on my arm. "But nothing. You're focused, you've always been focused. You can have a career and a life. It doesn't have to be a choice. She told me about China."

"Told you what?"

"Lake told me you flew to Beijing just to kiss her."

I bit my lips together, a little surprised Lake said that to my mom. "She did, huh?" My eyes remained set on the girls, but I saw my mom's grin out of the corner of my eye. "What kind of schmuck would do something like that?" I stood. "I'm going for a run. I think the rain looks like it will hold off."

"Okay. I love you, my dear *schmuck*."

LAKE

My unpacking revealed a notecard:

CHAPTER FIVE

My brain hurt because I couldn't piece it together, but nonetheless it sent the really good kind of chills along my spine. I finished unpacking and took care of Trzy's needs, which included cleaning out her litter box, lots of petting, and some laser play, then I knocked on Everson's door.

"Miss me, Apollo?" I flashed him my best smile when he opened the door.

"That might be taking it too far."

"Oh well, in that case I have other things to do—" I turned.

"Wait."

I looked over my shoulder. "Yes?"

Everson shook his head. There was no real need to make him beg, but I couldn't help myself.

"I missed you, but you're still not getting any of this." He motioned to his body.

I laughed, turning back around and throwing my shoulders back, chin up. "Don't flatter yourself, Apollo. I get mine." Oh Lord ... was I ever getting mine.

There it was—the full smile, pearly whites and all. "Coming from your mouth, it just sounds all kinds of wrong."

I frowned. How was I supposed to say it?

"Where's Shayna?"

He stepped out of the doorway. "Her room."

"Let me see the contract you have for your nanny candidates."

"Contract?" His brows stood erect.

"Yes, a contract. You know, the expectations you have, their duties, like: learning activities, recreational activities, meals, excursions, housekeeping, etcetera. And rules like: no smoking, drinking, or drugs, no napping, no parties or inviting friends over, no social media, no photos and sharing pictures or revealing locations, no television or gaming ...

"Please don't tell me you're interviewing nannies like looking for someone to mow your lawn. You had to sign an extensive contract to chase a ball and pat guys on the ass. For the love of God, Everson, you *need* a contract to hire someone to take care of a child, a fragile human being."

"I told you I'm not good at this shit. I told you—"

"Shh ..." I shook my head pointing toward the bedroom.

He rolled his eyes.

"It took you ten seconds to contact your attorney for help when you weren't going to keep her. A quick call to ask him for help with a contract for a nanny should be a no-brainer."

"Lake!" Shayna yelled, running toward me.

I bent down and hugged her, looking at Everson. How could he not be head-over-heels in love with her? Even if she did need a bath.

"I'll take care of it."

"Take care of it?" he asked.

"I'll hire a nanny for you."

Everson stared at me as if I had a "but" or a "you owe me" that I hadn't yet shared.

"Now, I think someone needs a bath again and maybe tomorrow I'll take you to the salon."

Perfect mocha eyes looked up at me. "Salon?"

"A haircut and maybe we'll paint your toenails too."

Shayna grinned then looked at her brother. "Evson, can I go?"

There it was, the little girl chipped away at his tough façade like I knew she would. The confusion on his face said he didn't expect her to ask him for permission.

She looked up to him.

She respected him.

She trusted him.

It was a gift and I knew he would start to see it a little more every day.

"Uh ... yeah, whatever."

Cage called to tell me goodnight. It was a short call with his sisters bugging him to let them say "hi." He planned on flying home late the next day. I planned on missing him.

The following day I took Shayna to the salon then shopping for more clothes. Silly me, I assumed Everson would have already done it. Wrong. Gah! Men.

"What the hell?" Everson gawked at the piles of bags we hauled into his apartment.

I glared at the TV. "Shut it off."

He shut off the X-Box game that was nothing more than horrific animated violence. "Yes, Mom."

"Time to grow up. She's six and if you want her to stop crawling in your bed in the middle of the night, then you need to stop letting her see things that will give her nightmares."

Everson didn't acknowledge my advice, instead he nodded to the bags. "Since we're on the subject of her being six, mind telling me why it looks like you bought out Macy's today."

I smiled at Shayna and found my happy voice instead of the condescending one Everson deserved. "Because a girl needs more than two outfits and one pair of underwear. Right, sweetie?"

She smiled, long lashes fluttering at Everson, and then she took off with one of the sacks to her room.

Everson shrugged, shoving his hands into his shorts' pockets. "How was I supposed to know what she had?"

"Oh, I don't know ... you could have looked in her tiny

backpack she showed up with, or maybe you could have asked her why she was wearing the same two outfits."

"I didn't want to invade her privacy or make her feel bad."

The crazy part? I believed him.

"Now I feel like shit. I didn't know."

"Doesn't matter. I'll be back later to help her put everything away. She has a bathrobe and her own toiletries now, so I'm going to help her figure out how to shower on her own here at your place. But she's young, Everson. If you see her naked it's not weird or a big deal unless you make it perverted, and if you do that, I'll bust your nuts with my robotic foot. Okay?"

"Fuck you," he said it in the most playful way it could be said, and he said it with a smile.

I blew him a kiss. "Language ... but, I like you too, Apollo. See you later. Call me if you need me ... now that you have my number." I shook my head. "Bye, Apollo."

My phone buzzed in my pocket as I unlocked my door.

Cage: *Flight delayed. Be home late. Early workout in the morning followed by two meetings to see if I still have a job. Dinner tomorrow night?*

Lake: *Yes!*

He texted me his address

Lake: *Your place? Can I bring anything?*

Cage: *An overnight bag.*

I smiled.

Lake: *Come home to me safely. I kinda like you—a lot. x*

Cage: *The feeling is kinda mutual.*

The next day consisted of testing more legs. Jerry and Thad shipped me a new jogging leg, two different ones for swimming, and one for biking. The wind made a commendable attempt at killing me on my bike, but I persevered. The training facility's pool was closed for a competition, so my swim legs had to wait.

I'd called several of Everson's nanny applicants to schedule an interview. One was available to meet that afternoon, so we met at a café for a casual interview. The previous day I did four over-the-phone interviews that didn't impress me enough to warrant a face-to-face meeting.

Too young.

Not enough experience.

Too stuffy.

Too flighty.

Then ... magic happened. I found *the* one. That was the one who met me for coffee.

Everson and Shayna pulled into the parking garage at the same time I returned from the interview.

"How'd it go?" Everson asked as Shayna smiled at me before running to the elevator.

"Perfect. Better than perfect. I hired your nanny. I set up a time to meet Shayna tomorrow at eleven. If they hit it off, then it's a go."

"Great. Thanks. I appreciate you doing this."

"My pleasure. This resumé is insane. I'm going to call the references tonight, but I anticipate it being a no-brainer." I walked toward the door.

"This isn't some ninety-year-old granny that's going to leave her teeth on my counter, right?"

I laughed. "Does it really matter what your nanny looks like?"

"No, but just give it to me straight. Is she hot?"

I shook my head. "No comment. See you both tomorrow." I shoved my key in the lock.

"WOW ... JUST ... WOW ..." I whispered after I typed in the code to the gate at the end of Cage's drive. His house was well hidden by tall trees, but once it came into view, I had trouble believing it was the least bit subpar compared to any of his teammates'.

I pulled around the cobblestone circle drive with a fountain in the middle and parked my car. Cage walked out of his ginormous, wooden front door with massive windows on three sides. I snapped my mouth shut before drool made its way down my chin. My heart rate doubled with each step my handsome guy in jeans, a white tee, and bare feet took toward me. His hair looked a little darker blond, like he'd just showered.

I stepped out, slung my bag over my shoulder, and shut the car door. My ridiculous grin had to look as goofy as it felt on my face. "I'm trying to play it cool, but I'm too damn excited to see you."

He didn't say anything. He just pulled a notecard from his pocket and held it up.

CHAPTER SIX

Cage grinned and tossed it aside. I made a mental note to get it later because I'd kept all of them, waiting for a shred of recognition to spark in my mind, but in that moment all I could focus on was his hands claiming my face then the kiss that made my legs go boneless.

The hello kiss didn't stop. It turned into a hungry kiss that said *I* would be dinner. Fine by me.

Grabbing the back of my legs, he lifted me up without breaking our kiss and carried me inside. All I caught were a few blurry images through my peripheral vision as he hauled me down one long, wide hallway and then another. The impact of a mattress broke our kiss, but he still didn't say anything.

I swallowed hard as he kept me pinned to the bed with hungry eyes while his hands stayed busy removing my clothes, and my leg. He took it off like removing my shoe, never letting his eyes leave mine.

"Nice place," I whispered. Crazy nerves.

He shrugged off his shirt, and then unzipped his jeans. "Thank you." He grinned and all it took were those dimples to make me sit up and scoot to the edge of the bed. They reminded me that three years earlier I fell in love with *the* boy. The Cage before me was *all* man and there was nothing I wanted more than to show my appreciation for *the man.*

I eased his briefs down, exposing his erection. When I looked up at him, his lips parted while his chest slowly rose and fell. There was just something so indescribable—so erotic—about the look in his eyes as I ran my hand down his length. It was desire mixed with pain. It said "you don't have to," but at the same time the darkness in his hooded eyes begged me to wrap my lips around him.

His hands threaded through my hair as my tongue eased along his warm flesh. I closed my eyes, seeing flashbacks of his mouth on me—the way he met my gaze with his tongue pressed to me and the way it made me fall to pieces.

The most beautiful surrender.

The heat.

The slow unraveling.

The seduction of tasting someone so intimately—desiring them so completely. I wanted him to feel that—all of it—all of me.

"Fucking hell, Lake ..." His face tensed around his heavy eyelids. He pulled back and finished removing his pants before trailing a path with his tongue up the inside of my legs. I leaned back, eyelids feeling as heavy as his looked. Within seconds I cried out, bucking my hips when his tongue found my clit.

"Cage ..." I fisted his hair, pumping my hips against him.

He didn't stay there long. He tasted every inch of my body, bringing me to the brink over and over again as I did the same to him. There was sex and then there was making love with a desire for it to go on and on, finding unfathomable pleasure in so much more than the release. We had the kind of sex that seemed to last for hours, and when we finally found that release, we started over again until reaching all-out physical exhaustion.

"I missed you," he mumbled in a sleepy voice with his cheek pressed to my stomach.

My new official favorite place in the world was naked, sweaty, and tangled in the dark gray sheets of Cage's massive, round bed in the center of a room that was far too big for a bedroom.

"I wouldn't have guessed." I laughed.

He dug his fingers into my sides.

"Stop!" I squealed, wriggling beneath him.

He licked my belly then bit the skin at my ribs. "Mmm ... you taste salty."

I chuckled as my fingers played with his hair. "That's sweat."

"It's sex. I love how it tastes on you."

My insides clenched. *He* was sex—the way he looked, the words he said, and the way he said them.

"So, am I going to get the grand tour of your bachelor pad, and can we start in the kitchen, specifically the refrigerator?"

His chuckle vibrated the bed. "Are you hungry?"

"No. I surpassed hungry over an hour ago. I'm starving, famished, withering away in the wind."

CAGE

"New rule. When you're at my house, you have to wear nothing but a white T-shirt of mine."

The sexy girl with wild, black hair and swollen lips that looked like they'd been thoroughly kissed peeked around the corner of my refrigerator that she helped herself to raiding, even though I'd just put salmon on the grill.

"Mmm, I like the feeling I get from knowing the shirt that hugged your sexy chest is covering my naked body." She winked and resumed her raiding.

"Yeah, well, imagine how I'm going to feel when I take it off your naked body to reclaim it."

"Reclaim the shirt or my naked body?"

I honestly couldn't remember a time in my life that I felt so completely happy.

Not when I won the Heisman.

Not when I went first in the draft.

Not when I signed my contract with Minnesota.

In that moment, I felt quite certain I'd give it all up just to watch Lake pop her lips over and over in contemplation of what would be her pre-dinner snack. Inexplicably, she owned a part of me from the moment she was born, and it took twenty-one years for her to find me and dangle it in front of my face in an are-you-missing-this sort of way.

"Do you have marshmallows?"

I crossed my arms on the counter, my feet resting on the rung of the barstool. "Sorry. No marshmallows. I don't eat much sugar."

"Hmm." She shut the refrigerator door, setting a glass bowl of red grapes on the counter. "You need marshmallows, and crispy rice." Popping a grape into her mouth, she grinned.

"I do, huh?"

She nodded. "Flax waffles and Justin's Chocolate Hazelnut butter."

"Anything else?"

Tapping a grape along her puckered lips, she rolled her eyes to the ceiling. "I'll think about it and let you know."

I tore off a stem of grapes. "You do that. Come on, I need to check on dinner." I walked to the deck.

"You're in jeans, no shirt. I'm in a shirt nothing else. What if your neighbors see me?"

"Nobody can see my deck. Come on out."

"It's dark and chilly."

"Come. Here." I laughed, turning the salmon on a cedar grill plank.

"Oh..." she stepped onto the deck. "It's warm."

I pointed to the two heaters on opposite sides and the one mounted above us.

"About five more minutes then I'll feed you before you 'wither away.'" Sitting on the end of a lounge chair, I tugged her hand, bringing her to straddle my lap, trying not to focus on her lack of panties.

"Thanks for inviting me for dinner." She placed a small kiss on my lips.

I nodded, contemplating my next words. Finding any words in the presence of the only woman who managed to leave me speechless was a nearly-impossible feat.

"You look so serious." She narrowed her eyes.

"Lake Jones ..." The words, where were the words and why was I scared out of my fucking mind to say them, but just as scared to not say them? "What would you say if I told you I love you?"

LAKE

Right then.

Right there.

In that moment.

Cage Monaghan turned his head and kissed me on the lips in a proverbial my-heart-felt-the-breath-of-eternity way. I had one goal: to make him turn his head.

I shook mine. "I wouldn't say anything. You'd leave me speechless."

He cradled my face. My eyes filled with tears.

"You're that girl, Lake. Had you not disappeared after that day in Omaha, I would be an elementary school teacher. I would not have chosen this life, because football *is* my life now. I don't know how to balance this anymore, and if I'm honest, I don't want to balance it. I want to give it up for you. I want being with you to be what I do every day because I swear to God I know I can do it better than anyone else. I love you, Lake. I love you in a way that makes me uncertain of everything in my life *but* you. I love you in a way that makes me want nothing *but* you."

It may have looked like my face was in his hands, but it was really my heart. He looked expectantly at me. I had nothing, so I shrugged and let big, fat tears roll down my cheeks.

He kissed away my tears.

"I love ... you too." The words caught in my throat. They'd been there for so long, growing with each day, needing so desperately to be said. Part of me regretted waiting for him to say it. If there was one thing my brush with death taught me, it was the true fragility of life and the importance of saying what matters the very moment it matters.

Ben died and I lived.

And right then, right there ... I knew why.

CHAPTER SEVENTEEN

NANNIES AND NEIGHBORS

Cloud nine carried me home late that night. I wanted to stay, but I had to be up and ready for Shayna's nanny, and the guy who made an official claim to the title Man of my Dreams was too much of a distraction. Leaving his bed in the morning would have been impossible after our perfect evening.

Following the best salmon ever, he made love to me on the deck, whispering that magical *love* to me over and over. I wasn't sure if there were depths to our love, but if there were, then I was in so far I knew I'd die before escaping.

I didn't want to escape. Cage quitting the NFL to be a teacher and spend more time with me? I didn't want that either. I'd watched him play in college. The euphoria on his face when he connected with a receiver in the end zone was not a look that said he wanted to be a teacher and spend his free time with a girl. We agreed the evening had left us both in a cloud of nostalgia and that making life-changing decisions was best done with a clear head.

What I did know for certain was Cage Monaghan was

the reason my life was spared. I didn't know how I knew it ... I just did.

"I'm not going to be able to stay too long. I have a meeting," Everson said as we waited for the nanny to arrive.

"That's fine. I have a feeling they'll hit it off in less than sixty seconds. Then you'll be dismissed and I'll expect a sizable finder's fee check at my door by dinner."

"Finder's fee?"

"For finding the world's best nanny."

"You sound pretty sure of yourself."

I grinned as Shayna came into the room. "This one's a sure thing. She's going to love Jamie, and Jamie is going to adore this sweet little girl." I hugged her.

"How old is Jamie?" Everson asked.

"Thirty-one."

Just on time, there were three quick raps at the door. Everson could take a lesson from Jamie on knocking properly, as in: I'm at your door but not trying to annoy the hell out of you.

Everson opened the door. "Can I help you?"

"Hi, I'm Jamie Law."

"No you're not." Everson shook his head.

"Everson!" I pulled at his arm to move him out of the way. "Don't be rude."

"Stick—"

"Lake." I shot him a scowl before flipping it to a smile for Jamie. The nanny didn't need to hear our pet names for each other. "Come in, Jamie."

"Lake, can I talk to you for a minute?" Everson asked in a tone that didn't actually ask, but rather demanded.

"Sure, just a second. Jamie, I'd like you to meet Shayna and her brother Everson Banks."

Shayna held out her hand for Jamie. Everson did not.

"A word. Now!"

I shot Everson another scowl followed by another apologetic smile to Jamie.

"Shayna, why don't you tell Jamie about your swimming lessons and what books you like. Excuse us for a few moments, we'll be right back."

"Take your time." Jamie smiled.

I shut the door to Everson's bedroom. "Oh ... my gosh. What is your problem? Do you have any idea how qualified Jamie is compared to every other person I interviewed? So help me if you blow this I'm going to be pissed at you."

He rested his hands on his hips. "Are you fucking blind? Jamie is a dude. I'm not hiring a dude to be my sister's nanny. That shit's just not right."

"Wow ... oh wow! Could you be any more sexist?"

"Yes, as a matter of fact, I could be, but I'll spare you and just keep it simple. No. Not hiring him."

"Because he's a guy?"

Everson nodded. "Correct."

"Two years ago he nannied for royalty in England. He has a degree in education. He's a part-time EMT. He speaks four different languages. He's completed seven Ironman competitions. AND he's hit the New York Times Bestseller list for a series of children's books he's written. Are you out of your mind? It doesn't get any better than Jamie."

"You gonna still help with her sometimes?"

"What? Yes. But I can't guarantee my time with the unpredictability of my job, so I can't be her nanny, otherwise I would have offered."

"I get that, Stick. But you'll be around when you can?"

I shrugged. "Of course."

"You'll hang out with Shayna and her nanny?"

"Yeah, sometimes."

"Great. Wait here."

I waited. Why? I wasn't sure.

"Jamie, man ... mind if I take your picture for security purposes?"

I peeked around the corner as Everson took Jamie's picture.

"What's that all about?" I asked when Everson came back into the bedroom.

He tapped the screen of his phone. "What were all those credentials again? Royalty ... teacher, EMT, four languages..." he continued to type into his phone "... Ironman competitions, oh and New York Times Best Seller."

"What are you doing?"

He held up his phone. "Just sent a picture of Jamie and his amazing resumé to Monaghan to see how he feels about me hiring him to work next door to you."

I rolled my eyes. "He's not going to care. If anything, he'll be impressed with my skills for finding the perfect person to watch Shayna."

Everson held up his phone as it dinged with a response from Cage. He smirked. "Yeah, that's what I figured he'd say.

Monaghan: *No. Fucking. Way!*

My jaw plummeted to the ground. I couldn't believe that was Cage's reaction. However, I refused to let Everson see my shock.

"You've got thirty seconds to make an intelligent case for not hiring Jamie, otherwise he's our guy. I know darn well you have plans over the next few weeks and I can't be your backup every time, so let's hear it."

"He's a dude!"

I grunted a buzzing sound. "Try again, twenty seconds left."

"It makes no sense that he'd want to be a nanny. That alone should raise enough suspicion."

Another buzzing sound from me. "Last chance, ten seconds."

"I'm going to catch shit from everyone I know for having a guy nanny..." he pointed toward the other room "...that looks like pretty boy out there."

"*That's* why you don't want to hire him? Because he's ..."

Everson crossed his arms over his chest. "He's what, Stick? Finish your thought."

I wasn't taking the bait. "Give him two weeks and if you don't like him then we'll look for someone else."

Our stare-off lasted for a good minute or more.

"One week and *I'm* the one who decides if we keep him. Got it?"

I nodded.

I followed Everson out and sat next to Shayna who'd been giggling and already having a great time with Jamie. Everson went through his whole spiel about a one-week trial to see if Jamie was really a good match, while I took a good look at the male nanny. Maybe a certain quarterback kept me from assessing Jamie's appearance or if I did do it, then it had to have been subconsciously.

Upon closer inspection, I had to admit Jamie was a little on the gorgeous side: tall, fit, a nice smile, dark hair and eyes. There may have been a hint of a Tom Hardy resemblance going on and a British accent that would have melted a certain amputee's panties in a pre-Cage lifetime.

"I'm not a big fan of American football, but I look forward to watching you play this fall."

I cringed. Jamie needed to just leave before he got any more strikes against him. It was clear from the way Everson's body tensed that he didn't like someone making it sound like there was any kind of football other than American football—*the* football.

"So, Jamie, thanks for coming by, it appears you and Shayna are going to get along just great. Tomorrow at eight?"

Jamie smiled. Yeah, he was a cutie.

"Great! Bye, Shayna, see you in the morning."

When the door closed, I leaned back against it. "Shayna, did you like Jamie?"

She nodded really big with a smile to match. I smirked at Everson whose face sustained a permanent scowl. It appeared as though I would not get to see his blinding smile anytime soon.

When I returned to my apartment, I took care of my first order of business.

Lake: *"No. Fucking. Way!" Really? Please tell me you didn't base a person's nanny qualifications on a photo.*
Cage: *Getting ready for an interview. TTYL*

Just as I blew out a breath of frustration, there was a knock at my door. A new type of knock, based on my knock expertise.

The peephole revealed a woman with long, red hair who moved in way too close, squinting one eye, attempting to look in my peephole from the other side. I jumped back. That was a first. So not cool on her part. I opened the door.

"Hi, are you Lake Jones?" she asked with an easy southern drawl.

Why did a stranger asking for confirmation of my name seem like a test?

"Who wants to know?"

She grinned a lovely smile that accented her soft, translucent blue eyes. They looked far less creepy than they did through the peephole. "I'm Penny Weiss, your new neighbor on the other side of the elevator. My husband and I moved in last week."

I peeked around the corner then nodded. "Oh, yeah, that place has been vacant for a while."

She wrinkled her nose. "The view's not great, but we don't mind. Anyway, I just wanted to introduce myself. We moved here from San Antonio, empty nesters now. My husband's parents are moving to an assisted living facility close by, so we decided to move here at least for a couple of years. Once our kids decide to marry and give us some grandbabies, we'll be out of here."

I nodded. Penny didn't look old enough to be a grandma. She looked maybe thirty-five, thin, with a silver arm cuff just beneath the bicep of her left arm, various sliver rings on her fingers, and large silver hoop earrings.

"Anyway, that's all. Just wanted to make the introduction. The apartment manager told me we might be a good fit. We left a great neighborhood, and I'm sure apartment dwellers don't socialize like homeowners in the burbs, but I'm old school. You drink wine?"

"I do." I smiled because chatty Penny was nice and unpretentious. Lord knows I needed a friend in my corner with all the testosterone in my life. No offense to Trzy.

She glanced down. "Wowza, never seen a leg like that before. Rupert, my husband, lost half his finger when he was fourteen. Came out on the short side of garbage disposal roulette.

I grimaced.

"I know, right?" She nodded slowly.

"Mine was a car accident. If Rupert ever needs an extra finger," *or eight* "I know a guy."

Penny laughed. "I'll tell him. He doesn't know what to do with the nine and a half he has, so I don't think it matters."

I'd known Penny for all of two seconds, and yet I felt pretty certain she was sharing cringe-worthy details about her sex life. It was official—I liked Penny Weiss.

"It's a little early for wine, but I have tea if you'd like to come in."

"You sure? I don't want to interrupt your day."

"I have a six-year-old to watch in an hour, so I have time."

Penny didn't freak-out over Trzy, but she did confess her cat allergy. It was a good test to Trzy's hypoallergenic trait.

"You look too young to be retired." I handed Penny a cup of tea and sat in the chair opposite her at my kitchen table.

"I'm forty-five and Rupert is fifty-nine." She gave me a sheepish grin. "We're the couple snobby people like to talk about. We were the hottest gossip topic for years. Rupert was a tenured professor of finance at the same college where my father was the dean. Rupert had two kids and was in a miserable marriage. I was eight weeks pregnant with two years of college under my expanding belt, but a master's degree in disgracing my father.

"Rupert and I saw each other for the first time outside of my father's office. I'd just told daddy dearest about my pregnancy, and of course I left in tears because my father was a total dick. An hour later there was a tap on my car window. I was bawling my eyes out, couldn't see to drive home. It was Rupert, a complete stranger to me at the time. He offered me a ride home. And because I was young and stupid, hence the unplanned pregnancy, I accepted his offer."

"When we got to my apartment, I invited him up for coffee, vomited the details of my tragic life, and drained all my tears into his shirt, using his silk tie like a hanky. Two hours later we were in my bed naked and completely satisfied. Can you believe a guy his age had never had a girl go down on him?"

Penny grinned. I'd lost all facial function as my jaw hung in midair.

"Oh, so to answer your retirement question. Rupert is retired; he made very wise investments over the years. As for me ... I don't need to work, but I've always had odd jobs. Just something to keep me busy and sane. I can't be with Rupert all the damn day. We'd kill each other."

Penny was such an unexpected part of my day, yet oddly refreshing. She had the power to break my Netflix addiction. I knew her how-I-met-my-husband story was just a morsel of her life.

"So was the father of your child out of the picture?"

"Honey, he was out of the picture before the picture ever came into focus. You know those things in life that really are not representative of your finer moments?"

I nodded, sipping my tea. I loved her southern drawl and the way she called me honey.

"Well, during the sowing-of-my-wild-oats phase, I kinda fell into a slut rut."

My brow lifted.

"I was stoned out of my mind most of the time and screwed anything with a dick." She tapped the rim of her cup with her fingernail. "Hell, who am I kiddin'? I'm pretty sure there were a few women in the mix too." Penny sighed. A faint smile grew on her face like she was reminiscing about the good ol' days.

"You've lived quite the life so far."

"I have. Lots of mistakes, but no regrets. What about you?"

"I'm not that exciting. Lost my leg and my boyfriend in a car accident. Moved here a few months ago from San Francisco. I make a living with my 'disability' by testing cutting-edge prosthetics and doing occasional photoshoots."

"What about a significant other? You're too pretty to not have a boyfriend ... or girlfriend. Equal opportunity, right?"

I chuckled, staring down at my tea. "I do have someone. It's kind of new and kind of old, but mostly kind of hard to explain, but he's ... quite the catch."

"I like the sound of that."

A knock at the door brought me back to reality just as memories of the previous night started to heat my skin.

"I'll get out of your hair." Penny stood.

"No, you don't have to go."

"Nope, I'm going. We'll chat later, honey."

I looked through the peephole.

"Aren't those things addictive? They don't work so well from the other side."

I grinned, partly from Penny's comment and partly from my handsome guy on the opposite side of the door.

"Yes, they are quite addictive. Peep-holing is one of my favorite pastimes." I opened the door.

"Oh sweet Jesus! You're Cage Monaghan."

Cage's eyes flitted between me and Penny.

"Yes, Penny, this is Cage. Cage meet Penny, my new neighbor." *And slut extraordinaire that I have a girl crush on.*

"Oh my Lord ... it's a huge pleasure. I follow football like a dog's nose to a cat's ass. Would you mind if I asked for your autograph?"

Cage looked at me again. I shrugged.

"I'll get a marker." I grabbed a Sharpie from the kitchen drawer. "Do you want a piece of paper or something, Penny?'

"Nope." She continued to gawk at Cage.

"Here." I handed the marker to Cage.

"Right here, doll, if you wouldn't mind." Penny pulled up her shirt about four inches, pointing to her lower back. "Right above my heart and wings tramp stamp would be perfect."

Cage looked at me again. Again, I shrugged. He signed her back and capped the marker.

"Ah, perfect. Rupert and I are going doggie-style tonight so he can stare at it. Nothing better than a guy who's a little jealous. Makes them up their game if you know what I mean." Penny winked then headed down the hallway.

Cage still had not said a word.

"She's great, huh?" I snatched the marker from him and walked back inside.

"I really have no words for *Penny*."

I shut the drawer and leaned against the counter. "But you have a few for Jamie, right?"

"Who's Jamie?" He slid his hands behind me, palming my ass while pulling me into his body.

I closed my eyes as he kissed the skin below my ear. "He's Shayna's nanny."

Cage stood straight, peering down at me with narrowed eyes. "So the picture wasn't a joke?"

I grabbed his ass as well, giving it a tight squeeze. "So the 'no fucking way' *was* a joke?"

"Yes. No ... I don't know. You seriously hired a male nanny for Banks's sister?"

"I hired the *most qualified* nanny who just so happens to be a guy. Please don't show me your sexist side if you have one. I don't want to see it. Yes, it's official: women can be pilots and doctors, and men can be nurses and nannies."

"Whatever, it doesn't affect me."

"True. Now kiss me so I can see if *I* still affect you."

Cage grinned as his lips showed mine that I did indeed still affect him. "I missed you in my bed this morning," he murmured over my lips while his hands slid up my shirt.

I pressed my hands to his chest. "We can't do this." I glanced over at the clock on my microwave. "Shayna is coming over while Everson does whatever the hell it is he does this time of year."

"Now?"

"Ten minutes."

"I can work with that." He kissed me hard, backing me to the counter as his erection pressed to my belly.

I giggled, wriggling from his hold on me. "Stop! Ten minutes is not enough." I rubbed my lips together. They were already numb from his assault on them.

Cage sighed. "Suit yourself, then. I'm meeting up with two of my wide receivers to practice some routes."

I righted my bra that he'd tugged down, exposing my

breasts. "Basically you're going to a park to play catch with your friends."

He captured both of my wrists behind my back in his right hand and bit my neck. Cage was a biter, and oh my God I loved what it did to me.

"Yes, basically," he whispered in my ear before leaving me puddled on my kitchen floor while he walked toward my door. "Later."

After the door already shut, I whispered, "Later."

CHAPTER EIGHTEEN

CATCH AND RELEASE

It happened. I found my village in Minneapolis. I found my life again in Minneapolis. Land of 10,000 Lakes. Duh, it was right there all along.

Jamie survived the one-week trial. In spite of Everson's intentions to be the decision maker, we took a vote. It was two to one. Jamie stayed.

Penny became my new BFF, which I didn't share with Lindsay for feeling-sparing reasons. I needed someone more messed-up than myself to truly accept me. Penny bridged the gap between my girlfriend and my mother. She listened to me like Lindsay, only less judgmental, yet gave motherly advice, only less ethical. Yeah, I loved Penny Weiss.

Shayna and Everson became my new siblings, although I felt much more like a mother to Shayna than a sister, and Everson was just ... Everson. I still hadn't broken through his tough outer layer to find what I knew had to be an ooey-gooey middle.

Another theory of mine.

Cage was the upside to every day, no matter what. The fact that we were just weeks from him leaving for training camp was bittersweet. My early morning peep-holing revealed a gathering of Everson and some other guys from the team in the hall, another upside to my life in Minneapolis. One of the other guys was my guy. I bent down and finished tying my shoe then opened the door. The boisterous laughter and chatter silenced as all eyes fell on me.

I smiled. "Boys."

"Damn, Monaghan!" One of the guys whistled. "You're choosing fishing over that today?" His eyes roved my body, clad in tight running shorts and a sports bra.

"Keep your fucking eyes off her." Cage playfully shoved the guy before moving toward me. He grabbed my head and kissed me, eliciting a few cat calls from the peanut gallery. "I missed you last night," he whispered in my ear.

I left him naked and sated in his bed to get home so I could video chat with Jerry about the fit of my newest leg. Clearing my throat, I took a step back before I started to sweat from his touch. "Fishing? So you were serious?"

"Your boy's got the sweetest fishing boat ever, Stick. Man, how have you not taken her fishing yet?" Everson asked.

I vaguely remembered Cage mentioning something about fishing once, but I didn't think much of it. "You have a boat? An actual fishing boat?"

The guys snickered.

"We go for the beer and banter, but Monaghan actually takes it seriously, giving us the stink eye if we get too loud."

I cocked my head to the side. Cage grinned as he shrugged.

"Catch and release, or do you eat the fish?"

"Depends." He shoved his hands into his back cargo shorts pockets.

I nodded, still a little surprised.

Cage gestured to my running leg. "Testing a new leg?"

I shook my head. "Underwear."

His brow wrinkled and the guys behind him inched a bit closer, ears perked.

"What?" Cage asked.

"My favorite underwear has been discontinued. I'm trying a new brand and the best way to test them out is to go for a jog. I want to know before I buy ten pairs if they're going to ride up on me. I'm not a thong girl. I don't like anything shoved up my ass."

His cheeks turned red while taking a hard swallow. The fishing crew tried and failed to hide their chuckling. One of the guys slapped him on the shoulder.

"We'll meet you out front." He cleared his throat. "Our condolences on the ass news."

That sparked a new round of laughter as the guys piled onto the elevator. When the doors shut, Cage pursed his lips and sighed. "Thanks for that."

I shrugged. "What?"

"What ..." It's possible his intention was to be serious or maybe upset, but he couldn't finish his thought without rubbing his hand over his mouth to hide his smirk. "You don't like 'anything shoved up your ass.' Really, Lake?" Rolling his eyes to the ceiling, he shook his head.

"So you're big into fishing, huh?"

"Don't change the subject." He narrowed his eyes at me. Too bad he still couldn't keep a straight face. It would have given his case a lot more merit. Those were favorite moments of mine, when he was ninety percent sure my actions were an embarrassing side effect of my Sahara Desert humor, yet still ten percent holy-shit-she's-serious.

I loved that ten percent. I worked my ass off for that ten percent.

"I'm sorry, what was the subject? Oh yeah, things I don't like in my crack. Sounds like a Jeopardy category or a Family Feud survey. 'Name something Lake Jones does not like up her crack. Underwear. Survey says? Ding ding ding ... ninety-four people surveyed said underwear, the other six said cock. And I do believe those six lascivious idiots are downstairs waiting for you."

Cage observed me; it was never just a stare or a lingering look. His eyes narrowed a fraction, but never lost their sparkle. The wetting of his lips was always followed by biting them together like he refused to speak until he'd figured me out. And just before he spoke, his dimples surrendered to his impending grin.

"I'm going to text you an address. Meet me there in three hours."

"What if I haven't sorted through this underwear situation by then?" My head tilted to the side as my poker face slipped a bit, revealing my own impending grin.

"Hmm ..." He pulled me to him, his hands easing into the back of my running shorts. "Don't fret over it," he whispered before sucking my earlobe into his mouth.

My lips parted, and eyes closed, as I held onto his biceps to keep my knees from buckling.

"Panties are optional."

Three words and my knees buckled. Thankfully—not really thankful at all—he fisted the back of my new panties and yanked up. My hero? No. The wedgie was underway a few seconds before my knees gave out.

I gasped.

He smirked.

"I think you should consider getting used to the idea—the feeling—of something in that sexy ass of yours."

Not much left me speechless, but my first non-brother-male-induced wedgie left me with cow eyes and a numb tongue.

He winked just before the elevator doors shut.

Being the youngest of five and having three older brothers made daily revenge plotting an integral part of my childhood. The address Cage texted me was to a lake. I parked next to his truck with the empty boat trailer attached to it.

Lake: *I'm here.*
Cage: *I'll pick you up on the dock. Please ignore any of the drunks.*

I laughed while shaking my head and grabbing my sunglasses. As I stepped onto the dock, echoing whistles and hollering ensued as a boat drew near.

"We're being ditched for a chick," one of the guys said as the boat crept alongside the dock.

I think there were five guys total, but I only had eyes for revenge ... or the lucky recipient of it wearing the goofiest khaki bucket hat with several lures hanging from it.

"There's my favorite Lake."

"You've got it bad, man. We're in the land of ten thousand Lakes and you have a favorite?" one of the guys said as they stepped onto the dock, some a bit more wobbly than others.

"Stick."

I raised a brow. "Apollo."

He grinned. Everson must have had some beer too; it was the only potion that seemed to bring out his full smile, at least for me.

"Later, Monaghan."

"Bender's driving, you dumb asses."

The last guy off the boat nodded with a polite smile. I recognized him as blond-bun guy from Everson's party, the one who seemed to know how to pronounce Trzy. He dangled a set of car keys.

"You must be Bender."

"Holden Bender, sober and at your service. How's your cat?"

He remembered me. Lovely.

"She's still a real party animal, one of the most sought after pussies in the building."

Holden's eyes raised for a second before he broke into a loud laugh, giving a quick glance back on the boat to Cage, who shook his head.

"I like her, Monaghan." He continued to chuckle as he walked up the ramp.

Cage and I had a stare-off until the sound of Bender's tires skidded in the dirt signaling their departure.

"I don't fish."

Cage grinned. "You grew up in Tahoe. How can you not fish?"

"Simple. I just don't. Boating? Yep. Skiing? Yep. Hiking? You betcha. Fishing? Not my thing." I tossed my purse into the boat and then stepped on without taking Cage's proffered hand. "When exactly did you become such a fisherman?" I flicked one of the lures attached to his hat.

Cage grabbed my wrist, giving me a warning glare that melted into a smile as he pressed his lips to the inside of my wrist. "My grandpa fished and so did my dad when I was really young. Fishing, camping ... basically anything outdoors." He hooked my waist with one arm and pulled me onto his lap with my back to the steering wheel as the boat hummed, sitting idle next to the dock.

"And wedgies? Who taught you how to give wedgies?" I narrowed my eyes.

He shrugged. "Kids in the neighborhood when I lived in Portland."

I kept the "you're going to pay for that, buddy" to myself. The element of surprise was my best bet for success.

"You look seventy in that hat."

"You don't like my hat?"

I liked his white muscle shirt and his defined legs beneath mine—the dimples were a given—but the bucket hat was ... anti-sexy. Yet, the guy managed to make it work.

"So, I'm your favorite lake, huh?"

His gaze fell to my lips. It was crazy how the slightest shift of his eyes affected me so much. My mouth dried up as my pulse accelerated.

I wet my lips.

His gaze descended to my chest.

My nipples hardened.

Mr. I Make Stupid Hats Look Sexy manipulated my body with nothing more than a look. It was subtle but profound, like the effect of the sun.

"You're my favorite everything." He met my eyes again and smirked. Of course he knew what he did to me. There was no hiding it.

"Your favorite everything, really?" I narrowed my eyes.

"Really."

"What's your favorite day?"

He grinned. "Any day I get to see you."

"Favorite color?"

"Blue, like your eyes."

"Favorite animal?"

"Elephant."

"Screw you."

His eyes danced with amusement.

"Favorite food?" In spite of the boat and all the fishing equipment on it, I couldn't reel that comment back in. Nope, I'd already cast it and he bit at it.

The arousal beneath me and the agonizingly slow way his tongue eased along his lower lip answered that question.

"Lake," he whispered. "I'm fucking starving right now."

Gulp.

I was a tad on the hungry side as well. "Um ..." I cleared my throat. "I think what you have in mind is more of a private dining meal."

He dipped his head and kissed my bare shoulder next to the thin black strap of my camisole top then licked a trail to my ear. "I love you."

Unexpected. It was like riding a roller coaster blindfolded. I anticipated the "I love you" two seconds before he gave me a wedgie, and when I expected a picnic-on-the-boat comment, he took my breath away like a plunging drop with those three simple words.

"I love you too." I grinned then tugged at his hat. "Even your hat is growing on me."

"Oh, yeah?" He sat back.

I nodded.

"Well..." he leaned to the side and flipped up a seat with a storage compartment under it "...then it's fate that I have one for you."

A lavender bucket hat with lures hanging from it. It was hideous and breathtaking at the same time.

"I don't want lice. How many women have worn this before me?"

"You're the first female to ever step foot on this boat. I bought it for you. I put the lures on it for you."

Losing my leg was easy compared to losing my heart to Cage, even if I did willingly hand it to him. With each passing day I knew I'd never get it back in one piece. Did he read the warning? Did he see the "Fragile. Handle with Care?"

"When your season begins and we don't see each other as much..." I took the hat and put it on, Cage smiled "...can you do me a huge favor?"

"Anything."

Pressing my palms to his cheeks, I whispered, "Don't forget to love me."

CAGE

The purple fishing hat fit her perfectly. I couldn't wipe the grin off my face. Total truth: Lake was the first woman to set foot on my fishing boat.

"I'll forget how to throw a football before I'll forget to love you."

Her lips brushed mine. I inhaled her flowery scent, which made me *need* to taste her sweet lips. Most of the time she tasted of cinnamon from her gum, but on my favorite occasions she tasted like marshmallows. I asked the man upstairs to twist fate in my favor: never let another man taste her lips.

"Both would be a tragedy."

I nodded, but if I were honest, the former would have sucked, the latter would have felt like the end of the world.

"Let's go catch some fish."

It took about fifteen minutes to get to my favorite spot. We could have made better time, but I went slow. I could have watched Lake all day with her smiling face in the sun, eyes closed, holding her hat to her head as her dark hair whipped in the wind.

"This is it."

She opened her eyes, head twisting in one direction and then the other. "Quite the cozy little cove."

"Yes." I grabbed my pole and tackle box.

"You're introverted."

"A bit. Here." I cast the line. "Catch me a fish."

"Your pole? You're going to let me use your special pole?"

"Babe, you can use anything of mine, anytime you want."

She sat next to me and took the pole. "Did you let your buddies use your pole?"

"Hell no."

We fished for less than an hour before the rain chased us back to the dock. I would have stayed dry had we not had to circle around to retrieve my hat that she tossed over the side when I asked how her new panties were working out. Apparently she kept score.

"Not cool, babe." I snagged my hat from the surface and put it back on my head.

She laughed as water dripped onto my face and body.

"I'm not laughing."

"Poor baby, don't get your knickers in a bind ... or do."

Thunder rumbled as a cool breeze wrapped around us.

"Do you need help getting the boat onto the trailer?"

I shook my head, too stubborn to say any more with my drenched hat on my head.

"Good." Lake hopped out as soon as we reached the dock. " 'Cause it's getting ready to pound on us." She hurried to her car.

Five seconds later the clouds opened up.

"Fuck." I shook my head, but didn't bother hurrying at that point as I was already drowned within seconds. After I secured my boat onto the trailer, Lake flipped me a grin as she pulled out of the parking lot past me. She was aggravating, and sexy, and that smile ... Damn! I wanted to suck that smile right off her face. I wanted to suck every inch of her until the only expression she had was the grimace that accompanied her loud moans and screams.

CHAPTER NINETEEN

GHOSTS

LAKE

Minnesota's Monaghan and Banks Caught in a Love Triangle with Amputee from San Francisco

Monaghan Dates Amputee – Proves He's the Real Golden Boy

Will Monaghan's Game Be Affected by His Demanding Girlfriend?

THE MEDIA BUZZ guaranteed me hot tea every morning, either at my apartment or Cage's house, compliments of Flint Hopkins.

"The nanny. You have to stay the hell away from the nanny!" Flint barged past Cage at the front door, making a beeline to me in Cage's kitchen. Normally he handed me my tea; that day he slammed it on the counter.

I spread chocolate hazelnut butter on my toaster waffles,

wearing nothing but Cage's white T-shirt and a grin. "Good morning, Flint. It's Sunday. Don't you ever take a day off?"

Just as I started to turn toward Flint, my protective lover held out a white terrycloth robe that I may or may not have taken from a hotel. I slid my arms in and Cage tied the front as he kissed me.

"I'm going for a run. Shower with me when I get back?" he whispered.

I squeezed my legs together and nodded.

Cage pointed a stiff finger at Flint as he passed him. "Upset her and you're fired."

Flint rolled his eyes, and so did I. It had become Cage's daily motto. I knew Flint's number one priority was protecting Cage's reputation. He knew I didn't give a shit about the headlines and pictures. We had a whole routine: Cage left, we did our usual verbal sparring, then plastered on smiles when our boy returned.

"I'm serious this time. Training camp starts in two weeks. The media is on high alert for absofuckinglutely any morsel of dirt they can run with." Flint jabbed his finger at a printed page of social media posts, newspaper headlines, and photos of me and Jamie with Shayna. The headlines all read "Secret Affair."

I watched Cage's truck pull out of the driveway. He liked to find a lake path to jog around for an hour or so in the mornings.

"Shayna's like a daughter to me. Jamie is her nanny. Sometimes I hang out with them when I have free time. Everson knows. Cage knows. What's the big deal? Shayna is always with us. He's worked for Everson for like ... two seconds, hardly enough time for a scandalous affair. I've never even been alone with Jamie since I interviewed him."

"Do you see Shayna in any of these pictures?"

I looked at the pictures. She wasn't in any of them.

Jamie and me on a park bench, laughing.

Jamie and me eating ice cream.

Jamie taking a bag from my shoulder, Shayna's bag, but it did look intimate.

I frowned. Shayna was right there, sitting beside me while we ate ice cream. She was walking next to Jamie when he took the bag. She was playing on the playground maybe ten yards away when we were laughing on the bench —probably about something goofy Shayna did. But she wasn't *in* any of the pictures.

"The tabloids said I was having an affair with Thaddeus last week because we were photographed having dinner when I flew out to San Francisco."

"He's your boss. That's easy to explain."

"So, Jamie is Shayna's nanny."

"But Shayna isn't your daughter or sister or anything that's easy to explain. That's why she's not in the photos, because people don't care about her. They care about the woman who took one of the most eligible bachelors off the market. They want to know that you're worthy of him, and if for one second they think you're not, then they're going to tear you apart because there are thousands of other women out there who'd love to have the chance that you've been given."

My head jerked back. "Excuse me? 'The chance I've been given?' Like my name was drawn out of a hat to be Cage Monaghan's girlfriend?"

Flint blew out a long breath. "I know it seems like my intentions are just to keep Cage's reputation squeaky clean, but you don't understand the impact this will have on your relationship with him, especially when the season starts and he's under twenty-four hour scrutiny of the media. The line between the truth and the lies begins to blur and doubt creeps in. He looks at this photo and starts to wonder. You see a photo of some girl's hand on his ass before he has time to remove it and you start to wonder.

"You're both young. Your relationship is in its infancy. Under perfectly normal, non-celebrity conditions it's hard to make it work. This ..." He shook his head. "This will destroy you if you're not proactive about keeping things simple."

Would that be my life forever? Tiptoeing around, worrying about finding clarity with that line between the truth and the lies? Was that why Cage wanted to give it up?

CAGE

I NEEDED to pound the hell out of the blacktop beneath my feet. I needed my lungs to burn. I needed something to erase the worry in my head. Flint did my worrying. He did my fixing. He did the shit jobs so I could focus on my career. But Lake wasn't my career. She was my ... everything.

Could I play professional football and have everything?

I let Flint have his talks with her because I knew his words didn't mean anything to her. She shrugged them off, and he felt better having "done his job." Being in the middle sucked, but the truth was I needed both of them. I didn't want to have to choose.

When I finally hit my exertion limit, I walked in a few circles with my hands laced on my head then collapsed onto the cool grass.

"Good morning, stranger."

I lifted my head, squinting against the sun. "Kelsey, hey." I let my head drop back and closed my eyes. Nothing like the ex-girlfriend appearing out of nowhere at the worst time.

"My guy's not usually this visible in the media during the summer."

"I'm not your guy." We were never together during the summer. She had no clue what she was talking about.

"We used to jog these paths together. Remember? Then we'd go back to your place and—"

"I'm twenty-four not ninety-four. My memory is just fine."

"Tell me, does she remove her leg when you're together? Is it kind of weird? I'd have to insist the lights be out—totally black in the room."

I rolled my head side to side. "You weren't a bitch when we were together; I never would have been with you. Why now? Why stoop so low?"

"Why her? Are the tabloids right? Is she a charity case? A puppy from the pound?"

I lifted up on my elbows and squinted at her again. Why was she so damn ugly? How did I not see it before?

"I love her. That's why."

Kelsey fake stumbled back a few steps. "Love?" She laughed. "You told me you weren't looking for love. You told me your career was your only love. Does she know that? Does she know your 'love' means nothing, because if you have to choose, you'll choose your love of the game?"

"I'm sorry."

"I don't need your apologies. I'm going to watch you break another girl's heart and that will be all I need to remind myself that you were a waste of my time."

I honestly thought we had an amicable split. Clearly I

was wrong. I stood and brushed the grass off my legs. "Enjoy your jog."

"Cage?" My name fell softly from her lips.

I turned back to her.

"Would you? Would you give it up for her?" The pain in her voice stung a bit. I underestimated her feelings for me.

"I'd give her my last breath."

Kelsey bit her lips together and nodded. I ignored the tears in her eyes. I had to.

"Take care, Kelsey."

LAKE

"Lake?"

"On the deck." I sat up in the lounge chair.

"Wine before noon? If Flint—"

I shook my head. "It's Sunday and past eleven. Close enough, right?" The wine had everything to do with Flint, but Cage didn't need to know that. Flint wasn't just his agent, they were friends. I could handle Flint. "I'm one lucky girl." My eyes perused his naked chest and the sexy way his jogging shorts hung low on his hips giving a tease of the V that my tongue had traced countless times.

"That's the wine talking." He squatted down in front of my chair and ran his large hands up my bare legs, stopping at my shorts. "You showered without me."

I nodded.

"What's wrong?"

I sucked at hiding my emotions, especially from Cage.

Setting my glass down, I scooted to the end of the lounge chair. "Did you see the pictures?"

His eyes tensed a bit, like he didn't want me to see his reaction. "Pictures?"

"Of me and Jamie?"

His Adam's apple bobbed. He saw them. I didn't need him to say it.

"I told Flint I've never been alone with Jamie since the day I interviewed him. I went with them because I had a free day and Shayna wanted me to go."

"It's fine. I trust you."

I teased my fingernails along his shoulders. "I know you trust me, but do you trust your head to separate the truth from the lies? Do you trust the jealousy you hate so much to not overreact? To not question? To not wonder?"

"This is my life. You didn't ask for this. I won't let it change you. I won't let you change where you go, what you do, and who you do it with. I trust you. Even if a million people reading trashy tabloids or who have nothing better to do than stick their noses in my business ... even if they don't trust you. I don't care and neither should you."

"Jamie is attractive. People are going to see that."

The muscles in Cage's jaw flexed.

"But I don't think of him. Not one minute..." my fingers teased down his chest "...not one second..." my hand slid under his waistband "...of the day." He hardened in my hand instantly as his jaw relaxed.

"You just showered," he whispered.

"Do you like me dirty?"

He nodded slowly, his eyes fixed to my lips as his breathing became more ragged with each stroke of my hand.

Leaning forward, I whispered in his ear, "I like you dirty too ... especially your mouth."

His hands slid under my ass and dug into my flesh like my shorts didn't exist. The pain turned me on. Why? I don't know. It just did. I kissed him. Our tongues warred as he moaned into my mouth before devouring the skin along my neck to the swell of my breasts exposed along my low-cut shirt.

"Show me," I whispered. "Show me your dirty mouth." Releasing him, I leaned back.

He rocked forward, dropping to his knees as he slipped his thumb under my panties. "I'm going to fuck you, Lake."

I closed my eyes, arching my back. "Why?" I breathed out.

"Because I love you ..." His voice dropped to something so deep and raspy, almost painful.

"And?" I moaned, rocking my pelvis into his touch.

Two of his fingers slid inside me as he crawled over my body, pressing his lips to my ear. "And you're mine, so I'll fuck you when, where, and how I want."

"Yesss ..." I seethed, reaching behind me, bracing my hands on the chair as he got me off with nothing more than his hand between my legs and his dirty mouth at my ear.

CAGE

Lake nudged me with her foot. The only thing she loved more than my indoor pool was the theater room. I thought she was joking about her Netflix addiction. She wasn't.

I pulled off my headphones. She watched *Sons of Anarchy* on the big screen while I watched game footage from the previous season on my laptop.

"What is it, sexy?"

She bit her thumbnail, a gesture I'd come to recognize as her way of getting the courage to ask me something important.

"I have a photoshoot in L.A. for a fitness magazine. Since it's so close to the Fourth of July, I'm going to fly to Tahoe to spend the holiday with the fam. Wanna meet me in Tahoe? Wanna meet my fam?"

I shut my computer. "Your fam, huh?"

She nodded, biting her nail again.

"All of your family?"

"Maybe. I'm not sure yet if Luke, Jess, and Grant will be there. I hope so."

I wanted to be with Lake and meet her parents, I just wasn't ready to see Jessica—Jillian. The memories of my father would come flooding back.

"I'll see."

"You'll see? What does that mean? Do you have plans in the next three days you haven't mentioned?"

I shrugged. "Not sure yet. I haven't really thought about it."

"'Lake, I have plans, sorry.' or 'Lake, I'd love to go.' I get those responses, but I don't get the 'not sure yet.' Are you waiting for a better offer?"

"No, I just ... I ..." Closing my eyes, I shook my head.

"Please don't let this be about 'Jillian.'"

"And if it is?"

She sat up. "It's not allowed be about Jillian or Jessica or your dad or my brother. That is over, and I don't mean it as any disrespect to you or your father's memory. I just want it to be Lake Jones introducing the man that she loves to her family."

"I don't know what happened."

"What do you mean you don't know what happened?"

Setting my computer aside, I stood, pacing the room, hands on my hips, head down. "I mean I don't know about Jessica Day. When she called me, she offered to tell me everything, but I didn't want to know how she ended up in our lives or why she was leaving. I only wanted ... only needed to know one thing."

"What was that?" Lake whispered.

"If she'd really loved my father."

Lake stood and walked toward the door.

"Don't you want to know what she said?" I called, hating the anger in my voice because I really wasn't mad at her.

"No." She kept her back to me, pausing at the door.

"Why not?"

"Because I already know."

"Then tell me what you think she said."

"I'm not doing this."

I chased after her. "It's because you don't know. I bet she never told you or your brother."

"I'm going home. I didn't mean to upset you."

"I'm not upset! I just want to know what you think she said."

Lake hurried into the bedroom and grabbed her overnight bag, shoving her stuff in as fast as she could.

"Tell me."

She ignored me. I grabbed her arm as she tried to walk past me. The look of shock on her face when her eyes flitted between me and my hold on her felt like a knife in my heart. It was a look like she didn't recognize me.

I released her; she didn't have to ask.

"Why won't you tell me?"

"Because it shouldn't matter." She opened the front door.

"It matters to me!"

Her head hung in defeat. I felt like every single word I spoke was a sucker punch to her, but something so deep inside of me needed to know. It was a part of myself I didn't recognize—a part I couldn't control.

"She told you she loved your father. That's what she told you. She told you she didn't regret one second with him. And you believed her, yet you hated her for finding happiness on the opposite side of your father's grave. You hated him for choosing to spend his final days with her. You hated yourself for being too young and scared to do anything about his situation."

Lake turned. "Does that cover it for you? Will it help you sleep at night to know that my family not only lost her, but in some ways we never got her all back because she gave a part of herself to your father? Does it make you feel good to rub it in my face?"

When she blinked, tears trailed down her cheeks, and I was the bastard of all bastards.

"You don't want the story. You don't want anyone to come along and disrupt your memories, but you're A-fucking-OK with digging up my past, a past you don't even completely understand because Jessica ... *Jillian* has been this no-go subject for us, and if I can't tell you that she was in a wedding dress, getting ready to walk down the aisle when I was on my way to the hospital, and that I woke three months later to not only the news of my leg and Ben, but that my brother didn't get married because of my accident *and* that she 'committed suicide' after her parents were murdered ... if I can't tell you that..." she batted away more tears and her voice cracked "...then you'll never understand that my greatest disability has nothing to do with my missing limb. It's the sleepless nights and the nightmares and the need to move on with my life and find something that makes me feel like I'm the one who deserved to live."

"Lake ..." I moved toward her.

She shook her head and stepped out the door. "I don't want your pity, and I don't want your apologies. I just wanted to spend the Fourth of July with all the people I love most in this world. But you've ruined that for me because somehow our losses in life have become a competition. Well ... you win. Sorry your dad died. Have a nice holiday."

CHAPTER TWENTY

CHASING THE SUN

LAKE

"**Wine**?" I held up a bottle of sauvignon blanc when Penny opened her door.

"You look like shit, doll face." She stepped aside. "Come in. Rupert went to visit his parents."

She poured the wine while I collapsed on her sofa.

"Boy trouble? Can't be that, can it?"

Penny knew about my past, so much more than Cage did. I recapped the fight we had. Twice. The first time I was sober and gave Cage a lot of slack because he'd been living with unaddressed demons for three years. The second time my ego stepped up to the mic, under the influence of three glasses of wine, and said every mean thing I wanted to say to Cage.

Reason five-hundred and fifty-one why Penny Weiss was just the absolute best: she never bashed Cage. Rupert? He was a 24/7 victim of being thrown under the bus. She somehow knew I needed a sounding board, yet at the same time she knew I loved Cage with ferocity. I was always on board with Flint and keeping our guy "squeaky clean" because in spite of everything, Cage Monaghan really was a kind, genuine soul.

My lover.

My friend.

My *reason.*

"I hope you're not too drunk to remember this." She giggled. "Hell, I hope I'm not too drunk to say this correctly. I could easily fuck up this advice and you'll leave here and dump his gorgeous ass. So whatever you do ... no matter what I say, don't dump his gorgeous ass."

I leaned my head back, closing my eyes. The alcohol made the room spin a bit too much. "Give it to me, Penny Poo."

"He gave you something very personal, and while I'm sure it came out a bit harsh, the fact is he trusted you explicitly with something so raw. It sounded ugly because it didn't just flow from him, it ripped past his heart to get to you. And from what you've told me, I think you reacted so much better than most, if not all other women, would have done. The love you have for each other is something so ... so real, so fucking amazing and earth-shattering that no matter what ... you will survive.

"You said it yourself, even when he tries to talk dirty to you, he can't do it without saying 'I love you.' That's rare and so special, doll face. Do you get it? I'm not sure any other guy, if given the chance to talk dirty to his woman, would waste three of his words on 'I love you.' You don't ask him to say it, hell, you practically give him permission not to say it, but he *has to*. For him. *He* can't be with you and not say it. It's that fucking important to him. *You're* that important to him."

I sighed. She was right. "I should go see him, make things right."

"Oh ... no way, honey. His actions are one hundred percent excusable, but they're still wrongdoings. You need to let him simmer with it and wait for him to come to you. Obviously, he has a lot of emotional shit he's dealing with. I know it sounds cliché, but time really is the answer."

I NEEDED OUT.

I needed to breathe.

I, too, needed time.

I flew out to L.A. the next morning. Penny agreed to look after Trzy; the hairless cat wasn't an issue for her allergies.

I also texted Cage before boarding the plane.

Lake: *I'm sorry. I just need you to know that I feel your pain, just differently. Have a safe holiday. I love you.*

I shut down my phone and watched Minneapolis fade into the distance through the window of the plane. It made my heart ache.

When I landed in L.A., I felt better. Maybe we both needed to say what we did even if it hurt the other to hear it. The only thing harder than dealing with feelings was allowing other people to have them also, especially when they weren't the same as mine. I had to trust time.

Time to heal.

Time to forgive.

Time to let go of the past.

Time to hold on to the future.

The hotel the magazine booked for me to stay at during the shoot didn't have any available rooms until my original check-in date, so I got a room at a less glamorous hotel, but it was on the beach, so it didn't matter. I needed the blue waters of Mother Earth to remind me of my insignificance and how my problems didn't matter because ... Ben died and I lived.

I hadn't been to the beach since my accident. At one point I felt certain I'd never go to another beach in my life. My remaining foot missed the feel of the sand between its toes. Parts of my skin hadn't seen the sun in years. Nothing compared to the feeling of the sun on my face, like it rose that morning just to shine on me.

Thank you, sun.

I didn't acknowledge the photos that I knew were being taken of me. Sports star's girlfriend, vacationing without him, pale body sprawled out on the beach with a prosthetic leg sticking out of the sand like a stick. Yeah, yeah, I didn't give a shit because really ... Sun. On. My. Face.

The moment felt tangible, like the elements were physically hugging me. So on a beach in Los Angeles, under a perfect sky with the wind whispering a beautiful lullaby along my skin ... I found what had eluded me for so long.

Sleep.

Three hours later I woke with a dried trail of drool from the corner of my mouth to my shoulder. It hurt to open my eyes. My whole face felt puffy and ... burnt.

"Oh my God!" I bolted up.

Red.

"No, no, no ..." I scrambled for my leg. It wasn't there.

It. Wasn't. There!

The beachgoers had dwindled to a few people walking along the shoreline in the distance. I flipped over, grimacing at the sand rubbing against my burnt legs.

"Ouch, ouch, ouch!"

Casting aside my pain, I dug like a dog in the sand. Why? Why would someone take my leg? Who does that?

I'm not sure when it started. At first I thought it was rain. Nope. The drops in the sand were my tears. I sat back on my towel and gently brushed the sand from my arms and legs.

"Ouch, ouch, ouch!"

So many thoughts fought for my attention. Thad would kill me. I lost his leg that no doubt cost more than my car. I was alone in L.A., stranded on a beach that looked more abandoned with each passing moment as the sun began to set. The last thought was the worst part: I couldn't walk. My hopping skills were quite good, but not in the sand. The photo shoot that would never happen. I didn't need a mirror to see my face. My arms and legs said it all.

Glancing down, I eased my top away from my chest just to confirm. "Holy shit!" I looked like a candy cane. The entrance to my hotel was a good two hundred yards away. I considered crawling it, but there was no way that would end well. Another scan of the area revealed no one within earshot. Luckily my bag that I'd used as a pillow was still there. I dug out my phone, frowning at the last bar.

"Come on, God. I don't want to believe that you hate me, but some days are really hard to swallow. Just saying ..." Time was running out on the day, and my phone battery. The problem was I had no idea who to call. Everyone I knew was at least six hours away, and I couldn't justify worrying friends and family who really couldn't help me.

A laugh released with my sob. I had to laugh. "Really, Lake? Are you going to be stubborn to your own demise?"

9-1-1 seemed to be the wisest choice, but I didn't want the news camera that could accompany that call. I needed someone who would know how to handle my epically stupid predicament.

"Please don't die," I begged my battery to holdout while I made my call.

"Flint," he answered.

"It's Lake and my battery is going to die so just listen and then respond as fast as you can. I'm stranded on Reef Beach in L.A. with probably second-degree burns from the sun and someone stole my leg. I'm by myself, and I don't want to attract media attention by calling 9-1-1, but honestly I don't think I have a choice." I tried to stifle a sob, but I knew he heard it. "I'm in pain." I gave up hiding my sobs. Truth? I was scared and my pulse could be felt along my skin and it hurt so damn bad.

"I've got you. Fifteen minutes. Someone will be there."

The lump in my throat was hard to speak past. "Th-thank you," I whispered.

Just before my phone died, I noticed a missed text from Cage he sent while I was frying myself.

Cage: *I love you too.*

It made me cry even more as my body shook with chills and my stomach roiled with nausea.

CAGE

Four hours of game footage later, I still couldn't get Lake off my mind. I was such an asshole to her. Everyone said, "You really should talk to someone about your dad." Nope, not me. I didn't need a shrink to analyze my feelings over my father's death and the events that led up to it. All I needed was to focus on the game. That's what he would have wanted.

Three. Fucking. Years of pent-up emotions and out of everyone, I chose to let them explode on Lake. I should have chased her. I should have been on the next plane to L.A. to beg for her forgiveness, but I needed to get things right in my head first. Her text shot a bullet right to my heart. Of course she'd forgive me before I ever asked her to. That was just one of the million reasons I loved her. I kept my reply simple because what I wanted to say could not be said in a text.

As I shut down my computer, surrendering to my lack of focus, my phone rang. I wanted it to be her. It wasn't.

"Flint, what's up?"

"Hey, buddy. I really hate calling you about this, and I know it's a mistake, but I have this feeling that if I don't tell you, you'll find out I knew and that threat you always make about firing me ... it will become my reality."

"Word efficiency, Flint. You never use this many words without making an actual point. What the hell is it?"

"Lake called me about thirty minutes ago."

I sat up straight as an unsettling feeling slithered along my spine. "Why?"

"She's in L.A."

"Yeah, I know."

"She got herself into a predicament."

"Words, Flint! Out with it!"

"She was stranded on a beach with second-degree burns and someone stole her prosthetic leg. I'm calling you because she sounded scared."

"Fuck! Are you serious?" I was halfway to my room to throw the rest of my shit into my bag before he answered. My bag was basically full because I already knew I was going to get my girl and make it right. I just didn't think it would be in a rush to a hospital. Life was good at packing a solid fuck-you punch to the gut when least expected.

"Sadly, yes."

"Why the hell did she call you instead of me?"

"Because her cellphone battery was about dead and she's smart ... well, I think. I'm reserving judgment on that until I hear the full details of her predicament. I'm guessing she knew if she called you, you'd ask too many questions and ultimately have to call yours truly to do what I do best."

Fix. That's what he did. I couldn't even refute anything he said because it was the truth.

"Where is she now?"

"Hospital."

"Get me the first flight out then text me the hospital and room number."

"Check your phone. I already texted you the information and your flight leaves in ninety minutes so get your ass going."

"Flint?"

He chuckled. "We'll hug it out later. For now ... you're welcome."

My heart rode in my throat the entire way to L.A. Loving a woman the way I loved Lake was so fucking painful. She made me feel *everything.*

A car waited for me at LAX; I didn't expect anything less of Flint. The driver knew where to go without instruction. I didn't wait for the vehicle to come to a complete stop before I hopped out and ran to the hospital entrance, then past the desk, ignoring the nurses telling me to stop and some bullshit about not being allowed down that hall that led to Lake.

324 ... 325 ... 326

With my heart pounding, I took a calming breath before opening the door to her room. A nurse stood next to her bed, tapping the screen of an iPad. She looked back at me and smiled.

"Are you family?"

At least that's what I think she said. I couldn't think, so I just nodded. Lake opened her eyes, a slight grimace tugged at her red, swollen, blistered face.

"Monaghan," she said with a gravelly voice.

"I'll give you two some privacy. Get some rest and you'll get to go home tomorrow." The nurse smiled as she walked past me.

"Let me guess, you just happened to be in the neighborhood."

I shook my head, sitting on the edge of her bed. "Not even close."

"A shame. I could have used your assistance when I had the equivalent of an amputee blowing a tire. Only someone stole mine."

"What kind of bottom-of-the-earth lowlife scum takes an amputee's leg at the beach?"

She laughed, but it didn't hide her grimace. "Exactly! Thaddeus is going to kill me. They're probably holding it hostage and by morning I'll receive a ransom notice."

The humor fizzled and reality set in.

"Lake, I'm so sorry. I'm sorry for what I said. I'm sorry I wasn't here. I'm sorry for everything."

"Don't." She rested her hand on mine. "Don't apologize for your feelings. You're human."

"Yes, humans have feelings, but inconsiderate bastards

unleash them on the one person they love most, and that's just messed up."

She held her arms out in front of her; the surface of her red skin was bubbled with tiny blisters. "I fell asleep in the sun with like SPF 2 on my skin, and I woke up a lobster missing a leg. *That's* messed up."

I leaned in until my lips hovered over hers. My hands itched to touch her, but I didn't want to hurt her. "Lake," I whispered. "Let me be sorry. Let me be scared that something so much worse could have happened to you today. Let me have all the emotions that come with loving you. Let me love you. Okay?"

"K," she whispered.

I feathered my lips over hers.

"The sun," she said.

I sat back.

"It felt so amazing. The sand. The ocean, just a few steps away from me. I really struggled with my self-image right after my accident. I didn't think I'd ever lie on a beach again." She shook her head. "But I didn't care what anyone thought of me or my leg stuck in the sand next to me. If there's a God, I'm certain he never meant to take the ocean, the beach ... the sun away from me. And sleep ... God, it's been so long since I woke up with drool down my face."

I chuckled.

"I know, gross, but I slept, Cage. I really slept. I didn't crash into my normal wall of exhaustion. I drifted into peace. So while I'll probably end up with skin cancer in a few years, I don't regret it. When the blisters heal and the burn fades, I'll still have the memory of beautiful, serene sleep."

"I know you're always awake when I fall asleep, and

you've said you have trouble sleeping and even some nightmares, but I had no idea just how bad it is for you."

She shrugged. "To explain it to you, I'd have to share my past, and my past can't be completely separated from yours —from Jillian Knight—so that's why you don't know."

Total bastard. How could I claim to love her and not *really* know her?

"It's late. You should sleep and I'm guessing they'll add something pretty awesome to your IV to help. Tomorrow we'll go to your hotel and you'll tell me your story—everything. Then we'll fly to Tahoe for the holiday with your family."

Tears filled her eyes.

"Don't cry."

She blinked them away. "I'm not."

I smiled as one escaped down her cheek.

"We're flying to San Francisco before Tahoe. I need to see a guy about a leg."

I kissed the top of her head. "Sleep, baby. Dream of me and know that I love you in a way that feels so much bigger than four little letters."

CHAPTER TWENTY-ONE

MEET THE JONESES

LAKE

DRUGS. Yep, that's all I needed to get some hardcore sleep. I woke to a tray in front of me with a cup of tea, a pink daisy, and a notecard.

CHAPTER SEVEN

I smiled. Maybe it was the drugs or maybe it was just time, but in that moment, I remembered.

Cage looked down, scratching the back of his head. "Yeah, my dad wasn't a collector or any sort of packrat, but my parents were divorced. I'm his only child and my grandparents live in Portland, so I guess it's my responsibility to decide what to do with everything. It's all mine now, including the house. The funny part? I don't want any of it."

"My brother's fiancée died a year ago. Her stuff still hangs in his closet. It's just stuff, but there has to be a finality to get rid of it. I bet you'll feel it when the last thing is removed

from here and someone else buys the place. The 'stuff' is the epilogue. The story is over, but part of it lives on like a ghost for just a few more pages. What's left at the end of the epilogue?"

"Nothing," he replied.

I cocked my head to the side and narrowed my eyes. "Depends on how you look at it."

"And how would you look at it?"

"I'm not sure yet. My boyfriend died in the accident that took my leg. When I came out of my coma, the funeral was over, his parents had cleaned out his apartment, and some other person lived there. I turned the page after the final chapter only to find no epilogue. The author of my life sucker punched me."

"Some would say the author of your life is God."

"And I'd agree. But no amount of faith can truly comfort a grieving heart that can't make sense of such tragedy. I didn't lose my faith, but I did feel like God sucker punched me. No epilogue. But he's God, so I'll probably forgive him some day."

Cage chuckled. "I'm sure he'll be grateful."

We flirted. I tried to pretend my brother wasn't waiting for me in the car, but before I walked out the door, I made one last reference to the story of life.

"Cage?"

He turned. "Yes?"

"You want to know what comes after the epilogue?"

"What?"

"A new book filled with endless possibilities."

Cage peeked around the corner, blowing the swirling

steam from his cup of coffee. "Good morning."

I pressed my hand gently to my chest. Something as imperfectly perfect as our journey to that point passed between us without a word. I saw the recognition in his eyes. He knew I remembered ... and he smiled.

"I'm your new book. I'm your endless possibilities," I whispered with the last bit of breath I had left after that realization knocked it from my chest, leaving my heart swelling with so much love.

"You are."

I cleared my throat, mustering something resembling an actual voice. "Do you feel it?"

"Feel what?" He sat on the edge of my bed.

"My heart beating in your hands."

Cage looked at me, more like through me. After a few moments ... he nodded.

THAT MAN—THE one of my dreams. He flew to Beijing to kiss me. Then he traveled to Los Angeles to really *see me* for the first time. My mom used to tell me to stop wishing my life away because the beginning and end were separated by nothing more than a blink. With Cage, I refused to blink.

"I can carry you."

I laughed as the driver pulled up in front of the hotel. "I can use the crutches. I need to get used to them anyway. I'm not going to be able to use my prosthetic legs until the burns on my leg heal a little bit more, at least until the blisters heal." I nodded toward his door. "Fans in L.A. Impressive."

Cage sighed. "Photographers. Not fans. Maybe there's a back entrance."

"Why? You embarrassed to be seen with me?" I perked a brow.

He smirked. "For the love of God, have you even looked in a mirror?"

I laughed. "I'm sure they'll spin it. Lake Jones, girlfriend to Minnesota's quarterback, suffered severe burns and loss of a limb in a meth lab explosion."

"Flint would love that. Come on, crispy." Cage hopped out and walked around to my side, opening my door while the two guys with cameras flashed a few shots.

"Cage, what happened to your girlfriend?" one of them asked.

I eased out as Cage held my crutches out for me.

"Nothing." He winked at the photographer with a cheeky grin. "Why do you ask?"

He could have ignored the photographer's question or said it was none of their business.

I grinned when Cage's smiling face focused back on me.

"Got it?"

I nodded, smiling through the pain while the cameras clicked again and again.

"What brings you to L.A.?" the same photographer asked me.

"Sex on the beach."

Cage adjusted his baseball cap low on his face, either to hide his amusement or embarrassment. I couldn't tell.

"Sex on the beach?" he asked after we left the reporters behind.

I shrugged as the elevator took us to the fourth floor. "It's a better headline than the meth lab scenario."

"Have you had sex on the beach?" he asked.

"Only in a shot glass. You?"

"No comment."

"What was her name? Bambi? Summer? Fantasia? I have it on good authority that sand is not genitalia-friendly. So hopefully you didn't drag your elephant trunk through the sand before slipping it into her delicate clamshell."

He fisted his hand at his mouth, and shook his head as the laughter he refused to share shook the rest of his body. "Only you ... only you ..."

Keeping my eyes trained to the elevator doors as they opened, a grin grew along my face. "Come on, Monaghan. No sense talking sex until you can look at me without grimacing."

"I don't—"

"Yes, you ..." My ears began to ring and my vision blurred with spots as the hallway seemed to move.

"Lake!" He caught me just as the light-headedness beckoned me to the floor.

"Not ... feeling so ... well. Weak." I closed my eyes as the stars in my vision made me nauseous.

"Stay with me. Which room, baby?"

I tried to focus on my breathing to keep from completely passing out. "412," I whispered.

"Is the key in your bag?"

"Uh huh."

"Everything okay?" an unfamiliar voice asked.

I was too weak to even open my eyes.

"Could be better. Would you mind looking in this bag for our room key?"

"Sure." It was a lady's voice. That much registered. "Here it is. Which room?"

"412," Cage answered.

"Here you go."

"Thank you so much."

"Are you sure you don't need anything else?"

"Nope. We're good. Just a touch of sun poisoning. She'll be fine. Thank you."

"Take care."

The door shut.

"Lake?"

"Uh huh?"

"I'm going to lay you down."

"K."

Riding the edge of blacking out was a miserably uncontrollable feeling.

I jumped as he pressed a cold washcloth to my forehead.

"Sorry. I don't want to hurt your burn, baby."

"F-fine," I whispered, because the cold really did feel good. I peeked open my eyes.

"Welcome back." He smirked. "Told ya I should have carried you the whole way."

All I had to give him was a weak smile, but it was his. He owned all my smiles.

"Feel better?"

I nodded, staring down at the empty plate on my lap, my legs stretched out on the bed, pillows propped up behind my back.

"I felt a little nauseous, so I can't believe I ate the whole thing."

"It was painful to watch, like a vulture on the side of the road with a fresh kill. I can't believe the plate survived." From the chair by the window, Cage smirked, tapping his fork lightly against his lower lip.

"Has the brash insult thing worked for you in the past

with ... Bambi, Summer, Fantasia? I mean, does your brain make a conscious decision between telling a girl she's sexy and beautiful versus a pig with Dumbo ears?"

He shook his head. "It's really not for your benefit, it's for mine."

I choked on my laugh. "*Benefit*? Enlighten me. How does insulting me benefit you?"

"It's my attempt to see you in a different light so my mind doesn't focus on doing very dirty things to you."

My jaw dropped.

Cage shrugged, like can't blame a guy for being honest.

"Sss ... so in Beijing you said my ears were big to keep from thinking about doing very dirty things to me?"

"Yes," he answered diplomatically.

"So you don't really think I have big ears?"

"I didn't say I made up shit. I just implied I tried to focus on something less sexy."

My hands inched toward my ears as they always did when he mentioned them. "Can, I mean ... do you think ears can really be sexy?"

"Lake?"

"Huh?" My brow tensed as I covered my ears.

"I love your ears."

"It's OK if you don't. It's not a deal breaker, right?"

"I love your ears."

"I'm trying to remember ... maybe one of my siblings pulled on them when I was younger. Maybe my mom dragged me to my room by them when I got in trouble."

"I love your ears."

"It really shouldn't matter though ... it's not like you stick your dick in my ears. Although, have you ever read any books or seen movies where guys say they want to fuck every hole or orifice of a woman's body? That would have to include ears and ..." I wrinkled my nose. "Nostrils too. Those guys must have pencil dicks. I think you'd have to have a pencil dick to even say something so ridiculous."

I twisted my lips as Cage threw his head back in laughter. "Lucky for me your dick is too big to fit in my nose or my ears. Do you suppose a guy's spunk dissolves wax or clears sinuses?"

"Stop!" He kept laughing. "You win."

"Yeah, I think so too." I smirked and heaved a pillow at his head.

He caught it and hugged it, hiding his shit-eating grin.

"Enough with my ears. Gah! You're giving me a complex. How would you like it if I pointed out your imperfections to keep from wanting to do very dirty things to you?"

He perked up. "I'm intrigued. So you think about doing very dirty things to me? What tampers your desire? My love handles?"

"You don't have love handles."

He pulled up his shirt. "True. Is it this tooth that I chipped years ago?" He opened his mouth and pointed to a lower tooth. I'd never notice it before. "Is it my hands? They really are too big for my body, but they come in handy for gripping a football."

His hands held a master's degree in doing the most incredible things to my body. They were perfect.

"I'm not telling you because I don't want you to be self-conscious about it, like what you've done to me." I had nothing. Absolutely nothing on him.

"Then tell me about the very dirty things you think about doing to me."

Second-degree burns didn't come in handy for much,

except for hiding my embarrassment. "I want to tell you about me. You said I could and I'm ready."

The jovial mood in the room died and his smile did too.

He cleared his throat and sat up in the chair. "Okay. Tell me. 'Lake I-don't-know-your-middle-name Jones was born ...'"

I shook my head. "Just highlights. The ones that matter."

He leaned forward, resting his arms on his legs. "I'm listening." It pained me to see him stare at the ground, like he needed to emotionally brace himself.

"I met Ben on a bike tour of San Francisco. My friend Lindsay insisted we take the tour because her boyfriend owned the small tour business. They hadn't been up and going long, so they needed people to take the tours, write a review, etcetera."

Cage looked up. "You're a very willing guinea pig."

I nodded. "I'm game for just about anything once. Anyway, Ben was our guide for the four-hour tour that morning. At the end he handed me a purple conversation heart candy that said, 'Say Yes.' I stared at it with confusion for a few seconds, and then he asked me out on a date. It was oddly romantic and totally unexpected. I felt certain no guy would top his unique gesture. Until I met you. Beijing for the win, baby."

His flicker of a smile encouraged me to continue.

"He gave me a conversational heart on every single date. It's how he told me he loved me. It was crazy how I lived for those two or three simple words. I never ate them. Instead, I kept them in a jar. On the morning of Luke and Jessica's wedding, I was supposed to go to the church with the rest of the bridesmaids, but I didn't. I wanted my heart. I wanted those little words that meant so much to me. So I had Ben pick me up and take me to breakfast before going to the church." I laughed, the kind that did nothing to ease the pain.

"Ben tried to talk me out of it. He said I should spend my morning with the other women. However, my insistence, my utter stubbornness, won over and he caved."

"You blame yourself."

My eyes met Cage's. I nodded. "How can I not? The truck hit us on a road we never would have been on had I not altered the morning's plans." I closed my eyes and whispered, "Ben died and I lived."

The bed dipped. I opened my eyes.

"Come here." He leaned his back against the headboard and spread his legs.

I eased over between them so my back rested against his chest. He brushed my hair off to one side and kissed the back of my neck.

"Death is filled with whys, what-ifs, and so damn much regret that it can swallow your whole fucking world if you let it. Ben died and you lived. It's just a fact. It's nothing more and nothing less. You can hold onto it or let it go, but either way, it won't change the fact."

I rested my hands on his legs and my head against his shoulder. "Is that what you tell yourself about your dad?"

"Every damn day."

"Does it help?"

"Sometimes."

"I don't remember the accident, but I remember the candy heart. It said 'Kiss Me.' So I did. I leaned over the console and kissed his cheek. I remember sitting back in my seat and adjusting the shoulder strap across my chest, and I remember him giving me the most adoring sideways glance. And that's it. That's all I remember until I woke from a coma three months later without Ben ... without my leg ... and without Jessica."

Cage's body tensed against mine. I kept going, like the proverbial ripping off a Band-Aid.

"Jessica's parents were murdered, and then she and her brother committed suicide, or at least that's what we believed. They received new identities and moved to Omaha while my family grieved for my leg, the uncertainty of my awaking from the coma, and my brother who was left so completely devastated by everything.

"Jessica is the strongest person I have ever known. I have her at rock star status, and I have no doubt that your dad loved her because she's impossible not to love. And she never told me what she said to you, but I know her, and her capacity to love is just enormous and her emotions are real, true, and completely unapologetic. But here's the thing, my brother loved her, my whole family loved her, and when he saw her—alive—it nearly killed him. If your dad wouldn't have died, I don't know what she would have done, who she would have chosen, but it doesn't matter anymore. And I'm sorry—I am so very sorry that it doesn't."

I lied. I lied to spare the last shred of his feelings. Jessica would have chosen Luke, I'd have bet my life on it.

"When my dad left to be with her—to die with her—I hated her for taking him. I hated him for choosing her. But ..." He pressed his lips to my head.

"But?"

"But now I have this person in my life, and she's melted butter and warm syrup on hot waffles, a blues song on the radio at sunset with a cold beer in hand, and the smile on my face when I'm all alone. And if someone asked me to choose a lasting image to take with me before I died ... I'd pick her face."

I was "her." I was "she." The words that left his lips would never really sink into my full conscience. The accident took so much more than my leg and yet Cage gave it all back to me tenfold. He didn't complete me with a part of himself; he just put me back together with all my own pieces. I shattered and he crawled around on the floor handing me my confidence, my hope, my dreams, my voice, my future. He mended me then kissed my scars and looked at me like I was nothing short of a timeless masterpiece.

Closing my eyes, I smiled. "I love our story. I love it so much because in every chapter you make me fall in love with you all over again. Let's never *be* in love. Let's *fall* every day without ever touching the ground."

"Fuck gravity." He rested his cheek on my head.

I chuckled. "Exactly, fuck gravity."

CHAPTER TWENTY-TWO

DADDY'S GOT A GUN

CAGE

"THEY'RE GOING to love you. More so when they recognize you. My parents follow football." Lake grimaced as she put pressure on the 'loaner' leg from Thaddeus.

She had three other legs packed but none that wouldn't 'kill' to wear them with the burns on her leg. Her face didn't lead me to believe the one from Thad was any better.

"Why don't you forego the leg and just let me carry you?"

"Yeah, not happening."

I retrieved our bags from the back of the rental car.

"My mom doesn't know about my beach mishap, and I'd rather not tell her. She worries enough as is."

"Sure. I get it. Because it's going to be real easy to hide when your entire front side looks like you lost a battle with a dragon."

"You've been putting aloe vera on me. I think it's better."

"I'm sure the look on your mom's face will confirm it

one way or another. And can I ask why you didn't tell your parents who I am?"

She stopped at the stairs, looking at them like a mountain. I set the bags down and scooped her up in my arms.

"I had it."

"Good to hear. In the meantime, I've got you."

"Stop," she whispered when we reached the door.

I didn't set her down because there really wasn't anything I liked more than having her in my arms.

"There's a part of my past I didn't tell you."

"You're adopted."

She laughed. "No. At least I don't think so. It's about you. When Jessica came home after your dad died, I wanted to ask her about you. I wanted to know if you had a girlfriend. I wanted to know your address, your phone number, just ... something. But I didn't ask her because she and Luke were trying to leave the past exactly where it belonged. I stalked you, but I couldn't come after you. I dreamed of you tracking me down, but you didn't, so I accepted you didn't want me the way I wanted you."

"You didn't know shit, Miss I Live in New York."

She rubbed my earlobe between her fingers. God, I loved when she played with my hair, feathered her hands over my face, or touched me in any way.

"My point is, if someone would have told me that we'd be here like this, I never would have believed them because you've been this completely out-of-reach dream since the day we met. Today the dream is real, and that's why I didn't tell them your name, but I've been talking about you for months. I think until this exact moment I didn't wholly believe you'd be here."

"Oh, sweet baby girl, please tell me you two didn't elope." Lake's mom held open the screen door.

We looked at pictures of her family on her phone when we stayed at the hotel in L.A. She thought I'd feel more comfortable if I could easily put names with faces. Her mom, Felicity, was easy to recognize with her chin-length black and gray hair, and her tall, slender frame.

"No, Mom, we didn't get married."

I eased her back on her feet.

"Oh, baby! What happened to you?"

Yeah, her skin was still *really* red.

"Minor sunburn. I was in L.A. with a low SPF. No biggie. It happens."

"Are you sure you're okay—Oh. Good. Lord! You're Cage Monaghan. Lake, what's he doing here?" Felicity smacked her hand against her chest. "Tom!?! Get in here. You're never going to believe this."

I grinned. "Nice to meet you, Mrs. Jones." I offered my hand.

She just stared at me with a wide-eyed look plastered to her face. "Felicity ... please, and ... w-what are you doing here?"

Lake took my hand and tugged me past her mom and into the foyer. "He's with me, Mom, he's my ..." She glanced up at me as if she needed my permission to finish her introduction.

"Boyfriend?" I said to Lake.

She grinned, like my confirmation in front of her mom made her whole day. "Yes." She continued to smile at me, even though her words were meant for her mom. "Cage Monaghan is my boyfriend. I didn't tell you at the time, but he flew to Beijing just to kiss me."

Felicity's mouth fell agape as she shifted her gaze to me.

With a shrug, I grinned. "True story."

"What's the hubbub about? Whoa!" Her dad stopped the moment he saw Lake. "What the hell, baby girl?"

"A little sunburn, Dad. No big deal."

His gaze lingered on her for a few seconds, like he didn't know if he should believe her. Of course he should not have, but I valued my life so I kept my mouth shut.

After the brief stare-down, which Lake won, her dad moved his attention to me. "Holy crap! You're Minnesota's quarterback ... Monaghan. What ... why are you here?"

Lake rolled her eyes. "Jeez ... thanks, parents, for not making the assumption that Cage is my boyfriend. Heaven forbid the girl with the missing leg find herself a real catch."

Tom pointed a finger at me while he met Lake's angry face. "This isn't a joke?"

I held out my hand. "It's not a joke, Mr. Jones. I'm dating your daughter. I'm Cage, but I gather you already know that. Anyway, it's nice to meet you."

Tom shook my hand. A generous grin formed along his face beneath his short gray beard that matched the gray in his hair mixed with a reddish-blond. "Nice to meet you, Cage. Not gonna lie, we're not Minnesota fans, but I've been a fan of yours since you played in college."

Nodding, I chuckled. "Thanks. And I appreciate your honesty. I doubt there are many Minnesota fans around here."

"I'm a fan." Lake hugged my back.

I rested my hand over hers. "Thanks. That means so much coming from such a football enthusiast such as yourself, babe."

Her parents laughed.

Tom winked at Lake. "If you're still together when the season starts, please don't waste good tickets on this one. It would make me sick to see her in the stands, completely bored and clueless. We've never been able to get her to watch football."

"Ugh ... really? Can we move on to a subject that doesn't involve throwing your daughter under the bus? Dad, why don't you help Cage bring in our bags."

Before I went back outside, the most incredibly crazy thing happened. Felicity gently grabbed Lake's ears and kissed her cheek then whispered loud enough for me to hear, "He's quite the catch, baby girl, but so are you and don't you ever forget that."

Lake's eyes bugged out as her lips parted and our gazes locked. My eyes matched hers, and I had to bite my grin because ... Holy shit! Her mom tugged on her ears.

As soon as we brought in the luggage, Lake stared at the stairs to the second floor—another mountain to tackle. I could see it on her face.

"Something wrong, sweets?" Felicity asked.

"Um ... I just ..."

"You don't still have trouble with the stairs do you? I thought you said Thad's legs felt like the real thing, not so much as a hint of a limp, even on the stairs."

"Yeah ... the leg is good. I just got a little bit of the *minor* burn on my leg so anything rubbing against it is a bit uncomfortable."

"I got her," I said, taking the stairs two at a time to set our bags at the top before coming back down.

"This is embarrassing," she mumbled as I lifted her in my arms.

"Your mom has your room ready, Lake," her dad said. "Cage can sleep in the blue room."

Their house. Their rules. I wasn't going to question one word. That's how military kids were raised. My spitfire of a girlfriend? She wasn't as submissive to their rules.

"Pu-lease, Dad. Newsflash, I'm twenty-four. We've had sex."

I closed my eyes, trying to pretend she did not just say that.

"Lake—" Her dad tried to speak.

"It's true. Deal with it. We've had lots of sex in a lot of different places and posit—"

"Lake!" Felicity stifled her laugh.

Tom was to my back, so I couldn't see him. I just prayed he didn't own a gun.

"Hold on," I mumbled through my embarrassment as I carried her upstairs.

"What?" She grinned as I plopped her on the bed in her pink room.

"'Hey, Mom and Dad, meet Cage. He's my boyfriend and just so you know ... we've had sex in a lot of different places and *positions*?' That's what you were getting ready to say, right?"

She eased back, resting her hands on her belly. "Sorry, was some part of what I said inaccurate? Do you want me to list all the times, places, and positions we've had sex, because I can. I remember every single one."

My cock was steel in my pants. Just talking about it left me so fucking hard, even if my brain still couldn't get past her saying that to her parents. My cock? Nope. All it heard was her say the word sex and its x-ray vision saw her naked and beneath me.

"You're thinking about it, aren't you?"

I moved toward the window, checking out the view of the less seductive lake as I adjusted myself. "I'm not thinking about anything except you embarrassing me. What are the chances your dad owns a gun?"

"One hundred percent." She giggled.

"Peachy. I'm not going to have sex with you here. First, you're still in a lot of pain, even if you don't want to admit it, and second ... I don't want to disrespect your parents."

She sat up. "First, you don't know my pain level, and second, my parents have gone skinny dipping in the lake with Jessica and Luke. My parents show an inappropriate amount of PDA all the time and just wait ... if we stay long enough, you'll hear them."

I turned, leaning my back against the pink-painted wall. "Hear them?"

She wiggled her eyebrows.

"No." I shook my head. She had to be making that up just to get a reaction out of me.

"It's true. They like their music loud and their sex even louder. If they still do their same routine, I can even lip-sync it for you. They have to keep it quiet when they have paying guests staying here at the B&B, but when it's just us kids, they don't hide it. I wonder if my dad shoves my mom's panties in her mouth to keep her quiet or—"

"No!" I shook my head. "No. No. No." I grimaced. "I don't want to know this. I just met them. When I see them, I want to see the two beautiful people who made you. I don't want to actually think of them 'making you.' And definitely not with your mom gagged by her own underwear."

"Oh ..." Lake shook her head. "Don't say anything to them about the underwear gagging. That's just speculation on my part. I'm not trying to spread rumors."

"Seriously!?! You honestly think I'd say something about that to them?"

She tried to hide her smile, but I saw it in her eyes before she let her lips free from the confinement of her teeth. "No." She laughed. "But oh my gosh! You should see your face. You look horrified."

"You're such a ..." I shook my head, rubbing my hands over my face.

"A what?"

"A pill. An evil plotter. A handful ... more than a handful. So all of that about your parents was just to get a reaction out of me."

Her head jerked back. "What? No. The only part I was joking about was mentioning the panty-gagging, because I know you never would. But the rest? The skinny dipping? The PDA? The loud sex? All true."

I rested one hand on my hip while rubbing the back of my neck with my other hand. "And the gun?"

"He probably owns at least a dozen, but he's never used one on my boyfriends. He came close with Ben, but my mom swooped in as the voice of reason to save the day."

"What did Ben do?" I looked up.

"Took my virginity ... in the green bedroom. Did you know they make dirty conversational hearts? It's true. I'm not proud of this, but all it took was a candy heart that said, 'Let's make love," for me to hike up my skirt and rip off my panties. It didn't even matter that he gave me two more right away that said, 'Bend Over' and 'Lick me.' I've been permanently banned from that room, which is a shame because it's the only one with a king-sized bed; the rest are queen. Hope you work well in small spaces."

"We're not having sex here." I shook my head, partly to affirm my declaration and partly to rid my head of Lake having sex with some other guy. I was jealous of a dead guy. That was a new, pathetic low for me.

"So you'd say no if I offered to wrap my lips around your cock right now."

"Jesus, Lake ..." I had to turn and adjust myself again. I needed a cold shower to cool my balls and wake me up from this nightmare of a long weekend that had only just begun.

Her laughter always left me powerless. I was such a sucker for her smile.

"I love playing with you," she snickered.

Yeah, I loved when she played with me too, but my preference was more physical and less psychological.

I turned. "Your mom grabbed your ears."

"Oh my God! I know. It wasn't until she actually did it that I realized it's been going on for years. If you would have asked me, I would have said she cradles my head, but no. She grabs my ears. She's ruined my ears! They'll never go back to their original position."

I grinned. Lake was her own universe, and when I had the pleasure of being part of it, I wasn't a famous football player and I wasn't the man still grieving his father. I was the guy who wanted to make being with her a full-time profession.

"I love your ears. I love the way you moan when I drag your earlobe between my teeth."

I also loved how her breath caught when I said things like that to her.

She swallowed hard. "Ivy"

"Ivy?"

"Yes." Her shoulders lifted. "The other day you said you didn't know my middle name. It's Ivy."

"Very earthy names."

"My parents claim they weren't hippies, but ... I'm not so sure."

"My middle name is James."

"I know." With a slight head shake she rolled her eyes.

"You do?"

"Duh. If you Google your name, the entire right column

is about you: full name, date of birth, height, current team, education, parents. Yep, it's all there."

"You've Googled me?"

"I may have." She picked at some peeling skin on her arm.

"To find out my stats?"

She shrugged. "Among other things."

I sat on the bed next to her, ducking my head to see her face that she tried to hide with her chin tipped down. "What other things?"

"Just stuff. Okay? Like places you've been photographed or ..."

"Or?"

"Or maybe who you've been photographed with."

"Did you go online to size up your competition?" I chuckled.

"Maybe." She pinched her lips together.

"And?"

"It's pretty stiff." Lake shot me a quick, wrinkle-nosed look. "You don't go for the average chick."

I shook my head. "Actually, I don't date that much."

Her jaw unhinged. "Uh ... I can do a search on my phone right now and prove that you are incorrect."

"Photos don't mean shit. If I lean too close to a waitress in a loud bar or restaurant to give her my order, some idiot snaps a picture and just like that, said waitress and I are an item."

"Yeah, well, then you must hang out at some pretty fancy places that only hire *really* sexy women to work there."

"Did the sun fry your brain a bit too? Because this is a new side to you. Jealousy doesn't suit you."

"I'm not jealous. I said I knew your middle name. You

asked how. I told you and it led into this conversation. I've said nothing out of jealousy. I've simply made observations, that's all."

I shrugged. "I don't know, it sounds a little like jealousy."

"You're such a dope. Jealousy is: Who was the blonde? How did you meet? Did you have sex? How much? Did you love her? Do you miss her? I bet you're thinking about her right now. When's the last time you talked with her?

But if you'd listened to me you'd know I didn't actually ask you anything. I said I looked at some online photos of you. Then I made the observation that the women in all the photos were very attractive. That's it. Period."

"Lake?" her mom called. "Get down here. Luke and Jessica just arrived!"

She sucked in a quick breath. The excitement in her eyes and the smile on her face eased my anxiety, but just a little.

CHAPTER TWENTY-THREE

MISSING VIRGINITY

LAKE

"GTO Jones!" I called from the top of the stairs. One step down left me seething with a few mumbled expletives. I was not ready to wear any prosthetic yet, but ... stubborn ... contumacious.

"I'll carry—"

Before Cage could finish his offer, I dropped to my butt and slid down the stairs. It didn't feel awesome, but at least my backside didn't feel like raw flesh. The messy, dark-haired boy at the bottom of the stairs giggled at me.

"Grant, Auntie Lake needs kisses." I held out my arms.

He jumped into them. I tried to hide my flinch as even his little body caused mine pain.

"Good Lord, Lake. What did you do?"

Keeping Grant captive in my embrace, I looked up at my brother Luke. He was the male version of me: black hair, blue eyes, and yep, upon inspection, his ears stuck out a bit too.

"Meth lab mishap."

He continued to stare at me with no reaction. Jessica laughed.

"Sunscreen, Lake," Luke said. "SPF 75 for your fair skin."

"Thank you, Dr. Jones. I'll take that into consideration the next time I fall asleep on the beach. Hi, Jess." Releasing Grant, I grabbed the stair rail to pull myself up without putting too much weight on my leg.

"We miss you. When are you moving back?" She winked and gave me a gentle hug.

Her body stiffened and in that moment I knew Cage had made his way down the stairs.

The son of her ex-lover.

The boyfriend whose name I never mentioned.

The man I wanted my family to love and accept more than absolutely anything.

Luke. He was the only one in my family who knew about my once-in-a-lifetime encounter with Cage. I let everything go after that day for him and Jessica. Luke looked at me and it was a very bittersweet moment. I saw the man who didn't want to remember that time in his wife's life, but I also saw the brother who remembered the day his sister found "the one."

Luke drummed the top of the steering wheel with his hands. He was tired of driving around the block.

"You didn't need to honk the horn." I slipped in the seat and slammed the door shut.

"So what did you find out?"

"He's gorgeous. He plays quarterback for Nebraska. Oh ... and I think he loves me and my prosthetic leg."

That wasn't the information he wanted. Luke needed to know if I found any clues to Jessica's whereabouts. I didn't mean to blurt out all of that about Cage, but I had to tell someone ... I just had to. We rode in silence back to our hotel in Omaha. Pain for his beloved radiated from him. I wanted to make it better, but just as we pulled into the parking garage, Luke reminded me why I loved him so much.

I rubbed the top of my leg, staring out the window.

"Your leg bothering you today?" Luke asked.

"No." I stilled my hand. "It's just a habit. That's all."

"I have no doubt that you're right."

I glanced at him. "What? That it's a habit?"

"No. I have no doubt that you're right about Cage. I'm sure he does love you and your leg. Any guy would be a fool not to."

It was crazy for me to even suggest that Cage could love me after one meeting, but it meant the world to me that Luke said that with complete sincerity.

"Cage," Jessica whispered as if he were a ghost. "What are you doing here?"

I stepped back, looking between her and Luke.

Luke cleared his throat and I knew ... I just knew he was going to say something to make everything right. That's what he did. He fought for the people he loved most in the world, and I was on that very lucky list.

"Lake and Cage met in Omaha when we were there looking for you. I think my dear sister fell in love with your neighbor, Jess."

And just like that ... Luke stole my heart. He let his past

go and gave me my chance at a future. I nearly cried when he smiled, the one that said he was happy for me.

Cage took the last two steps and gave Jessica a sad smile. Then he hugged her. Yep, I had the *very* best men in my life. Jessica hugged him tight, like she needed a minute to get her emotions together before he released her.

"I wondered if that's why you moved to Minneapolis of all places." Luke smirked while picking up Grant, who had his arms outstretched to him.

"What?" I narrowed my eyes. "*You* knew he played for Minnesota?"

Luke shrugged. "Of course. You mean..." he laughed "... you didn't?"

I shook my head feeling like the dumbest person in the world. How did everyone in my family know and follow the man of my dreams except me?

Jessica released Cage and took a deep breath. Both my brother and I waited for them to exchange something more than just a hug, but they didn't, and I loved them both for it.

"He's a damn good catch, Lake." Jessica squinted one eye at Cage. "But Lake's my sister, so fair warning, Monaghan, if you hurt her I'll kill you."

"Thanks, babe." Luke shook his head. "That was supposed to be my line. You're so emasculating."

"Whatever, Jones. I'm starving. Let's raid the kitchen. Carrying your baby takes a lot of energy." She rubbed her belly as they headed toward the kitchen.

I turned and fisted Cage's shirt, looking up at him. "Told ya they'd love you."

"Mmm," he hummed. His dimpled smile melting everything below my waist. "You know what I love?"

"Me, I hope."

Cage chuckled, threading his fingers through my hair. "Yes, and I love that you moving to Minneapolis had nothing to do with me ... that we just found each other." He pressed his lips to mine, kissing me slowly.

The truth for me wasn't explained by simple coincidence. Everything that had happened in my life forced me to find meaning and direction—a reason to keep moving forward. I believed my relocating to Minneapolis, out of endless possible destinations, had everything to do with Cage. Time told many stories and it was time for ours.

"I'M LEAVING your father and stealing your boyfriend. Is that going to be an issue, Lake?" my mom asked as we stared out the windows overlooking the circle of testosterone.

My dad, Cage, Luke, my other brothers, Lane and Liam, and my brother-in-law, Drake, stood around the grill drinking beer. Even Cage cheated on his no alcohol, treating-my-body-like-a-temple routine and had a beer with the other men I loved most in the world.

I giggled like a schoolgirl at my mom's comment. Thoughts of Cage did that to me. "I think it *could* be an issue, but feel free to ask him if he's interested."

"I might ask him too." Lara teased the rim of her wine glass along her bottom lip as she drooled over my guy. "Do you think he'd go for an older woman with stretch marks and deflated breasts?"

"Maybe." I shrugged, finishing off the last bit of wine in my glass. "I hear he's dated an amputee before. Must mean he's OK with some minor imperfections."

"How long did it take him to notice your missing leg?" my mom asked with a Cheshire cat grin on her face.

"Hmm ... I think it was maybe the fourth or fifth time we were having sex—in the same night of course." I winked at Anne, my sister-in-law.

She turned almost as red as me.

She knew our family was crazy and more times than not, inappropriately crude. But she never could jump in and role-play the bullshit quite like the rest of us. Jessica? She could do it like she'd been born into our family, but she was downstairs with all the kids since her knocked-up state prevented her from drinking with us.

"Anyway, he rolled his hot, sweaty, rippled-muscled body off mine and said between labored breaths, 'Baby, I think you're missing something.' I shrieked. He calmed me down and then we looked for my missing leg. Never found the damn thing."

We fell into a fit of laughter, except for Anne. She had a permanent grimace etched across her face. I'm sure she wondered how we could joke about my missing limb.

Easy. It happened.

It couldn't be undone.

We'd met our grieving quota years before.

Life was too damn short, so we did what the Jones women did best ... we drank until we collapsed into a giggling stupor.

"You're dating a celebrity, Lake. Has that sunk in yet?" Lara asked.

"Not really. I mean ... we haven't been dating during his regular season. There's always someone snapping a photo or asking for his autograph, but I have this feeling when training camp starts things are going to change ... a lot."

"There's going to be crap in the tabloids all the time," my mom added.

I nodded, refilling my glass. "Yeah, we've already had

some of that. Honestly, I can't believe any of you haven't seen me in some trashy magazine. I never dreamed I'd make it this long without you discovering the secret identity of my new boyfriend."

"You told me his name, sweetie." My mom gave me the stink eye. "Just not his last name."

I grinned behind my wine glass. "I wanted you to meet him before you got any preconceived ideas about my 'celebrity' boyfriend. And I wanted to feel secure in my relationship with him before bringing him to ... *this place.*"

"Good call." Anne smirked.

Cage looked up and caught us gawking at him through the window, and he grinned then winked.

"Oh. Dear. God. He winked at me. Do you think Drake saw him wink at me?" Lara fanned herself.

"Wine ... I can have a sip and not kill my baby, right?" Jessica came in the kitchen with Grant on her hip and exhaustion on her face.

"Shift change." Anne took Grant from her. "Besides, you can handle the inappropriate talk better than I can."

Jess kissed me on the top of my head. "Pour me an ounce of wine, Sis, and I'll give you my first born."

I laughed, pouring her an ounce, maybe two. "Don't let OCD Jones catch you."

Jessica sat down next to me and rolled her eyes, bringing the glass to her lips.

My mom's and Lara's eyes grew wide, their smiles pulled tight into grimaces.

"No. Way."

Jessica closed her eyes and grumbled as I turned. Luke stood behind her with the intercepted wine glass in his hand.

"Dammit, Jones! You're so controlling."

I giggled, missing their angry banter that always turned into Luke saying something that rendered Jess speechless. That day was no exception.

After setting the glass on the counter, he bent down and kissed her cheek while resting his hands on her belly. "How does it feel to carry such an important part of me inside of you?"

She frowned. "You don't play fair. You never have."

Luke stood with a proud smirk stuck to his face. "Dad's taking the hamburgers off the grill."

"I'll set out the salads and chips." My mom stood, draining the last of her wine with a satisfied sigh as Jessica glared at her. "Oh, did Tom remember your veggie burger?"

"Women who carry such an important part of your son don't get to have anything from the grill."

"Your quinoa dish is in the oven next to the rhubarb crisp," Luke called as he headed back outside.

I'm pretty sure out of the corner of my eye I saw Jess flip him the bird.

CAGE

Tom Jones. I'd gone almost two years without a drop of alcohol, and with one are-you-seriously-not-going-to-have-a-beer-with-me look, I had a cool bottle in my hand, the smooth lager coating my throat. The men in Lake's family were the opposite of her: they loved football. Even Luke, who Lake described as 'stuffy in a suit,' knew stats and players' names.

Red meat was also on the list of things I hadn't had in a long time, yet one of the burgers Tom flipped on the charcoal grill was mine. How did I become the schoolboy who wanted to fit in? It was crazy because I'd never been in that role, but I wanted every one of the men in Lake's life to like me.

After a good twenty minutes of discussing football with the guys huddled around the grill, and just when I started to get that fitting-in feeling, Tom asked me the question that made me choke on my beer.

"So how long have you been sleeping with my daughter?"

I looked at Luke, but he kept his head down, beer bottle to his lips, as did Lane and Liam.

Drake held up a finger. "I'm going to see if they need help with the kids."

Had Tom asked him the same question about Lara when they first met?

Either Tom had the world's best poker face or he was dead serious. Even his eyes narrowed a fraction.

"I love your daughter."

Luke peeked up and winked at me.

"Did you love her when you took her virginity?"

My eyes ping-ponged between Tom and her brothers who continued to keep their eyes trained to the grill.

My brow pulled tight. Lake told me her father caught her in bed with Ben. Didn't she? I began to doubt everything as the silence dragged on. I had no other choice, so I went with the best answer, the one that I liked too. It was the one where I was the only man who had ever been with Lake.

"Yes. I loved your daughter when I took her virginity." I

took a long swig of beer, praying for the buzz to kick in, but one beer could never give me a buzz.

My answer elicited all three of her brothers to glance up with their own confused faces. Just as I figured—she wasn't a virgin and everyone knew it.

"Did you *love* taking her virginity?"

The Jones men lasted all of two seconds before every single one of them busted into laughter. I smirked while shaking my head. I never expected the initiation to be quite so brutal. If I'd had a daughter would I have been able to joke about her sex life? Probably not. In all fairness, Lake warned me that her family was the complete opposite of normal.

"Fifty bucks if you answer him?" Liam laughed, still bending over to catch his breath.

"One hundred if you don't." Luke shook his head. The prospect of Liam's offer bringing a bit of worry to Luke's face as his smile faded.

I cocked an eye at Tom. He rested his hand on my shoulder, giving it a firm squeeze.

"You passed. No need to say anymore." He chuckled.

I pulled my T-shirt away from my chest. "Shit. I'm sweating. That was just ..."

"Fucking cruel." Liam winked. "Drake bailed because he went through the same torture over Lara. I think watching your hazing was too much for him."

"The psychiatry degree was more personal therapy from growing up in this family than a true dream job." Luke grinned before taking a pull of his beer.

"Mmm ..." I bit my lips together and nodded. "No comment."

"Tom?" Felicity called. "Luke said the hamburgers were about done. What's taking you guys so long?"

He scooped them off the grill. "Coming."

"We're not getting tickets to any games now are we?" Liam asked as we headed toward the door.

"Not a chance."

CHAPTER TWENTY-FOUR

HOW TO SAVE A LIFE

LAKE

WE STAYED two days with my family, ending with a stunning fireworks display along the lake. I'd seen it a million times, but I'd never watched it with Cage, which made it feel brand-new again. He made my whole life feel brand new again.

Jessica once told me that she really did feel a complete separation from Jillian Knight. She was always Jessica with Luke. I think she needed that clear distinction to let go of AJ and give her whole life to my brother. I never truly understood it until Cage. He wasn't with "Ben's girlfriend." Part of her died the day Ben died. It was a poignant realization.

Survivors sacrificed a piece of themselves to move on, a proverbial shedding of weight to keep from drowning. Jillian left part of her heart in the past to move forward as Jessica. The day I accepted the loss of my leg was the day the rest of Ben's girlfriend died, and in that moment I became a real survivor. That's who Cage loved, not the girl who wore a cloak of bitterness and hated the world —hated God.

We blinked and training camp swallowed up Cage's days and his presence. Minnesota still held their training camp away at a college campus—something to do with "bonding."

No Cage.

No sex.

No fun.

Even his birthday fell right in the middle of training camp. We talked for twenty minutes on the phone before he was taken away by his buddies.

Once my new layer of skin resembled something human again, I flew back out to L.A. for the photoshoot—without the beach time. Our jobs succeeded at keeping us apart. When he was free I was busy and vice versa. Shayna made claim to some of my free time as well, but the world's best qualified and hottest nanny still continued to make the news.

Jamie also continued to hold the title of best knocker. Three swift knocks. I grinned, knowing I'd be met with his usual shoulder shrug as Shayna pleaded her case.

Peephole check. Yep, they both stood on the other side of my door with beach towels draped around their necks.

"Lake! You have to come with us!"

I smiled at Shayna then met Jamie's shrug with the same smile.

"She's relentless," he said in his perfect British accent.

My responses to him always had a two-second delay because I enjoyed letting the way he said his words hang in the air.

"Yes, she can be." I pinched her nose and wiggled it until she scrunched her face.

"To the pool! We have to go!" Shayna clasped her hands under her chin.

I knew if I didn't answer soon she'd drop to her knees.

Why did my decision have to come after weighing the possible fallout of being seen in public with Jamie? Cage told me never to alter my life for his reputation or the media. Flint? He wasn't of the same opinion. I fell somewhere in the middle.

"The pool won't be open much longer ..." Jamie cocked his head to the side and pursed his lips.

Great. Just what I needed, both of them with the pleading puppy-dog eyes.

"I've been watching my sun exposure since my L.A. incident."

Shayna stuck out her bottom lip. Jamie looked at her and then at me.

"Wear a big hat and sit under one of the umbrellas. We'll only be there for two hours at the most."

Releasing a big sigh, I nodded. "Okay. Which pool?"

"The new natural swimming pool."

"Fine." I stepped back. "Come in, give me ten minutes."

After I packed my bag, I texted Flint.

Lake: *FYI I'm going to the new pool with Shayna and Jamie.*

Barely a second passed before he texted me back.

Flint: *No.*

I shook my head.

Lake: *Not asking permission. Just telling you out of courtesy.*

Flint: *Still no. 1st preseason game is coming up. Cage needs his head in it, not distracted by tabloids.*
Lake: *Haven't talked to Cage in two days. I think his head is "in it." I'll sit on the opposite side of the pool as Jamie.*
Flint: *Don't be naive.*

I tossed my phone in my bag. "Ready?"

Shayna jumped up. "Yes! Yes! Yes! Lake's going!" She gave Jamie a can-you-believe-it look.

He grinned at me. "Looks like you made her day."

"Hmm ... yeah, but here's the deal. We..." I motioned between us "...have to stay on opposite sides of the pool."

Jamie chuckled. "What? Like a divorced couple taking our daughter swimming."

"No. Like two people who've never met and won't meet, speak, or even glance at each other today."

"Deal."

Aaannnd that was just another reason Jamie was the best nanny. He took instructions without arguing.

"You suck at being part of the team."

Shutting off my Kindle, I flipped up the wide rim of my sun hat and squinted at Flint.

"You're overdressed for the pool." My eyes made a quick inspection of his black suit, no tie, top buttons undone. His expensive cologne announced his presence before his voice.

"You're underdressed for being in public."

I laughed. "It's a swimming pool."

"You don't own a one-piece swimsuit ... or maybe one of those long swim dresses?"

Narrowing one eye at him, I shook my head. "Sorry. If you're worried about me getting sunburned again, then I'd like to draw your attention to the big umbrella over my head."

He adjusted his sunglasses and looked around the crowded pool. "I thought we agreed Cage's reputation matters."

"Sure thing, *boss*. That's why I'm sitting here by myself."

"But lover boy is on the other side of the pool, you're not fooling anyone."

"Lover boy, huh? Well that explains it."

"Explains what?"

"Why a good-looking guy like yourself is never with a woman. You have a thing for Shayna's nanny."

"Fuck you."

Flint's *fuck you* was nothing like Everson's. I detected nothing playful or joking in his words.

"I don't care if you're gay. It's none of my business, and unlike *some* people, I know how to mind my own business."

Total bullshit. I was queen of the peephole. My favorite hobby was trespassing into other people's business.

"You don't know shit, Lake." Flint walked off. Not another word or even a quick glance back.

Jamie narrowed his eyes at me as he helped Shayna do her back float. I shook my head and flipped my hat back down.

A while later, Shayna called to me. "Lake, we're leaving now. I want to ride home with you."

Yes, we even took separate cars. Any bullshit issues Flint had about my outing was complete over-obsession on his part. I nodded and smiled as Shayna walked toward me, wrapped in a big pink towel that dragged along the ground.

Jamie held up his hand. "See ya at home."

"Ice cream! Please, Lake." Shayna clasped her hands again under her chin.

My willpower was no match for her adorable begging. "Yes, of course, ice cream." I took the edge of her towel and squeezed the water from her ponytail.

"Thank you, Lake."

"You're welcome. Let's go."

We stopped at her favorite place for ice cream, and she got her usual: rainbow ice cream with gumballs. I shook my head every time. How could she enjoy cold, hard gumballs that she had to spit into a napkin to chew when her ice cream was gone? I got peanut butter ice cream with chocolate cookie pieces.

"I miss Evson." Shayna swiped her tongue across her top lip, missing the smearing of pink on the tip of her nose.

"I know, sweetie. Training camp is almost over and you'll get to see him a little more often."

"I love Evson."

Of course she did. Love was all Shayna had to give.

"Have you said, 'I love you' to Everson?"

She nodded.

I jabbed my spoon into my ice cream. "Has Everson said 'I love you' to you?"

She nodded.

I wanted to cry, but I didn't. Instead I smiled. Every inch of me smiled. It felt like a huge victory. I knew he'd love her. I knew it would be impossible for him not to love her. It was no longer my illusion that she was going to be OK—that they were going to be OK—they were there.

I blotted a drip of ice cream from her nose.

She giggled then sucked in a breath. Her smile vanished

as her eyes widened with panic and her spoon dropped to the floor.

"Shayna?"

Her hand shot to her throat.

"Shayna?" I jumped up, sending my chair crashing to the ground behind me.

She was choking, really choking. Not so much as a cough or any sign of air exchange. Her eyes watered.

"Help!" My shrill voice broke through the air. I didn't even recognize it as my heart rocketed into my throat. I felt as if I, too, was choking. I'd taken CPR many years earlier, but I just couldn't think. I patted her back. Her lips turned blue.

"Step aside." A familiar voice appeared from seemingly nowhere.

"Flint! Oh my God, she's choking."

He held her against him, thrusting his fisted hands into her stomach.

"Call 9-1-1!" I screamed to anyone who would listen. My cell phone was a foot away from me at the table, but my brain would not function. Fear robbed me of everything, and I just panicked like when the prototype swimming leg fell off in the pool and Thad had to jump in to get me.

Shayna passed out and tears flooded my cheeks. "Shayna! Flint!"

He lowered her to the ground and I just stood there. Time slowed. Voices muffled into echoes. People gathered around. Shayna gasped and Flint rolled her to her side and out of her mouth fell a gumball. A fucking gumball. Why did I let her get gumballs? A few seconds later, sirens sounded, lights flashed, and everyone cleared as the paramedics pushed through the door.

I jumped when Flint's hands wrapped around my arms,

pulling me away from Shayna as the paramedics tended to her.

Ben died and I lived.

Shayna almost died and I would have lived. I made bad decisions that put other people in danger.

"Give them space, Lake," Flint said as he physically had to move me away from her.

I couldn't speak.

I couldn't even blink.

"We'll follow them to the hospital."

I shook my head. "I'm riding with her."

"Are you her mother?" One of the paramedics asked.

Flint said, "No," just as I said, "Yes."

The paramedic's eyes flitted between us. There was no way they were going to prevent me from riding with her.

"I'm her mom." I tugged out of Flint's grip.

"She's breathing fine, but we're going to take her to the hospital to have her checked out. You can ride with her."

I nodded.

"Lake ..."

I didn't look back at Flint. He saved her life and for that I would always be grateful, even indebted to him, but I didn't want to hear any bullshit about photographers, media, or how events of the day might tarnish anyone's reputation.

Shayna was smiling by the time we made it to the hospital. I was still a wreck. On the way, I texted Jamie. He was technically the one in charge of her while Everson was at training camp. He had her medical and insurance information.

"Hey." Jamie hugged me as they took Shayna back to be examined.

I lost it again. A new round of tears released from the flood gates.

"I-I-I'm so sorry. Sh-she almost died."

"Shh ..." Jamie rested his cheek against my head as sobs wracked my body.

The guilt and "what if" was so damn painful.

"She's going to be fine. Did you see the grin on her face?"

"But she could have—"

"It doesn't matter now. She didn't and she's fine. You're fine. It's fine, doll."

"Are you Shayna's parents?" A nurse interrupted.

Jamie released me and I wiped my face and eyes.

"I'm her nanny."

"I need to go over some medical information with you."

Jamie nodded, glancing at me with a tense brow.

I shook my head. "I'm fine. Go. They need you. She needs you."

When I turned, my body slammed into Flint. I sucked in a breath. "God! You scared me."

"I called Everson. He knows what happened and that Shayna will be fine."

"And Cage?"

Flint shook his head. "Everson won't say anything to him either."

"I'm calling him."

"He'll leave to come back here for you. Is that what's really best for everyone?"

"You mean for Cage."

"I do." Flint's tone held no regret. "After you see her, I'm taking you home. Jamie will take Shayna home and life will go back to being uneventful—not newsworthy."

Blink. Blink. Blink.

I just stared at him. Everything inside of me felt numb, including my tongue.

"We can see her."

My head jerked to Jamie. I nodded and followed him to the exam room.

"Hi, I'm Dr. Brody."

Jamie shook his hand.

"Lake!" Shayna jumped off the table and hugged me like she didn't nearly die an hour earlier.

I blinked back the third round of tears.

"She's fine. Her vitals are normal and you can take her home."

"Thank you," Jamie said to the doctor.

"My pleasure." He ruffled Shayna's hair a bit. "Maybe find a new flavor of ice cream next time."

She grinned.

Me? My heart ached and my gut churned with too much nausea to smile.

"Let's go, Shay." Jamie picked her up. I followed them out to the front.

"I want to ride with Lake."

That precious little girl had no idea that she almost died because I froze when she needed me most. Her innocence and unconditional love nearly shattered my hurting heart.

"Hi, Shayna. Lake's car is not here. I'm taking her home. You can see her tomorrow." Flint smiled at her. I wasn't used to seeing Flint smile. Maybe Shayna brought the best out of everyone.

"Sweetie, do you remember Flint?" I asked.

She nodded.

"Well, he got that gumball out of your throat. Flint's your hero today." I found a small smile.

Shayna's eyes grew big as she looked at Flint. "You did?"

Flint shrugged, like saving little girls from gumballs lodged in their throat was a daily occurrence for him.

"What do you say, Shay?" Jamie prompted.

"Thank you." Even Shayna wasn't immune to the aura of importance and authority that always seemed to envelope the space around Flint Hopkins. Her eyes stayed glued to him.

"You're welcome."

"I'm so relieved you're okay." I hugged her. "I'll see you at home."

She nodded as Jamie waved and took her to the exit.

"Shall we?"

I nodded, giving Flint a blank stare. The man was an enigma—a hard-ass with a million layers, and I had no idea what he kept hidden beneath them. I wasn't sure I really wanted to know.

FLINT ESCORTED me to my apartment. I must have been in really bad shape.

"My car—"

"I already have someone bringing it."

"My key—"

"I took it from your purse."

My eyes narrowed.

"You were a bit distracted."

I opened my door. "Did you steal my wallet too?"

"No, but I thought about taking your phone so you wouldn't be tempted to call our boy."

Needing Cage so desperately and feeling cut off from him held a special kind of pain. "How bad does it have to get?"

"What do you mean?" Flint stayed at the threshold to my apartment as I tossed my bag on the counter and picked up Trzy.

"If Shayna almost dying doesn't warrant bothering Cage, then what does?"

"Had she died, I would have called him myself."

"Fuck you." I glared at him. I didn't know if that was his messed-up version of trying to be funny, but I found no humor in it. I just needed Cage so badly it hurt all over.

"Ask any NFL wife and she'll tell you this is the life. Sacrifice. Sacrifice. Sacrifice."

"I'm not his wife."

"All the more reason to not call him."

"He might call me. He hasn't in a couple of days."

"I'm not doing this with you, Lake. You know what's best. Just go take a bath, have a glass of wine, whatever you need to do to let the day go." He went to shut the door.

"Flint?"

He turned.

"Thank you."

I didn't anticipate the pause, the diversion of his eyes to the ground between us, the wrinkle of pain on his forehead. "I drank."

Was it a statement or a confession?

My body froze. I feared a single move would scare him and he'd swallow back the words that I knew he needed to say.

"I had a wife ... and a drinking problem. I had a son ... and a drinking problem. It was my birthday. We went to dinner. I always drank. She tried to take the keys. I didn't let her. Told her I was fine ... I wasn't fine. Do you know how deafening screeching tires are to your ears?" He stared at the floor or into his past. "Do you know how the sound of bending metal embeds itself so deep into your mind you can never ever forget it?"

I did. I knew *exactly* what that sounded like and how it never went away.

"Cage was driving home behind us. She was trapped."

I gasped. *I* was trapped.

"The car was on fire. Cage got our son out. He got me out ... he couldn't get her out. She was trapped." He looked up. "Cage saved me and my son. I owe him. I'll always owe him. Football is his dream. I want to give him his dream."

I tried to nod. Maybe I did. From halfway across the country, Flint rescued me from the beach with just a phone call. He appeared like a guardian angel when Shayna wasn't breathing. And I knew if I asked him why, he would have said he did it for Cage. I finally knew why.

"Today you gave Shayna a second chance at life. I think your talent extends beyond sports stars and diffusing headline scandals."

Flint nodded once, still holding a world of confusion in his expression.

"Good night."

"Night, Flint."

CHAPTER TWENTY-FIVE

GAME DAY

"It sucks watching my teammates kiss their wives and girlfriends or play with their kids on the field between practices."

I barely slept. Between my normal torturous sleeping pattern and Shayna nearly dying the day before, my brain waded its way through a thick fog. But Cage's voice, like the rest of him, awakened me in every possible way.

"Then don't watch them." I yawned, sprawled out on the couch, rubbing Trzy's partial ear. She liked it. Why? Because she was Trzy.

"I have told you that you're welcome, even encouraged, to come visit me. Right?"

Tryz shook her head real quick. She'd hit her ear-rubbing limit.

"Yes. You've mentioned it a few dozen times."

"But ... I have yet to see you, and I'm missing you so fucking badly I'm beginning to..." he lowered his voice "... hate football."

I gasped. "No."

"Yes."

"You should quit and I'll quit my job too. We can play with Trzy all day, or go fishing. I bet Trzy would like fishing." I laughed.

"What a coincidence. We're both dreaming about quitting our jobs to play with pussy."

"That's crude."

Cage chuckled. "Ya think?"

"I do."

"Seriously. Why are you torturing me by staying away?"

I picked at my lower lip while formulating an answer that would make sense. "I've been busy."

"It's a day trip. You'd better have something more concrete than that."

I rolled my eyes. Good thing he couldn't see my guilty grin. "I don't know ... I haven't really heard any feedback from Flint or anyone else as to how you're doing—how you're playing. I mean ... you could totally be sucking it up on the field. For all I know, they may have drafted or traded some amazing quarterback who is ready to shove your ass to the bench. I have too many people who follow me or see me on social media. I can't be that girl with the over-hyped, second-string football stud. It's too embarrassing. I have my own reputation to think about."

"You need to come see me so I can put something in your mouth to stop your endless rambling of bullshit chatter. Seriously, why haven't you been here?"

I flipped on the laser pointer which sent Trzy into a spastic chase. "I think I distract you—"

"Flint. He said something, didn't he? Stupid fucker."

"No. Well, no more than his normal spiel. Let's face it. A month ago you were ready to quit the NFL to teach and be with me. On a scale of one to ten I was flattered by that gesture at a firm eleven. However, I think you're too young to throw this away. I'm not making you choose between me and your job. I'd never make you choose. I need to know your head is where it needs to be right now. You've said it yourself, nothing is worth doing half-assed. I'll be at your first preseason game this weekend. Camp is almost over, and then you can stick whatever the hell you'd like in my mouth. Okay?"

"Fuck me, Lake ... stop saying that shit. I'm so goddamn desperate to be buried inside of you."

I patted myself on the back, which I wasn't accustomed to doing, but it was crazy how those words just flowed from my mouth and I meant every one of them. They came out and blocked the pain of what had happened with Shayna. Flint was right. She was OK and the what-ifs didn't matter. Life existed in the what is, not the what was or what if. Ben died. Shayna lived. None of it needed to affect Cage in that moment.

"I've got to go, babe. I'll see you after the game. Okay?"

I nodded, swiping my tears. Gah! The emotions. I welcomed them. They confirmed every damn day that I was still alive. "Cage?"

"Yeah?"

"Don't forget to love me."

"Impossible."

"LAW?" I stared at the back of Jamie's Minnesota jersey.

"It's my last name."

"I know. But Shayna's has Banks. Why don't you have one with an actual player's name?"

Jamie led us to our seats like he owned the place. "Because you wear a jersey once and then the bloke with his name on the back, ups and leaves the team and you're stuck with a jersey that's no longer relevant. At least for Shayna it's her last name too. And why are you giving me a hard time? You're not even wearing a jersey or any team wear for that matter."

I laughed. "Flint told me to dress neutral. It's a preseason game, but he said fans can still get out of control, and since I've been in the media, wearing a Monaghan jersey could be like a target on my back."

"Oh. My. Gosh!" Shayna gasped as the stadium came into view, both teams on the field doing pre-game warm ups.

"Ahh ..." I smiled, closing my eyes for a brief moment. "Nothing quite like the smell of sweat and grass."

"It's artificial turf."

"Shut it, Jamie." I nudged his elbow as we squeezed past fans already seated. "I'm here. I'm excited to see Cage and Everson. Let me have my moment to get in the mood."

"Get in the mood?" He quirked a brow as we sat down with Shayna between us. "Look around you. I don't think these fans are getting into the mood. They've been dying for the start of the season since the final game of the last season. You make it sound like you don't like—"

I grimaced, biting my lips together.

"That's it."

I shook my head before he could finish.

"Yes. That's it." Jamie's eyes grew wide. "You don't like football."

My head continued to shake.

"I'm right. Does he know? Does your sports sensation know that you don't like his game?"

"I don't know what you're talking about and neither do you. I like his game just fine." My eyes homed in on said sports sensation playing catch with another player on the sideline while the rest of the team went through some stretching routine.

"Lake Jones doesn't like football." Jamie's chuckle escalated into a belly laugh.

"Shh ..." I glared at him.

"Mum's the word. Your secret is safe with me."

I rolled my eyes. Something told me my secret was far from safe.

CHAPTER TWENTY-SIX

A BAD JOKE

IN ALL HONESTY, I had to admit that watching a game from the fifty-yard line was a lot more exciting than watching a televised game. Drooling over my guy and feeding off the crowd's enthusiasm for him and his winning team that day also helped ignite my dormant football-fan status.

After the game, Jamie took Shayna home, and Flint escorted me to an area down from the locker rooms to wait for Cage to shower and make it through interviews.

"He was pissed that I didn't visit him at training camp." I twiddled my thumbs, feeling like an idiot leaning up against a concrete wall while players and press people ushered by in chaos.

Flint stood next to me, one leg bent, foot propped up on the wall behind us while he messed with his phone. "He killed it at training camp. His coaches are ecstatic about the season. Did you see him today? Three TD passes, no interceptions, no sacks. Monaghan's the real deal, something special that doesn't come along every day. He has the potential to be compared to the greats. You giving him space is the best thing you can do for him."

He *was* incredible. I couldn't deny it. The giving him space thing like I was some sort of bad influence stung a bit, but I'd learned arguing with Flint was futile at best.

"Jones, get your ass over here."

Just the sound of his voice burned my nose and sent a rush of tears pooling in my eyes. It wasn't until that very moment I fully realized how much I'd missed him over the previous three weeks.

I looked up. My smile owned my entire face as Cage walked toward me in a black suit, white shirt, and a violet, gray, and white tie. In his hand was a note card.

CHAPTER EIGHT

Screw Flint's motto of control and looking just right for the media. Screw the photographers and reporters. I ran into his arms and my God they felt so good.

"I missed you," I choked out.

Cage held me so tightly breathing became a challenge. I didn't care.

"If only someone would have invited you to visit me at training camp."

"Shut up." I laughed and swatted my tears before too many cameras zoomed in on my emotional state.

"Stick, are you seriously crying?"

Cage loosened his hold on me, letting me slide to my feet.

"Miss me, Apollo?"

His smile faded. "How's Shay?"

Cage furrowed his brow. I returned a tight grin.

"She's fine."

Flint, still perched against the wall, peeked up from his phone giving me a barely noticeable head shake.

"Was she sick?" Cage asked.

I looked at Everson.

"Yeah, but she's fine now. Right?"

My response was delayed. I still couldn't think about it without wanting to crawl into a corner and cry over what could have happened on my watch. "She's great. Loved the game and can't wait for you to get home."

"I'll call her. A few of us are going out for dinner. You guys in?"

My eyes shifted to Cage. "You can go ... I don't have to—"

"Some other wives will be there too," Everson added.

"She's not his wife." Flint felt it necessary to state the obvious.

"Fact." Everson rested his hand on Cage's shoulder. "But she's vying for that coveted spot." He smirked at me. "After the Twins game she said she was going to marry you."

I died, like a brutal town-square slaying. I couldn't believe he said that.

Cage squinted a bit as my eyes remained the size of silver dollars.

"No worries. I told her you were married to the game for now."

"Fucking right," Flint added. "Super bowl MVP, buddy. If you keep playing like you did today ... if you stay focused ..." I didn't have to look at Flint to know he was glaring at me. "Then I think we'll be dancing in confetti come February."

Cage nodded, his gaze still glued to me as I shriveled beneath it. "I think we're going home, Banks. But thanks ... next time. Come on, Lake." He grabbed my hand and pulled me toward the doors.

"Later." Everson smirked at me like a sibling who just pinned the broken vase incident on the younger child and watched them get hauled off for punishment.

By the time we made it to his truck, my heart was lodged in my throat. "It was a joke." I bit my lip and grimaced before he shut my door. It was a half-truth. Of course I wanted to marry Cage, but I didn't mean it like a goal, like my intention was to chase him and trap him.

"It's fine, Lake." He smiled and shut my door.

On instinct, my mind shifted into overdrive trying to analyze his smile, the tone of his voice, even his gait as he moved around the front of the truck. Was he mad? Scared? Confused? Disappointed?

"You mad?" I didn't even finish before I regretted asking the most clichéd couple's question ever. I was the youngest of five kids. I'd watched my parents and all my siblings and their spouses have the typical fights with the typical lines, and I swore I would never engage in that same behavior. Learning not to judge was a very humbling lesson.

"I'm not mad."

Great. Cage knew the typical answer. "I'm not mad" could mean "I'm not mad" or it could mean "I'm pissed, just not ready to talk about it."

I begged myself to just not speak, to dig deep and find control. Silence held an invisible power. If I could let it be—let us be—then maybe everything would be okay. Emotions needed time to find words.

When we got to his house, I eased out of his truck and followed him inside. He said nothing. I said nothing. He grabbed a sports drink from the refrigerator and guzzled it down with his back to me. Cage looked breathtakingly handsome in his suit. I wanted to tell him that. I wanted to tell him how much my hands ached to touch him. I wanted to tear open my soul and beg him to just love me as a friend, as a lover, as absolutely any person he wanted me to be, as long as that me was with him. That's all that mattered.

He was good at silence. Me? Not so much.

"I don't want to marry you." Lies. Why the lies? I just couldn't figure it out. The silence was killing me, and all I wanted was for it to stop. Like a gun to my head, I did whatever it took to make it stop. "In fact if you asked me to marry you, I'd say no, so ... really, just forget about it. I'm pretty sure I was still asleep when Everson knocked on my door."

Cage turned. God ... he was so handsome, my heart struggled to keep up with my lungs or maybe it was the other way around. Whatever it was, he left me so breathless, captivated, and at the complete mercy of his next move, his next word, his next breath.

A faint smile tried to claim his lips as he exhaled what sounded like the hint of a laugh. "I played to impress you today."

My lips parted as my body stiffened, eyes flitting side to side as if someone else was in the room, because the guy that Flint referred to as the future Super bowl MVP did not just say he played to impress *me*!?!

"It's the only way I can do this. I can no longer love the game unless I can convince myself I'm playing it for you. I used to play for my dad, but then I met you and..." he set the plastic bottle on the counter and shrugged, still staring at it like his next words were written on the label "...I kinda like you—a lot. I like our story. I like falling in love with you every day. I like seeing all your emotions in your eyes—"

"They're tears." I rolled said teary eyes toward the ceiling and fought them off with rapid blinks. "I'm so sick of you making me cry."

He laughed as he shrugged off his suit jacket, folding it

then resting it on the back of the barstool before threading his fingers in my hair. "Just so you know, I heard every word you said. I promise I'll never ask you to marry me. Okay?"

No. NO. NOOOO!!!

I'd have rather been the boy who got eaten by a wolf than the girl who never got proposed to by the man of her dreams. Lies. Damn the lies!

I cleared my throat, forcing myself to breathe as the horror show played out in front of me. Cage would never ask me to marry him. Fan-flipping-tastic. Why didn't we just declare abstinence and agree on pen pal status so we wouldn't even have to make time to see each other?

"Say something. You look like you just saw a ghost." He smirked.

My eyes moved—up, down, side to side—but the rest of my body remained paralyzed. I could see how I must have looked spooked.

"No. I-I'm happy." *Don't be contumacious, Lake. Don't let your stubbornness be the sword that slays your dreams.* Too late. "I can't tell you how ... uh ... *relieved* I am to know that I can just enjoy our relationship without the looming fear of you doing something ridiculous like proposing to me and ruining everything." Fucking idiot. Whoever came up with that term had me in mind. My picture belonged pasted in the dictionary next to it.

Cage brushed his lips against mine. "However..." he whispered "...I want kids someday."

Gulp.

"Would you consider being my baby mama?"

My head snapped back. "Baby mama?"

He nodded.

My lips moved but no audible words were formed at first. "Y-you want me to have your babies?"

"Absolutely. Not like a dozen or anything, and not right away. Maybe two over the next eight to ten years."

It was a joke, right? It had to be a joke, a classic calling of my bluff.

Contumacious.

Contumacious.

Contumacious.

I shrugged. *What the hell are you doing, Lake!* "Sure. Absolutely. Why not start now?" I couldn't say for sure if it was the adrenaline rush from his game, our weeks spent apart, or Shayna's near-death experience, but reason—all common sense—vanished from the room. The only thing that would prevent me from possibly being impregnated right there in the kitchen was Cage. Would he call mercy?

His eyes widened a fraction. "Now?"

"Sure. Carpe diem. It's August. Nine months would give us a baby in May—still off season for you."

He had to hear my heart. I could control my facial expressions, even my labored breaths were easy to stifle, but my heart surging in my chest felt like it was vibrating the whole house.

"Let's do it. Carpe diem!"

Oh. My. Holy. Hell!

Cage slammed his mouth to mine. He tasted like the mint he popped in his mouth on the way home mixed with a sweet essence from his drink. Within seconds, that vanished and all I tasted was his hunger. I felt his impatience. And I breathed him in so completely. He was oxygen and every cell in my body begged for more of him. Paralysis continued to grip my whole body, but it didn't matter. His hands made haste ripping off my clothes.

"I love you." Those three words melted from his lips as he brushed them past my ear. Those three words always affirmed what he told me in China. *This means something.*

Penny was right. Cage had to say them. Sometimes they came out jumbled with a string of dirty expletives, but he always ... *always* said it.

"I love you too," I whispered, searching for my breath as I tilted my head back and closed my eyes. "I missed you ... so much."

As he reached for the latch to my bra, I pulled away and shook my head slowly. A flirty grin played along my lips. "This is such a crime." I reached for his tie and loosened it. "I'm so conflicted. You in a suit is just so unfair to the rest of the male population. I know what lies beneath and my hands ache to feel you, but my thirsty eyes can't stop drinking you in. This suit was made for you." I laughed, sliding his tie from under his collar, loving how much it turned me on to unwrap him like the greatest of all gifts. "It *was* made for you. Wasn't it?"

He smirked then wet his lips, a piece of heaven alight in his blue eyes. "I wore it for you."

Setting his tie on the kitchen counter, I bit my lip and grinned. "For me, huh?" My fingers worked the buttons to his crisp white shirt. "That's a lot. You played to impress me today *and* you wore this sexy, makes-me-weak-in-the-knees suit for me too?"

He started unbuttoning his shirt at the bottom and we met in the middle, his fingers ghosting over mine, sending tingling chills along my skin. My body shimmied with a shiver. Cage laughed. I shrugged. There was no way to hide the palpable, visible, completely phenomenal effect he had on me.

My hands pressed flat to the hard planes of his chest.

He sucked in a long breath. Our smiles faded. His hooded eyes darkened as his jaw clenched.

"Lake?"

"Hmm?" My lungs drew in a shaky breath. Whenever we touched I felt the flames along my skin. The heat made it hard to breathe.

"I meant what I said."

I nodded. Every nerve along my flesh begged him for one look, one touch, one breath. The truth? In that moment I didn't make the connection. He'd said so many things to me.

He cradled my face and kissed me while I unfastened his pants. I ate up every bit of his hunger and made it my own. Cage touched me in a way that made me feel invincible and utterly fragile at the same time. The moment my back hit the counter, he lifted me onto it, never releasing my lips. My fingers eased into his hair as he unfastened my bra with deft fingers.

"Jesus, Cage ..." My mouth broke from his, gasping while he palmed my breasts, sliding his right thumb over my nipple. It fed the heavy ache between my legs.

"So much..." he dotted kisses down my neck to my chest "...love..." his tongue eased along the swell of my breasts as his hands gripped my hips "...for this woman."

My breath caught. *This woman* ... It's like his words weren't even meant for me. They felt like a whisper of gratitude to ... God?

Tilting my chin down, I just watched him love me. I would never forget the way his lips molded so perfectly to my skin or the way his long lashes rested on his cheeks, eyes closed like it was all just a dream.

Eyes that saw more of me than I saw of myself, looked

up at me. He stood straight and slid down his pants and briefs just enough to free his erection.

Holy fuck.

Messy bronze hair, sun-kissed skin peeking out from the white shirt that still hung from his broad shoulders, and his cock ready, and waiting for *me*. Wake up, Lake ... that's all I could think.

His fingers curled under the waist of my panties, and he pulled them down and over both my legs. As he let them drop to the floor his eyes lingered on my pretty prosthetic leg for a moment before meeting my gaze with a questioning look. My eyes flitted between his and his cock.

"Leave it," I said with a bit too much desperation in my voice.

That. That should have been the moment because that had always been the moment he used his magic to produce a condom out of thin air. Okay, his pocket, but really ... same thing. No magic that night. Just his fingers teasing my entrance until he deemed me ready for him—wet, breathless, desperate, and blind to anything but his touch.

Stop. Wait. Don't. Or a million other synonyms would have been appropriate in the moment.

He said nothing.

I. Said. Nothing.

Our mouths connected. He lifted me off the counter. I wrapped my legs around him and for the first time ever, I felt his warm, hard length slide inside of me—flesh to flesh. It was the most ineffable feeling. It was the most ineffable moment. It was love and lust and blinding emotions trumping every single ounce of common sense.

Fuck common sense.

Fuck gravity.

With Cage I never wanted to stop falling.

CHAPTER TWENTY-SEVEN

OH BABY!

CAGE

MY DAD KEPT ME GROUNDED. I never asked for more than I needed. Wants were a luxury for the greedy. Every action was preceded by intellectual contemplation. There was no room for impulsiveness if the mind stayed focused.

I never did drugs, not so much as a joint. I never drank beyond the legal limit unless I was in my own apartment, and by my senior year of college I abstained from all alcohol. Something shifted when my dad died. All the anger I had was channeled into this razor-sharp focus on being the best. My body became a temple. The game became everything.

But then ... Lake.

She became my drug, a heady cocktail of everything. The high I got from her was beyond anything imaginable. I was addicted and I acted like a fucking junkie around her. I *wanted* and I *took* over and over again. The greed was a drug of its own, so was the impulsiveness. With her I'd jump off any cliff without looking down ... without looking back.

I felt it. I could have stopped. I could have pulled out, but—addiction, greed, impulsiveness, *her*. With Lake's back pinned against the oversized door to my pantry, I rocked up into her one last time. Filling her with *all* of me. Her breathy cry and her tight pussy clenching my dick made me harder even as I came inside of her.

I came inside of her.

I should have pulled out, but I didn't. Instead, I grazed my teeth along her shoulder, nipping at her skin. The salty taste enticing me to *take* more. Ducking my head, I sucked her nipple into my mouth. When I bit down, her pussy clenched again around my cock, and just like that I was so fucking hard again.

"Cage," she moaned my name, her head falling back against the door as she ground against me. "More ..."

A drug ... Lake Jones was *the* drug for me. I'd happily die high on her. No regrets.

LAKE

My fingers relinquished their grip on his dress shirt that was no longer white and crisp. The wet, sweat-stained fabric clung to his chest as he eased me onto the bed, slowly pulling out of me as he stood. He could have dropped me to my feet in the kitchen, but he didn't. It was just another one of a million things Cage did that showed me how much he loved me.

With slightly-narrowed eyes on me, he tucked himself back into his briefs.

I felt his look. I felt it warm and starting to trickle out of me.

What. Did. We. Do?

I sat up and hurried to the bathroom.

"Lake?" he called after me.

"I'm ... I'm just going to take a quick bath." Reality shot through my veins, bringing on a whole new round of sweat, jolting my heart into overdrive, and robbing my lungs of all oxygen.

What. Did. We. Do?

After sitting on the toilet praying for gravity to be stronger than sperm, I turned on the faucet. I propped my prosthetic up against the wall and sat on the edge of the tub to remove the socket and peel off the liner. Easing into the steamy water, it felt so good I moaned. Would it be my last hot bath? Were pregnant women restricted to warm baths? Was I pregnant? Could I even be pregnant that fast?

A chaotic zoo of thoughts crowed my mind. There was always the morning after pill. Would that defeat the purpose of offering to be Cage's baby mama? Thaddeus ... he would kill me. I wasn't sure if he was serious about me needing new legs for pregnancy. Would an expanding belly really change my leg?

"Hey." Cage smiled as he cracked open the door, like he needed an invite to come into his own bathroom.

"Hi." I shoved as much enthusiasm, as much yay-we're-having-a-baby into my voice as possible. The lines along his brow reflected I failed to hit the mark. Maybe I wasn't such a good liar after all. "You look tired."

He peeled off his shirt. "Just a side effect of game day. When the adrenaline, especially after a win, wears off, all that's left are an aching body and exhaustion."

In that moment I felt guilty about the sex, beyond the

minor detail that we may have in fact created a life. I was the one who requested he nail me to the wall. Okay, I didn't use those exact words, but when he started to carry me out of the kitchen I said, "No. Right here." The only way he could make *here* work was to use the pantry door.

"Shit. I didn't even think about that. I'm sorry. We should not have—"

He shook his head. "It's fine." He removed his pants and briefs.

Fine. What was fine? Nailing me to the wall or unprotected sex? There was nothing awkward about that moment. The pathetic part was he had me so turned on again, standing there naked.

I closed my eyes and tried to do the impossible: clear my mind. I heard the shower and a few seconds later Cage groaned. He was in pain. I was a greedy little hussy. On a deep breath I slid under the water. I loved dull white noise that could only be experienced under water, like holding my breath stopped time, even if just for a few seconds.

"Ah!" I gasped as Cage pulled me from my abyss.

"Jesus, Lake!" He stood over me dripping cold water, eyes wide.

"What?" I coughed. Startled by unexpected hands gripping my arms, I inhaled a little water on the way up.

"You weren't moving."

I coughed a little more, clearing the last of the water from my windpipe. "That's because I was holding still."

He released my arms and stepped in the tub, wedging his cold body behind mine as he exhaled a heavy sigh.

"Why are you so cold?"

"Cold shower. Muscle recovery."

I leaned my back against his chest as he wrapped his

arms around me. He was like a gigantic ice cube stealing the heat from my water.

"I didn't mean to scare you."

"What were you doing?" His voice still held an edge of anger or maybe just concern.

"I was wetting my hair."

"For like ... five minutes?"

I laughed. "No, for like ten seconds."

"Lake ... we need to talk." His large hands covered mine, interlacing our fingers.

Even in the water I could feel the hard calloused patches on his fingers and palms. "About?"

"Everything."

I braced for the same lecture I'd already given myself a hundred times over since the incident in the kitchen. The fact that I thought of it as an "incident" just proved that we needed to discuss it.

"I have this love/hate relationship with my feelings about you."

"Oh God ... you're breaking up with me." I tried to sit up as my heart braced for impact.

Cage tightened his hold on me. "What? No. No. Why would you think that?"

"Because people have a 'love/hate relationship' with things they feel guilty about, and guilt is the equivalent of a flesh-eating bacteria for emotions."

"I regret nothing. Not even calling your bluff in the most dog-pissing-on-a-fire-hydrant way."

"Calling my bluff?" I knew. I just wanted him to say it. I was such a coward.

He kissed the top of my head. "I want to know more than your neighbors, Lake. If you're going to marry me, then I want to know before Banks."

"It was a jok—" I jumped as he bit the back of my ear.

"It wasn't a joke. Not wanting to marry me ... *that* was a joke."

"Now you're just being arrogant." I nudged my knee into his leg.

"I'm not. I'm just being honest. I don't ever want another man to touch you. I want every baby that ever grows in your belly to be mine."

Fuck the tears ... here they come.

"I want you to call me first when someone steals your leg ... even if I completely lose it and have to call Flint."

I laughed, biting my lips together to keep my emotions in check.

"And when I tell you to get your ass to my training camp because I'm fucking dying to see you, then I expect you to be there without worrying about how it will affect me. Football is my job. Let me worry about it. You are my life ... worry about that. Worry about keeping yourself safe so I don't lose another person I love. Focus on our future because, Lake ... you are my future and I *will* marry you, even if I have to drag you to the altar and fuck a yes out of you."

I practically choked on that statement. Promise? Threat? Then I waited. He addressed everything except the most looming issue of our future.

"Ask me," he whispered in my ear.

The lump in my throat had its own pulse like the timer to a bomb counting down. I had nothing to fear and I knew it, but I just couldn't will away my nerves.

"What if I'm pregnant?"

He chuckled. "You mean with the baby we agreed upon like ... an hour ago?"

I nodded. "Yeah, that one."

"I asked you."

"I know."

"I gave you a chance to change your mind."

All true statements.

"I know."

He pinched my waist, eliciting a jump. "Your turn."

"My turn?"

"To call my bluff."

My head inched side to side. "I don't know what you're talking about."

"Oh, come on ... this is the part where you tell me you're on the pill then scold me for being so irresponsible."

My eyes leapt from their sockets. "You've had this conversation before?"

"No, but friends of mine have."

I pried free from his arms and lifted myself to the edge of the tub.

"Where are you going?"

I grabbed a towel and dried off. "Home."

"What? It's late. Just stay."

My hands shook as I fought with my liner. It was a bitch to get on if my leg wasn't dried well.

"Are you mad?"

Once my leg was secured, I stood, wrapping the towel around myself. "Let's not be that couple that asks if the other is mad when *clearly* the other is mad. I said it to you earlier and I should not have. So ... I'm sorry—"

"I really wasn't mad, just confused by your reaction to what Banks said, that's all. But you ... *you're* really mad at me."

"Yes! Yes, I am." I marched out to retrieve my clothes from the kitchen, but I didn't have to because he had them neatly draped over the back of the chair next to his closet door. His considerateness irritated the hell out of me.

"What the hell? I don't understand."

I refused to look at him hovering over me with a black towel tied low on his waist, water rivulets racing down his skin.

"I don't play that game, you big idiot!" I fastened my jeans and tugged on my shirt, leaving my bra on the chair.

"Lake!"

I made a dash for the back door. "Dammit!" I pressed the heels of my hands to my forehead. "I didn't drive," I whispered to myself. So much for my dramatic exit.

When his hands gripped my arms to turn me toward him, I didn't even fight it. My eyes wandered over his bare chest and running shorts.

Cage sighed then lifted my chin with his finger. Defeat stole my tears, leaving me with a blank stare and the occasional blink.

"You're not on the pill," he said in a monotone voice like the answer to two plus two just came to him when he should have known it all along.

"I'm not on the pill," I whispered.

CAGE

My dad laughed at me from Heaven or Hell, or maybe it was his ghost shadowing me every day. I could hear him calling me young and stupid. The truth? I *was* still young and stupid.

Lake looked at me and I knew she was waiting for me to lie, but I wasn't going to lie to her. Yet I knew the hardest part would be convincing her that my words were, in fact, the truth.

"I'm sorry for making a terribly irresponsible assumption. I'm sorry if you're pregnant and you don't want to be. But if I'm completely honest with you, I wanted everything that happened in the kitchen. And even if I felt pretty certain you were on birth control, there was ... there *is* a very visceral part of me that wants to make a life with you. And for that, I cannot feel one ounce of regret."

She didn't speak. I needed her to say something. Anything.

"You agreed to be my baby mama, Lake. You let me come in you ... twice."

Her face turned crimson. "I don't have a car here."

"Just as well. You're not going anywhere." I grabbed her hand. "Come on. I'm starving. My baby probably is too."

"Not funny," she grumbled, following me into the kitchen.

"Have a seat. Put your feet up before your ankles start to swell."

"Still not funny. Actually ... it's a little funny. I only have one foot and ankle."

"Lake." Giving her a narrow-eyed look, I grabbed her waist and lifted her onto the counter, where everything had started earlier. She teased her fingers along my cheeks and into my hair. God, I loved her touch.

"What if we're having a baby?" she whispered.

I turned my head and kissed the inside of her wrist. I craved the feel of her soft skin in that very spot, maybe because it always smelled like flowers, like that was where she dotted her perfume.

"What if we're having a baby?" My lips, pressed against her skin, curled into the biggest shit-eating grin.

CHAPTER TWENTY-EIGHT

THE ITCH

LAKE

"Let me get this straight. He kinda sorta but not 100 percent thought you were on the pill and you just ... were OK with being his baby mama?" Penny handed me a glass of wine.

I shook my head. "Baby."

She rolled her eyes and tucked her leg under her as she sat at my kitchen table across from me. "A little red wine is good for baby and good for mama, that's assuming you're even pregnant. Please tell me you've considered the real possibility that you're not actually pregnant."

"I have, but I have this really strong feeling that I am."

"Nausea?"

I shook my head.

"Overly tired?"

I shrugged. "Well, no more than normal."

"Tender, swollen breasts?"

Head shake.

"Missed period?"

I rolled my eyes. "This just happened yesterday."

"Exactly, honey. Feeling schmeeling. Take it from the expert." Penny jabbed a thumb at her chest. "It's not as easy to get pregnant as you think. If it were ... I'd have twenty kids." She smirked. "With twenty different fathers."

"But we had it twice. That's a lot of sperm and they can live in my cervical fluid for three to five days."

"First, stop bragging about being nailed to the pantry door *twice*."

I giggled, shaking my head.

"And second, I think you need to stay off the internet. Google porn, my-young-sexy-quarterback-screwing friend. Don't Google the lifespan of sperm."

I stared into my boring glass of water. "It's so weird. We've been dating for three months and we could be having a baby together. My friend Lindsay will call me irresponsible. She abides by the time rule. No insta-love. Every event in life should be properly spaced on a timeline. She doesn't understand how coming so close to death changes all of that. Time is too precious to waste. I don't want to plan. I want to live."

"I hear ya, honey. But be prepared ... you're both pretty high right now. There's nowhere to go but down. Try to bring yourself back to the surface before life does it for you. Living comes with so much heartache, especially for those of us who *really* live." She winked. "But's it's worth it, even when you're up late reading porn while your husband snores and releases SBDs, the kind that burn your lungs and make your eyes water. The kind you can actually taste."

My nose scrunched. "No."

"Yes, ma'am. Not gonna sugarcoat it for you. Those pheromones that you crave? The ones that conceal garlic breath, armpit odor, and SBDs? You become immune to their power, and then you're left with one stinky son of a bitch. Don't get me wrong. It doesn't mean that you don't still love the stinky SOB, it just means it takes so much more than a look to wet your pussy. It takes a full moon, a recent shower, a bottle of cologne, a gallon of mouth wash, and at least three glasses of wine ... oh, and a bottle of lube." Penny sighed. "Damn hormones."

"That's so ..." I grimaced because that was my "delusional" life with Cage. It only took one look, and I honestly couldn't remember thinking he was stinky. I even loved—craved—his sweat after a workout.

"Life, honey. It's just life. I never promised Rupert forever ... not even in our wedding vows. I think the chances of going to my grave as his wife are pretty damn good at this point, but if not, I know we'll end it amicably. I don't really believe humans are meant to mate for life. I think that behavior is for animals who survive on instinct, not reason."

"And does he agree?"

"Absolutely. After all, I'm his second wife."

"I'm ... speechless. My parents still do it like rabbits."

Penny shrugged. "Maybe they're the exception. Or maybe they enjoy recreational drugs."

"I doubt my parents ..." I bit my lip and rolled my eyes to the ceiling. "Hmm, you could be right."

"Everyone has their own story." She winked and I knew she was referring to my "story" with Cage. "Make yours memorable. That's the best you can hope for."

"And if I'm pregnant?"

Penny chuckled a bit before finishing the last of her wine. "It's a crazy plot twist. That I can guarantee you."

Were we ready for a plot twist?

After therapy with Penny, I did some laundry and packed for my trip to San Francisco to meet with Thaddeus for a new fitting. Cage texted every chance he got to see how I was feeling. It was sweet and a little unnerving at the same time. Could I handle nine months of constant checking up on me?

There was a soft knock at my door. I checked the peephole, blinking several times before seeing the pint-sized figure with pigtails.

"Shayna! Hi sweetie, where's—" As soon as Jamie appeared at Everson's door I squinted my eyes. "Playing cops and robbers?" I inspected his bandana-covered face, kitchen goggles, and vinyl gloves. "Or did you clog the toilet?"

"Have you had chicken pox?" he asked.

"Um ... yeah. Why?"

Shayna pulled up her shirt, exposing her torso dotted with red, blistered spots. "I didn't eat chicken."

I smiled. "Of course you didn't."

"I haven't had them. Haven't had the vaccine either," Jamie mumbled behind the bandana.

"A nanny who hasn't had the chicken pox. That's crazy."

He shrugged. "Most kids are vaccinated. Flu vaccines are the most common request for my job."

"It's quite possible you've already been exposed."

"I fear that too." He sighed.

"I'm leaving for San Francisco in the morning."

"I messaged Everson. He hasn't had them either."

"What? Jeez, were you both raised in sterile homes?"

"I can check with Penny."

"Lake..." Shayna gave me her puppy-dog eyes and pouty lip "...I need you. I have a feeder."

"You mean a fever?"

She nodded.

"I'll owe you," Jamie added.

"You always owe me. Everson always owes me. Something tells me I'm never going to get paid."

"Hey, I'm keeping your secret safe."

"What secret?" My brow furrowed.

"Your I-hate-football secret."

"I don't h—"

"You hate football?" Shayna asked.

He was blowing it out of proportion. Cage knew I didn't "follow" football, but saying I hated it was just not good.

Jamie didn't have to worry about chicken pox; I was ready to kill him on the spot.

"No. I don't hate football. Go." I nodded to Jamie. "Go home and scratch yourself. I hope you get a heavy dose of the rash on your t-e-s-t-i-c-l-e-s."

"Testicles?" Shayna looked up at me.

My jaw plummeted to the ground. Jamie snickered.

"Forgot to mention we've been working a lot on spelling. She's really smart."

My lips twisted. "Hmm ... yes, she is."

"What are testicles?"

"A part of the body only boys have."

"Like a penis?"

I sighed. There really was no use trying to do anything but be honest with Ms. Smarty Pants. "Yes. Testicles are close friends with the penis."

She nodded with a thoughtful expression on her face.

"So ... you're good?" Jamie was halfway to the elevator.

"Peachy, just peachy." I glared at him then smiled at Shayna.

Lake: *Shayna has chicken pox. Neither Jamie nor Everson have had them so I'm not going to SF tomorrow because I have a little, itchy roommate for the next week or until she's no longer contagious.*
Cage: *I heard. Banks is staying at a hotel for the night until his cleaning lady can decontaminate his place in the morning.*
Lake: *Pathetic. Have you had them?*
Cage: *Of course. How are you feeling?*

I LAUGHED. There it was.

Lake: *Hungry. I have no food in the house since I was planning on leaving town, but now I'm not.*
Cage: *Got it.*

A well-earned eye roll followed his text.

Lake: *Please don't send Flint to the store for me.*
Cage: *Why not?*
Lake: *It's not his job.*
Cage: *His job is whatever I say it is for the day.*
Lake: *He doesn't know what to get.*
Cage: *I'll tell him.*
Lake: *You don't know.*
Cage: *Marshmallows, bread, flax waffles, almond milk, chocolate hazelnut butter, green-tip bananas, ripe avocados, organic eggs, low sodium Spanish rice … I know what you eat. ;) I'll have him get itch stuff for Shayna along with hummus and carrots for her. Banks said she eats a ton of it. Work calls. I'll come by later. 9 ish.*
Lake: *Don't forget to love me.*

Cage: *Impossible.*

He knocked me over with his astute observations of my eating habits and the fact that Everson knew that Shayna loved hummus was a bit endearing as well. I knew he loved her.

"You feel bad?" I frowned at Shayna curled up on my sofa.

"I think—"

"Oh, sweetie ..." I rushed to the sofa but not before she was bent over the side of it, vomiting. Luckily it missed my rug, staying confined to the hardwood floor.

"Lake ..." Tears filled her eyes.

I grabbed a few tissues off the coffee table and blotted her eyes and then her mouth. "I know. It's no fun to be sick."

Three hours later Flint arrived with bags of groceries.

"I really appreciate you doing this. I know it's probably not in your job description." I started to take the groceries out of the bag as Flint walked over to the sofa and looked a Shayna sleeping.

"What's this?" I asked.

"Stuff for Shayna. Everything in that bag is for her: Baking soda, Epsom salt, brown vinegar, ground oatmeal, homemade anti-itch cream, essential oils, Jasmine tea, coriander and carrot juice with honey, and I upped the fruits and vegetables on the list Cage gave me. She needs to eat well to heal properly."

Who was the guy in front of me?

"A 'homemade' anti-itch salve. Whose home?" I chuckled, looking at the amber glass container with no label, just 'itch salve' written in permanent marker on the white lid.

"I made it."

I looked up at him with wide eyes. "You?"

He shrugged. "A simple internet search and a trip to Whole Foods. No big deal. I also emailed you instructions on how to use everything."

Flint Hopkins was Mother Teresa in a custom-tailored suit. I imagined him concocting an itch salve in his kitchen, wearing a manly apron over his suit, maybe with his jacket off and sleeves rolled up to his elbows.

"Thank you. I'm sort of ... speechless."

He held up his hand. "Really it was nothing." He turned the door handle. "Call me if you have any questions or need anything else."

I moved to him, wrapping my arms around his neck. He stiffened like a board. Then I kissed his cheek. He cleared his throat as I released him.

"You're a good man, Flint."

He gave me a weak smile.

"Lake ..." Shayna called with a raspy voice.

I rushed over to her, making sure the vomit bucket was within reach. When I looked back, Flint was gone.

CHAPTER TWENTY-NINE

LET ME LOVE YOU

CAGE

I KNOCKED ON HER DOOR.

No answer.

I knocked again.

"I'm up to my ears in puke, let yourself in!"

A grimace plastered itself to my face before I even opened the door. It was wrong, so very wrong that I got hard instantly when her tiny, short-clad ass welcomed me, wiggling side to side as she scrubbed the floor on her hands and knees.

"Hey." I bit my tongue before "How ya doing?" came out. "Where's Shay?"

"Tub. Oatmeal bath slash vomit rinse off." She tossed the sponge and wad of paper towels into the bucket and stood, sweaty hair matted to her face. Even then, with blue kitchen gloves up to her elbows and her soiled shirt clinging to her chest, I wanted to grab her and kiss the life out of her.

"Anything I can do? Feed Trzy? Clean her litter box?"

Lake sighed. "Funny, but no. I'm going to get her out of

the tub, cover her with Flint's anti-itch salve, and put her to bed." She set the bucket on the counter and peeled off her gloves. After brushing past me toward the bathroom, she stopped and retreated a few steps. "Hi." A tiny smile graced her face, and she fisted my shirt and pulled me to her lips for a kiss.

"Hi." I grinned.

"Take a load off. You look tired." She continued toward the bathroom.

A few minutes later Shayna shuffled out in her jammies and wet hair then sat on the couch.

"Hey, pumpkin. Not feeling well, huh?"

She frowned and shook her head.

"I'll be out in a minute. I'm going to put some towels over the sheets so the oily salve doesn't stain them."

"We're good." I smiled at Shayna. "Did Everson come see you?"

She shook her head. "He called."

The guy was a pussy to not at least peek in on her to say hi.

"I staying with Lake. Jamie go home with his testicles."

I gave her words a few seconds to sink in, because there was no way I heard her right.

"What did you say?"

"I staying with Lake. Jamie go home with his testicles. Lake said ..." she scratched along her ribs, a slight grimace on her face.

"Lake said?"

She shrugged. "His penis and testicles ... I thinks she er ... they're friends cause ..." Her brow furrowed like she was searching for the right words. " 'Cause she hates football. But I like football."

"Okay, sweetie, let's get you in bed." Lake smiled at Shayna. "How's Flint's itchy stuff working?"

Shayna shrugged. "Itchy." She scratched again. "A little."

"Give it a bit and I bet you'll feel better. It was nice of Flint to make it for you. Too bad you were asleep, you could have told him thank you."

"I see him. I see you hug and kiss him before he go." Her gaze shifted to me.

Mine was rigid. I couldn't stop my jaw from grinding the hell out of my teeth. All I could see was red and the panic in Lake's face confirmed it.

"Nigh nigh." Shayna gave me a sad smile before shuffling toward the bedroom.

Lake held up a finger. "Wait here and *don't* overreact." After a short stare-off like she wanted to ensure I wasn't going to leave, Lake turned and followed Shayna.

Someone was going to die. That's all that went through my head.

"What the fuck, Lake?" I tried to keep my voice low and calm, but it was nearly impossible.

"It's not what you think." She moved closer and touched my arm.

I jerked away. It's not how I meant to react, but I did it anyway and regretted it the moment I saw the shock ... the pain on her face. I hated that part of myself. It reminded me of my father, and as much as I loved him, I didn't want to be him. He destroyed my mother. At least he had an excuse. I had no fucking excuse, but I also had no control.

"I don't know what to think since in the last five minutes I've been informed that you're 'friends with Jamie's penis and testicles.'"

She flinched as her face contorted, but not in shock ... in guilt.

"And that you "hate football," and for the win ... you kissed Flint!"

She held a finger over her lips to hush me. I had too damn much anger simmering inside to be hushed. I was going to let the Jamie thing go and write it off as a six-year-old misunderstanding, but after the Flint revelation, I just couldn't.

"I'm exhausted. Shayna has thrown up three times today, and Trzy had attempted to eat it three times and later made her own vomit mess for me to clean up. When Shayna wasn't vomiting, she wanted me to cuddle with her and her body temperature is like two hundred degrees and now I'm a sticky, yucky, mess in desperate need of a shower. So I'm simply going to tell you what happened and then we're not going to talk about it anymore."

I didn't move. All I could do was glare at her, my jaw set.

She released a long breath. "I made a snarky comment to Jamie saying I hoped he ended up with chicken pox on his t-e-s-t-i-c-l-e-s, not realizing how well Shayna could spell. She asked about them then asked if they were like a penis, so I said yes, they were friends. End of story. As for the Flint thing..." closing her eyes for a moment she shook her head "...he not only brought me groceries, but he brought all this stuff for Shayna that he didn't have to bring her. Flint has done a lot for me, and before he left I gave him a 'friendly' hug and quick peck on the cheek."

Jealousy. Worst fucking feeling ever.

"I've had a long day too ... I'm going home before I say something I might regret."

LAKE

Leaving. That was his response? To leave? Everything was so innocent and meant nothing. How could he not see that?

"Really? After yesterday, you honestly think I'm interested in some other guy?"

"I don't know what to think, it's just ..." He pressed the heels of his hand to his temples and rubbed them. "Do you kiss the package delivery guy? If some guy holds open a door for you or picks up something you dropped, do you kiss him?"

"Not fair. Flint's different."

His face hardened again. "Flint's my employee."

"Flint's your friend."

His eyes narrowed, chin jutting forward. "All the more reason to keep your fucking lips off him."

That was a nice jab. I didn't have the strength for the fight he wanted to have.

"I know you think he's good looking. You told him the first day you two met. You like his name. You call him when you're in trouble ..."

"Fuck you." I couldn't take back the words. I didn't say them playfully like Everson, and the moment they crossed my lips I felt a clenching pain in my heart.

Cage's eyes widened. He didn't expect me to say that either. After a few moments, he shook his head, running his hands through his hair. "I hate it," he whispered. "I hate this fucking—" He stopped so abruptly it felt like a car slamming into a concrete wall.

Words hurt so bad. My eyes filled with tears.

"I'm sorry ..." I saw as much pain on his face as I felt in

my heart. He blinked several times, his eyes softening a bit. "I'm tired. It's no excuse. I'm jealous. It's not an excuse either, but I'm human so I can't help it. I get it. He saved you that day at the beach, but I would have too. You could have called 9-1-1 or—"

"Jesus, Cage! He didn't just save me at the beach. He saved Shayna's life when I couldn't." That was it ... the tears could no longer be held at bay. "After the game, when Everson asked about her, he was referring to our trip that turned into Shayna choking on a gumball while I just stood there helpless. Had ..." I sucked in a shaky breath because the idea of what would have happened had Flint not been there was still too unbearable. "Had Flint not been following me ... she ..." My hand slapped over my mouth and I released a sob. "H-he s-saved her l-life ..."

Before I could take another breath, he had me in his arms. It's the place I'd felt so desperate to be since the day it happened. In the most literal sense, I fought my way every day to be strong and stand on my own two feet, but sometimes even strong people needed a safe haven to just fall apart.

"Lake ..."

I fisted his shirt and just cried. No expectations. No need for words. All I wanted was for him to be strong enough to take that pain I could no longer hold in my heart.

"I killed Ben and Shayna almost ..."

"Shh ... no ... you're so wrong." He held my head, brushing his thumbs over my wet cheeks. "Lake Ivy Jones ..."

I released a laugh that was still a partial sob.

"From this day forward ... You. Share. *Everything* with me. I want to know if you bump your knee or break a nail."

His voice dropped to a whisper and his brows knitted. "You should have told me."

"I want to protect you—"

"No." He shook his head. "It's a job."

"You love your job."

He rested his forehead on mine. "I love *you*."

CAGE

"I HAVE AN EARLY MORNING. Are you going to be okay?"

She pulled away and grabbed a tissue from the coffee table. "Yeah. If you don't think I'm the neighborhood whore, then I'm good."

That stung, but I deserved it. "I'm a jerk."

She grunted a laugh. "You're jealous. It equally pisses me off and turns me on at the same time."

When would she learn? "I don't like being jealous."

"So you've said." She tossed the tissue in the kitchen trash and filled a glass with water, drinking the whole thing without stopping.

I hated seeing her tear-stained eyes and her overall look of physical and emotional exhaustion. Mostly, I hated that I was responsible for part of it.

She wrapped her arms around me. "I need to feed Trzy, take a bath, and hopefully crash for a few hours before Shayna wakes up. I highly doubt she'll sleep through the night. Not that I'm one to talk."

"You seemed to sleep well last night."

"I sleep better with you."

"Yeah? Then you should move in with me."

"Whoa!" She held up her hands. "Stop right there. It's one thing to be your baby mama, but cohabitation too?"

My gaze shifted to her tummy. Why? Because I was an idiot, who for an insane moment thought that twenty-four hours after possible conception there would be something to see.

"Go." She rolled her eyes. "You have 'work' early in the morning."

"I'll stay ..."

She shook her head then grabbed my shirt, demanding my lips—just another thing that woman did that made it impossible not to want to spend every breath with her.

"Good night," she whispered.

"Night." I kissed her nose and turned, grabbing the door handle. "Lake?"

"Yeah?"

Keeping my back to her, I closed my eyes. "Ask me to stay."

"You don't have—"

"Ask me. If you *need* me the way I need you, then ask me. Ask me like your needs matter more than my job."

I swear I could hear her swallow so hard. I wanted her to tell her pride to fuck off around me. More than anything in the whole damn world, I wanted her to surrender her emotions, her *needs* to me the way she surrendered her body. Maybe that made me a greedy bastard, but I couldn't help it. With Lake I wanted absofuckinglutely *everything*.

"Stay," she whispered.

LAKE

"If you ever tell anyone I did this, I will have my man card ripped away in exchange for a pussy. I've never heard of a guy doing this, and if I'm honest ... my balls are shrinking a bit with each stroke."

I smirked. "I won't tell anyone." That meant I wouldn't tell anyone that couldn't keep it a secret from him. "On a scale of one to ten, how sore were you this morning? I mean, you shouldn't have been too bad. You never got sacked yesterday, but the kitchen sex ... standing ... with an encore performance, also standing ... that had to have a residual effect." I grinned at Cage's reflection in the mirror.

After my bath, he asked if there was anything he could do to ease the tension of the day, I opted against requesting a massage since his body was probably much sorer than mine. Instead, I asked him to brush my hair. I loved, loved, loved having my hair brushed.

He gave me a challenging look in the mirror as he stood behind me making repeated strokes with the brush.

I grinned, perched on my vanity chair in my Angry Bird tank top and shorts.

"On a scale of one to ten, I was maxed out and leaning toward eleven *because* while I did not officially get sacked yesterday, I was on the ground after nearly every pass I made. Out of probably five hard hits, only one was called as a late hit. But I wouldn't expect someone who *hates football* to understand or notice what happened in the game."

There it was. I'd been waiting for it. A small part of me held out hope that in the larger scope of our fight, the football comment would get buried beneath Jamie's testicles—figuratively of course—and kissing Flint. I was wrong.

"Kids say the darnedest things."

"Kids repeat what they hear grownups say. So who told Shayna that 'Lake hates football?'"

"Jamie. He's trying to break us up so he can whisk me away to London," I said in my best—which was the worst—British accent.

"I'm going to beat the living shit out of him."

I shook my head. "Can't ... your hands are worth too much money to waste them on the nose of that bloke. Besides, he may have come to the hating-football conclusion from something I said. Which..." I held up a finger and he exhaled slowly instead of butting in with an argument "...by the way, I never said 'I hate football.'"

Cage paused with the brush at the top of my head, brows raised. "Then what did you say that he may have misconstrued?"

"I think I said something about needing to get in the mood for your last game, and he took it the wrong way."

"I see. Well, I'm in the mood to have sex with you, or watch you talk in your sleep, or listen to you baby talk to Trzy, or really anything in life that involves you." He smirked. "Even brushing your hair or buying you tampons."

Turning, I took the brush from him, twisted my lips, and exhaled a slow breath. "Truth?"

He cocked his head to the side and crossed his arms over his chest. "Always."

"I followed you, sort of stalked you after we met. I followed most of your senior year at Nebraska. I watched the games." I grinned. "I watched you." With the next breath my grin faded. "But what started out as complete nostalgia over seeing the man of my dreams—the guy who kissed me and made me want to wear pretty shoes again—it just started to make me sad and depressed. Seeing you just made me miss something I thought I'd never have. Missing you began to feel like missing my leg. Then I met Thad and he gave me a reason to believe in new dreams. I let go of the dream of you. And football? Watching it was like looking at photos of myself before I lost my leg."

"And now?" He scooped me up and carried me to my bed. I was so *not* helpless, but even if I hadn't lost my leg, I think I'd have wanted to be carried around by my muscly man.

I kept myself monkey-bound to his torso when he sat on the bed. "Let's just say the second I spotted you on the field I became fanatical. Now everything about it makes me ... happy. Nervous, as in I'm scared to death that you could get hurt, but when I watched you walk off the field in one piece after the game yesterday, I was so damn happy and giddy."

He released me and I slid under the sheets while he shrugged off his shirt and pants then slipped in beside me. I nuzzled my face into his chest taking a deep inhale.

"So you no longer hate football. You no longer have to get in the mood for it?"

I smiled, tipping my chin up and pressing my lips to the crook of his neck as he pulled me close. "I'm in the mood to have sex with you, or listen to you snore, or watch you yell at yourself when you watch old game footage, or really anything that involves you. Even going fishing with you or playing in bounce houses with you at eight-year-olds' birthday parties."

He reached over and turned off the light on the bed stand. "Sorry ... I didn't hear a thing you said after 'I'm in the mood to have sex with you.'"

CHAPTER THIRTY

A LITTLE TOO LATE FOR LOVE

A WEEK LATER, Jamie was fully broken out with chicken pox, although supposedly not on his testicles. Shayna's were all scabbed over enough for her to move back in with Everson. I needed to catch up on work, so Everson asked Judy, Shayna's ne-ma's sister who originally dropped Shayna off, if she'd come stay a few days to watch Shayna until Jamie was over his rough stage and no longer contagious or until I got home, whichever came first. Judy agreed to come; she'd wanted to visit anyway.

Cage stayed with me every night until I left town. The truth was, I did sleep better with him. My nights without nightmares outnumbered the ones with them. I felt like he was serious when he said he *needed* me. Sex was extra, a true icing-on-the-cake. Just being together was all that mattered. There was something uniquely mind blowing about needing someone so much and them needing you back just as much.

And the baby? At night Cage rested his hand on my tummy in a gentle way he had never done before. Perfection. It was the only word to describe my life in those moments. I was desperate to feel something ... tender breasts, nausea, unusual fatigue, anything that would confirm that I was pregnant since it had been too early to take a pregnancy test. My family would lose their shit if they knew I'd been praying that I was pregnant.

"Love!" Thaddeus greeted me at the studio where the photoshoot was scheduled.

"Hey, sorry I had to delay this."

"Fine, fine. We're good." He hugged me, but tighter than he usually hugged me, and his quick 'fine, fine" brushoff was out of character for my anal retentive boss. Something was up.

I almost shared my possible baby news just because he was in such rare, agreeable form that day, but before I could open my mouth to speak, he said something that rendered me speechless and robbed all baby thoughts.

"So..." he smiled or grimaced, maybe a little of both "...I did mention today's shoot is nude, right?" He blinked rapidly.

I didn't blink at all. "Please tell me 'nude' is code for no makeup."

"Oh God no! You'll have full makeup, but ... aside from makeup and the new leg I've made for you, you won't be wearing anything else."

"Thad—"

"Wait! Before you try to object, let me tell you that this is going to be the most beautiful and artistic shoot you have ever done, *and* the write-up that goes with it will knock your socks off. I've already read it, except for the quotes from you and a few of the other models that will be added. It's about body image and what makes people beautiful. It's about confidence ... that little thing you were low on when we met. Remember?"

"But you're asking me to pose naked."

Thad tipped his chin down, pinning me with wide eyes.

I sighed. "It's just *a* body. Who I am existed before it and will continue to *be* long after it's gone. I'm so much more than the flesh that covers my remaining bones."

Thad grinned as he nodded once. "And?"

Another sigh. "And ..." It still choked me up to say the words—the same words I made Shayna say the day I got arrested. "I'm beautiful."

His metal finger tapped my nose. "I shouldn't have hired you."

I frowned.

Thad shrugged. "I should have dated you. Stupid me." He walked toward the photographers setting up their equipment as a woman with a blond ponytail longer than that of an actual pony and a fake-white smile smeared with a bit of red lipstick motioned for me to follow her. My steps felt heavy under the weight of Thad's confession, the one he said with the ease of announcing his regret of getting steak for lunch instead of chicken.

My phone chimed just as I dropped my bag in the dressing room to get into wardrobe, which did in fact turn out to be an actual white robe that would get discarded before I stepped in front of the camera.

Cage: *Penny has to leave town. Family emergency. Her dad had a stroke. I'm in charge of Trzy. Do you think she'll piss all over my place if I take her there?"*

Lake: *Is Penny's dad okay?*

Cage: *He's in the hospital but that's all I know. She was going to message you but didn't want to worry you since you seemed stressed over leaving Shayna.*

Lake: *Have you seen Judy? She's like 100!*

Cage: *Be nice. Banks said she's only 85.*

Lake: *Lol. Sorry. Trzy loves you. You can take her anywhere as long as she has a litter box and food. She's too much of a diva to piss on your floor. Just make sure you have a water bowl for her and take her laser pen to play with her.*

Cage: *So now I have to play with her too?*

Lake: *Do I have to beg you to play with my pussy?*

Cage: *Knock that shit off. I don't need an erection before my massage.*

Lake: *Another massage? It sure is rough being you. Play with Trzy and pet her too. Lots of petting.*

Cage: *She's hairless. I'm not sure she likes it.*

Lake: *The last pussy of mine you petted was also hairless and believe me she sure as hell liked you petting her … and licking her … and …*

Cage: *Fuck!! I've got to go whack off before my massage. Thanks a lot.*

Lake: *Monaghan … Don't forget to love me.*

Cage: *Impossible.*

I hoped the photographers wanted a smiling model because it would take a while to wipe the huge one off my face.

"It's … amazing, beautiful, and … wow." I smiled at Thad as I pulled up my robe and put on my new Thaddeus Westbrook original.

"My love said she wanted it all: fashion and function." He shrugged, but a rare vulnerability showed through that I'd never seen before. He looked like a nervous boy on his first date.

That heaviness returned to my heart. "The toenails are painted." I smiled like he hadn't tried to turn my world inside out thirty minutes earlier.

"I taught you function before fashion, but I guess you taught me that a brilliant inventor wouldn't sacrifice either."

I laughed. "Glad to know your ego is still larger than life." I walked a few feet in one direction, jumped up and down, then jogged to the other side of the room. The leg felt and performed just like my other robotic legs, but it looked like my pretty leg, maybe even prettier. "You're brilliant, Thaddeus Westbrook." I hugged him.

His body stiffened beneath my arms, something he'd never done before with any of the other million hugs I'd given him over the years. Even his arms draped around me, resting lightly on my back in the most awkward way. When I released him his smile faded as he cleared his throat and diverted his gaze toward the photographer.

"Ready?" he called.

"Whenever Lake is," the photographer replied.

"It's all you, love." Thad's sad smile broke something in me, but I couldn't even say for sure what it was.

"The photographer is a guy." I tightened the sash on my robe.

"His two assistants are women."

I looked over at them waiting for me. They smiled. I smiled, sort of. "I don't want you to watch."

Why did he have to look disappointed, like I'd rejected him?

"I'm going to see the photos, love. And you're going to change legs four times. Think of me as your assistant."

I nodded to the ponytail lady. "She did my makeup, she can bring me my legs."

"Did I mention I'm going to see the photos? The whole

world could potentially see the photos, love. This is going to be huge."

The whole world. *Cage.*

Thad grabbed the collar to my robe and pulled me close to his face. My breath caught in my throat.

"Change the world, Lake. Don't let the world change you," he whispered then pressed a soft kiss to the corner of my mouth.

He'd kissed my cheeks thousands of times, but that kiss was more intimate. That kiss crossed a line that hadn't existed between us since our first date because we didn't need it. We worked together. He became part of my family. That one kiss changed everything. I hated him for doing that. I hated him for taking something so perfect and ruining it.

I wasn't his.

I would never be his.

I belonged to Cage.

I belonged to the man who made me believe his sole purpose in life was to love me.

Turning, I dropped my robe, letting it pool at my feet just inches from where Thad stood behind me. He sucked in a tight breath. I smiled because ... fuck him for doing that to me.

The photographer, the handsome photographer that would have made my bones shake in my pre-Cage Monaghan days, nodded, keeping a neutral, professional expression. "Rae and Brit will get you in position."

The two assistants took over and within minutes all of my modesty vanished. Every pose was angled to hide fully exposing any part of my body that would qualify my photos being anything but tasteful. We shot for almost two hours with several short breaks. I made frequent leg changes, but most of the shots seemed to be without any prosthetic or robotic leg, truly bare naked photos of me.

"My boss will send you proofs for you to approve and sign off on the final shots for the publication." The photographer handed me his business card as I exited the dressing room, fully clothed again. "Call me if you want any of the photos for yourself."

"Thank you." I smiled. It was weird how awkward I felt at that moment. Naked? Nope. But with my clothes on the atmosphere changed like we had a secret. I suppose the secret was he'd seen me from some pretty intimate angles through a big-ass camera lens.

"By the way. I'm a huge fan of your boyfriend." The photographer called just as I reached the door.

Turning, I nodded. If Cage knew what he had seen over the previous two hours, the photographer would probably have his eyeballs physically extracted.

"You were amazing, love."

"Fuck you." I brushed past Thad waiting outside of the building.

"Excuse me?"

I whipped around. "Don't! Don't you dare act like nothing happened in there."

"What ... I don't—"

"You should have dated me? Really? Now you're saying this? The look? The kiss? What the hell?"

His stature shrank several inches as his chin fell to his chest, shoulders turned inward. "The timing is terrible. I know it. The events of my life thus far have been a compilation of terrible timing. I know my chance is slim at best, but what if you're the one for me? I chose my ambitions over love, and I shouldn't have. I should have chosen you."

I shook my head. "You want me because you can't have me. You like the challenge, the chase."

"I want you because you're in my head all the damn time. You've been in my head since the day we met, but the timing wasn't right, and now time's running out and I can't just let you go without a fight. My whole fucking life revolves around you. I spend more money and time on you than anything else. Do you have any idea how many deadlines I've missed, how many opportunities I've let slip away because all I could focus on was making a new leg for you, making you happy, making you ..."

That wasn't my life. There was no way I was standing in front of Thaddeus Westbrook hearing those words fall from his mouth. I didn't even feel like myself in my own body. It was a scene from a movie or a Netflix show, but it wasn't my life. It couldn't be my life.

"Making me what?" I whispered or I think I whispered. Maybe I didn't even speak. There was no reason to speak to something that wasn't really happening.

Thad stepped toward me, gently holding my shoulders. "Making you love me. I was trying to make you love me. I just didn't know how to show you in any other way. I was scared to tell you that I made the wrong choice. But then you met Mr. Wonderful and I don't want to let go because I would never forgive myself for not asking you to ... choose me."

Biting my trembling lips together, I shook my head. "Do you really love me?"

Thad's brow wrinkled like my question was somehow a slap in the face, like I should have known the answer. "Yes," he whispered.

"Then I'm going to tell you something and when I'm done you're going to forget about this day like it never happened and you're going to do it because love is giving all and taking nothing."

The defeat in his eyes told me he knew the answer, but I needed to say the words because I did love the tall, handsome geek before me, even if he made me hate him that day.

"I'm not the one for you. I can only be the one for *one* man and he's the reason you didn't choose me that day. The universe knew something we didn't at the time. Cage was the *one* for me before I took my first breath, and he'll be the one after I take my last."

"How can you say that?" Thad shook his head. "What about Ben? If he were standing right here would you still say Cage is the one?"

That hurt. I loved Ben and I would always love him. What hurt the most was the truth—fate took Ben so I could be with Cage.

"Yes. I'd choose Cage. Ben was my first love. Cage is my everlasting love. And you ..." I brushed the back of my hand along Thad's cheek. "You're the reason I'm changing the world. I don't want to lose you, but I also don't want to hold you back."

"You're breaking my fucking heart."

I wiped away a stray tear. "You're breaking mine."

He rolled his eyes toward the sky and shook his head. "You're just worried I won't make you any more legs."

"I'm not worried. I'm terrified."

His head snapped back down. I felt the tension between us lighten a bit, letting my heart slow and my lungs take a breath.

"What would you do for a Thaddeus Westbrook original?" I saw my Thaddeus again in his smirk, and I nearly cried because I honestly loved him like family. "Sex?" His brow raised a fraction.

The awkwardness melted away. My friend was back with a goofy suggestive wiggle of his brows. I didn't waste a minute letting him know that I needed "us" back—the playful banter that defined our *friendship*.

Twisting my lips, like I was actually giving it consideration, I narrowed my eyes then shook my head. "Blowjob."

"Hmm ..." he scratched his chin. "Deep throat?"

"Lollipop."

"Swallow?"

"Hand-job finish."

"On your tits?"

"On Jerry Chu's face ... oh, wait ... he's not gay."

His wide eyes danced with humor, and I bit back my smile, then we both erupted into laughter. And once again ... all was right in the world.

CHAPTER THIRTY-ONE

THE NAKED TRUTH

ALL WAS *NOT* right in the world again. Just before I was scheduled to leave for home, Penny messaged me that her dad died. Fate didn't seem to work for everyone, because Rupert's mother fell and broke her hip and he needed to be at the hospital while she had surgery since his dad wasn't well enough to be there. Penny's mother died several years earlier, and she had no siblings. Penny was a bad-ass, independent woman, and when a bad-ass, independent woman breaks down on the phone and begs her favorite neighbor to come to San Antonio, there was only one thing to do—go to San Antonio.

Lake: *Change of plans. Penny's dad died. Rupert can't be with her so I'm changing my ticket and going to San Antonio.*

Cage didn't answer until I landed in San Antonio.

Cage: *Give her my condolences. I miss you so damn much!*
Lake: *I will. Miss U 2! I have so much to tell you, but I don't want*

to do it over the phone. How's Shayna? Everson never answers my texts. How's Trzy?

Cage: *Judy left early after an incident, so Banks had to beg your nanny guy to come back to work before he was ready. So guess who's staying with me until nanny guy is no longer contagious?*

Lake: *Football guy, please tell me you know that 'nanny guy' has a name and it's Jamie.*

Cage: *I miss you.*

My heart constricted. God ... I missed him too.

Lake: *Call me when you're home and you've put the kids to bed.*

Cage: *Kids?*

Lake: *Trzy and Everson*

Cage: *How's my baby? I need some good news.*

My constricted heart ripped a little because all was not right in the world. I got my period that morning, but I sort of knew because I took a pregnancy test after the photoshoot and it came up negative. However, I thought it was probably too early to really detect it.

He needed good news. I had none to give.

Lake: *I'm good. Don't forget to love me.*

Oh the growing lump in my throat—the only thing growing in my body. My phone rang. It was him. He knew. Of course he knew. He knew my words. He knew me.

Just as a taxi stopped, I pressed ignore. If I'd answered, I would have lost it.

Cage: *I'm sorry and I'll never forget to love you.*

I cleared my throat and tossed my phone in my purse, then gave the driver the address.

CAGE

I HAD no business starting a family when my career was still in its own infancy. So why was Lake not being pregnant such a jab to my gut?

I knew she wouldn't answer until she was ready and able to talk about it. Penny needed her and it took everything I had in me to be the mature person and acknowledge I could wait. My needs were not as important. Our baby didn't die. She was never pregnant. But ... I still felt an unexplainable loss.

"Hey," she finally answered on my last attempt before going to bed.

"Hey, how's Penny?"

"She's okay. I think she's mourning the things that happened between her and her father before he ever died, more than his actual death. The unspoken apologies."

"When is the funeral?"

"Saturday. Visitation is tomorrow."

"You coming home Sunday?"

"Yes."

I sighed. "I'm leaving Saturday for Sunday's game in Detroit. I'll be back late Sunday."

"I'll keep my—"

I waited but she didn't finish.

"Your?"

"Nothing."

"Tell me."

She laughed, the kind that did a shit job of hiding the pain behind it. "I was going to say I'll keep my sex demands to the bed instead of ..."

I leaned back on my pillow and closed my eyes, rubbing them with my thumbs. "Instead of the pantry door."

"Yeah," she whispered.

"I want to say something to make you laugh. I love your laugh. I swear it's my favorite sound in the whole world, and I've heard some amazing things. But your laugh ... it's all consuming. I can't stop smiling when you laugh, and after a while I don't even remember what was said that made you laugh because I just get so lost in you. God ... I sound so fucking sentimental right now. I ... I just don't want to be Penny. I don't want to ever leave anything unsaid between us."

"I blame your weak sperm." She laughed and just like that I was lost in her. "Isn't that just how it is in life? The big jocks, with dicks the size of English cucumbers, have the most pathetic little swimmers with like ... zero stamina. And the scrawny little pencil dicks, you know the ones I'm talking about, the ones that could in fact fuck every orifice of a woman's body? Their pre-cum could impregnate half the world."

Her giggles brought a bittersweet smile to my face because I missed her So. Damn. Bad.

I cleared my throat. "Judy left because of a doll massacre. When she was putting away some of Shayna's laundry, she found a drawer full of dolls and they were all missing their left leg below the knee. In the back of the drawer was a serrated steak knife and a pile of amputated doll limbs. Banks talked Judy out of reporting it to CPS, but he couldn't talk her out of leaving. That's why your nanny guy, *Jamie*, had to suck it up and get back to work before he felt 100 percent."

"No!" She gasped. "She did not cut off her dolls' legs."

"She did. Banks still can't tell the story without nearly pissing himself. You're her idol, babe."

"Oh boy, oh boy, oh boy ... I love that girl."

I went to say something, but I couldn't. The hesitation said it for me.

"Cage, I feel it too. It's insane really. We're not married. Children? Why would we even consider them at this point? We're probably the only two people in the world who can understand why me not being pregnant is such a disappointment. It was a bet, or dare, or just some weird standoff that happened that day in your kitchen. I was terrified and exhilarated at the same time. I hadn't even considered kids yet, all I knew was I wanted you. But after we did it ... I realized I wanted *that* part of you too."

"But I have weak sperm?"

"Incredibly weak."

"Maybe you just have an inhospitable environment. Probably all the junk food you eat."

"Watch it, Monaghan. You have a pretty good record with me, but those are some fighting words. If you don't back it down, then I'd say the chances of you scoring anytime soon are pretty slim."

"We're separated by three states. I can't even see your end zone."

Lake giggled. "Just as well. It's really more like a war zone right now."

"I love you. I need sleep. Long day."

"You don't want to discuss my period anymore?"

"I'm sure Penny would be a better fit for that conversation."

"No. Penny lost her uterus. I don't think she wants to discuss this with me."

"Jesus, has she reported it missing? I bet the same asshole who stole your leg has her uterus too. I suspect they've both been sold on the black market."

There it was—her laugh. I'd make crazy shit up all night long for more of her laughter.

"Sweet dreams, my sports star. Don't forget to lo—"

"It's what I do best. Good night, sexy."

I AWOKE to a text from the woman who managed to unravel me a little more the farther she traveled away from me. Lake held me together. It was a frightening realization that any one person had such a profound effect on my existence.

Lake: *Where will Trzy be when you leave? Check with Mrs. Leonard in 2A, just flash her your dimples. Or ask Jamie. <3 U.*
Cage: *Flashed Mrs. Leonard my dimples. She fainted. Paramedics came. As the officer took my statement it hit me … you didn't mean my butt dimples, did you? So embarrassing …*
Lake: *Funny guy. My tongue loves your butt dimples. Did you get arrested? How cool would it be if we both had a police record? I hope you really did moon her, it will make the confession I have to give you so much easier.*
Cage: *WTF?*
Lake: *We're at the church. I have to go. Keep your ass off the turf Sunday. Tell your tackle guys to protect you. Good luck.*
Cage: *Linemen. Love you. I'll stay on my feet if you keep your damn clothes on!*
Lake: *Really, I have to go … but challenge accepted. I'm going to watch Sunday's game at a sports bar downtown and every*

time you land on your ass I'm going to remove a piece of my clothing. xx

I typed ten different responses, then deleted them. She had me by the balls. Stubborn woman.

"Get your ass on the bus, Monaghan. We have a plane to catch."

I nodded at my coach and slipped my phone into my pocket. Visions of Lake stripping in a sports bar haunted me. It was a joke. It had to be a joke.

Fuck!

What if it wasn't a joke?

DETROIT RACKED up three sacks on me. We had the number one defense, they had the number two. Every inch of my body fucking ached—throbbed. I had two seconds to get the ball off. Where the hell were the blocks? Don't throw an interception. Don't get sacked. See the whole field. Find my receiver. Stop thinking of Lake stripping.

I stopped for a few questions before making it off the field at the end of the game.

"Cage, you edged Detroit out in overtime. Did you anticipate their defense rushing as much as they did today and how will you adjust for when they come to Minnesota next month?"

"We played the number two defense, but our offense practices against the number one, so we were ready. Of course we expected them to come hard, but my line did a great job of giving me a few extra seconds to find my receivers. One game at a time, but right now we're three-

and-oh, so the plan is to just keep practicing hard and bringing it on game day."

Reporters spewed questions left and right, knowing damn well I'd only respond to the one from the network televising the game until I reached the locker room.

"What is your reaction to Lake Jones posing nude for *Breaking Barriers* magazine?"

I turned. Flint and several security guys nudged me to keep going.

"Locker room," Flint warned.

I glared at him for a moment then continued making my way off the field.

"What the fuck, Flint," I gritted between my teeth.

"I don't know."

"How the hell do you not know? I pay you to know this shit."

"You pay me to keep your reputation clean. Not hers. I can't control her any more than you can."

I turned before going into the locker room... "Find out."

He chuckled. "You want me to call her?"

"No ... yes ... dammit!" I shook my head, trying to not make any more of a scene. "Never mind. I'll handle it."

LAKE

My bed. I missed my bed.

Cage didn't reply to my message, but it was marked "read" so I knew he saw it. There was no doubt in my mind that he'd come straight to my apartment after he got off the plane—until he didn't. Through my peephole I saw Everson arrive home. Two hours later ... no Cage. No response. I had a monster headache from squinting into the peephole. I needed a new pastime.

I typed a text then deleted it, opting for a phone call since I knew he was off the plane. It went to his voice mail.

"Hey, um ... congrats on your game. I guess you're asleep by now, but if you're not, call me. I'm sure I'll be awake for another hour or more. So ... bye."

After brushing my teeth, I noticed my phone light up on my bed stand as I slipped off my leg.

Cage: *Tell me about the nude photos.*

He didn't answer on purpose. How did he find out? I called his phone. Again, no answer.

Cage: *Just tell me if it's true.*

I called again. Again, no answer. My eyes shifted from the call button to the time: 12:45 a.m.

Thirty minutes later I arrived at his door. The house was dark.

bang bang bang

The hall light illuminated, followed by the entry and the click of the door lock. He appeared in a pair of gray jogging shorts and nothing else, eyes squinted against the light.

"If you have more than ten pubic hairs attached to your balls, then you should have answered your phone like an adult."

He stood resolute, blocking the doorway.

My eyes widened a fraction as I slid my hands up into the sleeves of my purple hoodie, then hugged myself to keep warm. "Wow. Really? The silent treatment. How mature of you."

"Is it true?"

I laughed. "Does it matter?"

He looked at me like it mattered more than anything, and in an instant my smile fell flat. It was the look he gave me when he was upset about his dad and going to meet my family. I didn't know that Cage. I didn't even recognize him.

I said goodbye with a single, slow nod and turned, walking back to my car. As I fastened my seatbelt, a jarring bang to my hood brought my head up with a snap. Cage stood with his hands pressed to the hood, eyes locked to mine. Dropping his chin to his chest he just stood there and I waited. The occasional glimpse of his demons broke my heart.

A good minute later my door opened. I inched my eyes up to his, hoping I'd see my Cage again. He leaned in and unfasten my seatbelt, then took my hand and helped me out. After closing the door, he inched closer until my back pressed against it. I'm sure there were the right words to say, but I wasn't sure what they were. I refused to apologize for anything. I'd done nothing wrong. But I loved the man before me more than life itself so ... yeah, I waited for him to give me something I could work with, something I could help mend.

He threaded his hands in my hair and released a painful sigh as he leaned forward. His lips brushed along my lips like a soft breeze, skimming along my cheek. He breathed me in, burying his nose in my hair, his lips at my ear. My skin bloomed with a million tingly goose bumps.

"No," he whispered. "It doesn't matter."

CHAPTER THIRTY-TWO

LOVE

"I'LL TELL you about the photos if you tell me about the condom." Lying on my side, ghosting my fingers over his face, I took a hundred mental pictures of him. That's what my mind did when the vision before me felt like a dream. Cage Monaghan naked in bed, sheets draped low on his waist, one leg kicked out on top of the bedding was *the* dream.

"Condom? He peeked open one eye.

"Two weeks ago you were hell bent on getting me pregnant, but tonight you wore a condom."

He closed his eye again and smirked, but said nothing.

"You find a different baby mama?"

"Nope. She's still in bed with me. The kitchen was impulsive. You said it yourself."

"A mistake?"

He sighed. I could feel his exhaustion. It probably wasn't fair to ask him to mentally process anything at that point. "Nothing about us *is* or *ever* will be a mistake."

I nodded slowly to myself, keeping my fingers drifting over his face, neck, and down to his chest. I loved feeling him as much as he loved my touch. "I didn't know it was a nude photoshoot."

My hand paused as his body stiffened beneath it.

"I could have said no. I didn't. The magazine is not pornographic. It's about the power of humanity, technology, changing the world. Thaddeus has taken away my disability. He's changing the world, he's changing lives, and I'm the face that represents that right now. Even if Lake Jones doesn't matter to the world, my story does. It matters for every person born with a physical disability, for every soldier wounded in battle, every victim of a life-changing car accident. The only thing that sets me apart from anyone else in my proverbial shoes is opportunity. Thaddeus wants to give every physically-challenged person that opportunity."

Cage opened his eyes and shifted to his side, facing me with his head propped up on one arm. "What do Thad's inventions have to do with your nude body?"

"My body is just that ... a body. It doesn't define what I can do in life. I'm not ashamed of how I look, not anymore. We can't change the world until we change how the world views body image and disabilities." I flipped the sheets off me, exposing my naked body to him. "What do you see?"

His eyes roved along my body, eventually settling on my eyes. "You know what I see."

"I do, but I want you to say it."

"I see you."

"How much of me?"

"All of you."

I nodded. "And that's why I love you, but most people see only one thing ... they see that part of me that they believe is missing. They see everything they think I can't do, can't be, can't have, can't achieve."

His hand slid along my cheek as his thumb brushed my lower lip. "What does Lake Jones want to do?" he whispered as my temperature rose a few degrees.

My tongue teased the tip of his thumb. "You."

A grin twitched at the corner of his mouth. "What does Lake Jones want to be?"

My hand slid down his stomach. "Filled with you."

Cage's Adam's apple bobbed. "What does Lake Jones want to have?" His grip on my face tightened.

My teeth dug into his thumb for a few seconds before I kissed it. "A life with you."

He wet his lips before taking another hard swallow. "What does Lake Jones want to achieve?"

My hand made a slow stroke up his hard cock. "Everything," I whispered a split second before his mouth took mine and his body rolled onto me.

Our fingers intertwined over my head as my hips moved with his. Would he stop for protection? I didn't know. I didn't care. The passion we had fell deep in the realm of reckless, and reckless felt like the purpose for existing in that moment. I was *living*.

"I hate..." he kissed me hard, taking the air from my lungs "...that anyone else gets to see you like I've seen you..." his hips rocked into me, my back arched as a moan escaped my throat "...but if it will change the world..." his tongue dipped deep into my mouth again and my fingernails dug into his hands "...then I'll sacrifice my possessive side for the greater good."

He moved onto his elbows, rocking his pelvis into me harder, sweat beading along his brow. I wrapped my legs around him. Would he pull out? Did our impulsive needs make sense? Did they *need* to make sense to anyone but us?

My hands slid up his arms, his neck, stopping on his

face. "Monaghan, you're so stupid ..." My eyes closed for a moment as he angled his hips to rub my sensitive clit. God, dying in that moment was perfectly fine with me. My eyes locked to his again. "Nobody will ever see me like you see me."

THE NUDE PHOTOS MATTERED, but not in a way I ever imagined. They were the buzz-talk for a while in the sports community after the reporter leaked it. Cage perfected the "Lake is an Incredible Woman and I Fully Support Her" speech, and he did it before ever seeing the photos or reading the article. He apologized that night for having trust issues. I think I fell even more in love with him.

I could never have been with someone who demanded perfection. Those people were nothing more than judgmental assholes that lived in denial of their humanity. Cage's jealousy, his anger, his doubt ... they made him human, but his recognizing it? It made him extraordinary.

Love—the hand that pulls someone to their feet.

Love—the lips that kiss their wounds.

Love—the proffered tissue to wipe their tears.

Love—the smile that reminds them we are all human.

Love—the mind that doesn't judge.

Love—our soul's purpose.

Love—our sole purpose.

Cage was my love and I was his.

Once the magazine published the photos with the article about my journey from disability to superior capability, the inappropriate chatter in the sports community silenced. The proverbial jaw-drop was felt around the world thanks to the instant news phenomena of the internet.

Thaddeus Westbrook and Lake Jones trended on social media more than any NFL sensation.

"You're a big deal, baby girl," my mom said with pride as we talked on the phone early one morning a week after the photos were published, which didn't happened until November.

They sat on them, waiting to get the article just right. He never admitted to it, but I suspected anal-retentive Thaddeus Westbrook was part of the hold up. I was fine with that, anything to keep his mind focused on business and not the near fallout of our relationship. I couldn't say we were back to one hundred percent, but we were close.

"I'm not a big deal." I rolled my eyes as I fed Trzy in Cage's kitchen.

We weren't officially living with him; I still had my apartment. However, I hadn't slept there since returning to Minneapolis the previous month from visiting Luke and Jessica's new baby girl, Harley. Cage moved nearly everything except my furniture while I was gone. He said it was Trzy's idea.

"They're beautiful. They represent how I've looked at you your whole life."

"Says my mom."

"Lake ..."

I dropped two frozen flax waffles into the toaster. "Sorry. I know, and you're right."

"Are you going to make it home for the holidays?"

"I hope so, but football doesn't really take a break, and Thad can't keep up with all the interview requests. I'm flying to New York tomorrow. Thad and I have two different morning show interviews this week and three talk shows. Then I fly directly to L.A. for more interviews and talk shows. It's ... crazy. I'm just a girl who lost her leg. Thad is the real star. He's making certain physical disabilities non-existent. He's creating things that allow disabled people to outperform athletes without disabilities."

"True, but the article is about so much more than Thad's inventions. It's about the emotional struggle—your emotional struggle—things I never knew."

I nodded to myself. Even I never anticipated sharing so much of myself after the photoshoot when Brandon, the writer scripting the article, contacted me to answer a few questions. Everything I told him fit perfectly with the photos. It was me—honest, vulnerable, unplugged, and naked.

"I never knew you mourned the loss of your identity so much more than your leg."

Ripping off the top of the tea bag packet, I dropped it in my red mug and filled it with hot water. "I wasn't born with a disability. It wasn't a part of me for twenty years. I looked in the mirror and that's how I identified myself. In a blink I became dependent on everyone around me. I was so angry because I couldn't see that girl in the mirror anymore. I was on the cusp of my independence, in love, hopeful, and so ambitious. Then it just ... vanished."

"What you said about the shoes brought me to tears ... hell, who am I kidding. Every quote of yours in the article brought me to tears. But the shoes ... "

I smiled, licking the chocolate hazelnut butter off my finger then putting the lid back on the jar. "I loved shoes."

"I know you did. It broke my heart when you told me to get rid of them. Did Cage know? Had you told him he was the reason you wanted a new leg that you could wear pretty shoes with?"

"I told him the day he took me to the airport to fly to Beijing, but honestly, I don't think he realized the true life-changing impact it had on me until he read the article for the first time last week. He totally denies it, but I know he got teary eyed reading the article, and I know it was the part about him and the shoes. Had I not met him I don't think I would have bugged the hell out of Luke to help me get a prettier leg, and had I not had that pretty leg and the boost of confidence it gave me, I would not have made a profile on the dating site where I met Thaddeus."

"Well, I hope he's the one. It would be a crime for one of the Jones women to not be with the hunky quarterback with dimples, and as much as it breaks Lara's and my heart, you really are the obvious choice."

I laughed because in spite of the loss in my life, I still had the very best people. "He's the one, Mom."

I never told her about our almost pregnancy or our sporadic reckless behavior since then that left me in a constant state of wondering am I? That secret stayed between us, okay, and Penny, but she didn't count. Penny was my free psychiatrist, so we had an unspoken doctor-patient confidentiality.

"They play Green Bay this weekend at home."

"I'll be in L.A. I'll be gone for a total of ten days."

"How does Cage feel about that?"

I took a bite of my waffle and mumbled over my mouthful, "He thinks we should both be unemployed and just stay in bed naked all day."

"Damn! You're giving me a hot flash."

I giggled. Only Felicity Jones, part-time nudist, would say that to her daughter. "I'm kidding ... I think. I mean ... he *has* actually said those words, but he loves the game and I love the opportunities I've been given in my own life. I think we both feel this obligation to make the most of the lives we've been given. But it sucks too. I miss him all the time."

"It's a blink, baby. He won't play football forever, and this fame you have with Thad will not last forever either. Just don't forget why you're both doing it. Don't lose what you have together. When the spotlight no longer shines, you don't want to be standing alone."

"Love you, Mom."

"Love you too, Lake. Call me when you get to New York so I won't worry."

I laughed. "You'll always worry."

"*Less*. I'll worry less."

"So damn depressing."

I smiled as the voice I loved most sounded behind me, even though I could feel the frown on his beautiful face. Staring at the large suitcase on the bed, overflowing with clothes and shoes for the East to West Coast temperature swing, I had to agree with him.

"Our jobs suck."

"They do."

The hair on my arms stood erect as I felt him just a breath behind me. I turned, drinking in the sight of my handsome man in a Minnesota T-shirt and jeans.

"We should quit."

He pulled me into his arms that seemed to be bigger, firmer, and sexier every time he enveloped me in them. "You can't quit."

Fisting his shirt, I buried my nose into his chest and inhaled my favorite aroma: freshly-showered Cage. I couldn't even pinpoint what I was smelling. All I knew was it was the headiest aphrodisiac ever. "And you can?"

His mouth wasted no time devouring my neck. "Yes ..." His teeth came next and my whole body shivered. "I just play catch for a living." His hands slid down and palmed my ass, pulling me as close as possible to his body. "You're changing the world. You're inspiring. You're a fucking hero to every disabled person out there."

"I'm not ..." My words came out as nothing more than little puffs of air.

"Well you sure as fuck rock my world."

I laughed. "Say we just do it. We both quit. Then what do we do? It would have to be something so cool like ..." I shook my head. "I've got nothing."

He chuckled, lifting me up, spinning around, and plopping down on the bed with me hugged to his chest. "You could probably get a job in PR, getting professional athletes' faces on boxes of generic crispy rice cereal."

"Smart ass." I bit his lower lip and gave it a firm tug then sat up, straddling him.

"Well, I know what I'd do." He laced his hands behind his head.

"Teach?" That was his degree from Nebraska.

His lips twisted. "Hmm ... that would seem like the obvious choice, but no. I'd get my Master's in Lake Jones."

I narrowed my eyes. "Lake Jones?"

"Yes. Through close observation, experimentation..." he wiggled his brows "...and thorough research, I'd completely figure you out. It might take years, a lifetime even, but I think it's what I'm best suited to do."

"Fine, I'll bite. Tell me what you've already discovered."

"I've discovered tons of peculiar habits of yours. I just need to figure out why you do what you do, like ... the way you draw random designs on the glass door when you shower, or the way you chew one and a half pieces of cinnamon gum like one is not enough but two is too much, or why you put chocolate hazelnut butter on your waffles then spoon out every single indentation with your finger before eating the waffle. Why don't you just eat a spoonful of the spread then eat the waffle on its own?"

I started to speak.

"Shh ..." He shook his head. "Those were rhetorical questions. I don't want you to tell me. That would take away the fun of figuring it out on my own. Some things I think I've already figured out, but I'm not one hundred percent."

"Such as?"

"The way you touch me."

I wiggled my hips over his, attempting to accompany it with a sexy smirk.

Cage chuckled. "That's not the touch I'm talking about, but don't stop."

Frowning, I stopped.

He took my right hand and pressed it to his chest. "You touch me like this." Moving my hand to his shoulder he smiled. "And like this ... and everywhere else—all the time. When we're in my truck you play with my hair and I fucking love it. When we eat you always sit next to me, even when we get a booth you sit next to me and rest your hand on my leg. At night some part of your body is always in contact with mine, and you do so instinctively. Originally, I thought it was just an intimate gesture, but it's not that. Sometimes I don't even think you realize your body is searching for mine." He shrugged. "I think I ground you."

Could he read my blank stare too? "Maybe I'm just

claiming you in front of the women waiting for you to ditch me."

"Are there people, these women you speak of, in our bedroom watching us sleep at night?"

Did he hear his own words? *Our* bedroom? Without a doubt Cage grounded me, and maybe that's why I did it. Honestly? I didn't realize I did it. Maybe I subconsciously needed the constant reminder that he was a real, tangible part of my life.

"Is this really *our* bedroom?"

"Trzy thinks so."

I looked over at my feline slut licking herself at the top of her cat tower in the corner. "I feel guilty paying for my apartment when I'm not there."

"Then let it go when your lease is up."

"Just like that?"

"Just like that. We're already living together. You're going to have my babies. It's only a matter of time before you take my last name, so ... yeah. Just like that."

My body fought for neutral, no reaction, but it was impossible. I felt my brows raise all on their own, like they just didn't give a damn that my brain screamed, "Don't react!"

"I'm taking your last name?"

"Unless you want to keep Jones. I'm good with whatever you decide."

"Uh ... are you proposing to me?"

"Sure."

How could one guy be my greatest dream and worst nightmare?

"Sure? That ... that's it?"

"I'm not following."

Aliens robbed the man of my dreams. How? When? Who was this imposter?

Climbing off him, I shoved the top down on my suitcase and yanked on the zipper. It was full, too full. He sat up and pressed his hand to the top, releasing the tension so I could zip it.

"You're mad."

"Stop." I shook my head. "Remember, we're not the 'you're mad' couple."

"Then just say it." He smirked.

It was the first time I hated his stupid dimples. "I despise clichés, I really do. And I love how we make no sense and perfect sense at the same time. I even love having no damn clue if I'm pregnant or not. It makes me feel so ... *alive.* But ..." I shook my head.

"But?"

"But 'sure' ? Really? You flew to China to kiss me. Let me say that again. You. Flew. To. China. To. Kiss. Me!"

"You want to get married in China?"

"Gah!" I threw my hands up, turned, and stomped into the bathroom. "I need to shower and get to bed. I have an early flight."

"Early? Like what? Eight?" He chuckled.

I slammed the door. My flight was at nine, but screw him for making fun of me.

CHAPTER THIRTY-THREE

THE BRAWL

I FLEW to New York the next morning, with a back-breaking chip on my shoulder and a boyfriend oblivious to his douchebag-ness. It wasn't a glamorous word, or a real one for that matter, but it was the most fitting one. The notecard in my bag should have been a heart-melting gesture:

CHAPTER NINE

But it wasn't.

The following ten days were a complete blur. At every turn I had a camera or microphone thrust into my face—questions about the photos and article, questions about my relationship with Cage, questions about my secret affair with Everson's nanny.

Thad and I were supposed to be changing the world, but my personal life seemed to trump everything else. His incessant eye rolling and jaw grinding said he was fed up with the sideshow of my life. Even the scheduled interviews that were supposed to *only* be about the magazine article and Thad's inventions ended with slipping in a question or two about my relationship with Minnesota's famous quarterback.

Texting with Cage seemed to focus on the same shit. I was sick of it.

Cage: *I read you're having an affair with Thad.*

Lake: *Who's the blonde with you on the front page of the sports section?*

Cage: *I miss you.*

Lake: *I miss you more.*

Our schedules did their absolute best to keep us apart. After my ten days with Thad, and one missed game of Cage's, I returned home for swapping out the clothes in my suitcase, desperate, hot sex with Cage, and right back on a plane for another week of promotion.

I made it back in time for Cage's last game before Thanksgiving. It was a home game, so I went to it with Shayna and Jamie.

"You're quite the celebrity." Jamie smirked as we took our seats, bundled up for the cold evening game.

"I'm an exotic animal on display. I hate it. Thad is extremely agitated. I'm surprised I still have a job."

"Look!" Shayna jumped to her feet. "Evson?" she yelled, seeing him warming up on the field.

"He can't hear you sweetie."

She plopped back in her seat with a frown.

Two guys in front of us, dressed in apparel for the opposing team, turned around once, then the bigger guy directly in front of me stood and turned. "You're her." He smirked, the kind that made me cringe.

I returned a polite smile, praying he'd take a seat and not get anymore drunk than he already seemed to be.

"I seen them pictures of you."

I gulped down the thick knot in my throat, trying to hide my nerves as Jamie scooted forward in his seat.

Drunk guy's eyes shifted to my leg that was covered in jeans and tall, yellow Bogs boots.

"You're the naked chick without a leg."

Jamie stood.

"The leg makes me sick, but your body, I'd turn a blind eye and fuck you any—"

Aaannd he was tumbling into the people in front of us, grunting like a stabbed pig and bleeding from his nose like one as well. Jamie shook out his fist and Shayna cried, burying her face into my chest as I hugged her to me.

"You fucker!" Drunk guy's sidekick threw a clumsy punch at Jamie, but my British hero hammered in his nose as well.

"Lake, take Shayna and get out of here," Jamie warned as security headed toward the erupting brawl.

What started out as Jamie putting two pricks in their place turned into an all-out war in the stands. One team's fans against the other team's fans.

Shayna wouldn't let go of my leg.

"Come on, sweetie. We have to get out of here. Shayna!"

She refused to move, so I picked her up and maneuvered my way to the aisle. It was chaos navigating down the stairs as everyone else shoved their way toward the commotion.

"Shay!" I hugged her tight to me, cupping the back of her head and curling my body around hers as I lost my footing and fell forward down the steep incline of stairs.

Pain—my back, my arm, my head, my mouth. Lights, bodies, and voices blurred in chaos.

"Lake!" Shayna's voice echoed as her perfect little face hovered just inches from mine.

God ... the pain.

CAGE

It was a big game, but at that point, being one of the few undefeated teams left in the NFL made every game a big game. It was hard not to think about the playoffs, the Super Bowl.

One game at a time.

"Shit's getting real." Our offensive coordinator nodded toward the stands. "The bigger the game ... the bigger the fights in the crowd seem to be."

I threw the ball then turned toward the commotion.

"Lake."

"What?" he asked.

I never let her distract me during the game, but I always knew exactly where she was sitting, and the brawl in the crowd, peppered with security guards that didn't seem to have a damn bit of control over the fans, was exactly where her seat was with Shayna's and Jamie's.

"Monaghan? Where are you going? Stay the hell out of that," my offensive coordinator called.

Even though my stomach wanted to empty its contents onto the field because I had a really sick feeling about the scene before me, I kept going, picking up speed. Jumping to the first row, I hopped over the railing and shoved my way into the thick of it. Within seconds I spotted Flint at the bottom of the stairs along with paramedics.

My presence drew a whole new commotion as fans attempted to shove shit into me to sign, and everyone had a camera phone in my face. Flint looked up and shook his head. I couldn't see past the circle of people huddled around the paramedics, but when my eyes shifted to Shayna standing next to Flint, tears rolling down her face, I knew. The familiar yellow boot flopped to the side next to one of the hunched over paramedics confirmed my fear.

"Move ..." I shoved through the congestion of people on the stairs. "Move ... get the fuck out of my way!"

Flint had the nerve to try and step in front of me and block my pursuit.

"I'll handle this. You get your ass back on the field."

I narrowed my eyes at him. "Friends or not. I will plant your ass on the ground without a second thought if you don't get The. Fuck. Out. Of. My. Way."

"Cage!" Shayna hugged my leg.

Flint shifted his stubborn gaze to her then stepped aside.

"Lake's bleeding ..." Shayna cried.

"Stay with Flint." I peeled her fisted hands from my pants and took one more step forward.

"Fuck," I whispered as they lifted her body onto the stretcher.

She was strapped down, head in a neck brace and blood oozing from a slew of gauze pressed to her nose and mouth, but her eyes were open wide.

"Lake ..." her name broke from my throat; it had a hell of a time squeezing past my heart lodged at the base.

Her eyes rolled to the side.

"Fuck, baby ..." That's not what I meant to say, but I

just couldn't think of anything but wondering what the hell happened. "I'm here. I'm coming too. I won't leave your side."

"Cage—"

I turned toward Flint, daring him to say one word. "It's just a game."

The look on his face hardened. "It's not just a game and you know it. She's just a girl, and she'll be fine."

I grabbed Shayna's hand and pulled her toward me as I leaned forward and whispered in Flint's ear.

"Fuck you and ... you're fired."

LAKE

Two missing front teeth.

Stitches in my lip.

Bruised ribs.

And one pissed-off quarterback.

That summed up my Sunday night football experience.

"I'm quitting." Those were the first two words I heard when I opened my eyes and my first clue that I was dealing with a pissed-off quarterback.

My head eased side to side.

He rested his forehead gently on my stomach.

My hand eased to his head. I wanted to comfort him with a witty reply, but as my tongue grazed the jagged edges of the remaining stubs of my front teeth, I decided I would never speak or smile again.

He turned his head, looking up at me. "You can't talk, huh?"

I lifted my shoulders a fraction, feeling a twinge in my ribs.

"You have stitches in your lip."

I nodded.

He grimaced. "Your two front teeth are fractured.

I nodded.

"Your ribs are bruised."

That explained the twinge. I nodded.

"Jamie was arrested."

My eyes widened.

Cage sat up and rubbed his face. "I fired Flint, so I called my attorney to deal with getting Jamie out."

He fired Flint. My heart broke. Flint was his friend. What happened to me had nothing to do with Flint.

I tried to speak, but my first word ended in a grimace that only made the pain worse when it pulled at the stitches in my lip.

"Don't." Cage shook his head. "Everything is fine. Shayna is with Penny until Everson gets home. I called your parents. They're waiting to hear back from me. I said I'd call again when you woke. From the panic that was in your mom's voice, I'm guessing she's already on a plane."

Hearing voices close by, I scanned the room, realizing we weren't actually in a room. It was nothing more than a hospital bed and a chair enclosed by a wall of machines to my back and a sliding curtain on the other three sides.

"Lake."

My eyes shifted to the brunette in navy scrubs sliding open the curtain.

"How's your pain level? Do you need more pain management?"

I shook my head. Yes, I felt pain, but nothing unbearable.

"Okay. No concussion. You're free to go. You can thank this young man for your lip."

My eyes narrowed.

"He insisted we have a plastic surgeon come down to stitch up your lip instead of the oral surgeon on-call." She gave Cage a smirk.

He didn't seem to care.

"Our on-call dentist did what he could. You'll want to make an appointment with your dentist. Ice your face if you can and ice your ribs along with pain medication. Take it easy for the next few days. Nothing strenuous. Focus on your breathing when you can and try to take some slow, deep breaths even though it might hurt a bit. Okay?"

I nodded.

"We checked over your leg and it looks fine, so as long as you don't have any issues with your prosthetic, you should be fine."

Another nod. Damn! Worst injury ever for a chatty person like myself.

Cage thanked the doctor. As he stood, I noticed he was still wearing his uniform pants and cleats with a gray Minnesota T-shirt. Flint would have already been there with a complete change of clothes and his truck waiting in the parking lot. I think I saw the same thoughts go through Cage's mind as I looked him over.

"Easy does it." He helped me sit up, one inch at a time.

Blood-tinged saliva hung in a long string from my mouth. I couldn't even swallow properly yet. Attractive.

There really had to be a limit for how many hospital trips were allowed in the first six months of a relationship. Cage had to think, "She's going to the hospital *again*?" Could I be anymore clumsy?

"Shay ..." I tried to talk without moving my mouth at all.

It sounded like I was mad, gritting the word through my clenched teeth.

"I told you she's with Penny. She's fine. She said you were carrying her and you fell." He shook his head as he eased my gown from my shoulders. "Whatever you did, it kept her from getting as much as a scratch. You..." his eyes met mine "...didn't get so lucky."

That's all that mattered to me. Everything happened so fast, but I remember the moment I lost my footing all I thought about was Shayna and hugging her to me, protecting her.

He stared at my naked chest. I quirked a brow. It was not the time for that. Cage shook his head with a small smirk.

"I'm just wondering if we should leave off your bra. It might feel too tight around your ribs."

I nodded. He helped put my leg on, like the pro he'd become with it, then he helped with my shirt and pants.

"Easy." He helped me off the bed.

My ribs ... they hurt.

"You want me to get a wheelchair?"

I shook my head.

"Want me to carry you?"

I gave him the are-you-serious look.

"It was just an offer."

Big surprise. We were met with a small crowd of photographers as we exited the hospital.

I tipped my chin down, and Cage held one hand in front of my face as he guided me with his other hand. A familiar black Mercedes pulled up.

"We'll find a cab," he mumbled to me as Flint got out and opened the back door.

"No." Cage shook his head.

"Swallow your fucking pride and put your girl in the back of my car."

They had a brief stare-off.

"This means nothing."

Flint nodded.

"Easy," Cage whispered as I got in the back seat.

He made his way around to the other side, exchanging a few words with Flint that I couldn't hear, and then got in next to me. Camera flashes sparkled in the night as Flint pulled away from the curb.

"Your truck is at your house."

Cage didn't respond.

"Your team lost. Bennigan threw five picks, two that led to touchdown conversions."

Still no response, but the grip he had on my leg tightened a fraction with Flint's words. I looked over at Cage, but he kept his eyes trained to the window, watching the road pass by.

When we pulled up in front of Cage's house, he helped me out and led me toward the door without a word or glance in Flint's direction. I stopped.

Cage narrowed his brow. "You okay?"

I turned, pulling away from his protective arms and walked back to the car where Flint still stood by the driver's door. Flint shared the same confused expression as Cage had.

I looked up. "Thank you," I whispered as best I could, but not loud enough for Cage to hear.

Flint just stared at me for a few moments then nodded once.

As I walked back toward Cage, I could see the look of betrayal in his eyes, but he didn't say anything.

CHAPTER THIRTY-FOUR

ALL THE WRONG WORDS

The straw that broke the camel's back wasn't just a clichéd saying. There was truth to it. *One* seemed insignificant until it was the one that was one too many. My relationship with Cage felt invincible, until all of our ones began to multiply.

He didn't quit. In fact his coaches and the whole team supported his decision to miss the game to be with me even though they did lose. Cage said it wasn't the worst thing ever. A lot of pressure came with being undefeated. He said they were able to refocus on the bigger goal instead of worrying about the loss that could take away their undefeated record.

I only half-believed him. Nobody liked to lose.

Jamie went from embarrassing male nanny to brute hero in both Everson's and Cage's eyes. The guy ended up taking out four drunks all from the opposing team's fans—another bonus—before the police had him in handcuffs. Jamie still had a court date scheduled, but he was out of jail and Cage's attorney said getting the charges dropped would be a chip shot.

Flint Hopkins got his job back after I insisted Cage forgive him. I knew it was hard for Cage because he wasn't there, but I would never forget watching Flint save Shayna. He would have to do something far worse than suggest Cage play instead of go to the hospital for me to justify Cage firing him.

My parents stayed through Thanksgiving. I felt it was overkill for a sutured lip and a couple of missing teeth, but I kept that to myself because football players didn't get the holidays off. Their presence took the edge off only getting to see Cage for a few short hours on Thanksgiving. Those few hours were heartbreaking. Cage confessed it was the anniversary of his father's death. I found it hard to be thankful that day.

Thad was fine going solo to our scheduled interviews. I'm sure he was secretly thrilled to not have to deal with my personal drama. Me? I watched my face go through a rainbow of colors as my lip healed. The day I got my implants was the best day ever. It was easy to take teeth for granted until the two most prominent ones got busted out. Not pretty, and talk about feeling insecure ... I didn't feel that insecure when I woke up missing part of my leg.

Crazy.

Lake: *CHAPTER TEN – Hope I'm allowed to declare the beginning of new chapters too!*
Lake: *Cheese!*

I sent a photo of my new smile as I left the prosthodontist's office. Cage was busy. I knew and fully understood that, but he didn't reply at all, not even a smiley face.

"Seriously, who doesn't have time to push the damn smiley emoji?"

Penny chuckled as I refilled her glass of red wine. We watched the early December flurries dance in the air from the grand wall of windows in Cage's dining room overlooking his deep wooded lot.

"I can ask this because I'm a woman so you can't get mad at me, okay?"

"What?"

"Are you having your period?"

I laughed. She was right. Had Cage asked me that, I would have decapitated him. "No."

"Are you pregnant?"

"No." We haven't had sex since I last had my period.

"No sex?" Penny's back stiffened, wide surprise in her eyes.

"I've been traveling, and then I was having my period when the accident happened, and since then we just haven't. I think the front-teeth-knocked-out-stitches-in-the-lip thing put a damper on things—that and him always being gone or watching game footage until his curfew."

"Curfew?"

"Yes. Sleep is important for performance, recovery, testosterone, HGH, etc."

"And sex?" Penny wiggled her brows.

I grinned. "I miss it. I miss him."

She glanced at her phone. "Shouldn't he be home soon?"

"Probably. I don't know. He's been eating all of his meals there so anytime between eight and nine he shows up, watches footage, and goes to bed. It's crazy how lonely I feel, yet I wasn't really lonely before I met him. It's such a weird I-had-no-idea-something-was-missing feeling. His presence spoiled me and now I miss it. I miss us."

"But you're still pissed about his lack of response to your smiling selfie?"

"Correct." I scrunched my nose as I heard the door creak a bit. "He's home."

Penny gulped the rest of her wine.

"Can you drive?"

"Pfft …" She waved her hand. "Sadly, it takes more than two glasses to impair this chick. Take care, honey. I'm always here for you … if you have wine."

I smiled as she hugged me. "Thanks, Penny."

"Hey, Penny." Cage gave her a tired smile as he dropped his bag to the floor and tossed his keys on the counter.

"Hey, number one." She winked. "Great game. Way to kick some Chicago ass last Sunday."

"Thanks."

She brushed past him. "Throw your girl a bone. She misses you." She took two more steps past him. "Oh, and answer her texts."

I wanted to die. Damn Penny and her uncensored mouth.

Cage perked a brow, be it a tired one, at me.

My lips pulled into a firm line as I closed my eyes briefly while shaking my head. When the front door clicked shut I opened them. "Hi."

"What does throw my girl a bone mean?"

"Nothing." I shook my head, gathering our wine glasses and carrying them to the kitchen.

"Doesn't sound like nothing."

I turned, running my hands through my hair. "I miss you. So what? It's no big deal."

He held out his hands. "Well, I'm here. Are you still missing me?"

I grunted a cynical laugh. "No game footage to watch?"

"You're upset about me watching—"

I shook my head. "I'm not. That's why I haven't said anything."

"Well, you said something to Penny about it, and apparently I messed up by not responding to your photo."

He did see it. That pissed me off more than it should have. Crossing my arms over my chest, I shot him a closed-lip smile. "How was your day?"

"Really? You want to know about my day?"

No. I didn't. I just wanted to kick down the damn wall between us, and I wanted him to hold me because he *needed* me. I wanted him to need my touch as much as I needed his.

He took my hesitation as his answer. "I'll be downstairs."

"Cage ..."

His footsteps faded in the distance.

THE NATURAL STEP that came after a fight was forgiving. The problem was, I didn't know if we had been or were fighting. Things were off between us, but not in a pointing-finger sort of way. Cage wasn't around long enough to have an all-out fight. He wasn't around enough to have much of any interaction. I'd even started sleeping in the guest bedroom because ... I wasn't really sleeping at all.

Netflix.

Video chatting with Thad and Jerry.

Nightmares—because I started having them again.

That's what consumed my nights. At least Cage was getting undisturbed sleep, but I couldn't help the resentment that bloomed inside of me. After the first night I spent in the guest room, he asked why I slept in there and I told him because I didn't want to keep him awake with my restlessness.

He said "OK" and left it at that.

OK! He had no idea how the simplicity of his responses grated on my very last nerve.

By the time Friday rolled around, I was ready for him to get on that plane and fly to Texas. At least if he was out of town I didn't feel so utterly ignored.

"You look tired." He kissed the top of my head as he brushed by me in the closet, throwing clothes into his bag for the trip as I hung up the clean laundry.

"I am."

"Well maybe you can get some sleep while I'm gone."

"Maybe I can get some sex too," I mumbled to myself, not at all intending for him to hear me.

"What did you say?" He turned.

"Nothing." I shook my head.

"No. You said 'maybe you can get some sex too.' What the fuck is that supposed to mean? Who the hell are you having sex with?"

With my back to him, I rested my hands on my hips and looked up at the ceiling, an exhausted sigh mixed with a laugh escaped. "No one. Absofuckinglutely no one. That's my point. Just forget it." I grabbed a shirt from the laundry basket and slipped it on a hanger.

"I can't be everything, Lake. I don't know what you want me to—"

I turned, anger brewing in my belly. "Don't do this. Don't you dare say you don't know what I want you to do. That's such bullshit."

His defensive stance mirrored mine as the wall between

us accumulated another layer. "So everything I say is bullshit? Like I'm lying to you?"

It wasn't too late. All he had to do was take me in his arms. *Really* take me in his arms, not a kiss on the head, or a quick peck on the lips, or a hug that lasted less than a heartbeat. I should have just thrown myself into his arms, but my ego insisted on protecting me from my fears, and I feared he wouldn't reciprocate. I feared feeling even more rejected. I feared the void between us.

When did I begin to fear what I wanted very most in life?

"No," I whispered as regret kicked me in the gut.

"I'm under a lot of stress right now, and I'm not trying to take it out on you. I have this amazing team that could go all the way, and I've been given this opportunity and I don't want to let them down. Some of these guys have been playing for years and they're tired and they want to retire, but they want the ring first. So I have to work twice as hard as all the veteran quarterbacks out there because the probability of me making some rookie mistake that could cost my whole team their chance at the title is really fucking high because I am in many ways still a rookie."

Rubbing my hands over my face, I tried to get my shit together because the chance of me losing it with him at the moment was as high as his chance of making that season-ending rookie mistake. "I'm sorry."

Tongue bite.

I was sorry, but I was also pissed, and confused, and wondering why the hell this was happening to us and if we would make it out in one piece.

Cage sighed. "I didn't want this to be a mistake. I still don't want it to be a mistake. I want to make this work. I'm trying, but if it's too much for you then you need to tell me. I'll understand. Okay?"

Oh my God ...

He broke my heart, like no one had ever broken my heart before. Breathing felt impossible. My lungs refused to draw in air.

Don't cry, Lake! Hold it together. Hold it together. Hold it together ...

"I'll see you in a couple days. Love you." He slung his bag over his shoulder and grabbed the back of my neck pulling me in for a quick kiss.

"Bye," I whispered as he walked off.

When I heard the back door close, I pressed one hand to the wall and my other to my heart, clasping the knife he just jabbed into it, as I lowered to my knees, sobs wracking my body.

I was a mistake. We were a mistake.

CHAPTER THIRTY-FIVE

IT'S YOU

"I DON'T BELIEVE IT." Penny grabbed the bottle of wine from me. "And I'm cutting you off because you're a light weight. I bet you can't even stand straight now."

I stared at the bags of my belongings cluttering the floor just inside my front door. Trzy and I were home again.

"Funny ..." The word slurred from my lips. "I was going to let the lease on this place go in February. I guess fate knew something I didn't."

Penny shook her head. She could shake her head all she wanted, but it wouldn't change my situation.

"There's no way he thinks you're a mistake. I have never in my life met a guy who looks and talks about a woman the way Cage Monaghan worships you."

I wanted to cry more, but the alcohol had dried up my tears. "Bad timing, I guess. Maybe I can just be his off-season fling."

"The guy tried to get you pregnant, more than once. That's not a fling, honey. That's a lifetime commitment. He said he wanted to marry you."

I shook my head. "No. When I asked if he was

proposing he said, 'sure.'" I laughed because every other reaction hurt too damn bad. "I don't even want to be here. I want to leave him a note that says, 'good luck, hope you get your ring,' then I want to go back to San Francisco and hold my new niece, Harley, and go to lunch with Jessica, and bug Luke at work between patients."

Penny leaned forward and grabbed my hand, giving it a firm squeeze. "You want to feel loved."

After staring at her hand on mine for a few moments, I looked up and nodded. My tear ducts decided to work again. "I want to feel grounded again."

Penny stood. "I get it. And I don't regret most things in my life, but the running? That I regret. Wait until he gets home and if you still want to go, then walk away. But don't run. OK?"

I wiped the stream of tears from my cheeks. "Okay."

CAGE

We won. One more game until the playoffs, but we already secured a first round bye. The second I stepped off the bus, I ran to my truck, desperate to get home—desperate to get to Lake. I hated how we left things. It ate me alive for three days. I wanted to call. I wanted to text, but I needed to stay focused. I knew the words would mean more in person.

"Lake?" I called. Her vehicle wasn't in the garage, but it made no sense that she wouldn't be there, given the late hour.

I flipped on the light in the bedroom. No Lake. No Trzy. Dropping my bag on the floor I walked to the closet and switched on the light.

Empty.

All of her stuff was gone. It felt as barren as my heart.

"Fuck." I closed my eyes.

After looking for a note or any sign of her and coming up empty, I hopped back in my truck and drove to her apartment.

It was late or early. I didn't care, as I banged on her door. A good minute or so later she opened it, standing before me in a Hello Kitty top and matching shorts. It took all the strength I had to not drop to my knees and beg her to come home. Her eyes were red, her posture lifeless.

"Hey." She smiled and I hated how forced it was. I wanted to own each one of her smiles, but in that moment I didn't feel like I owned anything but her grief.

"You moved out."

A slow nod.

It hurt. It hurt so fucking bad.

I cleared my throat. "Why?"

She wet her lips and rubbed them together as her eyes shined with tears. "I hated being your mistake."

"What?" I narrowed my eyes.

"You said you didn't want this to be a mistake." She blinked and the tears broke free down her beautiful cheeks. "I- I can't sit around waiting for you to decide if we're a mistake. I can't handle feeling like your whole world one minute and then being proposed to with a 'sure' the next. I can't be with you and not *be* with you. I can't handle having you so close and not feeling like I can touch you." She wiped her face and sucked in a shaky breath.

"Jesus, Lake ..." I pressed my palms to the side of my head, shaking it side to side. "I didn't mean us." My hands went from my head to hers, clenching her hair a little tighter than I should have, but I needed her absolute, undivided attention to the words that I had to say. "Football ... my fucking job. *That* was what I meant when I said I didn't want it to be a mistake. *That* was what I meant when I said I understood if it was too much for you."

I bent down until we were at eye level, our faces just inches apart. "It's *you*, Lake. It's you every damn day of the week and twice on any game day. It's you today, it's you tomorrow, it's you a fucking millennium from now. Get. That."

A sob ripped from her chest, and I had to fight my own fucking tears. Nothing in my whole life had ever hit me as hard as the gut-wrenching realization that this woman—my whole damn world—didn't truly feel the infinite depth of my love for her.

LAKE

Harder.

I wanted him to hold me harder. I needed his hands everywhere at the same time. I needed his touch to breathe life back into me because leaving him felt like a slow death. When I opened the door, I barely had a pulse.

"Cage ..."

He kissed me, pushing me backwards and kicking the door shut behind him.

"You're everything," he murmured into my neck, pulling my top off. His mouth dropped to suck in my nipple as my shirt fell to the floor.

I slid his shirt up his torso as he continued to lead me backwards toward my bedroom. When my legs hit the edge of the bed, Cage dropped to his knees and pulled down my shorts and panties, his lips eager to devour every inch of my skin. "Sit," he whispered with his lips pressed to the top of my left leg.

I sat. He slowly removed my leg, and rolled down the sheath leaving me completely naked. We went from a hundred miles an hour to zero in a matter of seconds. Resting his forehead on my leg, he breathed in and breathed out like it took herculean strength to make each conscious exchange of air as his hand caressed my residual limb, feeling every angle as if he needed to memorize it.

"Lake?" he whispered with his head still pressed to my leg.

I ghosted my hand along the back of his head, feeling a little unsteady—a little afraid—because he seemed so vulnerable.

"Yes." I exhaled a slow breath, attempting to calm the surging march of my heart trying to break through my chest.

Cage inched his head up just enough to meet my gaze. "I love you." The pain in his expression brought more tears to my eyes. He owned every single one of my emotions. "Marry me."

Oh God ...

My eyes and nose burned with a whole new level of emotion desperate to break free.

"Give me you. Give me every tear. Give me every breath. Give me every fear. Give me every touch. Give me every smile. Give me every day."

He dipped his head and kissed a trail down my leg and over my knee to where it ended. He kissed every inch of skin until I swear to God I could feel the rest of my leg, until I could feel all ten toes touching the ground.

"Lake..." another kiss "Ivy..." another kiss "...Jones..." his eyes came back to mine "give me *forever*. Give me the *one* thing I cannot live without..." grabbing my backside, he scooted me closer to the edge of the bed and pressed his lips to my chest over my heart "...give me you."

I STARTED by giving him my body while my mind played catch-up. The only fear I had at that moment was the possibility that he'd try to make love to me with patient, calculated moves. That's not what I needed. I needed our physical love to be all-consuming. I needed it to feel as painful as my emotions. His touch—I wanted it to feel branded into my skin, into my soul.

He took every part of me and he took it unapologetically. I felt needed, possessed, and yes, *completely consumed*. The love? It decimated the pain and doubt that life had allowed to creep into my mind. His touch? It owned me and as if he knew exactly what I needed, he didn't wait for me to give him anything ... he took it. He took every single piece of me.

"Yes," I whispered into his neck, my sweaty, completely-spent body a rag doll on top of his.

"When?" he mumbled, like exhaustion had paralyzed his ability to speak.

"I'll marry you yesterday." My lips curled into a grin against his skin.

His hands cupped my ass.

"Perfect."

"My ass?"

He chuckled. "Everything."

"In case you're wondering, 'sure' was not a proposal. *This* ... what you said to me, the oh-my-god-that-was-sex-from-another-dimension thing that just happened, was the world's best proposal. I was right in China to worry about you fumbling, Monaghan. Textbook rookie mistake. But you redeemed yourself with the best game-winning Hail Mary of all time. Congratulations."

His grip on my ass turned into a bruising one. "Are you congratulating me on the sex or the proposal? If it's the sex, then I'm going to be pissed. Name one time I've fumbled with the sex? Name one time you've faked an orgasm with me. Name one time you haven't screamed my name so loud—"

"Down boy." I giggled. "You've never fumbled the sex."

He eased his grip. "I'm sorry ... so very sorry. I let the stress consume me. I was so afraid to give you a second of my time because I knew it would never be enough. I can't find the balance. I'm an addict with you. I can't just take one sip, one hit. It's never enough and that need consumes me."

"Well, in your all-or-nothing world, I can't be the nothing. However, I couldn't live with myself if you made me the everything right now. You have other people counting on you, and I want to see you do this just as much as they do. So don't make me the reason you hate it, make me the reason you love it. You can have both. Stop making it a choice."

Cage ghosted his fingers up my back and threaded them through my hair, lifting my head up to look at him. "But just to be perfectly clear on this: I asked you to marry me and you said yes. Correct?"

My grin gave him the answer first. "Yes. I'll marry you."

"Because at one point you said if I asked you, you'd say no. So technically you can't blame a guy for easing into it with a comment like 'sure.' No one likes to get rejected."

"I was confused that we even had that conversation.

You'd already told me you were going to marry me even if you had to 'drag me to the altar and fuck a yes out of me.'"

His chest vibrated with laughter as he bent an arm back behind his head, tipping his chin down toward me. "And you were OK with that being my official proposal."

"Well..." I shrugged "...yeah. It was hot and spontaneous and a little caveman-like."

"You want me to be a caveman with you?"

"I could think of worse things, and I bet you'd look good in animal skin, carrying a stick or wooden bat-looking thingy to protect your woman."

"I ... um ... sorry, no. The Neanderthal role doesn't work for me."

"Oh, so we're role-playing. Well then, I'm sure the football player/cheerleading thing is your area of expertise. Have you ever had sex with a cheerleader?"

Cage shook his head. "I'm not doing this. No way. I'm not doing the 'how many girls have you slept with?' You like to say what is and is *not* us. Well, this is not us. If you can think back to what has happened in the past hour, then you know what we have is a storm ... an explosive phenomena larger than life ... something so far beyond any comparison."

My breath caught in my chest. We were still falling. Fuck gravity. My love for that man was so beyond healthy, I should have been committed. I scooted up and kissed him, and then rubbing my nose along his, I smiled. "But seriously, how many women have you slept with?"

He flipped me over, pinning me to the bed. "Only *one* that I care to remember."

CHAPTER THIRTY-SIX

TOO. DAMN. HIGH

CAGE

I LEFT my Sleeping Beauty with a **CHAPTER ELEVEN** card by the bed.

Lake: *I think I'm going to really like this chapter! I was thinking of telling my family that I'm getting married. What do you think?*

I downed the rest of my breakfast before meeting with my coaches to watch the footage from the previous day's game.

"Porn?" Grayson, one of my wide receivers sat down across from me.

I continued to stare at Lake's text. "Better than porn."

"Not possible."

"Clearly you haven't met my favorite lake."

"Mmm ... no, but I've seen her photos."

Looking up, I narrowed my eyes.

He held up his hands. "It's all good. They're tasteful.

And out of respect to you, I have a copy of the magazine on my coffee table, not on my bed stand."

"Good to know you value your life."

Cage: *Who's the lucky guy?*

Lake: *The one with his face buried between my legs right now.*

Cage: *Watch it.*

Lake: *I'm shipping Christmas gifts today. I don't have anything for your family yet, and Christmas is in one week.*

Cage: *I've taken care of it.*

Lake: *For real?*

I laughed. Grayson gave me a smirk.

Cage: *For real.*

Lake: *What do you want?*

Cage: *I think you mentioned the area between your legs. Throw a bow on it and I'm good.*

Lake: *Yeah, so I'm going to call my family now and tell them.*

Cage: *I didn't ask your dad for permission. Maybe you should wait until I ask him. Huge oversight on my part.*

Lake: *Sure. You've been attempting to impregnate his daughter for weeks. I feel pretty certain nothing about the proposal was an oversight, but rather an afterthought by this point.*

A baby. God, I could hear Tom Jones grilling me about that. *"Did you knock my baby girl up? Did you 'enjoy' knocking her up?"*

Cage: *Would it be weird to get married and even have children without actually telling your family?*

Lake: *Um …*

Cage: *Forget I asked. Tell them hi. Gotta go. Love you.*

"Sexting?"

I shook my head. "Grayson, you need a life."

"Football is my life."

Standing, I wiped my mouth one last time and tossed my napkin on my empty plate.

"It's not a life. It's a game—one you won't play forever. A life ... get a life, dude."

LAKE

THE GUY.

The proposal.

The ring.

By January I had it all. I owed God an apology. Dreams really did come true.

"It's too big?"

With his nose in the refrigerator, back to me, how did he know I was staring at my ring?

"It is." I wiggled my fingers, grinning as the early morning light hit it, sending a kaleidoscope of colors splattering along the ceiling and walls.

"I should exchange it." He turned, pouring a tall glass of orange juice.

My eyes remained glued to my left hand while my right one scooped chocolate hazelnut butter out of my waffle divots. "You shouldn't."

"Do your parents know I have playoff tickets for them?"

"Uh huh." It really was perfect—a simple, round solitaire. A *big* solitaire sitting atop a diamond and sapphire platinum band.

"They are in the stands with my family. *You* are in the box with Shayna and the owner's family."

I cut my gaze to his. "You're being overprotective."

"Tough shit." He swept my hair off my back and kissed it, letting his lips linger until my skin was covered in goose bumps and my body shivered. "Your days of sitting in the stands are over. Besides, I didn't ask for a seat in the box, Gretchen, the owner's wife, insisted that's where you and Shayna sit after your incident."

" 'Cause they don't want to lose a game again because of their quarterback choosing his injured girlfriend over the game."

"It would be my injured fiancée now, but I'm sure there is more than one reason for their generosity. Again, I don't give a shit. Your safety is my number one priority."

I licked my finger clean and turned toward him, hooking my fingers through the belt loops of his faded jeans. "Does this scare you?"

He squinted. "What?"

"This life? Our life? Does it seem too perfect? Us ... your near-perfect season ... the real possibility of winning the Super Bowl?"

He shrugged. "One game at a time. One day at a time."

"One wife at a time?" I grinned.

Twisting my ring on my finger, he smiled. "One wife for a lifetime."

He was good—really good.

"I'm scared." My lips held a residual smile to hide the true depth of my fear.

Cage's hand slid behind my hair, gently holding my neck as he leaned down and kissed me. "What are you scared of?" he whispered over my lips.

"I'm afraid we're too high. I'm afraid the universe—

God—is going to demand balance again. I'm afraid we're going to stop falling when the ground hits us." I rested my hands flat on his chest. "I'm afraid of the ground."

Resting his forehead on mine, he rolled it side to side. "Fuck gravity."

UP.

Up.

Up.

Minnesota made it to the Super Bowl and they made it in the year that Minneapolis was hosting it. Things couldn't get any better. I was engaged to a sports rock star. It didn't even matter that all the trashy tabloids had us cheating on each other. Gravity? We weren't falling anymore. We were flying.

"Just keep moving." Flint and several bodyguards led me through the sea of fans flooding the field. Confetti snowed down on us as the NFC Championship celebration on the field reached its peak.

I couldn't see him.

I couldn't see him.

And then ... I saw him and only him. I could barely breathe. He stood behind the stage wearing his championship shirt and hat. He looked like a young boy who just lassoed the moon. Handing me a football, the one he ran into the end zone on the final play of the game, he shook his head. Then he wrapped his arms around me and lifted me off the ground.

"Now it's real. God, I love you! Nothing in my life is real until I'm sharing it with you." He kissed me and I loved that he couldn't even contain his grin long enough to kiss me.

"Congratulations! Way to not fumble, Monaghan." I grinned, biting my bottom lip, feeling the elation of it all on my own face.

Ten seconds. That's how much time we had in our own little bubble before Flint and the group of security guards succumbed to the throng of players, photographers, and fans.

"Come on." Cage took my hand and led me to the stairs going up the back of the stage where they were going to present the trophy.

I shook my head, trying to pull my hand out of his grasp. "It's all you."

"I'll throw you over my shoulder." His brows lifted.

My eyes did their customary roll as I gave in and followed him onto the stage.

Gretchen, the owner's wife, put her arm around my waist, keeping me steady as Cage took his place in the spotlight with her husband and the head coach as the announcer began the presentation. I needed her support. My whole body shook from the adrenaline.

"Show the cameras that beautiful smile of yours. They love you too, you know." Gretchen winked.

I wasn't so sure "they" loved me too. I'm pretty sure there was an "I Hate Lake Jones" Facebook group with thousands of jealous women bashing the girl with the missing leg. Facebook was a shit-fest like that.

I couldn't hear anything but my own heart pounding and the whoosh of blood in my ears. A few minutes later Cage turned, holding a big-ass football trophy in one hand and reaching for me with his other hand. He kissed me while a sea of flashes flooded the stadium and more cheers erupted.

"Fuck gravity," he whispered in my ear before turning toward the crowd again.

I smiled, but beneath it was the worst feeling in the world. A knot in my gut pulled so tight I thought I might buckle over. We were too high.

Too. Damn. High ...

I RODE BACK with my parents to Cage's while he finished his post-game interviews. We stopped by the drug store for me to get some toothpaste. The bag I carried back out to the car had a box of pregnancy tests, no toothpaste. My parents were none the wiser.

Brooke, Rob, and the girls beat us back and had boxes of pizza and beer waiting for everyone.

"You feeling okay, sweetie?" My mom asked as I headed toward our bedroom.

I turned, forcing a smile, which was hard to do even with everyone else practically glowing. "Yeah. It's just been a crazy day. Good but crazy. I'm going to put my toothpaste in the bathroom. I'll be right back."

My mom, nodded, but skepticism lined her brow.

Tearing into the box, I pulled out the first stick.

Negative.

The second and third tests were also negative.

"Shit." I looked at my disheveled reflection in the mirror. I wanted to be pregnant so badly because it would have meant the worst feeling ever was for the best reason ever. Instead, I was left feeling like a fucking bomb was waiting to go off. Why? I had no clue. It was just a feeling. A feeling so strong I felt on the verge of tears. I just couldn't define it yet.

"Cage!" Hayden and Isa screamed in unison.

I turned on the faucet and splashed cold water on my face. "Get it together," I mumbled into the towel as I quickly blotted my face.

I peeked around the corner to the celebration in the kitchen.

Smile. Just smile.

Cage turned, setting down the near-empty bottle of his electrolyte drink. "Hey."

I smiled. It felt all kinds of wrong, but I did it anyway. "Hey." Ignoring the cancer eating me up inside, I walked into his waiting arms.

His lips settled next to my ear. "We should have put them up in a nice hotel," he whispered. His firm erection pressed to my stomach told me why. Apparently making it to the Super Bowl caused extreme horniness.

I should have shared his desperate desires, but the-world-is-coming-to-an-end cloud that hung over me didn't allow any sunshine on my libido.

"Bedtime girls." Brooke smiled at us and so did my mom.

Heat climbed up my neck. They *knew* exactly what Mr. Sports Sensation was whispering to me.

"Mr. Jones." My mom nudged my dad who still had a beer in one hand and a half piece of pizza in his other hand. "Bedtime. Finish up."

It felt like a wedding reception where everyone knew exactly what the bride and groom were getting ready to go do, except in the wedding scenario they weren't doing it in the same house as both sets of parents *and* two eight-year-olds.

"Goodnight, my boy." Brooke hugged Cage then her

voice lowered a notch. "Your dad would have been so proud."

Cage swallowed hard and nodded. I looked away, blinking back my own tears.

My dad gave me a hug then pointed to Cage. Cage grinned. "Well done, Lake."

I rolled my eyes.

"He didn't ask for my permission to marry you, but I'll let it slide if he's named the Super Bowl's MVP."

A slight cringe wrinkled Cage's face. He wanted to ask my dad.

"Goodnight, Dad."

He released me and patted Cage on the shoulder as he followed my mom to the walk-out level.

"Bedroom," Cage mouthed to me as we stood alone in the kitchen.

"I should tidy up the kit—Cage!" I squealed, but not before he had me over his shoulder, hauling me toward the bedroom like the caveman he claimed not to be. "Take off your clothes," he demanded the second my feet touched the ground. The lock clicked. He eyed me with a hungry look. "Off."

Too. Damn. High.

On a deep breath, I pulled my sweater over my head. His eyes settled on my breasts for a few seconds before he shrugged off his shirt. "Keep going." A naughty smirk played along his lips.

"My boots," I whispered.

He kneeled before me, pulling off my yellow Bogs then sliding down my jeans, steadying me with one hand on my waist while his other finished peeling them off my legs. Rising up onto his knees, his lips pressed to my navel as his hands slid behind me, unclasping my bra. "So beautiful ..." he whispered over my flesh.

I closed my eyes, feeling nothing but the single tear that slid down my cheek.

"Baby ..." the pad of his thumb caught it, tracing its path back to my eye. "What's wrong?"

Too. Damn. High.

"I'm scared."

He shook his head, hugging me to his body as he stood, taking me with him. He eased me back on the bed, covering my mouth with his. Our tongues slid together and more tears clawed their way out as he moaned into me. When he pushed off the bed to remove his pants, I turned my head and quickly wiped my eyes.

"Lake, look at me."

On a hard swallow I gave him my eyes.

He slid down my panties as he crawled up my body, never taking his eyes from mine. "Don't be scared. You're my world. I'll protect you with my life. You know that, right?" His chin dipped.

My eyes closed as his tongue circled my nipple. Why was it such a beautiful pain? It should have just been *beautiful*.

He buried himself inside of me, his lips tasting the skin along my neck.

I felt ... nothing. My eyes remained fixed to the white ceiling.

I felt ... numb. My hands limp against the back of his head as he moved inside of me.

I felt ... *dead*. My heart slowed ... slowed ... slowed ...

CHAPTER THIRTY-SEVEN

DREAMS OF THE WORST KIND

"NOOOO!"

I shot up in bed. My lungs gasped for air like a baby taking its first breath, but it felt more like my last as sweat beaded along my brow and rolled down my whole body, soaking my nightshirt.

"Lake!" Cage pulled me into his arms. "Shh ... I've got you."

I sobbed.

"It's OK ... shh ... it was just a dream, baby."

It wasn't. Dreams didn't sink their claws into your soul and rip it to shreds. I wrapped my arms around his neck and squeezed him. "Don't go. Please don't go."

"It's three in the morning. I'm not going anywhere."

Keeping a death grip around his neck, I shook my head. "I'm scared."

"Hey." He pried my arms off his neck and turned on the lamp.

We both squinted against the initial burning of our pupils.

"Look at me." He cupped my face. "What's going on with you? This is your third nightmare in the past week."

"You're on the field ... h-hurt."

"I'm here. I'm fine. It's just a nightmare. Okay?"

"It's so real ..."

"It's not. I'm here. You can touch me. I'm fine. You're fine ... we're fine."

"Don't go ..." I whispered.

He peeled off my soaked shirt and grabbed his white tee from the end of the bed and slipped it on over my head. "I'm not going anywhere." After switching off the light, he pulled my back into his chest and held me tight until sleep came for me again.

"MUST BE SERIOUS." Luke smiled, standing at the door.

My whole family and Cage's were in Minneapolis for the Super Bowl that was just three days away. Cage had a big house, but not big enough for the entire Jones clan, so everyone except our parents stayed at a hotel.

"Where's Jessica and the kids?"

"They stayed back at the hotel. You said you needed to talk to me ... you said it was really important so I came alone."

I nodded, closing the door behind us.

"Where are Cage's parents?"

"They took Hayden and Isa shopping. Mall of America."

Luke nodded, making himself at home in the black and white striped side table chair nearest the kitchen windows.

"Coffee? Tea? Beer? Wine?"

"Water." He smiled. "You look off."

"You mean a fucked-up nervous wreck?" I handed him the glass of water and sat down across from him.

He took a sip. "Brother to sister? Yes. You look like a fucked-up nervous wreck. I was playing the polite doctor role."

"Do you believe in premonitions?"

"The sixth sense? I've dealt with patients who have had premonitions. It's not a well understood phenomenon, but I'm not opposed to the possibility that some people have them."

"God!" I shook my head, running my fingers through my hair. "This is why I never talk to you about shit. It was a simple yes or no question." And just like that ... it hit me how much this *feeling* had affected me. That's not what I meant to say to Luke.

His brow furrowed. He knew it too. "Yes," he said in a soft voice. "I believe people have premonitions ... *feelings* in their gut that are absolute truth. Sometimes it's just a feeling. Sometimes it's more vivid, something that comes to them in a dream. I had the *feeling* with Jess. My gut knew something was terribly wrong before my head could make sense of it. I just ... knew."

I nodded, staring out the windows at the sun shimmering along the snow like diamonds. Swiping the tears from my cheeks, I drew in a shaky breath. "It started out as a feeling for me, like cancer eating away at my gut. I had physical pain with it, but then..." I swallowed hard "...I had the dream—nightmare. It was so clear, so real. The field. The game clock, it had exactly one minute left. Cage was ..." More tears raced down my cheeks. The pain was real. The dream was real.

"Cage was?"

I looked up at Luke. "Lifeless."

Luke let my confession sink in as he nodded slowly. "Hurt?"

"Paramedics. Coaches. Players taking a knee. And the crowd ... silent. But Cage, he doesn't move—not one muscle."

After a few more moments of silence, I laughed through the tears. "Tell me it's crazy. Tell me I'm crazy. Tell me it's impossible. Please, *please* tell me something to make it go away."

Luke said nothing, he just eyed me with what felt like pity.

"Say something," I pleaded.

"I'm sorry." He shook his head.

I bolted out of my chair, sending it screeching across the tile floor. "You're sorry? What does that mean? You're sorry I'm going crazy? You're sorry there's nothing you can do? There's nothing I can do?" I tugged at handfuls of my hair. I was crazy. Crazy felt like shit.

"All of the above."

"This is not fair. You're a goddamn shrink! Tell me what to do."

"Tell him."

I laughed, the certifiable lunatic kind of laugh. "Tell him? Brilliant, Luke. I've told him I'm scared. He knows I've been having nightmares."

"Did you tell him why you're scared?"

I shook my head. "It was just a feeling for the longest time. There wasn't anything to tell."

"And you've told him about the dreams?"

"He knows I've had them, but he doesn't know exactly what they were about."

"Tell him."

I grunted. "And then what? Do you really think he's

going to not play? It's the pinnacle of a football player's career. It's the whole damn reason they do what they do. He's not going to just not play because I had a feeling or a dream."

"You're right. He's still going to play the game."

"Then what's the point?"

"The point is you will have done all that you could do."

"But he'll still play?"

"Yes."

"And get hurt or die or whatever the hell my dream meant."

"It might just be a dream."

"Or it might not."

Luke nodded slowly. "Or it might not."

"God hates me. I don't even know what I did, but he hates me."

"I think we give God too much credit for things he doesn't control and not enough for the things that he does control." He stood. "I have to go. I have a wife who wants a shower." Pulling me into his arms, he whispered next to my ear, "Tell him and then ... pray."

IT SHOULD HAVE BEEN easy to make Cage understand my *feeling*. After all, the whole team stuck to a rigid schedule—meals, practice, interviews, bedtime. No one changed anything. For a bunch of men who didn't want to deviate one bit from their normal schedule for fear of jinxing things, my premonition should not have been such an absurd phenomenon.

Wrong.

"Security will be tight. The number of crazy people will

be doubled. Stay with Flint or one of your brothers at all times. Got it?" Cage zipped his suitcase.

I didn't have a single fingernail left, and the inside of my cheek and my bottom lip were gnawed to about nothing. "How do you feel about premonitions?"

Cage laughed. "I get them all the time. Usually about plays in a game."

"And they're right?"

He shrugged as he shoved his feet into his sneakers. "Sometimes. Why?"

"My nightmares?"

"Yeah?"

"They've been about the game and in them you get hurt."

He eyed me, quirking a brow. "Seriously?"

I nodded.

Cage seemed to think about it and for a fleeting moment I thought he would do or say something to change what felt like fate. "I've had some crazy dreams lately too." He stood. "Come here."

I took cautious steps toward him. The impending-doom feeling felt like every step and every touch would be our last. "I'm not so sure it's crazy. What if it's not?"

He cradled my face in his hands and smiled. Everything about me in that moment was an illusion. I wasn't holding it together on the inside. I was dying and he couldn't see it.

"In your dream, did we at least win the game?"

"Fuck you." I pulled away.

"What? Hey ..." He grabbed my arm and pulled me back to him. "What's going on? I was kidding."

"Well I'm not! I've had this sixth sense about the game. Before I ever had the dreams, I felt physically sick and I just had no idea—no words—to adequately explain this impending sense of dread. But then I had the dreams and you were on the field completely lifeless with everyone surrounding you and the stadium was frozen in silence and ... and ... the clock was stopped at one minute. One!"

"Lake ..." he shook his head. "I'm not trying to dismiss your feelings. I just don't know what you want me to do? Not play? Is that what you're asking?"

I didn't know what I was asking. I wanted him to play as much as I didn't want him to play. It was the most impossible question to answer. It was the most impossible decision to make.

Wiping my face, I relinquished a sad smile. The pain reached a dull numb. All I could feel was the beat of my heart because it—*he*—stood before me. "I don't know what I'm asking, so I guess I'm not asking anything. I just had to tell you, and I'm sorry because I know how selfish it is of me to give this to you right now, but I—"

He hugged me so. Damn. Tight.

"I love you," I whispered. "That's all you really need to know."

CHAPTER THIRTY-EIGHT

ONE MINUTE

CAGE

MY LIFE IN FLASHES:

Lake.

My father.

The moment of impact.

The crowd.

Lake's lips moving along my skin.

The sweat.

The light at the end of the tunnel coming into focus.

My heart beat heavy in my chest.

The roar of 73,000 people.

My lungs fighting for breath.

Lake's back arched, eyes closed, lips parted, as I moved up her naked body.

My mother's voice in my ear.

Fisting my hand over and over to keep it from shaking as flags wave and someone draws out the final note to *The Star Spangle Banner*.

Lake's tears.

Drowning. Fucking drowning in her tears.

A coin rotating again and again in the air on its way to the turf.

The echo of my own voice shouting the play.

And then ... *silence.*

LAKE

Please, God ... this time ... just please don't take him. I'll do anything.

I had the card he left me in my purse:

CHAPTER TWELVE

Lake: *Keep your head in the game. My premonition was just a moment of insanity. Enjoy this moment. You deserve it! Loving you is my life's greatest pleasure. I cannot wait to be your wife. <3*

I didn't know if he'd see it before the game, but it took the edge off by pressing send.

"You good?" Jessica grabbed my hand before Flint escorted me to the owner's suite.

"Luke told you." I looked over her shoulder to the rest of the family alight with excitement. Luke had his back to us. We all owed Penny big time for watching the young kids.

Jess squeezed my hand. "I think you messed with his head too."

I nodded, forcing a smile. I never meant to bring back bad memories for my brother. "I shouldn't have said anything."

Jessica stepped closer, squeezing my hand harder. "He's strong like his father was ... maybe stronger. But you ..." She grinned. "You're me ... maybe even stronger. Survivors aren't made. They're born. You're one of us."

"He could get hurt."

She nodded. "He could."

"He could ..." I couldn't even say it.

She nodded. "He could."

The woman I'd idolized since the day I met her believed in me. I didn't feel deserving. I felt like the girl who built her dreams on a man—a mortal—and everything was ready to crash, taking me in its wreckage.

"He's my everything."

Jessica shook her head. "He's a moment."

"I'm not ready for this moment to end."

She smiled, small, painful, and filled with her own lost moments.

"Ready?" Luke took Jessica's hand.

I drew in a big breath and converted it to a smile for those who had held my hand my whole life. "Go, Minnesota! See you guys on the other side." Grabbing Flint's arm, I followed him to the owner's suite.

Gretchen greeted me right away. "There she is!" She hugged me. "Get a drink and something to eat. Are you ready for this?"

I wasn't. I was so. Not. Ready.

"You have no idea." My lips pulled into a tight smile.

"Not a bad place for him to be in just his second year."

It was the worst fucking place ever, and I was the only one who saw it.

ONE

Ben died and I lived.

I wanted the heart. I wanted his kiss. I wanted that moment.

There didn't have to be a reason he died and I lived. Life was a million things and something profoundly different to everyone, but stripped down to its most simplistic truth, life was always an *experience*.

If there was a God, maybe he didn't really hate me. Maybe he loved me. Maybe he loved me enough to let me *experience* life—without limitations.

I loved Cage. I loved him enough to let him *experience* life—without limitations.

As I eased into my seat, I spotted Monaghan on the field. It was *the* experience for him. Calling it once in a lifetime was such an understatement.

A little boy's dream.

A father's proudest moment.

I hoped AJ was watching his son.

If God was truly all-knowing, then he knew Ben was going to die and I was going to live. He let *life* happen. I had no other choice but to experience the day—the moment—with 73,000 other people.

"You're shaking." Gretchen rested her hands on mine that were folded in my lap. "Gene played for Baltimore many years ago. Did you know that?"

I shook my head. Cage didn't talk much about the team's owners other than to say how grateful he was for their offer to let me sit with them.

"He was a quarterback too. We met in college and got married the summer before his rookie season. I gave myself an ulcer his first season. I was so worried about every tackle, every hit ... for us it's not about the win. Every game that your guy walks off the field on his own is a victory." She squeezed my hands. "I smell victory today."

I wanted to know if her words were a premonition or just bullshit to keep me from vomiting on her expensive shoes. I didn't ask.

Sixty minutes of clock time and four opportunities for it to read 1:00.

Please let it just be a bad dream.

By the end of the first quarter Cage was still fine and Minnesota was up by seven.

By halftime they were up by fourteen and Cage was not only fine, he ran a quarterback sneak play and scored with three seconds left on the clock. He couldn't see me, but he knew just where I was. He kissed two fingers then pointed them in my direction. Gretchen hugged me. My heart still wasn't beating.

Denver tied it up with two minutes left on the clock in the fourth quarter. Just like I had done in the previous three quarters, I held my breath during every play as the numbers on the clock ticked down. I only had to survive one more time that clock would read 1:00.

One minute and ten seconds ... the center hiked the ball.

Nine seconds, Cage took several steps back and cocked his arm ready to throw.

Eight seconds.

Seven seconds.

I grabbed my stomach. That pain? It punched my gut. "NO!" I screamed forcing myself to standing like somehow he'd hear me on the field.

Everyone in the suite looked at me in wide-eyed shock.

Five seconds.

Four seconds.

"Noooo!" I fisted my shirt over my heart. "CAGE!"

He brought the ball back to his chest, protecting it, then he ran with it.

Three seconds.

Ducking his head and hunching his shoulders, he collided head first with a defender.

Two seconds.

All eyes in the suite shifted from me to him as he fell to the ground.

One second.

I banged my hands against the glass. "CAGE!"

With the clock stopped at one minute, my world lay *lifeless* on the field. Coaches, trainers, and doctors rushed to him and that fucking eerie silence spread through the stadium.

Gretchen hugged my back. "It's okay, he'll be okay."

I shook my head, tears bleeding down my face.

Fuck fate.

Fuck premonitions.

Fuck life.

Ben died and I lived. Bullshit ... in that moment I was far from alive. If Cage left, I wanted to go too.

CAGE

"HELP ... ME ..." My words found no voice. My lungs begged for air. I couldn't move.

Before the doctors got to me, I saw it on my teammates' faces—*fear*.

Why wouldn't my hands move? My legs ... I could feel them, but I couldn't move them. My lungs ... what the fuck was wrong with my lungs. Why couldn't I breathe? Tiny puffs of air, that's all I could take. It wasn't enough.

They asked me so many questions as they went through all their checks with me.

"Bring your legs together," one of the doctors instructed.

I couldn't.

Lake. She knew.

They screwed off my face mask and eased me onto the board, strapping me down while someone held both sides of my helmet.

I was paralyzed.

I couldn't breathe.

Lake. She knew.

"Can you give the crowd a thumbs up?" one of the doctors asked.

My thumb moved, more like a twitch, but that was all. Over seventy-thousand people in the stadium, and all I could hear was my heart. It felt weak.

Lake. Where was my Lake? I hated that she was seeing this. What was I going to do? I couldn't hold her and tell her everything would be fine. Would it? Would I ever hold her again?

Then it set in—fear. I was so fucking scared.

Was I paralyzed? Would I ever walk again? Why was it so damn hard to breathe?

Lake ... she knew ...

CHAPTER THIRTY-NINE

DEFINING LUCK

LAKE

HAVING BEEN HUNCHED over in his chair, with his head in his hands, Luke finally looked up at me. Had I not been *completely* numb, I think the pain in his expression would have cut deep into my heart.

Did I still have a beating heart? I couldn't feel it.

"I should have ..." He shook his head.

Jessica rested her hand on his knee. Aside from Cage, the three of us were the only other ones who knew about my premonition. I wanted to tell his mom that it was my fault. I should have done more to stop him. Before the game I had talked myself into believing whatever happened was nothing more than free will ... *life.*

Watching his limp body being taken off the field on a gurney changed everything. Guilt. That's all I had. In a matter of seconds it sucked me in and swallowed me whole.

Hours later they finished their tests and moved him to ICU.

"Come on, Lake." Brooke held out her hand when the nurse gave family permission to see him for the first time.

I stared blankly at her hand. Aside from my eyes shifting from one inanimate object to another over the previous few hours, I don't think I actually moved from my deflated position in the chair. If complete shock had a look, it had to have been me. Even as the waiting room overflowed its capacity with players who came to see him straight from the game, I didn't move. I couldn't.

"Sweetie, you can go see him now." My mom touched my arm.

My eyes shifted to her hand; it was something else to focus on until my eyes glazed over again, taking everything out of focus and back into the empty space of my mind where nothing made sense.

Jessica hunched down in front of me, taking my face in her hands with a firm hold. "This is it. This is where you sink or swim. This is where the survivors are separated from the victims." She grabbed my leg, my prosthetic leg. "You're a survivor. Get up."

I'm sure people around us thought she was being insensitive. I knew otherwise. She loved me too much to watch me ever be a victim. There was a reason I'd idolized her for so long.

She stood and held out her hand. "Up."

An eerie silence claimed the entire waiting room. The numbness began to wear off, and the first thing I felt was a roomful of eyes on me. My naked body circulated around the world in a magazine with a massive readership. I bared everything to everyone without fear, yet I was so fucking scared to take the thirty steps that separated me from Cage.

I stood.

Jess squeezed my hands. "Strength acknowledges weakness. It has a healthy respect for it, but it never submits to it. Got it?"

"Got it," I whispered. Turning, I followed Brooke to the ICU.

THE LOOK.

I refused to have *that* look. It was the look my mom and dad had when I came out of my coma. The we're-so-happy-you're-alive look followed with a chaser of your-body-is-so-messed-up look.

Brooke? She had it the second we walked into the room. I channeled all the damn strength I could from some unknown place and plastered it on my face to not have any reaction. It wasn't easy, given the gazillion wires and machines hooked up to his body, his neck in a massive brace.

"Hey." His voice was soft, a little labored, as his eyes shifted to Brooke.

"Hey." She rested her hand on his. It didn't flinch. "How are you feeling?"

"Not feeling much ... of anything."

I took another step toward him. His gaze cut to meet mine.

"Chapter Thirteen." He tried to grin.

It wasn't funny. I didn't want that chapter in our story.

"You knew ..." he whispered.

I didn't. Couldn't he see that? Had I truly *known*, I would have gone to absolutely any length to keep him off the field. The truth? I knew nothing and yet seeing him in that hospital bed, it appeared as though I'd known everything.

"Knew what?" Brooke looked at me.

I shook my head. "Nothing."

She returned her attention to Cage. "The doctor told us it's a spinal contusion and they're going to run more tests tomorrow, but he's hopeful that you'll regain all bodily function after the swelling goes down. You'll be back on the field in no time."

I grimaced. How could she say that? What mother watches their son take a hit that could have ended their life and says that? I loved Brooke, but in that moment I lost a little respect for her. I hoped she said it for his sake and not for hers.

"We'll see," Cage said.

"There's a ton of players in the waiting room wanting to see you, but they won't let them while you're still in ICU. Your doctor would like to move you out by tomorrow, Tuesday at the latest."

Cage chuckled a little. "He said I'm clogging up the ICU. Even a few patients that know I'm here want to come see me. Catheter bags, IVs, and all. It's crazy."

"You sound so out of breath."

"Hit the area that controls my breathing."

Brooke narrowed her eyes and nodded. "You won." She smiled a little. "Your teammates out there ... they're wearing their Super Bowl Championship shirts and hats."

Cage smiled. I hadn't seen any sign of movement with the rest of his body, but he managed to smile in spite of the gigantic elephant in the room—he appeared paralyzed from the neck down.

Brooke was smiling. He was smiling. Me? I couldn't take another second of it. That weakness? I was ready to acknowledge it, rather it demanded my acknowledgment.

Running into the bathroom, I grabbed my hair and pulled it away from my face as I vomited into the toilet.

"Oh, Lake ..." Brooke rubbed my back. "You poor thing. Here."

As I unfolded my body, feeling a bit of relief, she handed me a wet paper towel. I wiped my mouth.

"I'm sorry."

"Don't apologize. I can't tell you how many times I've felt like doing the same thing since they took him off the field. Nerves. Fear. It's taxing on the body."

Brooke was right. I needed to get rid of that feeling that had been plaguing me. It was ridiculous to fear what had already come to fruition. Cage was in the ICU, paralyzed—and I couldn't do a damn thing about it.

I stepped out of the bathroom and shrugged as Cage eyed me, his brow furrowed.

"Could you give us a few minutes, Mom?"

She brushed her hand over his again, then smiled at me. "Of course." The tears in her eyes didn't go unnoticed by me. Brooke held strong for everyone else, but at some point she too would have to let go of her emotions.

"Thanks," I whispered before she turned to leave.

I just stared at him. It didn't seem real.

"Lake ... touch me."

My eyes inched up his body. "Where?"

He chuckled. "Anywhere. My chest, my arm, my leg. Reach your hand under the blankets and stroke my cock—just don't pull out my catheter. Anywhere, just touch me because you look so fucking scared right now."

"Aren't you?" I fisted my hand several times before resting it on the blanket over his foot. "Aren't you scared?"

"Out of my mind," he said just above a whisper with a

rawness to his voice that hung in the air like it was the first true thing he'd said since he went down on the field.

I feathered my hand up his leg and over his hip and stomach to his bared chest, resting between the mess of wires and electrodes attached to him.

"You're clairvoyant."

I shook my head. "I'm not."

"You knew."

"I didn't." Stepping away from his bed, I ran my hands through my hair, drawing in a deep breath as I turned my back to him. "I didn't *know* a goddamn thing. I felt it. I dreamed it. I tried to hide from it—deny it. Since Ben died, I second guess everything. I live in constant fear of making the wrong decision."

Turning back to him, I pressed my hand to my mouth and slowly shook my head. "It wasn't a premonition about a plane going down that you could have taken a different flight, or a car accident that you could have taken a different route. It was the biggest day of your career. If you wouldn't have played, we never would have known for sure, but your career would have been over. You couldn't just not play because your girlfriend had a bad dream."

"Fiancée."

I paused a moment then nodded.

"You're not calling off the wedding for something as trivial as me not being able to walk or get an erection for that matter ... are you?"

"Not funny. You're trying to make a joke of something so ..."

"The alternative sucks. If I lose my humor, things could get really bad."

I didn't want to smile. It wasn't funny. "Screw you and your damn dimples."

"I love how irresistible I still am to you even with ninety-percent of my body not functioning properly and the stench that has to be wafting from my sticky, sweaty body."

"I'm sure the nurses are already fighting over who will get to give you a sponge bath."

"Hmm ... I'm partial to the blonde with blue tipped spikes."

"You are, huh?" I rolled my eyes. "I don't like to be jealous. If you're not careful, Flint will be bailing me out of jail again for using my bionic leg to kick a nurse's ass for touching yours."

"I think my dick just twitched." He blinked hard, but I was fairly certain it didn't have anything to do with his dick.

"You're in pain."

"My neck and head have had better days."

"Monaghan."

I turned. The doctor who talked to us in the waiting room came in.

"You're causing a ruckus in my ICU. The news of you has led to other patients requesting to see you, claiming it's their dying wish. And I've been told the parking lot has turned into a weird mix between a candlelight vigil and a Super Bowl celebration. Half or more of your teammates and coaches have claimed my waiting room, even though they've all been told they will not be allowed to visit you until tomorrow. So ... here's what I need from you. By tomorrow afternoon, if the swelling has gone down—which it should—I need you to move some body parts for me so we can transfer you to a different room, not in my ICU. Can you do that for me?"

Cage grinned as best he could. "I'll see what I can do."

The doctor looked at me. "He's in good hands. Of course you can stay, but I'd suggest you go get some rest because I have this feeling you're going to be my greatest asset tomorrow to coax our quarterback into sitting ... standing ..." He twisted his lips, looking at Cage. "You might even be a walker. You think he's going to walk for us tomorrow?"

My eyes grew wide and flitted between Cage and the guy in the white coat with the most amazing bedside manner. "Yes." I smiled and it felt real, like it held hope. "Otherwise, I know a guy who can make anyone walk." I winked at Cage.

Thaddeus would have a field day with Cage. Hell, he'd probably hope for Cage to not regain full function just so he could show off a new invention and make headlines again.

"Go home, baby."

"I want to stay."

"You vomited like, twenty minutes ago. You need sleep and food before you come back to give me a shower tomorrow." He grinned at the doctor.

I felt my skin heat with embarrassment.

The doctor kept his chin down, looking at his iPad. "Monaghan, if you walk for me tomorrow, I'll let you invite ten women to give you a shower as long as you and your fan club are out of my ICU."

"Just one, Doc. I only want *one* woman."

I leaned in cautiously, letting my lips hover over his. "Monaghan ... don't forget to love me." I pressed a light kiss to his lips.

"Impossible," he whispered.

CHAPTER FORTY

STEP BY STEP

CAGE

ONE BLINK.

Anyone could close their eyes and imagine what it would be like to be blind, or wear noise canceling earphones and try to imagine what it would be like to be deaf.

Losing all function of your arms and legs? No word could accurately describe that feeling. The "feeling" was not a sensation at all. It was how the brain unearthed fears I never knew existed: fear of never feeling the ground beneath my feet, fear of never feeling the woman I loved in my arms, fear of becoming a waste of space—a burden.

I wondered if my father felt the same fear before he died. When they wheeled me off the field strapped to the gurney, I feared for my life with each labored breath, each look from the doctors, each second of silence surrounded by 73,000 people.

"If you don't walk again, I have dibs on your fishing boat."

"Fuck you, Banks." I coughed, desperate for a drink of water, as I peeled open my eyes. "What time is it?"

"Time for you to get your ass out of that bed. You're going to miss the parade."

"I feel like I got ran over by a damn parade."

A nurse came in with a smile too bright for my mood. "Shall we sit you up and get you some water?"

I stood corrected. She was officially my new best friend.

"Yes, please."

She eased the back of my bed up. I grimaced. Then she held up a cup of water and guided the straw to my lips. I drained it in less than five seconds.

"Thirsty?" She laughed.

"Yeah." I panted. When did drinking less than eight ounces of water exhaust me as much as sprinting the length of the field?

She took my vitals and typed a few things into her iPad. "Doctor Feltz should be in soon."

"Thanks."

Banks watched her leave the room like he was enjoying her ass moving with each step a little too much. "Stop eye-fucking my nurse."

He chuckled. "Well, you weren't givin' her the appreciation she deserved, so I thought I should."

"I'm engaged, in case you didn't hear."

"Yeah, I know Stick worked her freaky voodoo on you. You crazy fuck. She's a handful. What the hell were you thinking?"

I looked down at my hands as my finger curled. They worked.

Thank God.

"I was thinking I should snag her before she realizes I'm nothing more than a boring guy who listens to country music with a fishing pole in my hand. Now I'm on the fast track to losing my body. She's gonna fucking dump my ass."

Banks grinned. "You think she just likes you for your body?"

"Hell yeah."

"You think your dick will work again?"

"God, I hope so. Like ... screw walking, if I have to choose between my dick and my legs—"

"You choose your pecker, no question."

We eyed each other with shit-eating grins plastered to our faces.

"We won."

"I heard."

"Named your weak ass MVP."

"Heard that too. As you can see, I'm clearly very *valuable* right now."

"The hit to you was a fifteen yard penalty; put us in field goal range. Chip shot for three to win the game with no time left on the clock. You earned it long before they took you off the field. Don't doubt that, man."

I shouldn't have been on the field.

The nurse peeked in the room. Banks winked at her.

"A Dr. Westbrook and his colleagues are here to see you. Dr. Feltz asked me to check with you because he was not aware that you requested to see anyone else today. Dr. Westbrook nor any of his colleagues are on staff with the hospital."

Banks stood, tipping his chin up. "I'm outta here. Check with you later."

"Thanks, man. Really."

The nurse gave me a tight smile.

"I'll see them. Thank you."

It surprised me that Lake didn't mention she called

Thad. Even more surprising was how fast he made it to Minneapolis.

"Mr. Monaghan." Thad smiled as he and two other men I'd never seen before followed him.

"Thad. I didn't know you are a doctor."

"I have a doctorate degree, so yeah ... I'm a doctor. If it makes you feel better, I brought two other doctors with me. Dr. Coleman has a PhD in Ergonomics with specialization in biomechanics, and Dr. Klein has a PhD in Machine Learning. Doctors, meet Cage Monaghan."

The two men nodded. Dr. Coleman looked maybe fifty with a thick head of gray hair. Dr. Klein had to be at least ten years younger with the world's thickest glasses.

"You realize I haven't lost any limbs or anything like that, right?"

"Cage, Cage, Cage ... it hurts that you don't really understand what I—*we*—do. I can build you a machine or a complete robotic exoskeleton if need be. Essentially, I can take the weakest part of your body and replace it, even if just temporarily, while at the same time using novel technologies such as computational methods that can emulate neural processes and incorporating electrodes that can measure electronic pulses of your muscles and stimulate movement when needed to reduce muscle degeneration during the healing process."

The wall behind me was splattered with his words because they all went over my head.

"This is the future, but for you it's now. You don't have to wait. Machines attached to our bodies can make us faster, stronger, and much more efficient. I give people with 'disabilities' the tools to outperform their 'non-disabled' peers."

"You're going to help me outperform other quarterbacks."

Thad and his two colleagues laughed, sharing little smirks. "We're not into robot boxing. Football is a barbaric sport. I don't build things to destroy them, like stuntmen trashing cars on a movie set. I simply believe everyone should have the right to live a full life without disability."

"What if I want to play football? Can you help me do that?"

The truth? Football was the farthest thing from my mind; I just wanted to walk out of the hospital on my own two feet. But I still wanted a sense of where Thad was going with his technological promises.

"Yes. If your doctors think there is even the slightest possibility you could get back on the field again, then I can take that percent chance, as small as it might be, and make it one hundred for you. Can I keep you safe on the field? No. Can I guarantee the next time you run into a defender that your head won't snap right off your shoulders? No."

"Knock, knock ... am I interrupting?" Dr. Feltz smiled.

"No. Come in."

Thad nodded. "By all means, do your thing. Don't mind us; we'll just be mice in the corner." He stepped back and the three geeks literally huddled together, shoulder-to-shoulder in the corner.

"How do you feel sitting up?"

"My neck is sore."

He nodded then proceeded to go through a series of tests. I think I did well. I had reflexes and feeling in my arms and legs. I needed to take a piss, but wanted to use the bathroom which meant I had bladder control. With four men in the room, it wasn't the best time to check out my dick, but I was hopeful it, too, worked.

Every time Dr. Feltz mentioned possible scenarios for my recovery, including estimated timelines, the peanut gallery rolled their eyes and gave me a slight head shake. Thad held up his fingers less than an inch apart to signal "less than," which he apparently thought he could make every phase of my recovery happen in "less than" the projection Dr. Feltz gave me.

"Any questions?"

"Can I go to the bathroom?"

Dr. Feltz smiled. "I hope so. You'll completely make my day if you do. It's not even nine yet and my waiting room is overflowing with your people." He held up a finger. "Let me get help."

"I have something in my hotel room that can have you jogging, running bleachers ... whatever by the end of the day." Thad smirked.

"I'll keep that in mind. For now I just want to test out my God-given parts to go take a piss."

"Good morning." Two nurses chimed as they followed Dr. Feltz back into the room. "Look who we found hanging around outside your door."

I narrowed my eyes, not *seeing* anyone. Then Lake stepped into the room like she was scared to see me.

"Hey." She relinquished a shy smile. "Thad?"

Her eyes shifted to him. The look on her face was not a look that said she expected him to be there.

"Love." He nodded with a tight grin.

I hated him calling her that. She wasn't his fucking "love." I made a mental note to kick his ass for saying that in front of everyone ... when I could actually make a fist and hold it for longer than two seconds.

"What are you doing here?"

"I watched the game. Got a flight here the second I saw his body being carted off the field."

"Oh ..." she eyed me for a second before returning her gaze to him. "Thanks ... I guess."

"If we can have the room for a minute we'll remove your catheter and get you up." The nurse looked around the room.

"We'll be in the hallway." Thad nodded to the door.

"Um ..." Lake started her own retreat.

"It's nothing you haven't seen."

Lake returned a wide-eyed look. "Um ... k." She moved toward the window, keeping her back to me.

"You might feel a little stinging. That's normal."

I gave her my small OK smile since nodding wasn't an option with a neck brace. She removed it while the other nurse draped a gown over me.

"We're going to take this slow ... really slow." The nurse instructed as she and the other nurse brought me to sitting, easing my feet off the side of the bed, and then helping my arms into the gown before tying it in back.

I felt a little light-headed and weak, so damn weak.

"Take all the time you need." She stepped back as the doctor proceeded to do some reflex checks with me sitting. Following his fingers. Touching my finger to my nose. Snapping his fingers next to one ear and then the other. Doing different crap with my hands and feet.

"Good. You're doing better than expected." He nodded.

I scooted toward the edge of the bed. Both nurses jumped to my side.

"Very slow and easy."

Lake held enough pain for both of us in her expression.

I grinned. "I'm coming for you, Jones."

Her eyes that were trained to my feet, shot up along with a grin. "You've got this, Monaghan."

I felt the ground beneath my feet, not in a stable way,

but I felt it and that's all that mattered. My head seemed to be the last on board because as I stood, both nurses holding on to me, all I wanted to do was let my eyes roll back in my head and collapse backwards.

"Focus, Monaghan. My three-legged cat's got more balance than you."

I loved that woman. I fucking loved her.

One step.

God, I feel like a baby taking its first step.

Another step.

Don't pass out!

Another step.

"You're doing great." Dr. Feltz watched me with a reassuring smile.

I looked up at Lake. Sweat pouring down me.

She yawned, patting her hand over her mouth. "I'm growing a beard over here."

Another step.

"I stink. My breath is even worse than the rest ... of my body."

Another step.

My heart raced in my chest.

Lake grinned and took the final step for me. Easing her arms around my body. My arms? They worked and I used them to hold on to her. If I were being honest, I think that's what my arms were made to do. I wasn't going to be able to throw her over my shoulder and haul her off to my cave anytime soon, but I'd get there.

"I love you," I whispered. Holding her in my arms released an avalanche of emotions. My eyes squeezed shut, lips trapped between my teeth, fighting them off. The intensity of that moment rivaled my father dying—a life-altering moment. *Physically* holding her to my body, after questioning if I'd ever hold her again, changed the course of my life. Fuck football. My hands were made to hold every single piece of that woman. Period.

"Love you more." She tipped her chin up and made my knees shake with one smile.

CHAPTER FORTY-ONE

THE FUTURE

LAKE

DR. FELTZ KICKED Cage out of the ICU that afternoon and told him to take his following with him—in the nicest way possible. A number of players' wives and coaches' wives reached out to me offering their support, letting me know Cage would most likely try to distance himself from me while he dealt with the physical and emotional ramifications of his injury.

Cage? Nope. When someone loves you so completely, it's almost heartbreaking. Cage Monaghan loved me like that. Being loved and trusted unconditionally by him was one of the greatest honors of my life. We didn't need generic wedding vows that promised love in sickness and health. The day he arrived in Beijing something unspoken passed between us—something that said we would always go to the ends of the earth for each other.

"Home." Cage grinned as Rob and Flint walked beside him to the door, just in case.

After seven days in the hospital, he was released.

Surgery was still a possibility to fuse two of his vertebrae, but we had second, third, and all the way to twentieth opinions to get before he would consider "going under the knife."

One day.

One step at a time.

"Okay..." Cage sighed as he sank into the leather sofa "... everyone can leave, at least for a few hours. No offense, but I've been fussed over for a week straight, and I just want to not be the center of attention for a bit. Okay?"

My family left three days earlier. Brooke and Rob sent the girls home with Cage's grandparents two days after the accident so they could get back to school. Therefore "everyone" was Flint, Brooke, Rob, and ... me.

Brooke gave him a kiss on the cheek. "We'll grab some dinner and run to the store to restock your fridge."

"Thanks." He returned an appreciative smile.

"I'll call you in the morning and let you know your schedule." By schedule Flint meant his doctors' appointments and therapy appointments.

"Thanks, Flint."

After everyone else left, I jabbed my thumb behind me, not having any clue where I was going to go. "So ... I'll just ... um ..."

"Lake?"

"Yeah?" Wringing my hands together, I smiled.

"Get your ass over here."

"But you said—"

"What I said was code for 'Get the hell out of here so I can be alone with my Lake.' Now, take off your shoes, ditch the leg if you want, clothing is optional and actually quite discouraged."

I laughed. "I think your eyes are bigger than your

appetite. It winded you to walk from the car to the couch. Your balance is still a bit off. Yet ... you think you can handle *me*?" I sat next to him.

He lifted his arm over me, but even that looked like its own feat. "Handle you, finger you ... your choice."

"Shut up ... how can you be so chipper?"

"Well, there's you. I'm above ground. I can walk without an 'exoskeleton' of Thad's. I have a Super Bowl win and an MVP trophy too. And now the pressure of that life is gone. I can work my ass off to recover, marry the woman who owns my heart, and spend the rest of my life knocking her up."

I scooted to the side to look at him. "What do you mean the pressure of that life is gone?"

His brow furrowed. "I'm ... not playing again."

"What? The doctors ... your coaches ... all the talk has been about what it will take to get you back on the field. That's why they've arranged for a million different opinions from the best doctors in the country. When did you tell them you're not playing anymore?"

"I haven't. I'm telling you now. I'm telling you first."

My jaw hung in midair.

"You can't possibly want me to play again."

I didn't. That was a fact. So why was I in such shock? I expected his plans of playing again to be a fight between us. He took that away, and I felt like someone standing to give a speech and having the teleprompter quit working. All I had to say was, "I'm so relieved." Three words. Instead, the Devil himself hijacked my brain to play devil's advocate.

"You love the game. How can you just give it up? Players get hurt all the time. It's part of the game. You know that. You've said it yourself a million times. Your team doctor said the chances of you being cleared to play next year are really good. This is your dream."

Wow. What the hell, Lake!

Cage's wide eyes said it all—I'd lost it. And I had. I just said everything I'd prepared for him to say to me.

"You want me to play again?"

No. The answer was no.

Say it, Lake. NO! Just say, no!

"Maybe ... I mean..." I shook my head "...I don't know. It's not my decision to make."

"It's *our* decision. This affects us, not just me."

"I can't make this decision."

"But you're trying."

I shook my head. "I'm not."

"Well, I just told you I'm not planning on going back and instead of relief ... elation ... I saw this epic disappointment on your face. Am I not appealing without my NFL status?"

"That's not fair. You know the answer to that." I stood, pacing the room to release some of the tension.

"Jesus, Lake. You saw everything before it fucking happened!"

"Exactly!" I stopped, fisting my hands at my sides. "And with Ben I saw nothing. For every right decision in my life there's been ten wrong ones that felt just as right at the time I made them. I didn't just lose my boyfriend and my leg. I lost my intuition, my confidence on a level far deeper than what meets the eye, and my instincts are shit!"

Cage sighed. "Just tell me what you *want* me to do, not what you think I should do."

I shook my head. "No. I can't."

"Why not?"

I sat on the coffee table in front of him with my legs

between his. Taking his hands, I squeezed them, demanding he look at me. "If I weren't in the picture, if you were single and in this exact situation what would you do? Would you give it up?"

It was still too early for him to answer honestly. His neck was still in a brace, his body was sluggish and off balance at times. Of course not playing again was the knee-jerk decision. But at some point he would feel better, stronger, and I had a hard time believing that he wouldn't miss the game and regret his decision.

"You can't answer me, can you? What does that tell you?"

Cage grumbled and grimaced like he wanted to shake his head at me, but his brace wouldn't allow it. He stood, easing to his feet an inch at a time.

I grabbed his arm to help steady him.

"I've got it." He pulled away. "You don't understand and it fucking drives me crazy that you don't." Holding onto the back of the couch for a few seconds, he shuffled his feet along the floor toward the bedroom.

He was right. I didn't understand *anything,* and it was a debilitating feeling to have such a disconnection from life.

CAGE

YES.

The answer was yes. I would have done every stupid thing in my power to get back on the field had Lake not been in my life. The game was my love, it was the greatest tribute to my biggest fan—my father. I knew a ton of guys who played the game like it was their entire life. Live or die on the field ... it didn't matter as long as the last thing they remembered was the field—as long as they died with a helmet on their head.

That was me before Lake.

My mom and Rob came back several hours later with bags of groceries as I finally emerged from the bedroom. There were a million things to say to Lake, but I didn't want them coming out as a string of anger. I wasn't angry with her. I was heartbroken for her. She was lost in an abyss of emotions, but she refused to let a single one go.

"You're fighting," my mom whispered in my ear as Rob helped Lake unload the groceries.

"Why do you say that?"

"Lake looks on the verge of crying."

I frowned. "It's complicated."

"We're flying out in the morning, but if you need me to stay—"

"No. We have some things to work out and it's probably best if we do them without an audience."

"Should I be concerned?"

"I hope not." I didn't know what it would take to get Lake to let go of all the shit that cluttered her mind and held her emotions captive.

My mom and Rob went to bed early since they had an early flight. Lake helped me bathe, saying no more than a few words such as "lean forward" and "sit back." After she helped me into bed, I watched her every move. She sulked between the bathroom and the closet like the whole world rested on her shoulders.

She sat on the bed and removed her leg.

"I'll play if they clear me."

She turned. "Don't do it for me."

I laughed, because really ... I had no other choice. "Don't quit for you. Don't play for you. I can't seem to win."

She tossed her leg on the floor and slid under the sheets with her back to me. "I don't want you to do any of it for me. I want you to do it for you. I'll be happy if you're happy."

"I'm happy. I'm happy. I'm happy. Just so ... fucking happy." I laughed again, knowing the sarcasm in it would probably piss her off.

She sat up, whipping her legs around to the side of the bed, sliding on her liner, then snapping on her leg like she was seriously pissed at it. "Wonderful. You just go to sleep and have your happy dreams. I'm going out in the other room. I'm not tired."

"Lake."

She took off in a blaze of anger.

I felt like shit. Had my body worked properly she never would have made it out the bedroom door, but I was the tortoise in the race—and far from steady. What felt like three days later, I managed to get to the living room. Lake stood by the window with her back to me. A new round of snow danced in the air, illuminated by the lights lining my drive on both sides.

"Ben died and I lived." All emotion was stripped from her voice. "Had he not died I would not be with you, and ... that feels more tragic than his death. Life is such a mind-fuck. We say what we're supposed to say, but feel what we're not supposed to feel. If God really hears my thoughts, then he knows I don't regret going to breakfast with Ben. He knows I don't regret Ben dying that morning. He knows I feel like a monster for having those feelings."

She turned. No tears. No emotion. It broke me to see her pain cut through every nerve, leaving her bleeding out without any more feeling.

"And my fear? It's that in time I won't regret you playing in that game. I won't regret not stopping you. I won't regret you getting injured because the only thing worse than hating God for tragedy that doesn't make any sense is hating Him for making complete sense of it in time. But the rawest truth is I don't think he has a damn thing to do with any of it. I think we make sense of it in our own messed-up minds. I think God is the greatest of all scape-goats. And if I choose to believe in him, then I have to acknowledge his greatest love for us is free will."

Lake shook her head. "*You* chose to play. *I* chose to sit there and watch. Free will. It's so damn scary. God's not a safety net. Living in fear, being guided by it, is a miserable life. It's me right now. I don't trust myself—my thoughts, my feelings, my instinct—and it's like a cancer inside of me. *One* time ... one time my gut was right. Do you see how debilitating that is? It may never be right again, but I'll always live in *fear* that it could be because *one* time it was."

I stepped closer. "You're afraid of me playing?"

Her eyes trailed up my body, landing on my gaze. "Yes," she whispered.

I took the final step. My hand ghosted along her shoulder and down her arm, she shivered under my touch. "You're afraid of me *not* playing?"

Tears filled her eyes. My touch made her feel again. I would *never* take for granted the visceral effect I had on her. It reaffirmed the *one* thing I knew to be absolute truth in my life—my hands were made to touch her.

"Yes." She blinked, releasing the tears.

CHAPTER FORTY-TWO

WE WOULD BE LAKE AND CAGE

LAKE

BROOKE AND ROB left and then life got real again. I went to a few appointments with Cage then Flint took over so I could get back to my job. Three weeks after he came home from the hospital, the neck brace was off, but surgery was still in question. I jumped at every chance to go to an interview about my magazine spread, or spend the day testing new legs, or anything to keep my mind off Cage and his decision. That's what it had become—his decision.

I gave up my shoes out of grief and an instant loss of myself after my accident. I didn't want Cage giving up football for the same reason. Of course, I didn't want him to play either, but ... free will, unconditional love, and all the necessary emotions that came with life.

"You're home early." Cage smiled as he chopped red peppers.

He was my new idol. The guy spent five to six hours a day in therapy, yet came home and made dinner every night with his signature dimply smile plastered to his face.

"Tired. I'm just tired." I lifted myself onto the counter a foot from his ninja chopping.

"Well you've been working seven days a week for the past two weeks." He held a slice of pepper up to my lips.

I opened my mouth then chewed it while nodding to acknowledge he was right, I'd been working too much. "So tomorrow is the day."

"Yep." He kept his head down, eyes trained to the sharp knife moving rapidly just millimeters from his fingers.

"You've made your decision?"

"We'll find out, won't we?"

We agreed his decision to play or retire would be his and his alone. I requested we not discuss it, and in true Lake Jones contumacious fashion, I told him I didn't want to know until he made the official announcement on TV. I said I wanted to watch and find out with the rest of the world. However, I felt pretty certain he was going to play. He'd had too many surgery consults and second opinions for a surgery that was only necessary if he planned on trying to return to football.

"I love you no matter what you choose."

Cage chuckled. "Good to know."

Gah! I wanted to know, but I did not ask. My stubbornness was a living, breathing being all of its own.

"We should start planning a wedding, don't you think?"

I smiled. "Yes. I think we should. Are you thinking spring, before training camp?"

Cage scraped the diced peppers from the cutting board to the salad bowl, a sly grin tugged at his lips. "I'm thinking we fly to Vegas and just do it."

"Ha! My mom would disown me. Lara and Drake did the Vegas thing, and I think my mom is still pissed about it. She has this wedding dress, a gawd-awful looking thing, which was her mother's dress. I don't think it was ever white, but it's now a piss yellow. Anyway, my mom promised her mom she'd wear it for her wedding, but after having Luke before they got married, her hips and boobs no longer fit into the ugly dress. Soo ... she promised my grandmother, before she died, that Lara or I would wear it. Honestly, I think that's why Lara went to Vegas."

Cage stuck his rice and vegetable dish into the oven. He ate a near perfect diet before his accident, but afterward, he went even stricter with it to help his body heal faster. I had to sneak my marshmallow treats because I hated the disapproving eye he gave me when I ate them in front of him.

"So you're going to wear a piss yellow wedding dress from two generations back just to make your mom happy?"

"Yes. I'm the only one who fits into the dress, so I'm going to pair it with some kick-ass heels and wear the hell out of it so my grandmother smiles down on me and my mother no longer feels her wrath."

He slipped off the oven mitts and grabbed the inside of my knees, spreading them so he could stand between my legs, pulling me close to him. "You're such a good girl, Lake Jones." Brushing his nose against mine, he palmed my ass.

I tried to play it cool, like I wasn't dying to be intimate with him, but it had been over a month since we'd had sex and I. Was. Hungry.

I cleared my throat, snaking my hands up the inside of his shirt. "I'm not."

"No?" His grin taunted me.

I sucked in a breath as he kissed my lower lip before drawing it into his mouth and dragging it through his teeth.

"No," I whispered, working the button and zipper to his jeans.

"Lake ..." His breath hitched as my hand slid into his briefs.

"Cage ..." I stroked him as he smashed his lips to mine.

Everything in that department seemed to work just fine, but I felt obligated to check it out to be sure, and it involved being anything but a "good girl."

Pushing him back a few inches, I eased myself off the counter and onto my knees.

"Lake ..." He tipped his chin down, lips parted, breaths becoming more ragged with each passing second.

"Keep saying my name, Monaghan ... it makes me so fucking wet."

That look, the one with dark eyes searing into mine as he grabbed the counter with one hand and fisted my hair with his other, it was the reason I was on my knees, yanking down his pants and taking him into my mouth. My f-bombs were dropped on very few occasions. I wasn't the dirty talker, but in that moment I felt it again—falling ... falling ... falling.

Fuck gravity.

We would be Cage and Lake.

We would be unpredictable.

We would be reckless.

We would push the boundaries of sanity and give normality the middle finger.

"Jesus, baby ... w-what are ... you doing?" His fist in my hair tightened.

I smiled around his cock, one hand gripping the base. He just realized where my other hand was—slid down the front of my jeans, beneath my panties.

"Lake ..." He said it with so much grit to his voice, I lost all control, surrendering to my orgasm.

I hummed over him.

"I'm going to ... Lake ..."

Sliding my hand out of my pants, I grabbed his hard glutes and took him as deep as I could until I tasted his warmth spilling into my mouth.

"Fuck ... Lake ..." Both hands fisted my hair.

Yeah, that's all the encouragement I needed to look up at him with my "good girl" grin and ... swallow.

ANOTHER DREAM or premonition brought me out of my sleep, sweaty and breathless. After putting on my leg, I made my way to the closet and slipped on my clothes. Cage was still asleep, as most people would be at 3:00 a.m. My trip took less than thirty minutes. I'm sure most people frequenting a twenty-four hour drug store at that time in the morning were probably in need of pain relievers or some other necessities, like cheese puffs and beer. The older woman at the register eyed me with a slight grin as I handed her a twenty in exchange for the three-pack pregnancy test.

"Lake?" Cage's tired voice called from the bed as I eased back out of my clothes in the closet, my box of pregnancy tests still in the bag waiting to enlighten me.

"Yeah?" I hurried back to bed.

He snaked his arm around me and pulled me close. "What were you doing?" The sleep in his groggy voice led me to believe I could say anything and he wouldn't question it.

"Forgot to floss my teeth." I rolled my eyes at my ridiculous response.

"K ..." he mumbled, burying his face in my hair on a long sigh.

I was trapped in his arms, which wasn't a bad place to

be any other time, but the sticks weren't going to pee on themselves. Eventually, I fell back to sleep, the kind that took an earthquake to resurrect me, the kind of sleep that didn't notice Cage waking or showering.

"I have to leave for my news conference in ten minutes." My side of the bed dipped.

It was that day. The. Day.

My eyes popped open to Cage reading something. I narrowed my eyes at the paper in his hands then my eyes shifted to the nightstand and the opened pregnancy test box next to a notecard.

CHAPTER FOURTEEN

"It says morning is the best time to do this. Your urine is most concentrated."

I jackknifed to sitting. "What are you doing?" I snatched the unfolded insert from him.

He smirked. "You missed out on the reproductive unit in junior high health class, didn't you?"

"What are you talking about?"

"Baby, you can't get pregnant just by swallowing. It doesn't work that way."

As much as I tried not to smile, I couldn't hold it back. "Shut up, you dumb ass." I shoved him until he moved so I could put on my leg.

"Why do you think you're pregnant?" He stood, straightening his amethyst tie, looking mouthwatering in his black suit and white shirt.

Grabbing the box, I brushed past him to the bathroom. "Because there are two things I can't remember very well."

"What's that?" He stood in the doorway. Nope, he

owned the doorway. I couldn't form a coherent thought, let alone actual words with him looking like sex in a suit.

"Mind turning around for a second?"

"You wanna see my ass in this suit."

Dear God, yes!

"No. I'd like to pee without you watching me."

He grinned then turned. "What two things?"

"I can't remember for sure when I last had a period *or* the last time we used a condom."

My cell phone rang on the nightstand. "Ugh!" I doused the three sticks as quickly as I could, tossed them on the counter, washed my hands, and ran to get my phone. "Hey, Mom."

Her timing was impeccable.

"Good morning, sweetie. So this is the big day. Are you nervous?"

Cage came out of the bathroom, giving me a wink and mouthing "gotta go."

I nodded, mouthing "love you." We both knew there was no such thing as a short conversation with my mom. I couldn't believe he wasn't going to wait to see the test results before leaving, but the sports world was waiting for his announcement—so was I.

"I don't know what I am. If he walks out on that field again, I'm not sure my heart will survive, but at the same time I love him. I want to watch him live his dreams no matter where they take him or how long they last. That's *living*." I walked back into the bathroom. "What the hell ..."

"Lake, what are you talking about?"

"N-nothing. I ... I have to go. I'll call you after the press conference."

"Lake!"

I ended the call and ran to the back door. His truck was

gone. I tried calling him. He didn't answer. After throwing on my clothes in less than thirty seconds, I grabbed my purse and jumped into my car. My key fob was missing. I ran inside to the rack by the backdoor that had spare keys. My spare fob was missing.

"Dammit, Monaghan!" I stomped my feet like an errant child.

My keys were gone.

He was gone.

The pregnancy tests were gone.

PERCHED on the couch with my back ramrod straight, I watched the sports commentators discussing everything Cage Monaghan. The buzz was just as I suspected. He was going to play again if the team doctors cleared him. Of course they had an interview with a doctor who stated the huge risk it was to play again. Even with the surgery, it would always be a weak spot in his body and another injury like it could be more devastating.

By the time the pregnancy-test snatcher appeared on my screen in front of a sea of press snapping picture after picture, all of them eager to ask the first question before he'd made any sort of statement, I had chewed off every single one of my fingernails.

I grabbed my phone.

Lake: *TELL ME, DAMMIT!*

He adjusted the microphone, tipping his chin down to the podium. A smirk spread across his face. He saw it. He saw my text.

"Thank you for coming today ..." He took his sweet time thanking every coach, player, and doctor for their support since the accident. Then he proceeded to thank his fans, family, and friends including Flint. Next he discussed his love for the game and what a dream it was to be drafted by Minnesota and lead his team to their first ever Super Bowl Trophy. "I'm young and my doctors feel if I opt for surgery, I have a good chance of getting back on the field with a promising career ahead of me."

I gulped again and again. It was coming ...

"However, I'm in a much different place now than what I was two years ago. Life isn't anything if not unpredictable. So as much as I'd like to say this has been an agonizing decision for me, I can't. It's been the easiest decision of my life. Thank you for the ride. While short, it's been everything I could have ever imagined, but I'm announcing my retirement from the NFL."

There was an audible gasp in the crowd. Me? I wasn't breathing.

"As most of you know my beautiful Lake has agreed to marry me ..."

Holy shit ...

He held up a stick. MY. STICK!

"Oh..." he grinned from ear to ear, dimples on full display "...and I'm going to be a dad."

Tears. So many tears. Cameras flashed like crazy. Questions were hurled at him from every direction, but all I could do was drown in my own tears as my hand pressed to my stomach.

I did it. I got the guy.

Ben died, but I *lived.*

CHAPTER FORTY-THREE

OUR EPILOGUE

CAGE

"Ugliest dress ever." I stared at our wedding photo on the wall in our bedroom.

"But the shoes ..."

"Yeah, yeah, kick-ass heels, baby."

Lake and her eight-month baby belly stood in front of me, adjusting my tie. "Are you nervous?"

"Terrified."

"You realize at least one will wet their pants, another will vomit and totally miss the trash, at least two will be sent to the office when you notice they have head lice, there will be name calling, crying because it's their first full day away from their mommies, but..." she grinned as I grimaced "...*one* ... one little girl, the quiet one with pigtails and maybe freckles too, she will fall in love with you and declare you as her future husband. That will be the highlight of your day."

I rested my hands on the sides of her belly and bent

down to nuzzle my nose in her neck. "You're the highlight of my day. Every day."

I loved my life. We were *living*, we were falling, we were our own unexplainable phenomena, and I wouldn't have had it any other way. Even our "village," as Lake liked to call them, seemed to move on to better things as well. Minnesota renewed Banks' contract, so he and Shayna moved into a house, a house whose previous owner happened to be Minnesota's recently-retired quarterback. He also found a girlfriend: Shayna's dance teacher. Lake said she didn't have *that* much to hold on to—whatever that meant.

The nanny 'Jamie' continued to work for Banks, contingent on him never looking at Banks' girlfriend. I felt his pain. Flint went back to school to complete his law degree so he could fight to get his son back since he was taken from him after the accident. As for Penny and Rupert ... they stayed in their Minneapolis apartment. Lake still met her for girl-talk, and Penny still violated me with her eyes every time I saw her.

"Your lunch is on the kitchen counter."

I stood up straight, taking a deep breath. "Okay. I have my first practice tonight too."

When we sold the house and moved into something smaller and closer to the private elementary school where I got a job teaching first grade, I decided to embrace my new, low-profile life by joining one of the Park and Rec's flag football teams.

"I can't believe you didn't get the quarterback position."

I shrugged. "I know, right? I don't understand why they think it would be such an unfair advantage to our team. I haven't thrown a football in several months."

Lake nodded. "Exactly. We spent the summer on the boat."

Best. Summer. Ever.

I fished. Lake sprawled out on the front of the boat in her bikini, baby belly growing a little more every day, a high SPF sunblock, a book in hand, and her fishing hat on.

"I just hope they let me play. I'm new to the team so I could end up riding the pine for a while until I earn my spot."

She tugged on my tie until I bent down to give her a slow kiss, then she grinned. "I sure like riding your pine."

I shook my head.

"Too corny?"

"A little." I adjusted myself. "But clearly it still does it for me."

"Monaghan?" She called after me as I walked toward the door, grabbing my lunch box on the way.

I turned.

"Don't forget to love me."

I smiled. "Impossible."

LAKE

Six Years Later

"He made me call him Mr. Monaghan." Amelia pouted, dropping her purple backpack onto the floor.

Cage picked it up, giving me an eye roll as I hugged our daughter after her first day of school. I stroked her loose, black ponytail that had lost its braid during the day.

"Then he took me to the hallway and said I can't raise my hand anymore."

I smirked. An exaggerated head shake accompanied my hubby's eye rolling.

"Well, we talked about this. At school, daddy is your teacher, so you should call him Mr. Monaghan like all the other kids."

"But he's my daddy."

Cage fisted one hand over the other, making a stabbing motion toward his heart. "The two women in my life are going to be the death of me."

"Here." I handed her a rice crispy treat on a plate. "Trzy is on the back porch. Go give her some love while I scold Mr. Monaghan for being so mean to my baby today."

Amelia smiled, flipping Cage a now-you're-in-trouble look over her shoulder, while traipsing out of the kitchen.

"Tell me about your day, Mr. Monaghan." I grabbed the bowl of leftover marshmallowy goodness and plopped down onto a chair at the kitchen table.

Twisting the top off a hard-earned beer, he smirked as his lips hovered over the amber glass. "We talked about what it means to do a good deed, and everyone took their turn sharing an example. Amelia said her daddy was helping wash her mommy in the shower this morning and that was an example of a good deed."

"W—" I coughed. "What? Are you serious?"

Cage took a long pull of his beer, then nodded. "Unfortunately. And the real kicker? The principal was sitting in on that discussion."

I pressed the pad of my finger to the corner of my eye, wiping away a tear. "That's hilarious."

"It's not." He tugged on my hair, forcing my head back. "Next time lock the bathroom door before joining me in the shower," he whispered in my ear, followed by a bite to my neck.

"I wanted to tell her we were conserving water. It was the perfect opportunity to discuss environmental responsibility. But no, you had to pipe up and say you were helping wash me."

He grabbed my waist and pulled me onto his lap as he sat in the chair next to mine. I draped my arms over his shoulders.

"Because environmental stewardship was going to sound so much more believable to my boss than my explanation."

Wrapping my hand around the neck of his beer, I brought it toward my lips.

"No way." He shook his head, pulling it away from me.

"A sip."

"You could be pregnant."

"That's the story of my whole life with you! You haven't used a condom once since we've been married. If it weren't for all the breastfeeding keeping my eggs at bay, we'd have ten kids."

"Your math is wrong baby. We've only been married for six years. Without multiples in there, we never would have been able to have ten kids by now."

"Don't be smart with me, Mister." I fisted his shirt.

He grinned. "Where *are* my guys?"

"Jeffrey is playing with Brock next door, and Colton is still napping." I rolled my eyes toward the ceiling. "That's it, right? We only have three kids. I can't keep track. Every time I blink I'm pushing a baby of yours out of my body."

Cage shrugged. "I love you pregnant."

"You love me naked and riding your cock."

He smiled. "That too."

I could not have dreamed of a more perfect life. Thad moved on after making me the ideal leg for pregnancy. The world was no longer 'ours' to change, it was his. I had my hands full with three young kids and my blog. We were offered an insane deal to do a reality TV show after Cage retired from football, but that wasn't our style. Instead, I started a blog. I never could've predicted *millions* of people following it, but it happened.

A familiar voice followed a quick knock at the back door. "Don't you two ever quit?"

Cage pulled me closer. "Nope."

I wiggled out of his hold and then resumed my marshmallowy obsession. "Hi, Flint. You staying for dinner or do you have a hot date?"

"No date. No more women."

Cage grabbed Flint a bottle of iced coffee with almond milk—that we kept on hand just for him—out of the refrigerator and handed it to him. "Is this about the new tenant?"

"New tenant?" My brows raised.

"She's getting evicted as soon as I can legally kick her out."

"Someone tell me what this is all about."

Cage smirked. "Flint found someone to rent the space above his law office."

"And that's not a good thing?"

Flint scowled at me. "No. *She's* not."

Cage continued, "Her business is loud and distracting."

"Oh? What does she do?"

"Drive me fucking insane."

Both Cage and I laughed.

"She's a therapist," Cage winked at Flint.

"Aannd ... therapists make too much noise how?"

Flint sighed. "She's a *music* therapist."

My eyes narrowed. "That's a thing?"

He held his coffee with one hand, gulping it down, as he loosened his tie with the other hand. "Apparently."

"Flint had a mile-long list of businesses that he would not allow to rent the space, but—"

"But I couldn't exclude some fucking profession that I didn't know existed, in the agreement."

"So, what are we talking? Piano? Guitar?"

"Depends on the day. Drums today."

"I don't see the problem." I shoved more crispy rice into my mouth. "If she didn't disclose her profession—"

"She did." Cage laughed. "But Flint didn't think to ask what exactly a music therapist does because he was too busy ogling her tits."

"Cage!"

He shrugged. "Flint's words not mine."

Flint pulled out the drawer to the recycling bin and tossed his bottle into it. "*Therapist.* Just the word implies lots of silence and a few quietly spoken words. I assumed a music therapist..." he rubbed the back of his neck "...I don't know ... let patients lie on an expensive leather sofa and listen to classical music, wearing noise-canceling headphones. Not autistic kids banging on bongos."

"Sounds like a cool profession."

Both Flint and Cage glared at me.

"What? It does." How was I the only one in the room perceptive enough to see the obvious? "Harrison loves music. Maybe you should send him to see her for therapy."

"My son doesn't need therapy," Flint said in a huffy voice.

"He does because his father has signed him up for every possible sport, yet, all he wants to do is play music." My nose wrinkled. "I know you hate it when I say this, but I think Harrison is a musical genius—a prodigy."

"He spent three very influential years of his life being raised by my single, ex-mother-in-law. She enrolled him in dance class. If he needs therapy, it's to channel the testosterone in his body."

"Says the guy who concocted his own herbal, anti-itch salve for Shayna when she had the chicken pox."

"I'm well-rounded. Harrison can play Bach and pirouette around the living room, but he can't make a free throw or catch a football to save his life."

"I don't think his lack of athletic ability is a life-or-death situation. Right, baby?"

Cage's gaze flitted between us. "I think it's time for Jeffrey to come home."

He jabbed his thumb toward the door. "I'll let you two work this out."

"Coward."

"Just smart," he called before the door shut behind him.

Flint and I stared at each other for a few seconds before we both chuckled. "Feels like the old days."

Flint nodded. "The second we'd start to argue, he'd flee."

"Those were the days."

"Think he misses it?"

"Us fighting?"

Flint shook his head. "Football. I've never wanted to ask."

I set my spoon in the bowl and stared at it for a few seconds. "Sure, I mean ... you both get together to watch every game. So you know he still loves it, but I don't think he's ever second-guessed his decision. And it's not that I haven't looked. When he's watching ESPN or looking through old pictures, I stare at him, waiting to see a tiny glimpse of sadness or longing for that life."

I shook my head. "But I don't. For over six years all I've ever seen is complete adoration for this life we have, our kids, and his job." A smile tugged at my lips. "He says football was just a fun way to make 'a little money' while he waited for his life to really begin—while he waited for me."

"Do you worry that when you're done having kids he'll get restless and start to feel a little regret?"

"Ha! I worry that we're never going to be done having kids, and if that day comes, I have a feeling he'll be too old and senile to remember that he ever played the sport."

"Mommy?" Amelia called.

"I hear him, sweetie." I held up a finger to Flint as I turned toward the bedroom to get Colton from his crib.

Flint grinned when I returned with my smiling six-month old in my arms. "Hey, buddy."

"Where's Harrison anyway?"

Flint ruffled Colton's head of thick, blond hair. "Birthday party." He looked at his watch. "I have to pick him up in an hour." His eyes latched back onto Colton then shifted to Amelia as she brought her plate back into the kitchen.

"You need a wife, Flint. And at least three more kids."

"No." He shook his head just as Cage and Jeffrey showed up.

"Jeffrey Aric Monaghan! What happened to your hair?" I gasped at his *mohawk.*

"Brock's mom thought they were playing in the basement. They were actually in the bathroom with his dad's beard trimmer."

Jeffrey smiled. "It's cool."

It was hideous. Only a complete head shaving would fix it.

Flint kissed me on the cheek and Colton on the head. "Sure, Lake. I *need* more kids and a wife."

I couldn't erase the grimace from my face as my eyes remained fixed to Jeffrey.

"Looks awesome, big guy." Flint held out his fist and Jeffrey gave him knuckles. Then he gave Cage a man hug and whispered something in his ear that brought a huge smile to Cage's face.

"Trust me. I know," Cage replied just before Flint closed the door.

AFTER DINNER, a complete head shaving and three baths, we finally collapsed into bed, enjoying the temporary silence around us. Cage slid down my panties then pulled off my T-shirt.

I loved how after three kids, he still looked at me like a miracle.

"What did Flint whisper in your ear before he left?" My words came out breathy as his tongue circled my nipple.

"Same thing he said to me on our wedding day when you were walking down the aisle."

"And what was that?" My hips jerked as his hand slid between my legs.

"He said, 'best decision of your life, buddy.'"

The End

ACKNOWLEDGMENTS

To my family, thank you for making this life a good one.

To my editing team, Max, Kiezha, Monique, Leslie, and Kambra, thank you for helping my words make sense.

To my assistant, Jennifer, thank you for making my life so much easier. It's such a cliché, but I really don't know what I did before you.

To Shauna, my name wizard, thank you for being a sounding board for all my random thoughts.

To the bloggers who promote my books, thank you for loving my stories enough to share them with your followers and for putting your emotions about my books into reviews.

To my Jonesies Facebook group, thank you for being my safe haven in the overwhelming world of social media, my cheerleaders, my relentless pimping warriors, but most importantly—my friends. I adore you.

To anyone with a disability, I may not have done the best job portraying the life of an amputee, but this story was about survivors. Thank you for being an inspiration. All it takes is *one* person to see your strength, and just like that ... you've changed the world. *One* is enough.

ALSO BY JEWEL E. ANN

One

Idle Bloom

Undeniably You

Naked Love

Only Trick

Perfectly Adequate

Look The Part

When Life Happened

A Place Without You

Jersey Six

Scarlet Stone

Jack & Jill Series

End of Day

Middle of Knight

Dawn of Forever

Out of Love (*standalone*)

Holding You Series

Holding You

Releasing Me

Transcend Series

Transcend

Epoch

Fortuity

The Life Series

The Life That Mattered

The Life You Stole

Receive a FREE book and stay informed of new releases, sales, and exclusive stories:

Mailing List

https://www.jeweleann.com/free-booksubscribe

ABOUT THE AUTHOR

Jewel is a free-spirited romance junkie with a quirky sense of humor.

With 10 years of flossing lectures under her belt, she took early retirement from her dental hygiene career to stay home with her three awesome boys and manage the family business.

After her best friend of nearly 30 years suggested a few books from the Contemporary Romance genre, Jewel was hooked. Devouring two and three books a week but still craving more, she decided to practice sustainable reading, AKA writing.

When she's not donning her cape and saving the planet one tree at a time, she enjoys yoga with friends, good food with family, rock climbing with her kids, watching How I Met Your Mother reruns, and of course...heart-wrenching, tear-jerking, panty-scorching novels.

www.jeweleann.com

Printed in Great Britain
by Amazon